THE CALLING OF THE GRAVE

www.transworldbooks.co.uk

*Also by Simon Beckett
featuring David Hunter*

THE CHEMISTRY OF DEATH
WRITTEN IN BONE
WHISPERS OF THE DEAD

and published by Bantam Books

THE CALLING OF
THE GRAVE

Simon Beckett

BANTAM BOOKS

LONDON • TORONTO • SYDNEY • AUCKLAND • JOHANNESBURG

TRANSWORLD PUBLISHERS
61–63 Uxbridge Road, London W5 5SA
A Random House Group Company
www.transworldbooks.co.uk

THE CALLING OF THE GRAVE
A BANTAM BOOK: 9780553825596

First published in Great Britain
in 2010 by Bantam Press
an imprint of Transworld Publishers
Bantam edition published 2012

Addresses for Random House Group Ltd companies outside the UK
can be found at: www.randomhouse.co.uk
The Random House Group Ltd Reg. No. 954009

The Random House Group Limited supports The Forest Stewardship Council
(FSC®), the leading international forest certification organisation. Our books
carrying the FSC label are printed on FSC® certified paper. FSC is the only
forest certification scheme endorsed by the leading environmental organisations,
including Greenpeace. Our paper procurement policy can be found at
www.randomhouse.co.uk/environment

Typeset in Sabon by Falcon Oast Graphic Art Ltd.
Printed and bound by CPI Group (UK) Ltd, Croydon, CR0 4YY

2 4 6 8 10 9 7 5 3 1

For Hilary

Prologue

One. Two. Eight.

The numbers of decay. That's the ratio by which all organisms, large and small, decompose. In air, in water, in soil. Provided it's the same climate, a submerged body will take twice as long to break down as one left on the surface. Underground it will take eight times as long. *One, two, eight*. It's a simple formula, and an inescapable truth.

The deeper something is buried, the longer it survives.

Bury a body, and you deprive it of the carrion-feeding insects that thrive on dead flesh. The microorganisms that would normally digest the soft tissues can't function without air, and the cooling insulation of dark earth further restricts the onset of decay. Biochemical reactions that would normally break down the cells themselves are slowed by the lower temperature. A process that would, under other circumstances, take days or weeks can last for months. Years, even.

Sometimes longer.

Starved of light, air and warmth, it's possible for a dead body to be preserved almost indefinitely. Cocooned in its cold burrow, it exists in near stasis, indifferent to the passing of seasons above.

But cause and effect applies here, as anywhere else. Just as, in nature, nothing is ever truly destroyed, so nothing is ever completely concealed. No matter how deeply buried, the dead can still make their presence known. *One. Two. Eight.*

Nothing stays hidden for ever.

Eight Years Ago

1

'What name is it?'

The policewoman's face was cold, in every sense. Her cheeks were chapped and ruddy, and her bulky yellow jacket was beaded with moisture from the mist that had descended like an earth-bound cloud. She regarded me with what seemed barely restrained dislike, as though holding me responsible for the foul weather, and the fact that she was standing out on the moor in it.

'Dr David Hunter. Detective Chief Superintendent Simms is expecting me.'

With a show of reluctance she considered her clipboard, then raised her radio. 'Got someone here to see the SIO. A Mr David Hunter.'

'It's Doctor,' I corrected her.

The look she gave me made it clear she didn't care.

There was a squawk of static from the radio and a voice said something unintelligible. Whatever it was didn't improve her mood. With a last sour look she stepped aside and motioned me past.

'Straight ahead to where the other vehicles are parked,' she said, gracelessly.

'And thank you,' I muttered, driving on.

Beyond the windscreen the world was draped with curtains of mist. It was patchy and unpredictable, lifting one moment to reveal the drab, wet moorland before wrapping white gauze around the car again the next. A little further along a makeshift police car park had been set up on a relatively flat patch of moor. A policeman waved me on to it, and the Citroën bumped and lurched over the uneven ground as I eased it into a clear space.

I switched off the engine and stretched. It had been a long drive, and I hadn't taken a break. Anticipation and curiosity had overcome any inclination to stop en route. Simms hadn't given me many details when he'd called, only that a grave had been found on Dartmoor and he wanted me to be there while the body was recovered. It had sounded routine, the sort of case I could be called out on several times a year. But for the past twelve months the words 'murder' and 'Dartmoor' had been synonymous with only one man.

Jerome Monk.

Monk was a serial killer and rapist who had confessed to murdering four young women that we knew about. Three of them were little more than girls, and their bodies had never been found. If this grave was one of theirs, then there was a good chance the others were also nearby. It would be one of the biggest recovery and identification operations of the past decade.

And I definitely wanted to be a part of it.

'Everyone's always thought that's where he got rid of his victims,' I'd said to my wife, Kara, in the kitchen that morning as I'd rushed to get ready. We'd been living in the detached Victorian villa in south-west London for over a year, but I still needed her to tell me where things were. 'Dartmoor's a big place but there can't be so many bodies buried out there.'

'David,' Kara said, looking pointedly at where Alice was eating breakfast. I winced and mouthed *sorry*. Normally I knew better than to mention the grisly details of my work in front of our five-year-old daughter, but my enthusiasm had got the better of me.

'What are vic-tims?' Alice piped up, frowning in concentration as she lifted a dripping spoonful of raspberry yoghurt. That was her food fad of the moment, having recently decided she was too grown up for cereal.

'It's just Daddy's work,' I told her, hoping she'd let

it drop. There was plenty of time for her to learn about the darker aspects of life when she was older.

'Why are they buried? Are they dead?'

'Come on, sweetheart, finish your breakfast,' Kara told her. 'Daddy's got to go soon and we don't want to be late for school.'

'When are you coming back?' Alice asked me.

'Soon. I'll be home before you know it.' I bent down and lifted her up. Her small body felt warm and ridiculously light, yet it never failed to amaze me how solid she was compared to the baby she'd been it seemed only minutes before. *Do they always grow up so fast?* 'Are you going to be a good girl while I'm away?'

'I'm always a good girl,' she said, indignant. She still had the spoon in her hand, and a glob of yoghurt dropped off and landed on the notes I'd left on the table.

'Whoops,' Kara said, tearing off a piece of kitchen towel and wiping it up. 'That's going to stain. Hope it's not important.'

Alice looked stricken. 'Sorry, Daddy.'

'No harm done.' I gave her a kiss and set her down before gathering up the notes. The top sheet had a sticky mark from the yoghurt. I tucked them into a folder and turned to Kara. 'I'd better go.'

She followed me into the hall, where I'd left my bag. I put my arms around her. Her hair smelled of vanilla.

'I'll call you later. I should have a better idea then how long I'll be away. Hopefully only a couple of nights.'

'Drive carefully,' she said.

Both of us were used to my going away. I was one of the few forensic anthropologists in the country, and it was the nature of my job to go wherever bodies happened to be found. In the past few years I'd been called out to investigations abroad as well as across the UK. My work was often grim but always necessary, and I took pride in both my skill and my growing reputation.

That didn't mean I enjoyed this part of it. Leaving my wife and daughter was always a wrench, even if it was only for a few days.

I climbed out of the car, treading carefully on the muddy grass. The air smelt of damp, heather and exhaust fumes. I went to the boot and pulled on a pair of disposable overalls from the box of protective gear I kept in there. Police forces usually provided them, but I liked to carry my own. Zipping up the overalls, I took out the aluminium flight case that contained my equipment. Until recently I'd made do with a battered suitcase, but Kara had persuaded me that I needed to look more like a professional consultant and less like a travelling salesman.

As usual, she was right.

A car pulled up as I began to make my way

through the parked police vehicles. The bright yellow paintwork should have been a tip-off, but I was too preoccupied to pay it any attention until someone shouted.

'Found your way, then?'

I looked round to see two men climbing from the car. One of them was small and sharp-featured. I didn't know him, but I recognized the younger man he was with. Tall and good-looking, he carried himself with the easy confidence of an athlete, broad shoulders swinging with his characteristic swagger. I hadn't expected to see Terry Connors here but I should have realized when I saw the car. The garish Mitsubishi was his pride and joy, a far cry from CID's usual bland pool cars.

I smiled, although I felt the usual mixed feelings at seeing him. While it was good to find a familiar face among the impersonal police machinery, for some reason there was always an edge between Terry and me that never quite went away.

'I didn't know you were on the investigation,' I said as they came over.

He grinned, cheek muscles bunching on the inevitable piece of gum. He'd lost a little weight since the last time I'd seen him, so that the square-jawed features looked more pronounced. 'I'm deputy SIO. Who do you think put in a word for you?'

I kept my smile in place. Back when I first knew

Terry Connors he'd been a DI in the Metropolitan Police, but we hadn't met through work. His wife, Deborah, had gone to the same prenatal clinic as Kara, and the two of them had become friends. Terry and I had been wary of each other at first. Except for the overlap of our professions we had little in common. He was ambitious and fiercely competitive, a keen sportsman whose career was another arena in which to excel. His self-assurance and ego could grate at times, but the success of the few cases he'd steered my way hadn't hurt either of us.

Then, just over a year ago, he'd surprised everyone by transferring out of the Met. I never did find out why. There had been talk of Deborah's wanting to be closer to her family in Exeter, but exchanging the high-octane policing of London for Devon had seemed an inexplicable career move for someone like Terry.

The last time we'd seen them had been shortly before their move. The four of us had gone out for dinner, but it had been an awkward affair. There was a barely suppressed tension crackling between Terry and his wife all evening, and it was a relief when it was over. Although Kara and Deborah made a token effort to keep in touch afterwards it was a lost cause, and I'd not seen or spoken to Terry since.

But he was obviously doing well if he was deputy SIO on an investigation as big as this: I'd have expected that sort of responsibility to go to someone more senior than a DI. Given the pressure he must be under, I wasn't surprised he'd lost weight.

'I wondered how Simms got my name,' I said. Although I was an accredited police consultant, most of my work came through recommendations. I just wished this one hadn't come from Terry Connors.

'I gave you a big build-up, so don't let me down.'

I suppressed the flare of irritation. 'I'll do my best.'

He cocked a thumb at the smaller man with him. 'This is DC Roper. Bob, this is David Hunter, the forensic anthropologist I told you about. He can tell more things from rotting bodies than you want to know.'

The detective constable gave me a grin. He had a snaggle of tobacco-stained teeth and eyes that wouldn't overlook much. A potent wave of cheap aftershave came from him as he gave me a nod.

'This should be right up your street.' His voice was nasal, with the distinctive accent of a local. 'Specially if it's what we think it is.'

'We don't know what it is yet,' Terry told him tersely. 'You go on ahead, Bob. I want to have a word with David.'

The dismissal was borderline rude. The other man's eyes hardened at the slight but his grin stayed in place.

'Right you are, chief.'

Terry watched him go with a sour expression. 'Watch yourself with Roper. He's the SIO's lapdog. He's so deep in Simms' pocket he could scratch his balls.'

It sounded as though there were some personality clashes, but Terry was always butting heads with people. And I wasn't about to get involved in internal politics. 'Is there some dispute about the body?'

'No dispute. Everyone's just falling over themselves hoping it's one of Monk's.'

'What do you think?'

'I've no idea. That's what you're here to find out. And we need to get this one right.' He took a deep breath, looking strained. 'Anyway, come on, it's this way. Simms is out there now, so you'd better not keep him waiting.'

'What's he like?' I asked, as we set off down the road towards a cluster of trailers and Portakabins.

'He's a humourless bastard. You don't want to cross him. But he's no fool, I'll give him that. You know he was SIO of the original murder investigation?'

I nodded. Simms had come to prominence the previous year, making his reputation as the man who had put Jerome Monk behind bars. 'That can't have done his career any harm.'

I thought there was a touch of bitterness in Terry's grin. 'You could say that. Word is he's got his sights set on the Assistant Chief Constable's desk in a few more years. This could clinch it for him, so he'll be expecting results.'

He isn't the only one, I thought, looking at Terry. There was an almost palpable nervous energy coming off him. But that was hardly surprising if he was deputy SIO of something as potentially high profile as this.

We'd reached the Portakabins. They'd been set up next to a track that ran from the road. Thick black cables snaked between them, and the misty air was tainted by diesel fumes from the chugging generators. Terry stopped by the trailer housing the Major Incident Room.

'You'll find Simms out at the grave. If I get back in time I'll let you buy me a drink. We're staying at the same place.'

'Aren't you coming?' I asked, surprised.

'Seen one grave, you've seen them all.' He tried to sound blasé but it didn't quite come off. 'I'm only here to collect some papers. Got a long drive ahead of me.'

'Where?'

He tapped the side of his nose. 'Tell you later. Wish me luck, though.'

He clattered up the steps into the MIR. I wondered why he needed luck, but I'd more to think about than Terry's games just then.

Turning away, I looked out across the moor.

Wreathed in mist, the barren landscape spread out in front of me. There were no trees, only patches of dark, spiky gorse. The year was still young, and patches of winter-brown fern and bracken sprouted amongst the heather and rocks and thick, coarse grass. Looking out from the road, the ground fell gently downhill before rising again in a long slope. Cresting it perhaps quarter of a mile away was a low, ungainly formation of rock that Simms had mentioned.

Black Tor.

Dartmoor had more impressive tors – outcrops of weathered rock that rose from the moorland like carbuncles – but Black Tor's wind-sculpted profile was unmistakable against the skyline. It sat on top of a low escarpment, a broad, squat tower, as though a giant child had stacked flattened boulders one on top of the other. It didn't look any blacker than any of the other tors I'd seen, so perhaps the name was down to some dark event in its past. But it sounded suitably portentous, the sort of detail the newspapers would gleefully seize on.

Especially if it was Jerome Monk's graveyard.

After Simms' telephone call I'd searched the internet for background to the case. Monk had been a journalist's dream. A misfit and loner who supplemented his precarious living as a casual labourer with poaching and theft, he was an orphan whose mother had died during his birth, leading some of the more lurid tabloids to claim that she'd been his first victim. He was often described as a gypsy, but that wasn't true. While he'd lived most of his life around Dartmoor in a caravan, he'd been shunned by the local traveller population as well as the rest of society. Unpredictable and prone to outbursts of terrifying violence, his personality matched his exterior.

If anyone looked the part of a murderer, it was Monk.

Freakishly strong, he was a physical grotesque, a sport of nature. The photographs and footage from his trial showed a hulk of a man, whose bald cannon-ball of a skull housed deep-set, sullen features. His black, button eyes glinted with all the expression of a doll's above a mouth that seemed curved in a permanent sneer. Even more unsettling was the indentation on one side of his forehead, as though a giant thumb had been pressed into a ball of clay. It was disturbing to see, the sort of disfigurement that looked as if it should have been fatal.

To most people's minds it was a pity it wasn't.

It wasn't so much the nature of his crimes that had been so shocking, though that was bad enough. It was the sadistic pleasure he seemed to take in selecting vulnerable victims from the Dartmoor area. The first, Zoe Bennett, was a dark-haired and pretty seventeen-year-old, an aspiring model who never returned home after leaving a nightclub one evening. Three nights after that a second girl disappeared.

Lindsey Bennett, Zoe's identical twin.

What had been a routine missing persons investigation suddenly became front-page news. No one doubted that the same individual was responsible, and when Lindsey's handbag was discovered in a rubbish bin, effectively ending any hope that the sisters were still alive, there was public outrage. Bad enough for a family to suffer that sort of loss once, but twice? And twins?

When Tina Williams, an attractive, dark-haired nineteen-year-old, went missing as well, it sparked the inevitable false alarms and hysteria. For a time it seemed there was a definite lead: a white saloon car was picked up on street CCTV cameras and reported by witnesses in the areas where both Lindsey Bennett and Tina Williams had last been seen.

Then Monk claimed his fourth victim, and for ever sealed his reputation as a monster. At twenty-five, Angela Carson was older than the others. Unlike them she was neither dark-haired nor pretty. There was also a more significant difference.

She was profoundly deaf and couldn't speak.

Afterwards, neighbours described hearing Monk's laughter as he'd raped her and battered her to death in her own flat. When the two policemen who responded to the 999 calls broke down her door they found him with her body in the wrecked bedroom, bloodied and crazed. They were big men, yet he'd beaten them both unconscious before disappearing into the night.

And then, apparently, off the face of the earth.

Despite one of the largest manhunts in UK history, no sign of Monk was found. Or of either the Bennett twins or Tina Williams. A search found a hairbrush and a lipstick belonging to Zoe Bennett hidden under his caravan, but not the girls themselves. It was three months before Monk was seen again, spotted by the side of a road in the middle of Dartmoor. Filthy and reeking, he made no attempt to resist arrest, or to deny his crimes. At his trial he pleaded guilty to four counts of murder, but refused to reveal either where he'd been hiding or what he'd done with the missing girls' bodies. The popular theory was that he'd buried them out on the moor before going to ground there himself. But Monk just smiled his contemptuous smile and said nothing.

With the killer behind bars, the story faded from the public eye, the missing girls just more victims whose fates were unknown.

That might be about to change.

Standing out like a beacon on the drab moorland was a bright blue forensic tent. It was roughly halfway between the road and the rock formation, a short distance off to one side of the rugged dirt track that linked the two. I stood for a moment in the fine drizzle, breathing in the fecund scent of wet peat as I wondered what I'd find inside.

Then I set off along the track towards it.

2

A corridor of police tape had been strung from the midway point of the track out to the forensic tent. The moor had been churned into black mud by the constant tramp of feet, and my boots squelched as I walked between the parallel lines of flapping tape. The area around the tent had been cordoned off, and a uniformed dog-handler stood guard at the opening. He shifted from foot to foot to keep warm as he and the dog, a German shepherd, watched me approach.

'I'm here to see DCS Simms,' I said, a little out of breath.

Before he could say anything the tent flap was thrown back and a man appeared in the gap. He was in his forties but seemed to aspire to be older. His face was remarkably unlined, and as if to offset the blandness of his features he'd cultivated a moustache that gave him a military bearing. The white overalls he wore somehow didn't look right on him. He'd pushed back the protective hood, and the black hair beneath it had managed to stay so neatly combed it looked moulded.

'Dr Hunter? I'm Simms.'

I'd have guessed as much even if I hadn't recognized his voice. It was peremptory and officious, confident in its authority. His pale eyes flicked over me and in that moment I felt that, for better or worse, I'd been swiftly assessed.

'We were expecting you half an hour ago,' he said, before disappearing back inside.

Nice to meet you, too. The dog-handler moved aside to let me through, tightening his grip on the dog's harness. But I was uncomfortably aware of the German shepherd's unblinking stare as I went past them and into the tent.

After the open space of the moor it seemed cramped and crowded inside, a confusion of overalled figures. The diffused light from the blue walls had an ethereal quality. The atmosphere was moist and clammy, with a mustiness disconcertingly evocative of camping. Beneath it was another odour, of freshly turned soil and something far less benign.

The grave was in the centre.

Portable floodlights had been set up around it,

steaming slightly in the damp air. Metal stepping plates had been put down around a rectangle of dark peat, framed by a grid of string. Someone I took to be a SOCO knelt over it, a big man who held his gloved hands poised in the air like a surgeon interrupted in theatre. In front of him, a muddy object was poking through the peaty soil. At first glance it could have been anything – a stone, a knotted root – until you looked more closely.

Thrusting out of the wet earth, its bones visible through rags of flesh, was a decomposing hand.

'I'm afraid you've missed the pathologist, but he'll be coming back when the body's ready to be removed,' Simms said, pulling my attention from the grave. 'Dr Hunter, this is Professor Wainwright, the forensic archaeologist who's going to be supervising the excavation. You may have heard of him.'

For the first time I took stock of the figure kneeling by the graveside. *Wainwright?* I felt my stomach sink.

I'd heard of him, all right. A Cambridge don turned police consultant, Leonard Wainwright was one of the highest-profile forensic experts in the country, a larger-than-life figure whose name lent instant credibility to an investigation. But behind the donnish public image Wainwright had a reputation for being ruthless with anyone he considered a rival. He was an outspoken critic of what he dubbed 'fashionable forensics', which amounted to pretty much any discipline that wasn't his own. Much of his ire had been focused on forensic anthropology, an upstart field that in some respects overlapped with his own. Only the previous year he'd published a paper in a scientific journal ridiculing the idea that decomposition could be a reliable indicator of time since death. 'Total Rot?' the title had crowed. I'd read it with amusement rather than annoyance.

But I hadn't known then that I'd have to work with him.

Wainwright heaved himself to his feet, knees cracking arthritically. He was around sixty, a giant of a man with mud-stained overalls stretched taut over his big frame. In the white latex gloves his meaty fingers resembled overstuffed sausages as he pushed off his mask, revealing craggy features that might charitably have been called patrician.

He gave me a neutral smile. 'Dr Hunter. I'm sure it'll be a pleasure working with you.'

He spoke with the rumbling baritone of a natural orator. I managed a smile of my own. 'Same here.'

'A group of walkers found the grave late yesterday afternoon,' Simms said, looking down at the object emerging from the soil. 'Shallow, as you can see. We've probed and there appears to be a layer of granite no more than two feet below the surface. Not a good place to bury a body, but fortunately the killer didn't know that.'

I knelt down to examine the gelid dark soil from which the hand protruded. 'The peat's going to make things interesting.'

Wainwright gave a cautious nod, but said nothing. As an archaeologist he'd be even more familiar than me with the problems presented by peat graves.

'It looks as if rain washed off the top layer of soil from the hand, then animals finished unearthing it,' Simms continued. 'The walkers found the hand sticking out of the ground. Unfortunately, they weren't certain what it was at first, so they dug away some of the soil to make sure.'

'Lord protect us from amateurs,' Wainwright intoned. It might have been coincidence that he was looking at me.

I knelt down on one of the metal stepping plates to examine the hand. It was exposed from the carpal bones of the wrist. Most of the soft tissue had been gnawed away, and the first two fingers, which would have been uppermost, were completely missing. That much was only to be expected – larger scavengers like foxes, and even bigger birds like crows or gulls, would have been more than capable of detaching them.

But what interested me was that, beneath the teeth marks left in the bone, the broken surfaces of the phalanges looked smooth.

'Did any of the walkers tread on the hand, or damage it while they were digging?' I asked.

'They claim not.' Simms' face was expressionless as he looked at me. 'Why?'

'Probably nothing. Just that the fingers are broken. Snapped cleanly by the look of things, so it wasn't done by an animal.'

'Yes, I had noticed,' Wainwright drawled.

'You think that's significant?' Simms asked.

Wainwright didn't give me a chance to answer. 'Too soon to say. Unless Dr Hunter has any theories . . . ?'

I wasn't about to be drawn. 'Not yet. Have you found anything else?' The area inside the tent would have already been picked clean for evidence by SOCOs.

'Only two small bones on the surface that we think are a rabbit's. Certainly not human, but you're welcome to take a look.' Simms was looking at his watch. 'Now, if there's nothing else, I have a press conference. Professor Wainwright will brief you on anything you need to know. You'll be working under his direct supervision.'

Wainwright was watching me with an expression of mild interest. While the pathologist would have final say over the remains, as a forensic archaeologist responsibility for the excavation would naturally fall to him. I didn't have a problem with that, at least in theory. But I knew of cases where interred bodies had been damaged by inept or

33

over-enthusiastic excavations, and my job wasn't made any easier when a skull had been shattered by a pickaxe or a spade.

And I'd no intention of being treated like Wainwright's assistant.

'That's fine, as far as the excavation goes,' I said. 'Obviously, I'd expect to be consulted on anything that might affect the remains themselves.'

There was a silence inside the tent. Simms studied me coldly. 'Leonard and I have known each other for a long time, Dr Hunter. We've worked on numerous inquiries together in the past. Very successfully, I might add.'

'I wasn't—'

'You came highly recommended, but I want team players. I have a very personal stake in this investigation, and I won't tolerate any disruptions. From anyone. Do I make myself clear?'

I was aware of Wainwright watching, and felt sure that Simms had been primed by the archaeologist. I felt myself bristle at his attitude, but I'd worked with enough difficult SIOs to know better than to argue. I kept my own face as studiedly neutral as his.

'Of course.'

'Good. Because I'm sure I needn't tell you how important this is. Jerome Monk may be behind bars, but as far as I'm concerned my job isn't finished until his victims have been found and returned to their families. If – *if* – this is one of them, then I need to know it.' Simms stared at me for a moment longer until he was satisfied he'd made his point. 'Now, if we're done I'll leave you gentlemen to your work.'

He brushed out through the tent flaps. Neither Wainwright nor I spoke for a moment. The archaeologist cleared his throat theatrically.

'Well, Dr Hunter, shall we make a start?'

Time seemed suspended under the glare of the floodlights. The dark peat was reluctant to relinquish its hold on the body, clinging wetly to the flesh that gradually emerged from below the surface. Progress was slow. With graves dug in most types of soil, the grave shape or 'cut' is usually easily defined. The infill soil that's been removed and then replaced is looser and less compact than the undisturbed earth around it, making it relatively easy to identify the edges of the hole. With peat the demarcation is less obvious. It soaks up water like a sponge, so it tends not to break up like other soils. The grave cut can still be found, but it requires more care and skill.

Wainwright had both.

His sheer physical presence dominated the enclosed space within the gently billowing blue walls. I'd half expected to be delegated to the sidelines, but he'd been unexpectedly happy for me to help with the excavation. Once my pride had stopped stinging, I was forced to appreciate just how good the forensic archaeologist was. The big hands were surprisingly deft as they carefully scraped away the moist peat to expose the buried remains, the thick fingers as precise as any surgeon's. We worked side by side, kneeling on the metal stepping plates laid out beside the grave, and as the body gradually emerged from the dark earth I found myself revising my earlier impressions of the man.

We'd been working in silence for a while when he used his trowel to scoop up two halves of an earthworm severed by a spade. 'Remarkable things, aren't they? *Lumbricus terrestris*. Simple organism, no brain and barely any nervous system to speak of, and they'll still grow back when you chop 'em in half. There's a lesson for you: overcomplicate at your peril.'

He tossed the worm into the heather and set down the trowel, wincing as his knees cracked loudly. 'This doesn't get any easier with age. But then what does? Still, you're too young to know about that. London man, aren't you?'

'Based there, yes. You?'

'Oh, I'm a local. Torbay. Driving distance, thank God, so I don't have to be put up in whatever fleapit the police have found. Don't envy you that.' He rubbed his lower back. 'So how're you finding Dartmoor so far?'

'Bleak, from what I've seen of it.'

'Ah, but you aren't seeing it at its best. God's own country, especially for an archaeologist. Largest concentration of Bronze Age remains in Britain, and the whole moor's like an industrial museum. You can still find the old lead and tin mine workings dotted about like flies in amber. Wonderful! Well, to old dinosaurs like me, anyway. You married?'

I was having trouble keeping up. 'Yes, I am.'

'Sensible man. A good woman keeps us sane. Although how they put up with us is another matter. My wife deserves a medal – as she frequently reminds me.' He chuckled. 'Any children?'

'A little girl, Alice. She's five.'

'Ah. A good age. I have two daughters, both flown the nest now. Enjoy them while they're young. Believe me, ten years from now you'll be wondering where your little girl went to.'

I smiled, dutifully. 'We've a while yet before she's a teenager.'

'Make the most of it. And may I give you a tip?'

'Go ahead.' This wasn't the Wainwright I'd been expecting.

'Never take your work home with you. I'm talking figuratively, of course. But detachment is essential in our business, especially when you have a family. Otherwise this will suck you dry. No matter what you see, no matter how appalling, remember that it's just a job.'

He picked up his trowel again and turned back to the remains.

'Actually, I was talking to someone recently who knew you. Said you'd originally trained as a medic?'

'I did a medical degree before switching to anthropology, yes. Who told you that?'

He frowned. 'Do you know, I've been racking my brains trying to remember. My memory's not what it was. I think it was at some forensic conference. We were talking about the new generation making their mark on the field. Your name was mentioned.'

I was surprised that Wainwright would admit even having heard of me. Despite myself I was flattered.

'Quite a leap, anthropology from medicine,' he went on, busily scraping the soil from around an elbow. 'I gather you trained in the US? That research facility in Tennessee, wasn't it? The one that specializes in decomposition.'

'The Anthropological Research Facility. I spent a year there.'

It had been before I'd met Kara, after I'd switched careers and exchanged working with the living for the dead. I waited for the put-down. It didn't come. 'Sounds like quite a place. Although probably not for me. I have to confess I'm not a great fan of Calliphoridae. Disgusting things.'

'I'm not a big fan myself, but they have their uses.' Calliphoridae was the family classification for the blowfly, whose life cycle provided an effective clock for charting decomposition. Wainwright was obviously keen on Latin names.

'I expect they do. Though not in this instance, sadly. Far too cold.' He pointed with his trowel at the remains. 'So, what do you make of it?'

'I'll have a better idea once the body's at the mortuary.'

'Of course. But I'm sure you've already drawn some conclusions.'

I could see the mouth smile under the face mask. I was reluctant to commit myself, knowing how easily things could change once the remains were cleaned. But Wainwright was nothing like the ogre I'd been expecting, and it was just the two of us there. Given his past antipathy to forensic anthropology, it wouldn't hurt to let him know he wasn't the only expert there.

I sat back on my heels to consider what we'd uncovered.

Peat is a unique substance. Formed from partially decayed plant, animal and insect remains, it's an environment that's inimical to most of the bacteria and insects that usually populate the earth beneath our feet. Low in oxygen and almost as acidic as vinegar, it can effectively pickle organic matter, tanning it like specimens in a lab jar. Whole mammoth tusks have been found in peat bogs, while human corpses buried hundreds of years before can emerge uncannily intact. The body of one man discovered in the village of Tollund, Denmark in the 1950s was so well preserved that at first it was thought he was a recent murder victim. Given the rope tied around his neck he probably had been murdered, though if so it was over two thousand years before.

But the same properties that make peat an archaeological gold mine can also make it a forensic nightmare. Determining an accurate time-since-death interval is difficult at the best of times: without the natural markers supplied by decomposition it can be all but impossible.

In this instance, though, I doubted it would be such a problem. About half of the body was now exposed. It was lying more or less on one side, knees roughly pulled up, upper body curled in a crumpled foetal position. Both the thin top that clung to the torso, through which the outline of a bra could be seen, and the short skirt were synthetic, and contemporary in style. And while I couldn't claim to be an expert, the high-heeled shoe on the now exposed right foot looked to me like a relatively new fashion.

The entire body – hair, skin and clothes – was caked in viscous black peat. Even so, nothing could disguise the horrific damage that had been inflicted. The outlines of broken ribs were clearly visible beneath the muddy fabric, and jagged bones poked through the flesh of the arms and lower legs. Beneath the clinging mat of hair, the skull was crushed and misshapen, the cheeks and nose caved in.

'Not much yet, apart from the obvious,' I said, cautiously.

'Which is?'

I shrugged. 'Female, although I suppose there's an outside chance it could be a transsexual.'

Wainwright made a scoffing noise. 'God help us. In my day that would never have been an issue. When did things get so complicated? Go on.'

I was beginning to warm to my theme. 'It's difficult to say yet how long the body's been buried. There's some decomposition, but that's probably explained by how close it was to the surface.'

Proximity to the air would allow aerobic bacteria to break down the soft tissues even in a peat grave, albeit at a slower rate. Wainwright nodded agreement. 'So the right timeframe to be one of Monk's victims? Less than two years, say?'

'It could be, yes,' I conceded. 'But I'm not going to speculate just yet.'

'No, of course. And the injuries?'

'Too soon to say if they're ante- or post-mortem, but she was obviously badly beaten. Possibly with some kind of weapon. Hard to imagine anyone breaking bones like that with their bare hands.'

'Not even Jerome Monk?' Behind his mask

Wainwright grinned at my discomfort. 'Come on, David, admit it. This does look like one of his.'

'I'll have a better idea once the body's been cleaned and I can see the skeleton.'

'You're a cautious man: I like that. But she's the right sort of age, you can see that just from the clothes. No one over twenty-one would dare wear a skirt that short.'

'I don't think—'

He gave a bass chuckle. 'I know, I know, that isn't very politically correct. But unless this is a case of mutton – or even ram – dressed as lamb, then we've got a teenage girl, young woman or whatever, who's been savagely beaten and buried in Jerome Monk's back yard. You know what they say, if it looks like a fish and smells like a fish . . .'

His manner grated, but he was only saying what I'd thought myself. 'It's possible.'

'Ah, a palpable hit! I'd say probable myself, but still. Which leaves the question of which one of Monk's unfortunate paramours this might be. One of the Bennett twins or the Williams girl?'

'The clothes might tell us that.'

'True, but this is more your province than mine. And I suspect you already have an inkling.' He chuckled. 'Don't worry, you're not on the witness stand. Humour me.'

He was a hard man to refuse. 'I'd only be guessing

at this stage, but . . .'

'Yes?'

'Well, the Bennett sisters were both quite tall.' I'd learned that from my hurried research after Simms had called: Zoe and Lindsey had the willowy grace of catwalk models. 'Whoever this is, she's more petite. It's hard to get an accurate impression of height with the body curled like this, but you can get enough of an idea of the femur's length to make a pretty good guess. I don't think whoever this was could have been more than five foot three or four at the most.'

Even when it was fully cleaned of soft tissue, which wasn't the case here, the thigh bone was only a rough indicator of stature. But I'd developed a reasonable eye for such things, and even with the remains contorted and caked in mud I was reasonably sure they wouldn't have been tall enough to be one of the Bennett sisters.

Wainwright's forehead creased as he stared down at the uppermost leg. 'Blast. Should have seen that myself.'

'It's just a guess. And as you say, it's more my area than yours.'

He shot me a look that held none of the joviality of a moment ago. Then his eyes crinkled. He gave a booming laugh.

'Yes, you're quite right. So, the odds are that this is Tina Williams. Good.' He clapped his hands together before I could say anything. 'Anyway, first things first. Let's finish digging her out, shall we?'

Picking up his trowel he set back to work, leaving me with the obscure feeling that the conversation had somehow been my idea.

We didn't speak much after that, but we made good progress. The only interruptions came when a SOCO arrived to sift through the peat from the grave. Except for a few more rabbit bones, though, it held little of interest.

It was dark outside the tent by the time the body was ready to be removed. It lay at the bottom of the muddy pit, filthy and pathetic. Simms had returned as we were finishing, accompanied by the pathologist, who he introduced as Dr Pirie.

Pirie cut an odd figure. He couldn't have been much more than five feet tall, so that his pristine overalls looked too big for his small frame. The face looking at me from beneath the hood was so fine-boned it could have belonged to a child, except that the skin was lined and wrinkled, and the eyes behind the gold half-moon spectacles were old and knowing.

'Good evening, gentlemen. Making progress?' His voice was precise and waspish as he came to the graveside. Next to Wainwright's towering bulk the pathologist looked smaller than ever, a chihuahua to the archaeologist's Great Dane. But there was no mistaking the authority he brought with him.

Wainwright stood back to give him room. Reluctantly, I thought. 'Nearly done. I was about to hand over to the SOCOs to finish off.'

'Good.' The small mouth pursed as he crouched beside the shallow hole. 'Oh yes, very nice . . .'

I wasn't sure if he was referring to the excavation or the remains themselves. Pathologists were renowned for being an eccentric breed: Pirie was apparently no exception.

'The victim's female, probably in her late teens or early twenties, judging by her clothes.' Wainwright had lowered his face mask now he'd moved away from the grave. His mouth quirked in amusement. 'Dr Hunter thought she might be a transsexual but I think we can discount that.'

I looked at him in surprise. Simms gave a dismissive sniff.

'Quite.'

'You can see her injuries for yourself,' Wainwright boomed, all business now. 'Probably caused by either a clubbing weapon or someone with prodigious strength.'

'A little early to say, I think?' Pirie commented from beside the grave.

'Yes, of course. That's for the post-mortem to decide,' Wainwright corrected himself smoothly. 'As for how long it's been here, if I was pushed I'd say less

45

than two years.'

'You're sure?' Simms asked sharply.

Wainwright spread his hands. 'It's only a guess at this stage, but given the peat conditions and the level of decomp I'm fairly confident.'

I stared at him, unable to believe I'd heard right. Simms nodded in satisfaction. 'So this could be one of Monk's victims, then?'

'Oh, I'd say that was a distinct possibility. In fact if I had to hazard another guess I'd say this filly could well be the Williams girl. The femur's far too short to belong to anyone as tall as the Bennett twins, but if memory serves she was, oh, five three, five four? That'd be about right. And the injuries certainly point to Monk after what he did to Angela Carter.'

Carson. Angela Carson, not Carter. But I was too angry to speak: Wainwright was shamelessly stealing credit for what I'd told him. Yet I couldn't object without seeming petty. Pirie looked up from his position by the grave.

'Hardly enough to provide an ID, surely.'

Wainwright gave a self-deprecating shrug. 'Call it an educated guess. At the very least I think it's worth seeing if this is the Williams girl first.'

He raised his eyebrows at Simms. The policeman looked energized as he slapped his hand against his thigh. 'I agree. Dr Pirie, how soon will you be able to confirm if it's Tina Williams?'

'That all depends on the condition of the remains once they're cleaned.' The diminutive pathologist looked up at me. 'It'll be faster if Dr Hunter works with me? I expect skeletal trauma is more his field than mine?'

He had an odd, sing-song cadence. I managed a nod, furious and stunned by what Wainwright had done.

'Whatever you need.' Simms no longer seemed to be listening. 'The sooner we can announce who this is the better. And if Monk buried one of his victims here it's reasonable to assume the others aren't far away. Excellent work, Leonard, thank you. Give my regards to Jean. If you're both free this weekend perhaps you'd like to come over for Sunday lunch?'

'We'll look forward to it,' Wainwright said.

Simms turned to me as an afterthought. 'Anything you'd care to add, Dr Hunter?'

I looked at Wainwright. His expression was politely enquiring, but his eyes held a predatory satisfaction. *OK, if that's the way you want it . . .*

'No.'

'Then I'll leave you to it,' Simms said. 'We'll be making an early start in the morning.'

3

I was still fuming later that evening when I arrived at the pub I'd been booked into. It was a few miles from Black Tor, a place called Oldwich I'd been told was less than a twenty-minute drive away. Either the directions were overly optimistic or I'd made a wrong turning somewhere, because it was three-quarters of an hour before I saw the smattering of lights in the darkness ahead.

About time. It had been a long day and driving on the moor in the pitch blackness wasn't my idea of fun. The memory of how I'd let Wainwright outmanoeuvre me still burned. Given his reputation I should have known better. A misty drizzle flecked the windscreen, refracting the glare from my headlights as I pulled into the pub car park. A flaking sign hung outside, the words *The Trencherman's Arms* faded almost to nothing.

The pub wasn't much to look at from the outside, a long, low building with peeling whitewash and a sagging thatched roof. First impressions were borne out when I pushed through the scuffed and creaking doors. An odour of stale beer complemented the threadbare carpets and cheap horse brasses hanging on the walls. The bar was empty, the fireplace unlit and cold. But I'd stayed in worse places.

Just.

The landlord was a sour-faced man in his fifties, painfully thin except for a startling pot belly that looked as hard as a bowling ball. 'If you want food we stop serving in twenty minutes,' he told me with poor grace, sliding a broken key fob across the worn bar.

The room was about what I'd expected, none too clean but not bad enough to complain about. The mattress squeaked when I set my bag on it, sagging under the weight. I would have liked a shower, but I was hungry and the shared bathroom had only a rust-stained bath.

But food and freshening up could wait. My mobile phone had a signal, which was a bonus. I pulled the hard-backed chair next to the room's small radiator as I called home.

I always tried to call at the same time, so that Alice could keep to something like a routine. Kara worked three days a week at the hospital, but her hours meant that she was able to pick our daughter up from school when I was away. She was a radiologist, a fact that had been the source of many long discussions between us when she'd become pregnant. We'd not planned on having children for another few years, by which time I hoped to be getting enough police work to supplement my university wage so Kara could stay at home and look after the baby.

Naturally, things hadn't turned out quite as we'd planned. But neither of us regretted it. Even though Kara didn't really need to work any more, I hadn't argued with her decision to go back part-time when Alice started school. She enjoyed her job, and the extra money didn't hurt. Besides, I could hardly object, given the demands of my own career.

'Perfect timing,' Kara said when she picked up. 'There's a young lady here hoping you'd call before she goes to bed.'

I smiled as she passed the phone over.

'Daddy, I did you a picture!'

'That's great! Is it another horse?'

'No, it's our house, except with yellow curtains because I liked them better. Mummy says she does too.'

I felt some of my anger and frustration slough away as I listened to my daughter's excited account. Eventually Kara sent her off to brush her teeth and came back on the phone herself. I heard her settling down into the chair.

'So how did it go?' she asked.

Being outmanoeuvred by Wainwright no longer seemed so important. 'Oh . . . could have been worse. Terry Connors is deputy SIO, so at least there's a familiar face.'

'Terry? Well, tell him to give my love to Deborah.' She didn't sound too pleased. 'Do you know yet how long you'll be there?'

'At least another couple of days. I'll be at the mortuary tomorrow, but they're going to start looking for more graves, so it depends on how that goes.'

We spoke for a while longer until it was time for Kara to put Alice to bed. Wishing I was there to read her a story, I washed and changed before going down to the bar. I'd forgotten the landlord's warning that they would be stopping serving food, and the twenty-minute curfew was almost up. He looked pointedly at his watch as I ordered, mouth set in a disapproving line.

'Another two minutes and you'd be too late,' he snapped.

'Lucky I was in time, then.'

Tight-lipped, he went off to get my order. There were other people in the bar now, more than a few of them police officers or connected with the investigation in some way, I guessed. There was only one free table, so I took my drink over to it. A solitary young woman sat at the next table, absently forking up food as she read from an open folder next to her plate. She didn't look up when I sat down.

The landlord came over with cutlery. 'You can't sit here, this table's reserved.'

'It doesn't say it's reserved.'

'It doesn't have to,' he said with petty triumph. 'You'll have to move.'

I couldn't be bothered to argue. I looked around for somewhere else to sit, but the only space nearby was at the young woman's table.

'Do you mind—' I began, but the landlord pre-empted me by slapping the cutlery down.

'You'll have to share,' he declared before stalking off. The young woman looked from him to me in surprise.

I gave an embarrassed smile. 'Service and charm. This place has it all.'

'Wait till you try the food.' She closed the folder, looking irritated.

'I can find somewhere else if it's a problem,' I offered.

For a second I could see she was tempted, but then she thought better of it. She waved a hand at the chair.

'No, it's fine. I've finished anyway.' She set down her fork and pushed away her plate.

She was attractive in an unobtrusive way. She wore old jeans and a loose sweater, her thick auburn hair pulled casually back with a plain band. She struck me as someone who didn't worry too much about how she looked, but didn't have to. Kara was the same. She could throw on anything and still look good.

I glanced at the folder she'd been reading. Even upside down I'd recognized what looked like a police report. 'Are you here on the investigation?' I asked.

She pointedly picked up the folder and tucked it into her bag. 'Are you a reporter?'

There was frost in her voice. 'Me? God, no,' I said, surprised. 'Sorry, my name's David Hunter, I'm a forensic anthropologist. Part of Simms' team.'

She relaxed, giving me a self-conscious smile. 'You'll have to excuse me. I get a little paranoid when anyone starts quizzing me about work. And yes, I am on the investigation.' She held out her hand. 'Sophie Keller.'

Her grip was firm, her hand strong and dry. She was clearly used to negotiating her way through the traditionally male police environment.

'So what do you do, Sophie? Or is that being nosy again?'

She smiled. She had a good smile. 'I'm a BIA. That's Behavioural Investigative Advisor.'

'Right.'

There was a pause. She laughed. 'It's all right, I'm not sure what a forensic anthropologist does either.'

'Is a BIA like a profiler?' I asked, reminding myself

to be diplomatic. That wasn't a field I had much faith in.

'There's a psychological aspect, yes, but it's a little broader than that. I advise on offenders' characteristics and motivations, but I also look at strategies for interviewing suspects, assess crime scenes, things like that.'

'How come I didn't see you at the grave today?'

'Sore point. I didn't hear about it until this afternoon, so I'll have to make do with photographs. Not ideal, but that wasn't really why I was brought in.'

'Oh?'

She hesitated. 'Well, I don't suppose it's a secret. They asked me here because if this is one of Monk's victims the others might be buried nearby. They want me to advise on the most likely places the graves could be. That's sort of a speciality of mine, finding where things are hidden. Especially bodies.'

'How do you do that?' I was intrigued. There had been a number of technological advances to help locate buried bodies in recent years: everything from aerial photography to geophysics and thermal imaging. But grave location was still a hit and miss affair, especially on a place like Dartmoor. And I wasn't sure how a behavioural specialist could help anyway.

'Oh, there are ways,' she said, vaguely. 'Anyway, now you know what a BIA does. Your turn.'

I gave her a potted outline of what my work involved, breaking off when the landlord arrived with the food. He set the plate down in front of me hard enough to slop the gravy on to the table. At least I hoped it was gravy: the greasy brown liquid could have been anything.

Sophie and I considered the mess of over-boiled vegetables and grey meat. 'So you decided against the smoked salmon and fois gras,' she said after a moment.

'It's the perks that make the work worthwhile,' I said, trying to spear a disintegrating carrot on my fork. 'So where are you from?'

'Bristol, but I live in London these days. I used to come on holidays around here when I was a girl, though, so I know Dartmoor quite well. I love the openness. I'd like to move out here some day, but with work . . . Well, you know how it is. Perhaps if I ever get tired of being a BIA.'

'I'm reserving judgement on Dartmoor, but I know Bristol a little. It's nice country round there. My wife's from Bath.'

'Oh, right.'

We smiled at each other, knowing that parameters had been drawn. Now we'd established I was married we could relax without worrying about putting out any wrong signals.

Sophie was good company, sharp and funny. She

talked about her home and her plans for the future; I told her about Kara and Alice. We both spoke about our work, although the subject of the current investigation was avoided. It was an ongoing case, and neither of us was about to give away too much to a virtual stranger.

But when I looked across the room and saw Terry and Roper heading towards me I knew that was about to change. Terry looked startled when he saw the two of us at the table. His expression became guarded as they approached.

'Didn't realize you two knew each other,' he said. Roper hung back just behind him.

Sophie gave Terry a smile that seemed to have an edge to it. 'We do now. David's been telling me what he does. It's really fascinating.'

'Is it,' Terry said, flatly.

'Do you want to join us?' I asked, made uncomfortable by the sudden atmosphere.

'No, we won't interrupt. Just came over to give you the news.' He spoke over his shoulder to Roper. 'Get the beers in, Bob.'

Roper blinked but hid any displeasure he felt at being ordered around. A trace of aftershave lingered behind him as he went to the bar.

'News?' I said.

Terry addressed me as though Sophie wasn't there. 'You know this morning when I told you I'd got to go somewhere? Well, I went to Dartmoor prison to see Jerome Monk.'

That explained Terry's secrecy earlier: no wonder he'd seemed keyed up. But Sophie jumped in before I could ask anything.

'You've been to *interview* him? Why wasn't I told?'

'Take it up with Simms,' he shot back.

Sophie was furious. 'I still can't believe you questioned him without consulting me first! Why bring a BIA in and then not use them? That's just *stupid*!'

I tried not to wince. Tact obviously wasn't her strong point. Terry's face darkened.

'I'm sure the SIO'll love to hear how stupid he's been.'

'You said you'd got news?' I said, trying to head off the row.

Terry gave Sophie a final glare before turning to me. 'Monk claims he can't remember who he buried where, but he's agreed to cooperate.'

'Cooperate how?'

Terry hesitated, as though he didn't entirely believe it himself. 'He's going to take us to the other graves.'

4

The prison van bumped along the narrow road. Police cars and motorbikes flanked it front and back, blue lights flashing. The procession made its way past the grassed-over ruins of an old waterwheel, one of the remnants of the tin mines Wainwright had told me about, and pulled up near where a helicopter stood on a patch of clear moor, its rotors turning idly. The doors of the police cars opened and armed officers climbed out, the snub shapes of their guns gleaming dully in the early morning drizzle. Now the front doors of the prison van opened as well. Two guards climbed out and went to the rear. The clusters of uniforms there obscured what they were doing, but a moment later the doors swung open.

A man stepped out of the back. The police and prison guards quickly formed a tight cordon around him, screening him from clear view. But the big, shaved head was clearly visible, standing out like a white football in the centre of the encircling figures. He was bustled across the moorland to the waiting helicopter, hunched over as the two guards hurried him beneath the whirling rotor blades. He climbed into the cabin clumsily, as though unused to the exercise. As he pulled himself up he slipped, going down on one knee. Hands reached out from inside the helicopter, grabbing his arm to steady him. For a second he could be fully seen, shapeless and doughy inside the prison-issue jacket.

Then he was inside. One of the guards followed him aboard and the door slammed shut. The rotors picked up speed as the other guard retreated back towards the prison van, clutching his hat to his head as the downdraught from the blades rippled the grass. The helicopter lifted from the ground, tilting slightly as it turned, and then it was angling away across the moor, shrinking until it was little more than a black speck against the grey sky.

Terry lowered the binoculars as the sound of its rotors diminished. 'Well, what did you think?'

I shrugged, hands stuck deep into the pockets of my coat. My breath steamed in the fine drizzle. 'Fine, apart from when he slipped. Where did you find him?'

'The double? He's some slaphead PC from HQ.

Nothing like Monk when you see him up close, but he's the best we could do.' Terry gnawed at his lip. 'The guns were my idea.'

'I wondered about that.'

He gave me a look. 'What's that supposed to mean?'

'It seems a lot of trouble to go to, that's all.'

'That's the price of a free press. This way they get something to photograph and we can get on with the job without the bastards getting in the way.'

I couldn't blame him for sounding disgruntled. Even though it was supposedly a secret, word had inevitably leaked out about Monk's involvement in the search. Keeping the press off open moorland would have been impossible, so the decoy would distract their attention while the real business was under way. Finding a grave out here would be hard enough without journalists trampling all over the moor.

'Looks like something's happening,' Terry said, staring through the binoculars.

About a mile away a line of cars and vans was racing across another road in the direction the helicopter had taken. Terry gave a grunt of satisfaction.

'Good riddance.' He glanced at his watch. 'Come on. The real thing should be here soon.'

It had taken two days to finalize all the necessary paperwork and arrangements for Monk's temporary release. I'd spent most of that time in the mortuary. Cleaned of the thick coating of peat, the full extent of the young woman's injuries was shockingly apparent. There seemed hardly any part of her skeleton that wasn't damaged: in places only the decaying tendons and soft tissue held the bones together. It was the sort of trauma you'd expect from a car crash, not something inflicted by a human being.

'The post-mortem wasn't able to establish a definitive cause of death,' Pirie told me, apparently unperturbed. 'There are any number of injuries that could have been responsible. Many of the internal organs and soft tissues are ruptured, the hyoid bone is broken and there are fractures to several cervical vertebrae. The damage to the thoracic cavity would almost certainly have proved fatal, as the splintered ribs penetrated the heart and lungs. In fact, the injuries suffered by this young lady are so severe that shock alone would probably have killed her.'

Young lady sounded curiously old-fashioned. Prim, almost. For some reason it made me warm to the odd pathologist. 'But . . . ?' I prompted.

I was rewarded with a thin smile. 'As I said yesterday, skeletal trauma is more your field than mine, Dr Hunter. I can't rule out strangulation, but the blows to her head were so forceful that her vertebrae and hyoid would probably have broken anyway. The attack must have been quite frenzied.'

'How do the injuries compare with Angela Carson's?'

I'd only been given a copy of the earlier post-mortem report that morning. I hadn't had a chance to read it fully, but the similarity of their injuries seemed undeniable.

'The soft tissue was too degraded to distinguish any signs of sexual assault, unfortunately. I'd hoped the peat might have preserved it adequately, but the physical trauma and shallowness of the grave worked against us. A pity.' He sniffed regretfully. 'The Carson girl also suffered mainly facial and cranial trauma, although nowhere near so severe as this. But as I understand it in that instance Monk was interrupted by the police, which perhaps explains why these injuries are so much more . . . pronounced.'

They were that, all right. Against the dull silver backdrop of the examination table, the features barely looked human. The front of her skull had been crushed in like a dropped egg, while the remaining skin and soft tissue of the face were pulped into the fragmented bones of the cheeks and nasal cavity.

'I believe psychologists claim this sort of facial disfigurement is an expression of the killer's sense of guilt. Eradicating their victim's accusing gaze. Isn't that the accepted explanation?'

'Something like that,' I agreed. 'But I can't see Jerome Monk as the remorseful type.'

'Quite. In which case he either has a truly terrifying temper, or he disfigures his victims for pleasure.' He looked at me over the tops of his half-moon glasses. 'Frankly, I'm not sure which is the most disturbing.'

Neither was I. A fraction of the force used would still have been fatal. Whoever this was, she hadn't just been beaten to death: she'd been pulverized. It was overkill in a very literal sense.

I'd expected the pathologist to leave me to work with an assistant, but he stayed to help with the grisly task of cleaning the remains: first cutting away the soft tissue then helping me disarticulate the skeleton so it could be soaked in detergent. It was a necessary part of my work but not one I enjoyed. Especially not when the victim was little more than a girl, and I'd a daughter myself.

But Pirie showed no such qualms. 'I'm always keen to learn new skills,' he said, delicately teasing a tendon away from its connected bone. 'Although I accept that these days that probably puts me in a minority.'

It took me a second to realize he'd been making a joke.

In the end, confirming that the dead woman was Tina Williams was relatively straightforward. The clothes and jewellery the body was buried in matched those the nineteen-year-old was last seen wearing when she'd disappeared from Okehampton, a market town on the northern edge of Dartmoor, and dental records confirmed her identity beyond doubt. Although the jaw and mandible were shattered and the front teeth broken, enough remained to provide a positive ID. The attack had been extensive but not methodical. Either Monk didn't realize his victim could be identified from her dental records, or he didn't care.

But then he probably never expected her body to be found.

I'd been able to add little to what we already knew. Tina Williams had suffered horrific blunt trauma injuries. Most of her ribs and the clavicle had simple fractures caused by a swift downward force, as did the metacarpals and phalanges of both hands. Although her face had LeFort fractures, formed when force from an impact dissipates along certain buttressing areas of the cranium, the rear of her skull was intact. That suggested she'd been lying face up on soft ground when the injuries had been inflicted.

Yet she seemed to have made no attempt to defend herself. Typically, when the forearm is raised to block a blow, it's the ulna that takes the brunt of the force, causing a wedge-shaped break called a 'parry fracture'. Here the ulnae and radii in both forearms had a combination of simple and more complex, comminuted fractures. That pointed to one of two scenarios. Either Tina Williams was already dead or unconscious during the attack, or she'd been trussed and helpless while Monk broke most of the bones in her body.

I hoped for her sake it was the former.

It was hard to say what had caused the injuries, but I thought I could guess. While Monk was powerful enough to have inflicted many of them with his bare hands, the frontal bone of Tina Williams' skull – her forehead – bore a distinctive curved fracture. It was too big to have been caused by a hammer, which would in any case more than likely have punched straight through. It looked to me like something that might have been caused by a shoe or boot heel.

She'd been stamped on.

I'd worked on any number of violent deaths, but the image conjured up by that was especially disturbing. And now I was about to come face to face with the man who was responsible.

The sound of the helicopter rotors had all but disappeared as Terry and I went back to the small township of police trailers, cars and vans that had now sprung into life around the moorland track. The constant traffic was churning the moor into a quagmire. Duckboards had been set down as temporary walkways, but black mud oozed up through their slats, making them treacherously slippery.

I hadn't expected to be here more than a few days, but the convict's surprise offer to show us where Zoe and Lindsey Bennett were buried had changed all that. While Wainwright would remain in charge of any excavation, Terry had told me Simms wanted me on hand when – if – any more bodies were found.

'Are you nervous? About meeting Monk, I mean?' Kara had asked the night before.

'No, of course not.' I had to admit I was more curious than anything. 'It isn't every day you get to meet someone like him.'

'So long as you don't get too close.'

'I don't think there's much danger of that. We're all supposed to keep our distance. Besides, I'll be the one hiding behind the police.'

'I hope so.' Kara didn't laugh. 'How's Terry?'

'He's OK, I suppose. Why?'

'I called Deborah last night. I haven't spoken to her in ages, so I thought I'd see how she was. She sounded funny.'

'Funny how?'

'I don't know. Distracted. Down. She didn't want to talk. I wondered if everything was OK between them.'

Terry wouldn't have told me even if it wasn't. We'd never had that sort of relationship. 'I haven't had much chance to speak to him. He's under a lot of pressure, though. Perhaps it's just that.'

'Perhaps,' Kara said.

Whatever might be going on in Terry's home life, the strain of this operation was beginning to tell. He had an intense, overwound look about him that spoke of too little sleep and too much caffeine. It was hardly surprising, since as far as I could tell Simms was delegating everything to his deputy. Except for press conferences, which he insisted on doing himself. He'd claimed the glory for identifying Tina Williams, and it seemed that every time I turned on the news I saw his wax-like features holding forth in front of flashing cameras and microphones. There was one quote from him which had been aired repeatedly:

'The man responsible for the deaths of Angela Carson, Tina Williams, and Zoe and Lindsey Bennett might be behind bars, but this investigation isn't over. I won't rest until all *of Jerome Monk's victims have been found and returned to their families.'*

It was suspiciously similar to what Simms had said in the forensic tent on the first day. I wondered if he'd been trying out potential soundbites even then. And while his superior courted the cameras and became the public face of the investigation, Terry was left to carry the brunt of the search operation himself. He'd been no stranger to high-profile cases while he'd been at the Met, but nothing like this.

I hoped he was up to it.

He glanced nervously at his watch yet again as we

clattered along the boards. 'Everything OK?' I asked.

'Why shouldn't it be? We've got one of the most dangerous men in the country about to be let loose and I've still no idea why the bastard's suddenly decided to cooperate. Yeah, everything's fucking great.'

I looked at him. He scowled, passing his hand over his face.

'Sorry. I just keep going over all the preparations, trying to make sure we've not overlooked anything.'

'You don't think he's serious about showing us where the graves are?'

'Christ knows. I'd feel happier if . . . Ah, screw it. We'll soon find out.' He stiffened as he looked ahead of us. 'Oh, great.'

Sophie Keller had emerged from the trailer serving as a mobile canteen, carrying a polystyrene container of steaming coffee. Bundled up in bulky overalls, the BIA looked like a young girl dressed in her father's workclothes. The thick hair was tied back with a no-nonsense band, the drizzle misting it with fine silver beads. A middle-aged man I didn't recognize was with her, stocky and pleasant-faced. She'd been nodding at something he said, but a coolness crossed her features when she saw Terry.

The two of them had made little secret of their dislike for each other. Whether it stemmed from something that had occurred on a previous investigation or was simply bad chemistry, they were textbook cat and dog. Terry's face hardened into cold planes as we approached.

Sophie ignored him as she gave me a warm smile, resting a hand lightly on my arm. 'Hi, David. Have you met Jim Lucas?'

'Jim's our POLSA,' Terry said, blanking her in return. 'He's been trying to keep some order in this three-ring circus.'

The police search advisor's handshake was just the right side of bone-breaking. His thick grey hair looked like a wire pan scourer. 'Pleased to meet you, Dr Hunter. Ready for the big day?'

'I'll tell you later.'

'Wise man. Still, not every day someone like Jerome Monk decides to work on the side of the angels, is it?'

'If that's what he's doing,' Sophie said, looking at Terry. 'I'd have a better idea if I'd been allowed access to him.'

Here we go again, I thought as Terry's jaw muscles bunched. 'We've already been through this. You get to accompany the team with Monk, but there's to be no direct contact. If you don't like it, take it up with Simms.'

'He won't return my calls.'

'I wonder why.'

'But it's ridiculous! I could assess Monk's state of

mind, gauge if his change of heart is genuine, but instead—'

'The decision's been made. Monk's not talking to anyone, and for the time being the priority's getting him to show us the other graves.'

'You mean Simms' priority.'

'I mean the priority of this investigation, and last time I checked you were a part of it. You want that to change, then say the word!'

The cords on Terry's neck stood out as they glared at each other. Lucas looked as uncomfortable as I felt. It was a relief when Roper came over. The DC's gaze flicked between Terry and Sophie, missing nothing.

'What?' Terry snapped.

'Just had the transport on the line. They'll be here in ten minutes.'

The anger drained from Terry. He straightened his shoulders. 'Right.'

'Hang on,' Sophie protested. 'What about—'

But Terry was already walking away, feet clumping on the duckboards. Roper hesitated long enough to give Sophie a toothy smile that exposed a line of pale gum above his incisors.

'Never mind, love. He's got a lot on his mind.'

She shot him an angry look as he hurried after Terry. Lucas rubbed the bridge of his nose, embarrassed.

'Well, I need to get on as well.' He hesitated, giving

Sophie an uncertain glance. 'Look, it's none of my business, but I wouldn't push too hard. There's a lot riding on today.'

'All the more reason why I should be able to do my job properly.'

Lucas looked as though he were about to say something else, then thought better of it. 'Just watch yourself. Monk's a dangerous bugger. You ask me, you're better keeping well away.'

For a second I thought Sophie was going to snap at the search advisor as well, but then she gave a reluctant smile. 'I can look after myself.'

Lucas kept his thoughts to himself. He gave me a nod. 'Dr Hunter.'

We watched him walk away. Sophie blew out an exasperated breath. 'God, sometimes I hate this job.'

Sophie had made no secret of her displeasure at being left out of the decision-making process. 'You don't mean that,' I said.

'Don't bet on it. I just can't understand why Monk's suddenly so keen to *help*. And please don't say it's his guilty conscience.'

'Perhaps he's planning an appeal and thinks it might help him get a reduced sentence.'

'He's got at least another thirty-five years to serve. I can't see him planning that far ahead.'

'You think he's hoping to escape?' I asked.

I wouldn't have dared mention that to Terry, not

given the pressure he was already under to see that didn't happen. The most dangerous part of any prisoner transfer was the transit, but everyone was well aware of what Jerome Monk was capable of. Even so, it was hard to see how even he could hope to escape out here, surrounded by guards and with a helicopter standing by only minutes away.

Sophie thrust her hands into her pockets, scowling in frustration. 'I can't see how he can, but I'd feel happier if he'd at least give us a bloody clue where the graves are. But no, he insists he'll only come out and *show* us. And Simms is letting him! He's so fixated on finding the Bennett twins so he can announce he's got the full set he's letting Monk dictate his own conditions. That's plain stupid, but I can't get anyone to listen.'

Not for lack of trying. I had the sense to keep that to myself, though. 'Even if the other graves are around here we'll be hard pressed to find them without Monk. I hate to sound like I agree with Simms, but what choice does he have?'

Sophie raised her eyes in exasperation. 'He could do what I've been suggesting for the past two days. I've already mapped out a few of the likeliest sites, but without more to go on I'm working blind. If he got Monk to just give us some *idea* of where the Bennett twins are buried, even a landmark, I might be able to find them myself.'

I looked at the blasted landscape of dead bracken, heather and rock spread out before us. It stretched for miles. I didn't say anything, but I must have looked sceptical. Twin patches of red bloomed on her cheeks.

'You don't think I can do it either.'

Oh, hell. 'No, it's just . . . Well, it's a big area.'

'Have you ever heard of Winthropping?' I hadn't, but she didn't give me chance to answer. 'It's a technique the army developed in Northern Ireland to find hidden arms caches. Anyone looking to make a hide – or bury a body – automatically follows the contours of the land, or uses reference points like a tree or distinctive rock to help them get their bearings. Winthropping's a way of reading a landscape to find the most likely places something would be hidden.'

'And it works?' I said without thinking.

'Amazingly enough, yes,' she said tartly. 'It isn't foolproof, but it's useful in situations like this. I don't care how well Monk's supposed to know the moor, it's still been a year since he killed the Bennett sisters. Their graves will be overgrown by now and he probably buried them at night anyway. Even if he wants to, I can't see him being able to remember exactly where they are. Not without help.'

As a rule I liked my science more clear-cut, not verging into crystal-ball territory. But she made a convincing argument. Still, it was academic now anyway. We both fell silent as we saw a distant convoy of vehicles creeping along the road towards us.

Monk was here.

5

After the drama of the decoy's arrival, the real thing was almost an anticlimax. There were no flashing lights or motorcycles, no waiting helicopter. Just an unmarked van escorted by two police cars. A stillness seemed to fall as they headed for where Terry was waiting with Roper and a group of uniformed officers. A dog-handler stood with them, the intent-looking German shepherd kept on a short leash. The van and cars pulled up well away from the other vehicles. In the silence after their engines died the sound of the doors clunking open carried clearly in the damp air. Unlike those with Monk's 'double', none of the police officers were armed: there had to be a realistic threat of escape to merit that. But they were all big, bulky men, whose hands immediately went to the batons clipped to their belts as they fanned out around the rear doors of the van.

'Very melodramatic,' Sophie commented.

I didn't answer. There was movement in the shadowy recesses of the van. Something round and pale solidified into a bald head as it emerged into the light. A crouched figure filled the opening, ignoring the step-board below the doors to jump down. Then it straightened, and I had my first look at Jerome Monk.

Even from where we stood, twenty yards away, there was no mistaking his sheer, hulking presence. His hands were cuffed awkwardly in front of him, and I realized with a shock that he was also wearing leg restraints. Neither seemed to bother him, and the hunched shoulders looked powerful enough to snap the handcuff chain without effort. His upper body was immense, yet the shaved head still seemed outsized.

'Ugly brute, isn't he?'

I'd been so preoccupied I hadn't noticed that Wainwright had joined us. The forensic archaeologist was dressed in well-worn but expensive outdoor gear, a scarf thrown flamboyantly around his neck. He made no attempt to keep his voice down, and his words carried clearly in the still air. *That's torn it*, I thought, as Monk's moon head swivelled towards us.

The photographs I'd seen hadn't done him justice. The indentation in his forehead looked far worse in the flesh, as though he'd been struck with a hammer and somehow survived. Below it, the skin of his face was pitted with scar tissue. A scabbed, yellowing graze on one cheek suggested that at least some of it was recent, while the crooked mouth was curled in the same half-smile he always seemed to wear. It seemed to acknowledge and mock the revulsion he provoked.

But it was his eyes that were the most disturbing. Small and unblinking, they were flat and empty as black glass.

I felt chilled as they settled on me, but I warranted only a fleeting interest. The dead eyes went to Sophie, lingering on her for a moment before shifting to Wainwright.

'The fuck you looking at?'

The accent was local but the voice was a surprise: gruff and disconcertingly soft. Wainwright should have let it go. But the archaeologist wasn't used to being spoken to like that. He gave a derisive snort.

'My God, it can talk!'

Monk's leg restraints snapped taut as he stepped towards him, feet swishing awkwardly through the wet grass. That was as far as he got before the two prison guards grabbed his arms. They were big men but the convict dwarfed them. I saw them brace themselves, tensing with effort as they tried to hold him.

'Come on, Jerome, behave yourself,' one of the guards said, an older man with grey hair and a lined face. The killer continued to stare at Wainwright, handcuffed hands dangling loosely. His shoulders and upper arms were massive, as though he had bowling balls packed inside his jacket. His black eyes remained fixed unblinkingly on Wainwright.

'You got a name?'

Terry had looked startled at the sudden confrontation, but now he moved forward. 'His name's none of your business.'

'It's all right. If he wants to know who he's dealing with I'm more than happy to tell him.' Wainwright drew himself up, using his full height to glare at the convict. 'I'm Professor Leonard Wainwright. I'm in charge of recovering the bodies of the young women you murdered. And if you've any sense, then I strongly advise you to cooperate.'

'Jesus,' I heard Sophie breathe beside me.

Monk's mouth curled. 'Professor,' he sneered, as though trying out the word. Without warning his eyes flicked to me. 'Who's this?'

Terry seemed at a loss, so I answered. 'I'm David Hunter.'

'Hunter,' Monk echoed. 'Name to live up to.'

'So's Monk,' I said automatically.

The black eyes bored into me. Then there was a slow wheezing, and I realized Monk was laughing.

'Smart-arse, aren't you?'

Only now did he turn to stare at Sophie. But Terry didn't give him a chance to ask about her.

'Right, you've been introduced.' He motioned to the guards to lead him away. 'Come on, we're wasting time.'

'You heard the man, laughing boy.' The other prison guard, a thickset man with a beard, tried to haul Monk away. He might as well have tugged at a statue. The convict swivelled his head, levelling that basilisk stare at him.

'Don't fucking pull me.'

The atmosphere was already tense, but now the air suddenly felt charged. I could see Monk's chest rising and falling as his breathing grew more rapid. A bubble of spittle clung to the corner of his mouth. Then a man pushed his way through the encircling police officers.

'Detective Inspector, I'm Clyde Dobbs, Mr Monk's solicitor. My client's agreed to cooperate in the search voluntarily. I hardly think assaulting him is called for.'

He had a thin, nasal voice that managed to sound bored and wheedling at the same time. I hadn't noticed him before. He was in his fifties, sparse grey hair swept across an expanse of pink scalp. His briefcase looked ludicrously out of place with his wellingtons and waterproof jacket.

'No one's assaulting anyone,' Terry snapped. He shot the bearded guard a look. The man grudgingly let go of Monk's arm.

'Thank you,' the solicitor said. 'Please carry on.'

Terry's jaw muscles tightened. He jerked his head at the guards. 'Bring him.'

'*Fuck off!*' Monk yelled, as the guards strained to pull him back. His eyes were suddenly manic. I watched, stunned, unable to believe this could go wrong so quickly. I waited for Terry to do something, to take charge, but he seemed frozen. The moment stretched on, taut and ready to shatter into violence.

And then Sophie stepped forward.

'Hi, I'm Sophie Keller,' she said easily. 'I'm going to help you find the graves.'

For a second there was no response. Then the black eyes flicked from Terry to her. They blinked as Monk's mouth worked, as though remembering how to form words.

'Don't need any help.'

'Great, then it'll be a lot easier for all of us. But I'm here just in case, OK?' She gave him a smile. It wasn't flirtatious, or nervous. Just a normal, everyday smile. 'Oh, and you'll probably want to lose the leg restraints. You're not going to get very far with those on.'

Still smiling, she turned to include Terry in that last comment. I could see the other police officers exchanging glances. Terry's face was red as he gave a nod to the guards.

'Just the legs. Leave the cuffs on.'

He spoke brusquely, but there wasn't anyone there who didn't realize how close he'd just come to losing control. I saw Roper watching nervously as Terry tried to regain some semblance of authority, and there were knowing looks on the faces of the other officers. If it hadn't been for Sophie there was no telling what would have happened. Not only had she defused the situation, she'd also managed to establish at least a tentative rapport with Monk.

After the outburst of a few moments ago, the convict seemed sullen and subdued. As he was led off down the track, the massive head turned to stare at Sophie.

'It looks as though Ms Keller's got a new pet,' Wainwright said as we followed on behind, our breath steaming in the cold morning.

'She did well.' Terry wasn't the only one to have just lost face, I reflected.

'You think so?' Wainwright's eyes were unfriendly as he watched them walk ahead of us. 'Let's hope it doesn't decide to bite her.'

The moor seemed to do its best to hinder us. The temperature dropped around the same time as the rain started to fall. It flattened the stalks of the grass and heather, a dull monotonous downpour that chilled the spirit as much as the flesh.

Jerome Monk seemed oblivious. He stood by Tina Williams' empty grave, rain running across his bald skull to drip from features that could have graced a medieval church gargoyle. He seemed to neither notice nor care.

The same couldn't be said for the rest of us.

'This is hopeless!' Wainwright snapped, brushing the rain from his face. The archaeologist had pulled on heavy-duty overalls that made his big frame look more outsized than ever. Stretched over his clothes and smeared with black mud, they were starting to look as frayed as the archaeologist's temper.

For once I sympathized. My own overalls chafed at my wrists and neck, making me sweat despite the chill. Water dripped from the top of my hood in silver beads, a cold trickle occasionally finding its way inside. The police tape was still draped around the area but the forensic tent had been taken down, and the empty grave was already filling with muddy water. In the days since I'd last been out, foul weather and the constant tramp of feet had turned the ground around it to a treacherous mire. There was cursing from the police officers as we picked our way out there, and once Wainwright slipped and almost fell. The archaeologist snapped a curt 'I'm all right' when I reached out to steady him. Even Monk seemed to be having difficulties, his balance hampered by having his hands cuffed together.

Except for his solicitor, the civilians – Wainwright, Sophie and myself – stayed a little way away from the group surrounding the convict, a token concession to our instructions not to approach. We'd been joined by a cadaver dog and its handler. The springer spaniel was trained to sniff out even the faintest taint of gases produced by decomposition, but first we had to find a grave. And Monk seemed in no hurry to help us with that.

Flanked by the two guards, he stared down at the shallow pit where Tina Williams had been buried, lips curled in his habitual sneer as though at some private joke. But I'd come to realize that it was just the natural set of his mouth: it bore no more relation to whatever thoughts went on behind those button eyes than the sickle grin of a shark.

'Bring back memories, Monk?' Terry asked.

There was no response. The convict could have been carved from the same granite as the rocks of Black Tor for all the notice he took.

The bearded guard prodded him. 'You heard the man, laughing boy.'

'Keep your fucking hands to yourself,' Monk grated without looking round.

His solicitor gave an exaggerated sigh as the guard bridled. 'I'm sure I don't have to remind anyone that my client is here voluntarily. If he's going to be subjected to harassment we can call this off now.'

'Nobody's harassing anyone.' Terry's shoulders were hunched, but not from the rain: tension snapped from him like static electricity. 'It was your "client" who wanted to come out here. I'm entitled to ask why.'

Dobbs's wispy hair flapped in the wind, giving him the look of an irate baby bird. The solicitor still had his briefcase. I wondered if it contained anything important or whether he just carried it out of habit.

'The terms of my client's release clearly stipulate he's here to assist in locating the graves of Zoe and Lindsey Bennett, and nothing more. If you wish to question him about anything else we can return to the prison so you can conduct a formal interview in the proper environment.'

'Yeah, whatever.' Terry didn't try to hide his disgust. 'Time's up, Monk. You've done enough sight-seeing. Now tell us where the other graves are, or you can go back to your cell.'

Monk raised his eyes from the pit and stared out across the moor. His restraints chinked as he raised his hands and rubbed them over his skull.

'Over there.'

Everyone looked where he'd indicated. It was even further away from the road and track. Except for occasional smaller outcrops of rock or islands of gorse, there was nothing to see except a featureless plain of heather and grass.

'Whereabouts?' Terry asked.

'I told you. Over there.'

'They're not near where you buried Tina Williams?'

'I never said they were.'

'Then what the hell did you bring us out here for?'

The look in Monk's black eyes was impossible to decipher. 'I wanted to see.'

Terry's jaw muscles bunched. I'd never seen him so edgy, but he couldn't afford to lose his temper now. I wished Lucas was there. The older man was a calming presence, and it was becoming obvious that Terry was getting out of his depth.

'How far away?' Terry asked, making a visible effort to restrain himself. 'Fifty yards? A hundred? Half a mile?'

'I'll know when I get there.'

'Can you remember any landmarks nearby?' Sophie asked quickly. Annoyance flickered across Terry's face, but he didn't interrupt. 'A big rock, a clump of gorse, anything like that?'

Monk looked at her. 'Can't remember.'

Wainwright gave a disdainful sniff. 'Hardly the sort of thing one would forget, I'd think.'

Again, the archaeologist's bass rumble carried

clearly in the damp air. Monk's head swivelled towards him.

'What *can* you remember, Jerome? Perhaps if you tried to—' Sophie began, but Terry cut her off.

'All right, let's get this over with. Just show us.'

Sophie looked furious but people were already moving away, a cluster of uniforms surrounding Monk's unmistakable figure.

'This is farcical,' Wainwright grumbled as we trudged after them, boots squelching on the boggy moor. 'I don't believe that creature has any intention of telling us anything. He's making fools of us.'

'It might help if you'd stop antagonizing him,' Sophie said, still angry.

'You can't afford to show weakness to creatures like that. They need to know who's in charge.'

'Really?' Sophie's voice was dangerously sweet. 'I tell you what. You don't tell me my job, and I won't tell you how to dig holes.'

The archaeologist glared at her. 'I'll be sure to pass on your thoughts to DCS Simms,' he said, before walking on ahead.

'Prick,' Sophie said under her breath, though not so softly that he couldn't hear. She glanced at me. 'What?'

'I didn't say anything.'

She smiled wryly. 'You didn't have to.'

I shrugged. 'If you want to fall out with the whole task force, don't let me stop you.'

'Sorry, but it's just so bloody *frustrating*. What's the point of me being here if they won't let me do my job properly? And as for Terry Connors . . .' She sighed and shook her head. 'They're handling this all wrong. We shouldn't just be letting Monk lead us around by the nose, not without pushing him for some indication where the graves are. How's he going to find them again if he can't remember any landmarks?'

'You think he's lying?'

'Hard to say. He seems vague one minute and certain the next. He's acting like he knows where he's going now but it's a hell of a long way for anyone to carry a body.' She frowned, staring at where Monk's pale head stood out amongst the dark uniforms up ahead. 'I'm going to have a wander round. I'll catch you up.'

She struck off back towards the track that led to Black Tor. I could understand her doubts, but there was nothing I could do about them. The going became more difficult as we headed further into the moor. The rain-soaked peat sucked at our boots while the heather and long marsh grass snagged our legs. Monk was struggling more than ever, giving lie to the myth of how at home he was out here. Several times he stumbled and tripped, snarling at the guards as they steadied him.

I noticed that Roper had dropped back and was

talking on his radio. He kept his voice down, but as I approached the wind carried snatches of his words over to me.

'. . . not confident, sir . . . Yes . . . yes . . . Of course, sir. I'll keep you informed.'

He ended the call as he saw me. The 'sir' had sounded ominous, and it didn't take a genius to guess he'd been reporting back to Simms. I wondered if Terry knew.

'Enjoying the walk, Dr Hunter?' The DC grinned, falling in step beside me. 'Turning into quite a marathon, isn't it?'

There was something about the man that grated. He couldn't be blamed for the rat-like teeth, but his grin was just a little too ready and too sycophantic for me to trust.

'The fresh air does me good.'

He bobbed his head, chuckling as though I'd cracked an after-dinner joke. 'A little too much of it for my taste, but there you go. So what do you think of Monk? He's something, isn't he? Face like a bloody Picasso.'

You're no oil painting yourself. 'How did he get the bruises? Was he in a fight?'

'Not exactly.' Roper's grin broadened, but his eyes were shrewd as they stared at Monk's back. 'He kicked off on one last night and had to be "restrained". Almost made us cancel the whole thing.

One of his party pieces, apparently, having a tantrum after lights out. That's why the guards call him laughing boy. He seems to find it all very funny if no one else does. Hello, now what's happening?'

There was a commotion up ahead. The German shepherd was being held back by its handler, barking at the group with Monk. At first I couldn't see what was happening for the surrounding uniforms, then two of them moved aside.

Monk had fallen. The big man was down in the muddy grass, struggling to get up. Police officers and the prison guards swarmed round him, unsure whether to haul him to his feet or not.

'. . . get the fuck off me!' He was clumsily trying to lever himself up in his handcuffs as his solicitor confronted Terry.

'Now are you satisfied? This is completely unacceptable!'

'He's not hurt,' Terry said, but he sounded sullen and defensive.

'I hope not, because if he is I'm holding you responsible. There is absolutely no reason for my client to remain handcuffed out here. He doesn't pose any escape risk, and in this terrain it's positively dangerous.'

'I'm not taking them off.'

'In that case you can take us back to the van, because we're done here.'

'Oh, for—'

'I will not have my client injured because of police intransigence. Either the restraints come off or he stops cooperating with the search.'

Monk was still lying in a heap, breath steaming as he glared up at them. 'You want to try walking with these on?' he demanded, holding out his cuffed hands.

Terry took a step towards him, and for a second I actually thought he would launch a kick at his face. Then he stopped, his entire body clenched and rigid.

'You want me to call the SIO?' Roper asked.

If I hadn't heard him reporting back to Simms I might have believed he was trying to help. His suggestion decided Terry.

'No.' Tight-lipped, he gave a nod to a police officer. 'Take them off.'

The officer stepped forward and unlocked the handcuffs. Monk's expression never changed as he climbed to his feet, clothes soaking wet and smeared with mud. He flexed his wrists, the big hands opening and closing like clamps.

'OK?' Terry asked Dobbs. Without giving him a chance to answer he stepped up to Monk. They were of a height, but the convict somehow seemed twice his size. 'You want to make me really happy? Try something. Please.'

Monk didn't speak. His mouth was still curved in

its illusory half-smile, but the black eyes were stone dead.

'I really don't think—' Dobbs began.

'Shut it.' Terry didn't take his eyes off Monk. 'How much further?'

The convict's big head turned to look back out at the moor, but then there was a distant shout.

'Here! Over here!'

Everyone looked round. Sophie was standing on a low rise some way away, waving her hands over her head. Her excitement was obvious even through the drizzle and mist.

'I've found something!'

6

A buried body always leaves signs. At first the body will displace the earth used to refill the grave, leaving a visible mound on the surface. But as the slow process of decay begins, causing flesh and muscle to leach their substance into the soil, the mound begins to settle. Eventually, when the body has rotted away to bone, a slight depression will be left in the earth to mark the grave's location.

Vegetation, too, can provide useful clues. Plants and grasses disturbed by the digging will take time to re-establish themselves, even when they've been carefully replaced. As months pass and the corpse begins to decompose, the nutrients it releases will feed the flora on the grave, causing faster growth and more luxuriant foliage than in the surrounding vegetation. The distinctions are subtle and often unreliable, but there if you know what to look for.

Sophie was standing by a low mound that lay in the centre of a deep hollow, perhaps fifty yards from the track. It was covered in marsh grass, the tangled, wiry stalks rippling in the wind. I went over with Wainwright and Terry, leaving Roper with Monk and the other officers. The three of us had to detour around a thicket of gorse and an impassable section of bog to get to her. She made no attempt to meet us, staying impatiently beside the mound as though she were afraid it might disappear if she turned her back.

'I think this could be a grave,' she said breathlessly, as we slithered down the sides of the hollow.

She was right: it *could* be a grave. Or it could be absolutely nothing at all. The mound was about five feet long and two wide, perhaps eighteen inches tall at its highest point. If it had been in a flat field or parkland it would have been a lot more likely to be significant. But this was moorland, a rugged land-scape full of random depressions and hummocks. And the grass covering the mound looked no different from that growing anywhere else.

'Doesn't look like much to me.' Terry turned doubtfully to Wainwright. 'What do you think?'

The archaeologist pursed his lips as he considered the mound. This was more his territory than mine. Or Sophie's, come to that. He prodded it disparagingly with his foot.

'I think if we're going to get over-excited about every bump in the ground it's going to be a very long search.'

Sophie coloured up. 'I'm not over-excited. And I'm not an idiot. I know what to look for.'

'Really.' Wainwright put a wealth of meaning into the word. He hadn't forgiven her for the earlier snub. 'Well, I beg to differ. But then I only have thirty years of archaeological experience to draw on.'

Terry turned away to go back. 'We don't have time to waste on this.'

'No, wait,' Sophie said. 'Look, I might not be an archaeologist—'

'That's something we agree on,' Wainwright put in.

'—but at least hear me out. Two minutes, that's all, OK?'

Terry folded his arms, his face shuttered. 'Two minutes.'

Sophie took a deep breath before plunging on. 'Where Monk's taking us, it doesn't make any sense. Tina Williams' grave was exactly where I'd have expected it to be—'

'Easy to say, now we know where it is,' Wainwright sniffed.

She ignored him, concentrating on Terry. 'It wasn't far from the track, which meant it was relatively easy to get to. And it followed the contours of the land: anyone leaving the track around there would naturally find themselves at that point. It made *sense* for it to be where we found it.'

'So?'

'So Monk won't specify where the other graves are. He's just leading us further out into the moor, which means he'd have to have carried the bodies all this way across moorland, in the dark. I don't care how strong he is, why would he do that? And he says he can't recall any landmarks to guide him back to where they were buried.'

Terry frowned. 'What's your point?'

'I'd expect him to remember *something* at least. When people hide something they use landmarks to align themselves, whether they realize it or not. But where Monk's heading just seems random. Either he's forgotten or he's deliberately leading us in the wrong direction.'

'Or you could just be wrong,' Wainwright said. He turned to Terry with a supercilious smile. 'I'm familiar with the Winthrop techniques that Miss Keller refers to. I've used them myself on occasion, but it's mainly common sense. I find them overrated.'

'Then you're not doing it right,' Sophie shot back. 'I went back to the track to find the most likely spots where anyone carrying a body could have left it. Where the going is nice and easy, not too steep or permanently boggy. I've found a few of them over the past few days, but this time I tried a little further out.'

She levelled a finger back towards the track, some distance from where we'd left it to go to Tina Williams' grave.

'There's a spot back there where the moor slopes gently away from the track. It's a natural point for anyone struggling with the weight of a body to access the moor. The way the ground runs funnels you to that big patch of gorse. It's easier to go around the bottom side of it than the top, and then you find yourself in a gulley that brings you right here. To a concealed hollow, where there just happens to be a grave-sized mound of earth.'

She folded her arms, defying Terry to find a hole in her argument. His cheek muscles jumped as he looked back at the mound.

'This is a nonsense,' Wainwright blustered, no longer bothering to hide his animosity. 'It's wishful thinking, not science!'

'No, just common sense like you said,' Sophie retorted. 'I prefer it to pig-headedness.'

Wainwright drew himself up to respond but I beat him to it. 'There's no point standing round here arguing. Let's get the cadaver dog to check it out. If it finds something then we'll need to open it up. If it doesn't, we've only wasted a few minutes.'

Sophie flashed me a smile while Wainwright looked more constipated than ever. I couldn't resist twisting the knife a little further.

'Unless you're absolutely certain there's nothing here?' I asked, trying not to enjoy his discomfort too much. 'You're the expert.'

'I suppose it wouldn't hurt to make sure . . .' he conceded, as though it had been his idea.

Terry stared down at the mound, then sighed and strode up to the top of the hollow. 'Get over here!' he shouted at Roper and the rest, then turned to Sophie. 'I want a word.'

The two of them moved out of earshot. I couldn't hear what was being said, but it seemed heated. Meanwhile Wainwright prowled around the mound, testing it with his feet.

'Definitely softer,' he muttered. He was wearing a thick leather work belt, the sort used by builders to hold tools. He took a thin metal rod from it and began opening it out. It was a lightweight probe, a metre-long extendable tube with a point at one end.

'What are you doing?' I asked.

He was frowning in concentration as he unfolded short handles, so the instrument resembled a slender spade without a head. 'I'm going to probe, of course.'

Disturbed soil was usually less compacted than the surrounding ground, and often another indication of a grave. But that wasn't what I meant.

'If there's anything buried in there you're going to damage it.'

'We need air holes for the dog anyway.'

That was true enough. Even though cadaver dogs could sniff out decay through several feet of soil, the holes would help them detect the gases produced by decomposition. But there were less invasive ways of making them.

'I don't think—'

'Thank you, Dr Hunter, but if I want advice I'll ask for it.'

Gripping the probe by its stubby handles, Wainwright jabbed it forcefully into the mound. Knowing he wasn't going to listen, I clenched my jaw shut as he wrenched it free and rammed it back in. Probing was a basic archaeological technique, but it had its drawbacks in a forensic situation. While it was possible to distinguish between damage to bone inflicted before death and that caused by a pointed metal probe afterwards, it was an unwelcome complication. Wainwright knew that as well as I did.

But then it would be my problem, not his.

Sophie and Terry broke off their discussion as Roper and the others reached us. Neither of them looked happy. Terry went straight to Monk and his solicitor, standing on the edge of the hollow so they could see the mound.

'This ring any bells?'

Monk stared down at it, hands hanging loosely at his sides. His mouth still seemed twisted in a mocking smile, but I thought there was a wariness in his eyes now.

'No.'

'So this isn't one of the graves?'

'I told you, they're over there.'

'You seem pretty sure all of a sudden. Not long ago you said you couldn't remember.'

'I told you, they're over there!'

The bearded guard clapped a hand on Monk's shoulder. 'Don't raise your voice, laughing boy, we can hear you.'

'Fuck off, Monaghan!'

'You want the cuffs back on?'

Monk seemed to swell, but Sophie spoke before he could do anything else. 'Excuse me, Jerome?'

She smiled as the big head snapped round. This time Terry made no attempt to interrupt, and I guessed her involvement was what at least part of their discussion had been about.

'Nobody's doubting you. But I just want you to think about something. You must have dug the graves out here at night, is that right?'

It was a safe bet: few killers risked burying the bodies of their victims in broad daylight. But Monk's solicitor wasn't having any of it.

'You don't have to answer that if you don't want to. I've already made it clear—'

'Shut up.'

Monk didn't so much as glance at him. His button eyes seemed muddied as they fixed on Sophie. After a few seconds he jerked his head in a nod.

'It's always night.'

I wasn't sure what that meant. Judging by Sophie's slight pause neither did she, but she covered it well.

'Things get confused in the dark. It's easy to make mistakes, especially when you try to remember later. Is it possible you could have dug at least one of the graves here? Or even both of them?'

Monk's eyes went from Sophie to the mound. He rubbed a hand over his bald scalp. 'Might be . . .'

For an instant he seemed confused. Then Terry spoke and whatever I thought I'd seen was gone.

'I don't have time for this. Which is it, yes or no?'

Suddenly the heat and madness were back in the convict's eyes. The curved smile looked manic as he faced Terry.

'No.'

'Wait, Jerome, are you—' Sophie began, but she'd had her chance.

'Right, that's it. Let's get back over there,' Terry said, starting to leave the hollow.

'But the body dog's here now,' she protested. 'At least give it a chance.'

Terry paused, indecision on his face. I think he might have overruled her if it hadn't been for Wainwright. The archaeologist had carried on probing the mound while the scene played out.

'Almost done,' he said, thrusting the probe into the soil again. 'The ground here feels less resistant, although since it's peat I doubt—'

There was an audible *crunch* as the probe hit something. Wainwright stopped dead. He composed his features into a thoughtful expression, avoiding looking at me.

'Well, there seems to be something here.'

Terry went over. 'A stone?'

'No, I don't think so.' Wainwright beckoned to the dog-handler, quickly asserting control. 'Start with the hole I've just made.'

The dog-handler, a young policewoman with red hair and wind-chapped pale skin, took the springer spaniel towards the mound.

'No! We're in the wrong place!' Monk shouted, his huge fists balled.

'Tell your "client" if I hear one more peep out of him he's back in handcuffs,' Terry snapped at Dobbs.

The solicitor looked reluctant, but the threat worked. Monk's mouth twitched as he cast a look behind him at the open moor and unclenched his fists.

'No handcuffs,' he mumbled.

The spaniel was almost falling over itself in its eagerness as it snuffled across the mound. There were only a few cadaver dogs in the country, and I'd heard nothing but good things about them. Still, I had my doubts now. Peat inhibited decomposition, sometimes virtually halted it. No matter how sensitive a dog's nose, it couldn't smell something that wasn't there.

But the spaniel's ears pricked up almost immediately. Whining with excitement, it began scrabbling at Wainwright's last probe hole. The handler quickly pulled it away.

'Clever girl!' Fussing the dog, she looked at Terry. 'No two ways about it. There's something there.'

A sense of anticipation ran through the hollow. Terry seemed nervous, but given the pressure he was under I didn't blame him. His career could be changed by what we found here.

'What do you want to do, chief?' Roper asked. The solemnity of the moment had wiped the nervous grin from his face.

Terry seemed to snap back to himself. 'Let's take a look.'

Wainwright clapped his hands together, his earlier scepticism evidently forgotten. 'Right, let's see what we've got, shall we?'

A CSI brought a holdall containing mattocks, spades and digging tools into the hollow, dumping it on the grass with a clank. Wainwright unzipped it and took out a spade.

'I'll help,' I said, but I was wasting my time.

'Oh, I don't think that'll be necessary. I'll let you know if I need any assistance.'

He made 'assistance' sound like a snub. The archaeologist had become suddenly proprietorial now that it looked as though we'd found something. If this was a grave I could guess who'd take credit for it.

There was nothing for the rest of us to do but watch as Wainwright used a spade to cut the outline of a narrow rectangle across the mound. Sinking an exploratory trench was a much more effective way of opening up a potential grave than excavating the whole thing at once. It would give us a better idea of what we were dealing with, allowing us to see which way the body was aligned and how deeply it was buried before the real digging started.

Wainwright made it look easy, though I knew from experience it was anything but. The spade's blade chopped into the earth with brisk efficiency, levering out neat slabs of turf.

'Signs of disturbance to the peat,' he grunted. 'There's been something going on here.'

I glanced at Monk. The convict's doll-like eyes were watching without expression. The only sound was the crunch of the spade and a gentle tearing of roots as the last piece of turf was lifted free. Once the covering of grass was removed Wainwright began sinking the trench deeper. The peat was wet and fibrous. He was about a foot down when he suddenly stopped.

'Pass me a trowel.'

The instruction wasn't aimed at anyone, but I was nearest. *You aren't doing anything else.* I took Wainwright the trowel, standing at the other side of the narrow trench as he squatted down to scrape peat off whatever he'd found.

'What is it?' Terry asked.

The archaeologist frowned, peering closer. 'I'm not sure. I think it might be . . .'

'It's bone,' I said.

Something smooth and pale was visible in the dark mulch. There wasn't much of it showing, but I'd cut my teeth differentiating between the smoothly ossified texture of bone and stones or tree roots.

'Human?' Sophie asked.

'I can't see enough to say yet.'

'Certainly bone, though,' Wainwright said, his voice betraying his displeasure at my interruption. The scratch of the trowel filled the hollow as he began digging away at the surrounding peat. Everyone's attention was fixed on the archaeologist. Sophie hugged herself anxiously. Terry stood with his shoulders bunched, hands jammed deep in his pockets as though to brace himself, while just behind him Roper gnawed his lip. Only Monk seemed unconcerned. He wasn't even bothering to watch, I saw, big head twisted to look back over the moor behind him.

Then Wainwright spoke again. 'There's some sort

of fabric here. Clothing, perhaps. No, wait, I think it . . .' He bent closer, obscuring whatever he'd found. Abruptly, the tension seemed to leave him. 'It's fur.'

'Fur?' Terry hurried forward to see for himself.

Wainwright was gouging the peat away now with savage strokes. 'Yes, fur! It's a bloody animal.'

The bone he'd uncovered was revealed as part of a broken pelvis, jutting through a bristly pelt that was coated with peat.

'What is it, a fox?'

'A badger.' Wainwright tugged a muddy paw free of the ooze, the dirt-clogged claws curved for digging. He let it drop. 'Congratulations, Miss Keller. You've Winthropped your way to an old badger sett.'

For once Sophie had no response. She looked as though she wanted to crawl into the hole herself as everyone moved closer for a better look. The badger was badly mangled, broken bones visible through the matted bristles.

'We had to make sure,' I said, annoyed. 'It could have been a grave for all we knew.'

Wainwright gave a wintry smile. 'Neither Miss Keller nor you are forensic archaeologists, Dr Hunter. Perhaps in future you'll—'

I didn't see what happened next, only heard the sudden commotion. Someone cried out behind us and I looked round to see both prison guards and a policeman on the ground.

Beyond them, Monk was running from the hollow.

He'd waited for his moment, when everyone's attention was distracted. The convict didn't so much as pause as another officer lunged for him. He charged right through the man, knocking him aside as though he'd been hit by a bull.

Then there was nothing in front of Monk but open moor.

'Get after him!' Terry yelled, breaking into a sprint.

Brute force and surprise had given Monk a few yards' lead but it was never going to be enough. The air rang with curses as heavy boots pounded after him. Then he jinked and changed direction, and suddenly the men who'd been about to catch him found themselves splashing through a grassy bog. Within seconds they were floundering to a halt as the soft mud sucked and dragged at their feet.

Monk barely slowed. The clumsiness that had led to his handcuffs being removed had vanished. He ran without hesitation, finding solid ground that looked indistinguishable from the bog around it. I realized now why he'd been looking back at the moor instead of watching Wainwright.

He'd been planning his route.

'Use the dog! Use the bloody dog!' Terry shouted, trying to detour round the mire.

The handler didn't need any prompting. As soon as he'd released it the German shepherd streaked over the moor towards Monk. Either luck or its lighter weight helped it through the mud, and in seconds it had closed the distance between them. I saw Monk's pale face glance back at it, losing yet more ground as he slowed to shuck out of his coat. *What the hell is he doing?*

A moment later I understood: as the dog caught up he spun round, thrusting out a forearm wrapped in the coat. He took a step back under its weight as the animal leapt at him, its jaws clamping on to the thick padding. Bracing himself, he slapped his other hand on to the back of its neck and heaved. There was a shrill yelp that suddenly cut off, then Monk flung the dog's limp body aside and carried on running.

The stunned silence was broken by a cry as the German shepherd's handler began sprinting towards the dog's unmoving form.

'Jesus Christ!' Roper breathed. He scrabbled for his radio. 'Get the chopper in the air! Don't ask fucking questions, just *do it!*'

Monk was going flat out, hammering across the uneven moorland as easily as if he were in a park. Most of the police were still struggling through the bog, but Terry had managed to bypass the worst of it. And the dog had cost Monk his lead. From the top of the hollow where I'd gone to help the injured men, I felt my breath quicken as I saw that Terry was going to catch him.

Sophie's hands had gone to her mouth. 'He's going to get killed!'

She was right. Terry could handle himself against most men, but we'd just seen Monk snap the neck of a police dog.

But so had Terry. He launched himself at the convict's legs in a rugby tackle, hitting him just below the knees. Monk fell as if he'd been poleaxed, crashing to the ground with Terry's arms still wrapped around his legs. It didn't even seem to wind him. He twisted round and began clubbing wildly at the man clinging to his legs, trying to reach him. Terry ducked his head into his shoulders and held on. Then one of the punches connected, and Terry jerked and let go. Monk kicked himself free and scrambled on to his knees, but that was as far as he got before a mud-spattered policeman rammed into him, bowling him away from where Terry sprawled on the ground. Another launched himself on to them, and then uniforms were swarming over the convict like ants over a wasp.

'*Come on then, bastards!*'

Batons rose and fell as Monk lashed out, knocking his attackers away. But sheer weight of numbers carried him to the ground. He regained his feet once, surging up again before a baton cut his legs from under him. Face down, he struggled to rise as his arms were wrenched behind his back. Before he could free himself he'd been handcuffed and it was over.

He howled like a wounded animal as the police pinned him down and fastened restraints round his ankles. Then they stood back while he thrashed on the ground, raging and helpless. Some of them had gone to attend to Terry. He was on his hands and knees, still dazed. As we watched he shrugged off the attempts to help him and stood up by himself. We were too far away to hear what he said, but he must have made some quip. A burst of laughter came from the men around him, raucous and slightly hysterical.

Sophie sagged against me. 'Oh, God.'

I put my arm around her automatically. Both prison guards and the policeman Monk had knocked down to escape were back on their feet. The older guard had blood smeared down his face from a broken nose but he was able to walk. Pale and shaking, he tilted his head back, staunching the blood with the tissues I'd given him. Of the two guards he'd been the more humane towards Monk. It hadn't done him any good.

Monk's solicitor had been conspicuously silent, but seemed to feel obliged to speak as we hurried over to Terry and the other officers.

'You realize this marks a failing of the police force's duty of care to my client,' he panted to Roper, brief-case tucked under his arm as he struggled to keep up. 'He should never have been allowed to escape. I intend to lodge a formal complaint about the whole handling of this exercise.'

'Please yourself,' Roper said.

Dobbs took his indifference as encouragement. 'And as for justifiable force . . . The way he was subdued was completely excessive, a textbook example of police brutality.'

Roper turned to him, baring his rat's teeth in a feral grin. 'If you don't shut up I'm going to shove that briefcase up your arse.'

The solicitor was silent after that.

The police officers around Monk all bore the scars of their encounter. Smeared in mud from the bog, there wasn't one of them who wasn't bleeding or nursing some injury. Terry himself had a grazed lump the size of an egg on his forehead, but wasn't badly hurt. He seemed pumped up by what had happened, adrenalin giving him a manic edge.

'Nice one, chief,' Roper said, slapping him on the back. 'How's the head?'

Terry gingerly touched the bump. 'I'll survive.' He grinned at Sophie. 'Doesn't spoil my good looks, does it?'

'Anything's an improvement,' she said coolly.

Wainwright strode up to where Monk lay trussed in the grass and heather. The convict's chest was heaving, and his face and mouth were slick with blood. He'd stopped struggling except for jerking against the restraints from time to time, testing them. The handcuffs were tempered steel, and the strap round his legs wasn't going to break any time soon, but I was still glad I didn't have to take him back to prison.

Fists planted on his hips, Wainwright glared down at him. 'My God, to think society wastes money keeping animals like this alive!'

Monk stilled. Blood stained his teeth as he twisted his head to stare up at the archaeologist. There was neither fear nor anger in his eyes, only cold appraisal.

'Oh, for God's sake leave him alone,' Sophie said. 'You're not impressing anybody.'

'Neither are you,' Wainwright shot back. 'And after your display back there you'll be lucky to find another police force willing to hire you again.'

'That's enough,' Terry said, coming over. The energy that had buoyed him moments ago seemed to have gone. 'We're finished here. We'll wait for the helicopter but the rest of you might as well go back.'

'What about the graves?' Sophie asked. She seemed subdued: Wainwright's jibe had struck home.

Terry watched as the dog-handler carried the body of the German shepherd towards us, its head dangling loosely. 'What do you think?' he said, turning away.

Sophie and I began making our way back to the track. She was quiet, but I didn't say anything until

I saw her angrily brush the tears from her eyes.

'Don't take any notice of Wainwright. It wasn't your fault.'

'Yeah, right.'

'It could have been a grave. We had to check it out.'

Something flickered at the edge of my mind as I spoke, but I couldn't quite pull it into view. It didn't seem important: I let it go, concentrating on Sophie.

She gave a bleak smile. 'I'm sure Simms will see it that way. God, I made a real fool of myself, didn't I? Offering to help Monk remember, so sure I knew what was going on. And he was playing us. He only said he'd show us where the graves were so he could try to escape.'

'You weren't to know that.'

She wasn't listening. 'I just don't *understand* it. How far did he think he was going to get out here? Where did he think he could *go*?'

'I don't know.' I felt too dispirited myself for a post-mortem on why things had gone wrong. 'He probably wasn't thinking at all. Just making it up as he went along.'

'I don't believe that.' Sophie looked troubled. She pushed a strand of hair from her face. 'Nobody does anything without a reason.'

7

Spring came and went. Summer moved into autumn, then winter. Christmas approached. Alice had another birthday, started ballet classes and caught chickenpox. Kara was promoted and given a small wage rise. To celebrate we spent the money in advance on a new car, a Volvo estate. Something nice and safe for the two of them. I flew to the Balkans to work on a mass grave and came down with flu in the freezing conditions. Life went on.

And the abortive search for Jerome Monk's missing victims receded further into the past.

I'd expected there to be more hue and cry over his failed escape attempt, but Simms managed to keep the story out of the press. The operation continued afterwards, but the heart had been taken out of it. Simms brought in technicians with geophysical equipment, hoping that the ground's electrical resistivity and magnetic field might reveal a human body. But they were desperation measures, not designed for rugged peat moorland, and everyone knew it. After a few more days the search was quietly called off.

Wherever Lindsey and Zoe Bennett were buried, they were going to stay there.

I wasn't sorry to leave. It hadn't been a good experience, and I'd missed my family. The only thing I regretted was that I didn't get a chance to say goodbye to Sophie. She went before I did, still berating herself over what had happened. I hoped she'd get over it. Incidents like that had a habit of following you around, particularly if the SIO was looking for someone to blame. But Simms had another scapegoat in mind.

I only spoke to Terry once before I left. It was on my last morning, when I was just loading my bags into the car outside the Trencherman's Arms. I slammed the boot as his garish yellow Mitsubishi pulled in alongside.

'Getting off?' he said as he climbed out.

'It's a long drive. You look rough. Everything all right?'

Terry seemed tired. The grazed bump on his head had started to scab over, making it appear worse than before. He ground the heels of his hands into his already reddened eyes.

'Peachy.'

'How did it go with Simms?'

'Simms?' He looked startled, as though for a second he didn't know what I was talking about. 'He's not about to put me up for a commendation, that's for sure.'

'He's blaming you?'

'Of course he is. You don't think he's going to take any flak himself, do you?'

'But he's SIO. It was his responsibility.'

'Simms will hang me out to dry if it takes some heat off him. And you think there aren't people here who aren't dying to see the new boy from the Met taken down a peg or two?'

He was right. I wondered if I should mention how I'd overheard Roper reporting back to Simms. But it was only a suspicion, and Terry had enough to contend with already.

'Is there anything I can do?'

He gave a bleak laugh. 'Only if you can wind back the clock.'

I'd never seen Terry like this. 'It's that bad?'

He made an unconvincing effort to shrug it off. 'Nah. I didn't get much sleep, that's all. Is Sophie around?'

'She left last night.'

'Last *night*? Why the hell didn't I know about it?'

'I didn't see her go either. I don't think she wanted

to hang around. She feels pretty bad about what happened.'

'Yeah, she's not the only one.'

'It wasn't her fault. In her position I'd have probably done the same.'

Terry looked at me: there was no friendliness in it. Suddenly it felt like I hardly knew him. 'How come you're standing up for her all of a sudden?'

'I'm only saying—'

'I know what you're saying. The whole operation's gone pear-shaped and my neck's on the block, but you're more concerned with looking out for Sophie bloody Keller. But then I noticed the two of you were getting pretty friendly.'

'What's that supposed to mean?'

'It means—' He stopped himself. 'Forget it. Look, I've got to go. Say hello to Kara.'

He went back to his car, slamming the door and accelerating away so quickly that gravel sprayed over my legs. I stood there for a while, torn between anger and bewilderment.

But I didn't worry about it for long. There was too much else going on in my own life to dwell on Terry, and the events on Dartmoor were soon put behind me. Alice seemed to be growing up more every time I turned my back, and Kara and I began talking about giving her a brother or sister. Professionally, I was busier than ever. The search might not have been a success, but my own role in it hadn't hurt my profile. I found myself in demand with more police forces, and if I occasionally wondered at my anticipation when the phone rang with news of another mutilated or decomposing body . . . Well, I told myself that was understandable. This was what I did for a living. I had to stay detached, and who wouldn't be pleased that their career was going well?

Then came the mass grave in Bosnia. I went as part of an international team charged with exhuming and, where possible, identifying the victims. It was a gruelling, month-long trip, three days of which I spent feverish in bed from flu. I came back half a stone lighter and chastened by our capacity for inhumanity on such an industrial scale. I'd never been so glad to be home, and at first I put Kara's quietness down to giving me space to adjust. It was only when I'd read Alice a bedtime story on my first night back, as we sat with a bottle of wine after dinner, that I realized it was more than that.

'OK, are you going to tell me what's wrong?' I asked.

She'd been staring into space for several minutes. It wasn't like her to be so withdrawn, especially when we hadn't seen each other for weeks. 'Hmm? Oh, sorry, I was miles away.'

'I know. What is it?'

'Nothing. Really, I'm just a bit preoccupied.' She

smiled, trying to brush it off. 'Come on, let's get the dishes cleared away.'

'Kara . . .'

She set down the plates with a sigh. 'Promise me you won't do anything.'

'Why, what's happened?'

'Terry Connors called round a few nights ago.'

I hadn't seen or spoken to him since Dartmoor. 'Terry? What for?'

'He said he was in London and thought he'd drop round to see you, but . . . Well, I got the impression he already knew you were away.'

I felt something cold spread through me. 'Go on.'

'There was just something . . . *off* about him coming round like that. I could smell he'd been drinking, but why didn't he phone first to make sure you were in? I made him a coffee but he made me feel . . . uncomfortable.'

'How do you mean, uncomfortable?'

Kara's face had flushed. 'Do I have to spell it out?'

I realized I was gripping the edge of the table. I made myself let go. 'What did he do?'

'He didn't do anything. It was just the way he acted. I told him he should leave but . . . Well, he asked if I was sure that's what I wanted. He said . . . he said I didn't know what you got up to while you were away.' She picked up her wine glass, then put it down again without drinking from it. 'Alice

118

woke up then and shouted downstairs asking if you were back. I was actually *relieved*. It seemed to shake him up, and he left.'

My vision was starred as though I'd stood up too quickly, even though I hadn't moved. 'Why didn't you tell me?'

'You were knee deep in a grave in eastern Europe. What good would that have done? Besides, nothing actually *happened*.'

'Jesus! He just came here and . . .'

'David, calm down.'

'Calm *down*?' I pushed my seat back, unable to keep still any longer. 'What he said about me . . . It isn't true.'

Kara stood up and came over. She touched my face. 'I know that. Terry just thinks everyone's like him.'

'How do you mean?'

'You must know what he's like. The affairs?'

'Affairs?' I repeated stupidly.

She gave me a quizzical smile. 'Seriously? You didn't realize? I don't know why Deborah's stayed with him as long as she has. She told me she gave up hoping he'd be faithful years ago; now she just wants him to be discreet. I got the impression that's why Terry had to transfer out of London. He was having an affair with someone he worked with, and it turned messy.'

That was news to me. But it explained the tension

the last time the four of us had gone out. Even I hadn't been able to miss that.

'Why didn't you say anything before?' I asked, putting my arms around her.

'Because it was none of our business, and I didn't want to make things awkward. Not when you had to work with him.'

Not any more. Kara leaned back to look at my face.

'Promise me you won't do anything stupid.'

'Like what?'

'Like anything. Just let it go. Please? He's not worth wasting time on.' She slid her hands around my lower back. 'And I really don't want to spend any more of your first night back talking about Terry Connors.'

Neither did I. So we didn't.

But I couldn't forget about it altogether. Terry had gone to my home intending to seduce my wife. If that wasn't bad enough, he'd tried to make her believe I'd been unfaithful to her. Just thinking about it made me light-headed with anger, but I told myself not to do anything for a few days, to give myself a chance to cool down.

I lasted until the following afternoon.

I was easing myself back into work after the Balkans trip and had arranged to finish early anyway. The plan was for me to collect Alice from school, but my fury at Terry had been festering overnight. I stewed over it for a few hours before phoning Kara at the hospital.

'Sorry about this, but can you pick Alice up later?'

'I suppose so. Why, has something come up?'

I was already regretting calling her. Kara's hours were part time and flexible, and she often switched to help out colleagues. But this was our daughter, and I'd only just got back from a trip. I should be focusing on what was important, not charging off to confront someone like Terry Connors.

'Look, it doesn't matter. Forget it.'

'No, it's OK. I was only staying for a staff meeting anyway, so I'm glad of the excuse.' A wariness entered her voice. 'Why, what's happened?'

'Nothing. Let's keep things—'

I was about to say 'as they were', but there was a commotion in the background down the line. I heard raised voices and the banging of heavy doors.

'Sorry, I'm needed,' she said in a rush. 'I'll collect Alice, you can explain why later. Bye.'

She broke the connection before I could say anything. I lowered the phone, feeling shallow. I made up my mind to call her back later and say I'd pick up Alice after all. I left it half an hour but when I tried her line it was engaged. And already I was starting to think about Terry again, letting a head of anger build up against him. There didn't seem much point in bothering Kara when she was obviously busy, and by now she'd probably made arrangements anyway.

Instead I phoned Terry.

I wasn't even sure he'd answer if he saw the call was from me. But he did. His voice sounded as cock-sure and breezy as ever. 'David! How're you doing?'

'I want to see you.'

His hesitation was only slight. 'Look, I'd love to meet up, but things are a bit hectic right now. I'll give you a call when—'

'Would you rather I wait for you at your house?'

I'd no intention of involving his family, but I wasn't going to let him brush me off. This time the pause was longer.

'Something you want to say?'

There was, but I wanted to do it in person. 'I can be in Exeter in a few hours. Name a place.'

'I can save you the trip. I'm still in London. I'll even buy you a pint.' His tone was condescending. 'It'll be just like old times.'

I willed myself not to lose my temper as I went to meet him. He'd suggested a pub in Soho, and when I walked in I saw why. It was obviously a police watering hole: most of the clientele had the in-definable swagger of off-duty officers. The place was decorated for Christmas, the same faded streamers and baubles they'd obviously been dusting off for years. Terry was at the bar, laughing with a group of men. He excused himself when I went in. The usual smile was on his face, but his eyes were watchful.

'Want a drink?'

'No thanks.'

'Please yourself.' Glass in hand, he propped himself comfortably against a table. 'So. Where's the fire?'

'Stay away from Kara.'

'What are you talking about?'

'You know what I'm talking about. I don't want you at my home again.'

He was still smiling, but a flush spread up from his neck. 'Whoa, hang on a minute. I don't know what she's said but I didn't know you were away—'

'Yes, you did. The mass grave was all over the news; it didn't take a genius to work out I'd be over there. That's why you didn't phone first, because then you wouldn't have an excuse to go round.'

'Look—'

'You even tried to make her think I'd been seeing somebody else. Why the hell would you do that?'

I thought something that could have been either guilt or regret showed in his eyes, but it was gone so quickly I might have imagined it.

He hitched a shoulder in a shrug. 'Why not?'

'And that's it?'

'What do you want me to say? Kara's a good-looker. You should be flattered.'

His grin was mocking. *Easy. Don't let him bait you.* This was comfortable territory for him. If I lost control he could wipe the floor with me and still have a pub full of friendly witnesses to vouch that I'd started it. I didn't know what I'd done to him, but I no longer cared. And realizing that I also realized something else.

'Things not going so well, Terry?'

His eyes narrowed. 'What're you talking about?'

'That's why you're here, isn't it?' I nodded around the pub. 'Recapturing the glory days. Your reputation must have taken a knock after what happened with Monk.'

The smile had gone. His expression was ugly. 'I'm doing fine. Just having a few days off.'

But his eyes gave the lie to that. There had always been something reckless about Terry; that was part of his charm. Now I saw there was something self-destructive as well. He relied on luck and momentum to carry him through: both had let him down and he was lashing out in frustration.

I just happened to be a convenient target.

There was no point in staying any longer. Kara had been right: confronting him had accomplished nothing. As I walked out, I heard him saying something to the group at the bar. Their raucous laughter followed me through the door, then it had swung shut behind me and I was back in the street.

I went straight home. It was too late for me to collect Alice, and I half expected them to be home before me. They weren't, so I began preparing dinner. I was already regretting going to see Terry, berating myself for making Kara do the school run. I resolved to make it up to them both. I'd take them somewhere that weekend, perhaps the zoo for Alice, and then find a babysitter so Kara and I could go out by ourselves in the evening.

I was so busy planning it that it was a while before I realized how late they were. I called Kara's mobile but there was no answer. Her voicemail didn't cut in, which was unusual. But I didn't have time to worry about it before the doorbell rang.

'If this is somebody cold-calling . . .' I muttered, drying my hands as I went to answer it.

But it wasn't. Two police officers stood outside. They'd come to tell me that a businessman drunk from an expense-account lunch had lost control of his BMW and hit Kara and Alice's car. It had shunted it in front of a container lorry that had crushed the new Volvo's frame like balsa. My wife and daughter had died at the scene.

And as quickly as that my old life ended.

The Present

8

I'd just come out of the shower when the doorbell rang. I swore and grabbed my bathrobe. Still towelling my hair, I glanced at the kitchen clock as I hurried into the hall, wondering who would be calling at nine o'clock on a Sunday morning.

I paused to look through the peephole I'd had installed in the front door. I was expecting to see a pair of polite young men with evangelical eyes and ill-fitting suits, hoping to sell me the dream of everlasting life. But I could only see one man through the distorted bubble of glass. He had turned to gaze at the street, so all I could see of him was his broad shoulders and short dark hair. It was thinning at the crown, exposing a palm-sized patch of scalp that he'd unsuccessfully tried to hide with a comb-over.

I unlocked the door. I'd been advised by the police

to fit a security chain after I'd been attacked the previous year, but I'd never got round to it. Even though the person responsible still hadn't been caught, the peephole seemed paranoid enough.

I'd take my chances.

The pewter sky cast a cold light when I opened the door. The lime trees lining the road outside my flat had shed most of their leaves, covering the street with a whispering mat of yellow. Although the October morning was cold and damp the visitor wore a suit without any sort of coat. He turned and gave a thin smile, eyes taking in my bathrobe.

'Hello, David. Not disturbing you, am I?'

What struck me afterwards was how ordinary it felt. It was as though we'd only seen each other a few weeks ago, not the eight years it had been.

Terry Connors hadn't changed. Older, yes; the hairline was higher than it used to be, and the skin of his face held a tired pallor that spoke of long hours spent in cars and offices. There were lines around his eyes that hadn't been there before. But while the good looks were more weathered, the square jawline a little heavier than I recalled, they were still intact. So was the cockiness that was part and parcel of them. He still looked down on the world in a literal and figurative sense: even though he was on the lower step, the muddy eyes were on a level with mine. I saw them flick over me, no doubt taking in changes just as mine were doing. I wondered how different I must look myself after all this time.

It was only then that the shock of seeing him hit home.

I had no idea what to say. He glanced back down the street as if it led to the past that lay behind us. I noticed that his left earlobe was missing, as though neatly snipped off with a pair of scissors, and wondered how that had happened. But then I bore scars of my own since the last time I'd seen him.

'Sorry for turning up unannounced, but I didn't think you should hear it on the news.' He turned back to me, his policeman's eyes unblinking and unapologetic. 'Jerome Monk's escaped.'

It was a name I hadn't heard in years. I was silent for a moment as it caught up with me, bringing back echoes of the bleak Dartmoor landscape and the odour of peat. Then I stepped back and held open the door.

'You'd better come in.'

Terry waited in the sitting room while I went to get dressed. I didn't rush. I stood in the bedroom, my breathing fast and shallow. My fists were clenched into tight balls. *Calm down. Hear what he has to say.* I pulled my clothes on automatically, fumbling at the buttons. When I realized I was delaying facing him I went back out.

He was standing by the bookshelf with his back to

me, head canted at an angle so he could read the spines. He spoke without turning round.

'Nice place you've got here. Live by yourself?'

'Yes.'

He pulled a book from the shelf and read the title. '*Death's Acre*. Not much for light reading, are you?'

'I don't get much time.' I clamped down on my irritation. Terry always had a knack of getting under my skin. It was part of what had made him such a good policeman. 'Can I get you a tea or coffee?'

'I'll have a coffee so long as it's not decaf. Black, two sugars.' He replaced the book and followed me to the kitchen, standing in the doorway as I filled the percolator. 'You don't seem very concerned about Monk.'

'Should I be?'

'Don't you want to know what happened?'

'It can wait till I've made the coffee.' I could feel his gaze on me as I put the percolator on the heat. 'How's Deborah?'

'Thriving since the divorce.'

'I'm sorry.'

'Don't be. She wasn't. And at least the kids were old enough to decide who they wanted to live with.' The smile crinkled his eyes without warming them. 'I get to see them every other weekend.'

There wasn't much I could say. 'Are you still in Exeter?'

'Yeah, still at HQ.'

'Detective Superintendent yet?'

'No. Still a DI.' He said it as though daring me to comment.

'The coffee'll be a few minutes,' I told him. 'We might as well sit down.'

The kitchen was big enough to double as a dining room. It was more comfortable in the sitting room, but I didn't want Terry in there. It was strange enough having him here as it was.

He took a seat opposite me. I'd forgotten what a big man he was. He'd obviously kept himself fit, although the signs of encroaching middle age were still there.

The bald spot must kill him.

The silence built between us. I knew what was coming next.

'Lot of water under the bridge.' He was looking at me with an undecipherable expression. 'I always meant to get in touch. After what happened to Kara and Alice.'

I just nodded. I'd been waiting for the inevitable condolences, in the same way you tense yourself against a blow. Even after all these years the words seemed wrong, as though my wife and daughter's death contravened a fundamental law of the universe.

I hoped he'd leave it at that, duty done. But he wasn't finished.

'I was going to write or something, but you know how it is. Then later I heard you'd moved, packed in forensics to be a GP in some Norfolk backwater. So there didn't seem much point any more.'

There wouldn't have been. Back then I hadn't wanted to see anyone from my old life. Especially Terry.

'Glad you're back in the traces now, anyway,' he went on, when I didn't say anything. 'I hear on the grapevine that you've been doing some good work. Back at the university forensic department, aren't you?'

'For the time being.' I didn't want to talk about it. Not to him. 'When did Monk escape?'

'Last night. It'll be on the lunchtime news. Bloody press is going to have a field day.' His expression matched the sourness in his voice. Terry had never liked journalists, and that much clearly hadn't changed.

'What happened?'

'He had a heart attack.' He gave a humourless grin. 'Wouldn't think a bastard like that had one, would you? But he managed to convince the doctors at Belmarsh to transfer him to a civilian hospital. Halfway there he broke his restraints, beat the shit out of the guards and ambulance driver and disappeared.'

'So it was staged?'

Terry shrugged. 'Nobody knows yet. He had all the symptoms. Blood pressure sky high, erratic heartbeat, the works. So either he faked them somehow, or it was real and he escaped anyway.'

Ordinarily, I'd have said both were impossible. A high-security prison like Belmarsh would have a well-equipped hospital wing, with blood pressure and ECG monitors. Any prisoner displaying cardiac symptoms bad enough to be considered an emergency wouldn't be in any condition to escape: the attempt alone would probably kill them. But this wasn't an ordinary person we were talking about.

This was Jerome Monk.

The percolator had started to bubble. Glad of something to do, I got up and poured the steaming coffee into two mugs. 'I thought Monk was at Dartmoor, not Belmarsh.'

'He was, until the bleeding hearts decided Dartmoor was too "inhumane" and downgraded it from a Category A to C a few years ago. After that he was shuffled round to a couple of other maximum-security prisons before Belmarsh drew the short straw. Hasn't mellowed him, by all accounts. He beat another inmate to death a few months back, and put two wardens in hospital when they tried to pull him off.' He raised his eyebrows at me. 'Surprised you didn't hear about it.'

It might have been an innocent comment, but I

doubted it. I'd been in the US earlier that year, and before that I'd been recovering from a knife attack and hadn't been paying much attention to the news. It was impossible to tell if Terry knew about that, but something told me he did. It was like him to probe for a response, just for the sake of it.

Keeping my face neutral, I spooned sugar into one of the mugs and handed it to him. 'Why are you telling me all this?'

Terry took the coffee from me without thanks. 'Just a precaution. We're warning everyone Monk might have a grudge against.'

'And you think that applies to me? I doubt he even remembers who I am.'

'Let's hope you're right. But I wouldn't like to predict what Monk's going to do now he's escaped. You know as well as I do what he's capable of.'

There was no denying that. I'd examined one of his victims myself, seen first hand the savage damage Monk had inflicted on a teenage girl. Even so, I still couldn't see that I was in any danger.

'We're talking about something that happened eight years ago,' I said. 'It isn't as if I had anything to do with Monk's conviction, only the search operation afterwards. You can't seriously think he'll care about that?'

'You were still part of the police team, and Monk's not one to discriminate. Or forgive. And you were there at the end, when everything went pear-shaped. You can't have forgotten *that*.'

I hadn't. But I hadn't thought about it in a long time, either. 'Thanks for the warning. I'll bear it in mind.'

'You should.' He took a careful sip from the mug before lowering it. 'You keep in touch with any of the others?'

It seemed an innocuous enough question, but I knew Terry better than that. 'No.'

'No? I thought you might have worked with Wainwright on other cases.'

'Not after Monk.'

'He retired a while back.' Terry blew on his coffee to cool it. 'How about Sophie Keller? Ever see anything of her?'

'No. Why should I?'

'Oh, no reason.'

I was growing tired of this. 'Why don't you tell me why you really came here?'

His face had grown red, and I could feel my own had matched it as the old antagonism flared. *Didn't take long, did it?*

'I told you, it's just a precaution. We're notifying everyone—'

'I'm not an idiot, Terry. You could have phoned, or got someone else to phone. Why come all the way to London to tell me yourself?'

There was nothing friendly in his manner any more. He fixed me with the cold-eyed stare of a professional policeman. 'I had some other business to attend to in town. I thought I'd stop by and give you the news myself. For old times' sake. My mistake.'

But I wasn't going to be fobbed off that easily. 'If Monk's going to go after anyone from back then, it's not going to be me, is it?'

Terry's face had darkened more than ever. 'I came here to warn you. Consider yourself warned.' His chair scraped as he stood up. 'Thanks for the coffee. I'll see myself out.'

He strode to the hallway, then seemed to change his mind. He stopped and turned. His mouth was a bitter line as he glared at me.

'I thought you might have changed. I should have known better.'

He walked out without a backward glance. I stayed at the table, the past so close I felt I could almost step into it. *Can you pick Alice up later?*

The flat seemed subtly different somehow, less my own. But my hands were steady enough as I collected the mugs. I hadn't touched my coffee but I no longer wanted it. I poured it down the sink and watched the dregs swirl down the drain. I didn't know why Terry had really come to see me, but the years hadn't changed one thing.

I still didn't trust him.

9

Monk's escape was the main story on the lunchtime news. An audacious prison escape by a notorious killer would have made headlines no matter who it was.

When it was Jerome Monk it was guaranteed.

The story was on the radio as I drove into the lab. I listened to the headlines, then switched it off. There'd be nothing I didn't already know, and despite Terry's warning Monk's escape didn't concern me. I was sorry he was free, and sorry he'd hurt more people in the process. But Jerome Monk wasn't my problem. Eight years was a long time, too long for him to care about me. Or me about him.

Still, try as I might to pretend otherwise, I couldn't shrug off Terry's visit as easily as that. I was long past apportioning blame for what had happened, but seeing him again had dredged up painful memories, stirred up an emotional sediment that refused to settle. I'd been looking forward to a leisurely Sunday, and a rare day off. I was supposed to be meeting two colleagues and their wives for lunch in Henley-on-Thames, something I'd been promising to do for weeks. But Terry's reappearance had changed all that. Knowing I wouldn't be very good company I'd called and made my excuses. I needed time by myself to come to terms with what had happened, to pack my memories back in their box.

I needed to work.

The past blew around me like a cold wind as I pulled into the Forensic Sciences car park. When I'd returned to London from Norfolk I'd been uneasy about returning to my old department, wary of being swamped by past associations. But in the end there hadn't been enough reason not to. I'd been based here for the past three years, technically a part of the faculty but with freedom to concentrate on police consultancy work. The university had offered me tenure, but so far I'd been reluctant to take it. The present arrangement seemed to work, even if there was still a temporary feel to it. I could live with that, though. Experience had made me reluctant to put down roots.

The building was closed on Sundays, but I often came in to work. I had my own keys, and I was used to being there alone. Still, I glanced around the empty car park as I made my way to the entrance. There's always something slightly unsettling about being alone in a normally busy public space. And while I might not be worried about Monk coming after me, there were others whose grudges were more tangible.

I still bore a scar on my stomach to warn me against complacency.

The forensic anthropology department was in the basement of a former Victorian hospital. It was accessed either by a cranky old lift that always seemed to smell of disinfectant or by two flights of stairs. As usual I took the stairs. The building was listed, and the stairwell still had the original tiles and stone steps. My footsteps rang as I descended, their lonely echo emphasizing the weekend quiet.

Once through the doors at the bottom, though, I was back in the twenty-first century. There were several labs, all of them modern and well equipped. My office was attached to one at the far end of the corridor. Not large, but big enough for my purposes. I unlocked it and flicked on the lights. There were no windows down here, and I paused in the doorway as the bright overhead fluorescents stuttered to life.

It was cool inside, the heating system turned down over the weekend. But I was used to that. My office was utilitarian, most of the space taken up by the old steel filing cabinets and desk. Switching on the computer, I left it to start up and pulled on my white lab coat which hung behind the door. Then I went out into the lab.

The grislier aspects of my work – carefully cutting away the decaying soft tissue from a cadaver, or degreasing human bones in detergent – were normally done at a mortuary. Most of the remains that came here had already been through that process, or were so long dead that time and decomposition had reduced them to dry bones anyway.

The case I was currently working on was one of the former. Stripped of its flesh and neatly set out on the aluminium examination table was the partial skeleton of a man in his thirties. At least, that was my best guess. His gender had been relatively easy to determine because of the shape of the pelvis and large size of the bones. I'd estimated his age from the condition of his vertebrae and the amount of wear evident on the pubic symphysis – the part of the pelvic girdle where the two pubic bones meet.

But while the skeleton normally provides other indicators to help confirm age and sex, as well as identification, that didn't apply in this instance. The advanced state of decomposition had suggested that, whoever this was, he'd died at least two years ago, but I'd been unable to be more precise than that. And I couldn't even begin to offer a probable cause of death. In fact the only thing I could state with any real confidence was that he'd been murdered.

I'd yet to come across a suicide or accidental death where the arms, legs and head had been severed.

The man's torso had been found by a builder, dumped inside the well of a derelict farmhouse in Surrey. Neither the well nor the rest of the property had yielded the missing body parts, and without any teeth to compare against dental records, or any notable characteristics on the remaining bones, identifying the victim would be a difficult task.

Still, I hoped to at least establish how he'd been dismembered. There was none of the trauma that would indicate an axe or cleaver had been used, which pointed to it being a knife or saw. Any blade would leave distinctive marks on the bone, and from the cleanness of the ones I'd seen so far this was likely to be some sort of power tool. My money was on a circular saw, but I'd need to examine each surface under a microscope to be sure. It was dull, methodical work, but identifying what cutting tool had been used might be the first step on the long road to catching the killer.

Stranger things had happened.

I set up the first slide and tried to concentrate on what I was supposed to be doing. But I stared at the magnified section of bone in the viewfinder without really seeing it. *Clean cut, no sign of splintering . . .* Something scratched away at my subconscious, an irritating connection I couldn't quite unearth. I straightened, feeling it on the verge of surfacing, but then a final chime from my office as the computer started up distracted me.

Whatever I'd been trying to remember vanished. I sighed and gave in to the inevitable. *OK, just get it out of the way. Then you can forget about it and do some work.* Going into my office I went online to a news website. I'd expected Monk's escape to be the lead story. It was. I just hadn't realized what a shock it would be seeing that face again.

Jerome Monk's photograph stared from the screen like a still from a horror film. The sickening indentation in his forehead still made you queasy just to look at it, and the eyes . . .

His eyes were still dead.

I scrolled down the screen to the photographs of his four victims. The images looked dated, their subjects frozen in time. The Bennett sisters would be . . . what? Twenty-six or twenty-seven now, and Tina Williams twenty-eight or nine. Angela Carson, the oldest, would be about thirty-five. Old enough to be married, to have children of their own. Instead, their lives had been cut brutally short.

And now their killer was free.

I rubbed my eyes, the taste of failure as bitter now as it had been all that time ago. Again, I had the feeling that there was something I needed to remember. It wasn't so strong as before, just a niggling presence at the back of my mind. I started to scroll back to re-read the story and jumped as the phone on my desk rang.

The picture on the screen doubled in size as I accidentally clicked on the zoom. Swearing under my breath, I grabbed for the phone. 'Hello?'

There was a slight pause on the other end. 'Is that David? David Hunter?'

It was a woman's voice, strong and slightly husky, though now with an edge of uncertainty. There was something familiar about it.

'Yes. Who's this?'

'Sophie Keller?' she said, and another part of the past clicked into place. 'We worked together a few years ago. On the Jerome Monk case?'

She phrased it as a question, as though unsure I'd know who she was. She needn't have worried: it was only a few hours since Terry Connors had asked if I'd heard from her.

'Sure, of course.' I made an effort to gather myself. 'Sorry, it's just weird timing. I was just reading about Monk.'

'You've heard that he's escaped?'

'Yes, I have.'

I wasn't sure whether to mention Terry, so I didn't. The two of them had never got on. There was an embarrassed pause. 'I got your office number from the university website, but I only called to leave a message. I didn't think you'd be there on a Sunday. I hope you don't mind.'

'No, I'm just a little surprised, that's all.'

'I know, I'm sorry, this is really out of the blue, but . . .' I heard her take a breath. 'Well, could we meet some time?'

The surprises were coming thick and fast today. 'Is this because of Monk?'

'I'd rather tell you when I see you. I promise not to take up much of your time.'

She tried to disguise it, but I could hear the tension in her voice. 'That's OK. Are you still in London?'

There was another pause. 'No. I'm living in Dartmoor now. A little village called Padbury.'

That surprised me. Sophie had never seemed the rural type, although I remembered she'd said how much she liked the moor. 'You made it out there, then.'

'What? Oh . . . yes, I suppose so.' She sounded distracted. 'Look, I know it's asking a lot, but if you could spare me a couple of hours I'd really appreciate it. Please?'

There was no mistaking the need in her voice, or the anxiety underlying it. This sounded a far cry from the confident young woman I remembered.

'Are you in some kind of trouble?'

'No, it's just . . . Look, I'll tell you everything when I see you.'

I told myself not to get involved in a cold case, that digging up the past would be painful and pointless. But then the case wasn't really cold any more. Now that Monk had escaped it was very much alive again.

And there was that subconscious itch at the back of my mind. Until today everything about this investigation had lain dormant for the best part of a decade. So why should it all of a sudden feel like unfinished business?

'How about tomorrow?' I heard myself say. It was too late today: I wouldn't arrive there till evening.

Her relief was evident even down the line. 'That'd be great! If you're sure . . .'

'I'll be glad of an excuse to get out of London.' *Are you certain that's the only reason?* I ignored the sardonic voice.

'Do you remember the Trencherman's Arms in Oldwich?'

The name brought back another blast of memory, not all of it good. 'I remember. Is the food any better than it was?'

She laughed. I'd forgotten what a good laugh she had, unselfconscious and full-throated. It didn't last long. 'A little. But it's easier than directing you to where I live. Can you make it in time for lunch?'

I said I could. We arranged to meet at one o'clock and exchanged mobile numbers. 'Thanks again,

David. I really do appreciate this,' Sophie said before she rang off.

She didn't sound grateful, though. She sounded desperate.

I lowered the phone thoughtfully. It had been quite a day for reunions. First Terry Connors, now Sophie Keller. Whatever she wanted to see me about, I doubted it was an accident that it coincided with Jerome Monk's escape. And it had to be something serious for her to get in touch after all this time. The Sophie I'd known hadn't seemed prone to panicking.

Still, eight years was a long time. People changed. I found myself wondering if she'd altered, if she still looked the same.

If she was married.

You can cut that out, I told myself, but I smiled all the same. Then without warning I shivered. I looked at the computer monitor, where the gargoyle face of Monk filled the screen. The black button eyes seemed to be watching as it smiled its mocking half-smile. I closed the connection and the photograph winked out.

But even after it had gone I still seemed to feel his eyes on me.

10

A few wisps of purple still clung to the heather, but autumn had already leached the colour from the landscape, cloaking the moor in dead greens and browns. It stretched as far as the eye could see, bleak and windblasted. The thigh-deep lakes of bracken were starting to die off, leaving nothing to break the monotony but house-sized rocks and thickets of impenetrable gorse.

A recent case had taken me to a remote Scottish island that if anything had been even more desolate, but there had still been an impressive sweep and grandeur to it. To my mind, this part of Dartmoor seemed brooding and oppressive, although I had to admit I wasn't exactly impartial.

I didn't have good memories of this place.

The sky had promised rain, but so far none had

materialized. Despite the low clouds the sun kept breaking through, picking out the heather in startling clarity before being shut off once more. I'd made good time from London, except for a traffic jam on the M5. It was the first time in years I'd been this far west, but I found myself recalling parts of the route, recognizing villages I'd forgotten till then. Then I reached the moor itself, and it was like driving back in time.

I passed signposts for half-remembered places, landmarks that nudged rusty chords of memory. I drove by the grassed-over ruins of the old tin mine's waterwheel, where Monk's decoy had lured the press away. It was even more overgrown and looked smaller than I remembered. I felt the past thicken around me, then the road curved away and in the far distance I could make out the rocky jumble of Black Tor.

I slowed for a better look. Even though I'd been expecting it, the sight still brought back the chill mists and *snap* of police tape vibrating in the wind. Then I'd passed the turn-off. Shaking off the memories, I drove on to meet Sophie.

Oldwich was on the edge of the MOD training area, a sizeable chunk of the national park that the military had annexed for its firing and combat exercises. Most of it still granted public access, except on days when training was taking place.

Today wasn't one of them. I passed a warning post, but there was no red flag to indicate the area was off-limits. Oldwich itself was an odd place, apparently undecided as to whether it was a town or a village. It didn't seem to have changed much; there were newer houses on its fringes, but its centre was still as drab and unprepossessing as I recalled. The pebble-dashed cottages had always put me in mind of a coastal town, facing out to the empty moor as though to a static green sea.

A two-carriage train was unhurriedly pulling away as I drove by, slowly dragging itself across the moor as if exhausted. The Trencherman's Arms wasn't far from the tiny train station. The last time I'd been here the pub had looked dilapidated and depressing; now the roof had been rethatched and the walls were freshly whitewashed. At least some things had changed for the better.

The small car park was round the back. I felt oddly nervous as I pulled in and turned off the engine. I told myself there was no need, and made my way to the entrance. The doorway leading into the pub was low, and I had to stoop to avoid banging my head. Inside was dark, but as my eyes adjusted I saw it wasn't just the thatched roof that was new. The exposed stone flags were a big improvement on the sticky carpet I remembered, and the flock wallpaper had been replaced with cleanly painted plaster.

A few tables were taken, mainly by walkers and tourists finishing lunch, but most were empty. It took only a moment to see that Sophie wasn't there, but then I was early. *Relax, she's probably on her way.*

A cheerful, plump woman was behind the bar. I guessed the sullen landlord had gone the same way as the flock wallpaper and beer-stained carpets. I ordered a coffee and went to one of the stripped-pine tables by the fireplace. It wasn't lit, but it was stacked with fresh-cut logs, and the ash in the grate suggested they weren't only there for decoration.

I took a drink of coffee and wondered yet again what Sophie might want. It had to be connected to Jerome Monk's escape somehow, but for the life of me I couldn't see how. Or why she'd contacted me. We'd enjoyed each other's company but I wouldn't have called us friends, and neither of us had made any attempt to keep in touch.

So why would she want to see me again after all this time?

My coffee had gone cold. Looking at my watch I saw it was nearly half past one. I frowned: after the way she'd sounded the day before I wouldn't have expected her to be late. But I wasn't sure how far she had to travel, so she could easily have been held up. I picked up the menu and restlessly flicked through it, glancing at the entrance every few minutes.

I gave it another quarter of an hour before calling Sophie's mobile number. At least there was a signal, which wasn't always certain out here. I listened to the clicks of connection, then I heard her voice: *Hi, you've reached Sophie. Please leave a message.*

I asked her to call me and hung up. Perhaps one of us got the time wrong, I told myself.

But two o'clock came and went with no sign of her. Restlessly, I checked the time again. Even if she'd been held up, I would have expected to hear something by now. Unless she was coming by train? I'd assumed she'd be driving but I hadn't asked. Pushing away my cold coffee, I went to the bar.

'Can you tell me when the next train's due in?'

The barmaid looked at the clock behind the bar. 'Nothing now for another two hours.' She gave me a bright smile. 'Late, is she?'

I smiled politely and went back to my table. But there seemed little point in waiting any longer. Grabbing my coat, I went out.

The sun had disappeared behind a high blanket of cloud, casting a diffuse, opalescent light as I walked the hundred yards to the train station. It was too small to have a ticket office, just two uncovered platforms linked by a short bridge. Both were empty, but there was a timetable on the noticeboard. The barmaid was right: there was nothing else due for a couple of hours. The only other train listed must have been the one I'd seen leaving as I'd arrived. Sophie obviously hadn't been on that.

So where was she?

A crow *caw-cawed* as it circled overhead; otherwise there was silence. I stood on the edge of the platform, staring up the line. The tracks were rusted but for the very tops, testament to how few trains used them. They ran straight, curving out of sight just before they reached vanishing point.

Now what?

I'd no idea. I wasn't even sure what I was doing there. I'd driven over two hundred miles for a woman I hadn't seen in eight years, and been stood up for my trouble. But although I tried to convince myself there was a mundane explanation, I couldn't quite believe it. Sophie had sounded desperate to see me: if she knew she was going to be late she would have called to let me know.

Something was wrong.

I went back to my car and took my road atlas from the boot. I had satnav but a large-scale map would give me a better feel for the geography of the place. Sophie had said she lived in a village called Padbury, which the map showed was several miles away. I didn't have her address, but it couldn't be that big. I'd just have to ask around until I found somebody who knew her.

Padbury was signposted well enough, but each

marker seemed to direct me further and further away from civilization. The roads grew increasingly smaller, until I found myself on a narrow, single-lane track hemmed in by high bramble hedgerows. Bare except for dead scraps of leaves, they towered above the car like a maze. In snow or icy conditions the place would be completely cut off. As I shifted down yet another gear to negotiate a blind corner I wondered what the hell had brought Sophie out here.

But then I'd no reason to talk: I'd made a similar choice once myself.

Within another mile or two the hedgerows gave way to thickets of stunted oak. They seemed to soak up what was left of the daylight, and although it was only mid-afternoon I had to switch on my headlights. I began to wonder if I could somehow have missed Padbury after all, and then I rounded a bend and found myself in it.

And out of it again, just as quickly. It was more a hamlet than a village, and I had to carry on for another half-mile before there was anywhere wide enough to turn around.

I was already starting to have a bad feeling about this. I'd hoped for at least a pub or post office where I might find someone who knew where Sophie lived, but other than a few stone cottages there was only a small church, set back from the road. I pulled up outside but left the engine running. Now I was here it seemed ridiculous. Even if I could find her house, turning up on her doorstep unannounced like this was starting to seem more and more like an overreaction.

But I was here now. With a sigh I got out of the car and made my way up the church path. Ancient stone gravestones flanked it, many of them set flat into the overgrowing turf, their inscriptions eroded to illegibility. The church door was wooden, black with age and hard as iron. It was also locked.

'Can I help you?'

The accent was pure Devon, sounding like something from an older, more peaceful age. I turned to find an elderly woman standing by the church gate. She wore a quilted jacket and tweed skirt, and an expression that was as watchful as it was polite.

'I'm looking for someone called Sophie Keller. I think she lives in the village?'

She pondered, slowly shaking her head. 'No, I don't think so.'

'This is Padbury, isn't it?' I asked, wondering if I might be at the wrong place.

'It is, but there's no Sophie Keller lives here.' Her face brightened. 'There's a Sophie Trask, though. Are you sure you've got the right name?'

It was possible that Sophie could have changed it – or married – since I'd last seen her, but she'd made no mention of it when we'd spoken. Still, I might as well make sure. I agreed that I might have made a mistake and asked for directions.

'You can't miss it,' the woman called after me as I got back into my car. 'Watch out for the kiln.'

Kiln? That made less sense than ever. But I realized what she meant soon enough. I followed the road out of the village, passing the point where I'd turned around earlier, and saw the curving shape through the bare trees about a quarter of a mile ahead. It was a squat, inverted cone, built of the same rusty-coloured bricks as the house it stood next to. When I drew closer I saw it looked on the verge of collapse. A rickety framework of scaffolding clung to one side, either to repair it or prop it up.

I pulled on to the verge in front of the overgrown garden fence. The dusk was thickening, but the house windows were unlit. Whoever lived here didn't appear to be home. A neat contemporary sign was fixed to one of the wooden gateposts: *Trask Ceramics*.

I almost drove away when I saw that. This had to be someone else. Yet Sophie had said she lived in Padbury, and according to the map there was only one in Dartmoor. *You've come this far . . .*

A stone-flagged path led to the house through a voguishly overgrown garden. A small orchard grew at one side, its scrubby apple trees now bare of leaves and fruit. The kiln sprouted on the other, tall and

157

faintly sinister. The air held an autumnal odour of woodsmoke as I pushed open the gate. A vague sense of trespassing mingled with embarrassment that I was here at all. I told myself again how ridiculous this was, but there was also an uneasy sense of déjà vu. I'd been in this situation once before, gone to check on someone to convince myself I was worrying about nothing.

I hoped history wasn't about to repeat itself.

Blown leaves from the orchard crisped underfoot as I walked up the path. There was still no sign of life from the house, its windows sheer panes of black. If someone was in I would simply make my apologies; if not . . . Well, first things first. I reached out to knock on the door.

And saw the freshly splintered wood where the lock had been forced.

All the doubts I'd had seemed to congeal in that second. The door was partly ajar, but I didn't push it open. The possibility that this could still be a stranger's house, that there might be an innocent reason for the smashed door, flashed through my mind, but I dismissed it. I looked around, half expecting to see someone behind me. But there was only the dark path, and the whispering branches of the trees.

The door creaked as I pushed it open with my fingertips. It swung back to reveal a darkened hallway.

'Anyone home?'

The silence was deafening. If I went inside I could be laying myself open to all sorts of trouble, but I didn't see that I'd any choice. If I called the police what would I say? That there were signs of forced entry at a house that might or might not belong to someone I knew?

If somebody's just lost their key you're going to look really stupid, I thought, and stepped into the hallway. Everything looked normal, but then I saw an old pine cabinet at the foot of the stairs, its drawers pulled open and their contents scattered. A vase lay shattered nearby, the broken pottery looking like pieces of bone on the floor.

'Sophie!'

I hurried inside, turning on the lights. There was no answer. I knew I should call the police but if I did I'd be told to wait outside until a car arrived.

That might be too late.

I quickly checked the downstairs rooms. They'd been ransacked, drawers and cupboards torn open and emptied, cushions flung off sofas and chairs. There was no sign of anyone so I ran upstairs. I noticed now that the carpet had wet patches on it, but I ignored it when I realized it was only water. All the doors at the top were closed, except for the bathroom. It was slightly ajar.

Through the gap I could see a pair of bare legs on the floor.

I rushed forward. A woman's body lay behind the door, blocking it so that I had to squeeze through. She was lying on her back, a towelling bathrobe fallen open. One arm was flung across her face, and a tangle of still-damp hair covered it further.

No blood. That was my first thought, but when I knelt beside her I saw that one side of her face was swollen in a livid purple bruise.

But even with that, and the fact that it was eight years since I'd last seen her, I still recognized Sophie Keller.

I moved aside the spill of hair and felt her throat. Her skin was cold but the pulse was steady. *Thank God*. I eased her into the recovery position, gently pulling the bathrobe down to cover her. There was no mobile reception, so I ran back down to the phone I'd seen in the kitchen. My voice wasn't quite steady as I called emergency.

Hurrying back upstairs, I covered Sophie with a quilt from the bedroom. Then, sitting next to her on the hard floor, I took her hand and waited for the ambulance to arrive.

11

I had to stay behind to give my statement while the ambulance ferried Sophie to hospital. I watched it go from the path just outside the front door, no siren yet but the blue light was bright and urgent, strobing through the dark branches as it disappeared up the lane.

It took nearly forty minutes for the first paramedics to arrive. During that time I'd not moved, sitting cramped on the bathroom floor with Sophie, talking to her constantly to reassure her that help was on the way, that everything would be all right. I'd no idea if she could even hear me. But there are different degrees of consciousness: if Sophie was aware on some level there was always a chance.

It wasn't as if there was anything else I could do.

The paramedics couldn't tell me much. Her vital

signs were stable, which was something. But there was no knowing how serious the head trauma was, or if she had any other internal injuries. The police arrived as the ambulance crew were bringing her down the stairs. The blackness of the country night was broken by flashing lights, giving the bare trees in the orchard an eerie, spectral hue. I stood by help-lessly as Sophie was carried out to the waiting ambulance, answering the flat-voiced questions of a policewoman. When she asked what my relationship was to Sophie I hesitated.

'I'm an old friend,' I said, not even sure if that was true.

As I'd waited for help to arrive I'd debated what to say. I'd no way of knowing if this had anything to do with Jerome Monk or not. The ransacked house looked like a burglary that had gone wrong, except for the timing. Sophie had called me asking for help, not long after Terry Connors had shown up to warn me of Monk's escape. And whoever had attacked her had done so before she could meet me and explain.

In the end I told the police everything, letting them decide whether or not to act on it. The policewoman's interest pricked up on hearing Monk's name, and so did her questions. Finally, frustrated with repeating 'I don't know,' I gave in to the inevitable.

'You need to call DI Terry Connors,' I told her.

I was loath to bring him into this, but I hadn't much

choice. Feeling like a criminal myself, I sat in the back of the police car with the policewoman's partner while she made the call. Finally, she came back.

'OK, you can go.'

It wasn't what I'd expected. 'Doesn't he want to speak to me?'

'We've got your statement. Somebody'll be in touch.' She gave me a smile that wasn't unfriendly. 'I hope your friend's all right.'

So did I.

The ambulance was taking Sophie to hospital in Exeter. As I drove there myself I tried not to dwell on the fact that the last time I'd been on this route, eight years before, I'd been going to the mortuary. The hospital had undergone some modernization since then, but not so much that I couldn't recognize it. The receptionist behind the Emergency desk was an over-weight woman with a neat fringe of greying hair. She frowned as she stared at her computer screen after I gave her Sophie's name.

'No one called that's been admitted tonight,' she said. 'You sure you've got the right hospital?'

I was about to argue when I realized my mistake. 'Sorry. Try Sophie Trask.'

She gave me an odd look but tapped at her keyboard. 'She was admitted to intensive care about an hour ago.'

Even when it's expected, there's still something

ominous about the phrase *intensive care*. 'Can I find out how she is?'

'Are you a family member?'

'No, just a friend.'

'We're not allowed to give out that information unless you're the partner or a relative.'

I sighed, trying not to snap. 'I only want to know if she's all right.'

'I'm sorry. Perhaps if you phone tomorrow morning . . .'

Frustrated, I went back outside. The hospital was a black rectangle behind me as I returned to my car, the bright squares of its windows deceptively cheerful in the darkness. *Now what?* I'd have called Terry myself, but I didn't have his mobile number and I doubted he'd be at his desk at this time of night.

But there was no point in staying here. I hadn't packed for an overnight trip, and if anything happened I'd find out as quickly at home as anywhere else. Even so, it felt like running away as I started the car engine and left the hospital behind. I stopped at the first garage I came to and bought a sandwich and caffeine drink. One was tasteless, the other sickly sweet, but I'd had nothing to eat or drink since breakfast and it was a long drive back to London.

The day's events replayed in my head as I drove. I'd gone to meet Sophie expecting to have at least some questions answered. Now there were more than ever.

The roads were quiet and I made good time to start with, but then the rain increased into a deluge that hazed the road with spray, smearing the windscreen like Vaseline despite the furious efforts of the wipers. I was forced to slow down, peering to make out the road ahead as the tail lights of the cars in front were reduced to dull red smudges. The downpour eased as I reached the outskirts of London, but not before a tension headache had settled into my neck and temples. I squinted against the street lights and brightly lit shops, the glare made worse by their mirror images on the rain-shiny pavements.

It was a relief when I finally turned on to my own road and parked outside my flat. It was after midnight. There were no other lights on, which meant my neighbours were either out or asleep. Unlocking the door, I bent to retrieve the usual assortment of bills and fliers, and as I straightened I felt a sudden sensation of being watched.

I quickly turned round, but the dark street was empty. I realized I was holding my breath, waiting for something to shatter the quiet, and forced myself to relax.

You're tired and imagining things. It's nothing.

Still, as I closed the door I was annoyed at myself. It was over a year since I'd almost been killed on my own doorstep: I'd thought I was past flinching at shadows.

Obviously not.

I went inside the flat, switching on lights. It seemed too quiet, as it always did. I switched on the TV and automatically flicked to a news channel, turning down the volume until it was no more than a murmur in the background.

I wasn't tired any more. Adrenalin had washed away the fatigue, and I knew if I went to bed now I wouldn't sleep. I went to the cabinet in the sitting room and took out the odd-shaped bottle of bourbon with the miniature horse and jockey on top. It was almost empty. I'd brought it back with me from Tennessee earlier that year, and had been eking it out to make it last.

But I felt I'd earned a drink now. And I'd need one for what I was about to do.

I poured myself a stiff measure and took a long swallow. The bourbon was raw and smooth at the same time, and as its burn ran through me I went out of the sitting room and opened the door at the end of the hallway. Technically, it was a third bedroom, but a bed would barely have fitted inside. A lot of people have a boxroom, where old furniture and belongings are stored and forgotten rather than thrown away. But in this case the description was literal.

The room was full of boxes.

I switched on the light. They were stacked one on top of the other, an assortment of plain cardboard and document boxes that filled the floor-to-ceiling shelves. Everyone has a past. Good or bad, it's what helps make us what we are.

This was mine.

After Kara and Alice had been killed I'd tried to run away from my old life. I'd dropped friends and colleagues, severed ties with anything and everything that connected me to what I'd lost. I'd sold or given away most of my belongings, but there had been some things that I either hadn't known what to do with or couldn't bear to let go. I'd put them in storage and done my best to forget all about them, until I'd felt able to come back and pick up the threads of my old life. Now all that remained of it was in these boxes. Photographs, diaries, memories.

Work.

I took another drink and set the glass down on a shelf. The boxes weren't in any order, but everything personal was in the plain and mismatched ones, flung into them in a barely remembered daze. I still wasn't ready to look in those. My research and case files were in the document boxes, and these at least were labelled.

I was dusty and sweating by the time I located the one I wanted. Carrying it into the living room, I set it on the low coffee table and opened it. The dry smell of old paper wafted out. The files were in alphabetical order, so it wasn't difficult to find the one containing my notes from the Monk case. There were several bulging cardboard folders, bound together with a thick rubber band. The band had perished with age, and disintegrated when I pulled them out. The folders themselves stirred echoes of memory: they were distinctive, blue and marbled, and I could remember I'd bought them in bulk to save money.

Shutting out that thought I laid them down and opened the first one. A bundle of old floppy discs slid out, meticulously labelled but useless on modern computers. Setting aside the outdated squares of plastic, I pulled out the rest of the folder's contents. There was a transparent folder containing the photographs of the grave inside the forensic tent. I flicked through them, the peat-caked remains caught starkly in the camera's flash. Each image brought a pulse of memory, but they could wait till later.

I turned to the case notes themselves. Most were printed hard copies, but mixed amongst them were pages I'd written in biro. While the script was obviously mine, it looked subtly different. Everything changes over time, including handwriting.

I wasn't even sure the person who'd written this still existed.

One of the sheets of paper was smeared with a dark smudge. It was only a few preliminary notes, hastily scribbled, and I'd started to put it to one side before I realized.

Kara mopping up the yoghurt Alice dropped on to the papers. 'Sorry, Daddy.'

I felt as though I'd been punched in the heart. Suddenly there was no air in the room. Dropping the smudged sheet on to the table I hurried out into the hallway. The cold, rain-freshened air braced me when I opened the front door. I gulped it in, no longer caring who might be out there. Outside, the wet street glistened in the streetlights. The night held that fresh, post-storm silence, heightened by the drip and run of water in the gutters and the distant swish of traffic. Gradually, some measure of calm returned. The emotional jack-in-the-box was back in the compartment I'd made for it, where it would lie coiled and waiting.

Until next time.

Closing the front door, I went back into the living room. The document box and papers lay on the table where I'd left them. I picked up the page with the dark smudge and carefully tucked it away in the folder.

Then, taking a long drink of bourbon, I sat down and started to read.

12

I guessed it wouldn't be good news when my doorbell rang next morning. It had been after three before I'd finally gone to bed, having pored over my old notes on the Monk investigation until my eyes swam. I'd felt sure I must have overlooked something, that there was some vital piece of information hidden among the dry pages. But they'd revealed nothing I hadn't known already. Tina Williams' injuries were horrific but hardly unique. I'd encountered worse since then, and even worked on a still unsolved serial-killer investigation in Scotland that bore chilling similarities. It was depressing to realize that there were others like Monk out there, still waiting to be caught.

In the end all I had to show for my efforts was another tension headache and a feeling that eight years was both a lifetime and no time at all.

I'd phoned the hospital first thing to see how Sophie was, only to be told they couldn't release any information. I'd left my number anyway, then debated what to do next. Though not for long. Whatever answers there might be, I wasn't going to find them in London. I called the university to tell them I'd be taking a few days off. I was owed holiday and Erica, the department secretary, had been telling me for weeks I needed a break.

Although this probably wasn't what she had in mind.

I didn't know how long I'd be away, so I packed enough to see me through. I'd almost finished when the chime of the doorbell echoed through the flat. I paused, tension knotting my stomach.

I knew who it would be.

Terry looked as though he'd hardly slept. Which perhaps he hadn't, given how long it would have taken him to drive here. His face was pouched and sallow, his jaw blued with stubble, and not even the mint of his chewing gum could hide the sour smell of alcohol on his breath.

'Getting to be a habit, isn't it?' he said.

I reluctantly stood back to let him in. 'Any news about Sophie?'

'Nope. No change.'

'So why are you here? It's a long way from Dartmoor.'

171

'Don't flatter yourself. I didn't come all this way just to see you. I've got other people I need to talk to while I'm here.'

He went into the sitting room without being asked. My notes from the Monk investigation were still on the coffee table, waiting for me to pack them away. Terry went over and picked up the top sheet.

'Been doing some homework?'

'Just going over a few notes.' I took it off him, put it in the folder and closed it. 'So what can I do for you?'

'No coffee this time?'

'I'm going out.'

He glanced at the bag. 'So I see. Anywhere nice?'

'Just tell me what you want, Terry.'

'I want you to tell me what happened yesterday, for a start.'

I'd been through this with the police numerous times the night before, but I knew there was no point in arguing. I went through it again now, from Sophie's phone call to how I'd found her unconscious on the bathroom floor. When I'd finished, Terry continued to stare at me without speaking. It was an old policeman's trick, but I'd seen it done too often before to fall for it. I looked back at him and waited.

'I thought you said you hadn't kept in touch with Sophie Keller,' he said at last.

'I hadn't.'

'You expect me to believe she just called you out of the blue? After eight years?'

'That's right.' He stared at me impassively, jaw bunching rhythmically on the gum. I sighed, annoyed. 'Look, I've no idea what sort of trouble she was in or why she called me. I wish I could tell you more, but I can't. Have you spoken to any of the people in the village? Friends, anyone who might know why she was attacked?'

'Are you trying to tell me how to run an investigation?'

I held my temper in check. 'No, but it seems a co-incidence it happened so soon after Jerome Monk escaped. I don't mean he was the one who attacked her, but there must be some connection.'

Terry had stopped chewing. 'What makes you so sure it wasn't him?'

'Why would he have anything against Sophie? She was the only person who tried to help him. And how would he even know where to find her?'

'You think you can't find out stuff like that in prison? Grow up. And if you're looking for a reason, she was probably the last woman he set eyes on. He's had years of lying in his cell, thinking what he'd like to do to her.'

That invited a question I'd not wanted to ask. But Terry had brought it out in the open. 'Was she raped?'

'No.' Terry's eyes were cold.

I was thankful for that, at least. 'Then it doesn't sound like Monk, does it? And he doesn't normally leave his victims alive.'

'He could have been disturbed or scared off.'

'Monk?' That was so far-fetched I almost laughed. 'Who by?'

'All right, since you don't think it was him just remind me what you were doing at Sophie's house yourself?'

'I've already told you.'

'Oh, that's right! Someone you haven't seen for years phones you up asking for help, so you jump in your car and drive two hundred miles, for *lunch*. And when she doesn't show up you track down where she lives, wander into her house and find her unconscious.'

'That's what happened.'

'So you say. But let's try this instead: you go to her house and force your way in. She's naked underneath her bathrobe, you get carried away. Boom. Then you panic and call it in as if you'd just found her.'

I stared at him, appalled. 'That's ridiculous!'

'Is it? The two of you always seemed pretty close on the search. I always wondered if there was something going on between you.'

I realized my fists were clenched. I opened them, fighting not to lose my temper, knowing that was what he wanted.

'Not everyone's like you, Terry.'

He gave a laugh. 'Oh, here we go! I was wondering how long it'd take.'

'If you don't believe me, ask Sophie. She'll tell you the same when she wakes up.'

'If she wakes up.' That stopped me. Terry nodded. 'A head injury like that, there's no knowing. Which puts you in an awkward position, doesn't it?'

I couldn't believe I was hearing this. Terry took a card from his wallet and tossed it on to the coffee table.

'Anything else happens, call me. My mobile number's on there. Don't bother with the office landline, I'm never there.' He went to the hallway and paused, his expression ugly. 'Don't pretend you're any different to me, Hunter. You're no better than anyone else.'

He slammed the door hard enough to shake the walls. I didn't move for a while, then went to the nearest chair and sat down. I felt stunned by Terry's hostility as much as his accusation. There was no love lost between us, but could he seriously believe that I was capable of doing something like that? Attacking Sophie?

Apparently.

Anger began to kick in again. I went to finish packing. Brooding wouldn't help, and neither would sitting around here.

I almost threw Terry's card away, but at the last minute I tucked it in my wallet. Then I set the alarm on my flat, threw my bag into the car boot and drove away. If I didn't get snarled up in traffic I could be in Exeter by mid-afternoon.

If I was going to start digging around in the past, an archaeologist was as good a place as any to start.

I hadn't given Leonard Wainwright a thought in years. I would have been more than happy to keep it that way, but it made sense to talk to him, at least. Now that Monk had reared his ugly head again, it couldn't hurt to see if he could add anything to the little I already knew.

The weather had steadily worsened as I'd neared Exeter, and by the time I arrived the rain was coming down in a sullen downpour. I booked into an anonymous hotel not far from the hospital. It was one of the bland chains that spring up in most city or town centres, with piped music in the lifts and plastic menus offering pre-cooked food. But it was cheap and convenient, and as well as a view of a car park my room had a Wi-Fi connection. Unpacking my laptop, I ordered a sandwich and set to work.

Finding Wainwright proved harder than I expected. I didn't have his address or phone number, and Terry had said he'd retired. I tried his old department at

Cambridge anyway, hoping that someone there would be able to help. The receptionist soon set me right on that score.

'We can't reveal personal details,' she told me waspishly.

I spent a fruitless half-hour searching on the internet before it occurred to me to try the obvious. Years before Wainwright had said he lived at Torbay. There was no guarantee he still did, or wasn't ex-directory. But I typed his name into an online phone directory and there he was: *Wainwright, Prof. L.* The entry gave both phone number and address.

Genius, I thought ruefully, massaging my stiff neck.

The phone rang for a long time before anyone answered. 'Hello, Wainwright residence?'

It was a woman's voice, clipped and officious. 'Can I speak to Leonard Wainwright, please?'

There was a pause. 'Who is this?'

'My name's David Hunter. I worked with Professor Wainwright several years ago,' I added, not sure if he'd remember me.

The pause wasn't quite so long this time. 'I don't recognize your name. Would he know you from Cambridge?'

'No, we were . . .' I searched for the right phrase, then gave up. 'It was on a police investigation. I'm in the area, and—'

I didn't get the chance to finish. 'Oh, I *see*. I'm

afraid Leonard's unavailable, but I'm his wife. You're in the area, you say?'

'Yes, but—'

'Then you must pop round! I'm sure Leonard would love to see an old colleague.'

I doubted it. 'Perhaps I should just call back later . . .'

'Nonsense! Are you free for lunch tomorrow? We usually have something light around one o'clock. Unless you have another appointment, of course.'

Lunch? That was the last thing I'd expected. 'If you're sure it's no trouble . . .'

'No trouble at all. Oh, jolly good! Leonard *will* look forward to it.'

I hung up, bemused by the invitation and wondering exactly what 'unavailable' meant. The prospect of lunch with the archaeologist and his wife wasn't something I relished, and I doubted Wainwright would thank his wife either. Still, I'd accepted now. That left me the rest of the evening to fill. I was wondering what to do when my phone rang. It was the hospital.

Sophie was conscious.

13

Traumatic brain injury isn't like a broken arm. Its unpredictable nature makes any sort of prognosis difficult, but in general the longer a victim remains unconscious, the more chance there is of serious damage.

Sophie had been lucky. Although the blow to her head had left her with bad concussion, her skull wasn't fractured and the scans had revealed no sign of complications such as haemorrhaging or haematoma: cranial bleeds that could go undetected, only to incapacitate or kill days after the initial injury.

She'd woken the night before, a few hours after I'd left the hospital. She'd been groggy at first, slipping in and out of consciousness, but the fact that she was awake at all was good news. It had been at her insistence that the hospital had called me. Now she was propped up in bed in a gown, the pillows splayed untidily behind her. Her tawny hair was tied back with a band, so that the injury to her face was clearly visible. Her skull might not be fractured but her cheekbone was. Although the swelling had started to subside, the bruising extended from temple to jaw in a startling kaleidoscope of colour.

'Thanks for coming,' she said as I sat down. She absently touched the plastic ID bracelet on her wrist. 'I'm not sure whether I should thank you or apologize.'

'There's no need for either.'

'Of course there is. I've put you to all this trouble, and if you hadn't found me . . .'

'But I did. And you haven't put me to any trouble.'

She gave me a wry look. 'Yeah, right.'

I smiled, still relieved that she was all right. Especially after Terry's visit. Rain drummed against the window, which reflected a reversed image of the stark hospital ward under the fluorescent lights. Sophie had a corner bed, and the one next to hers was empty, allowing us to talk without being overheard.

'How are you feeling?' I asked.

Sophie gave a wan smile. 'Apart from like I've got the world's worst hangover, about the same as I look, I expect.'

Given what she'd been through, she looked

remarkably good. Eight years had barely left a mark. Her face was unlined, and apart from the bruising she didn't appear much changed from the last time I saw her. But then Sophie had the sort of bone structure that would always age well.

She looked down at her hands. 'I suppose I feel more embarrassed than anything. And confused. I don't know which is worse, the fact that somebody broke into my house and did this to me, or that I can't remember anything about it.'

Short-term memory loss is common enough after a head injury, but that doesn't make it any less distressing. 'You can't remember anything at all? Nothing about who attacked you?'

'I can't even remember *being* attacked.' Sophie plucked distractedly at her ID bracelet. 'I feel really stupid, but it's like I told the police. I'd just finished showering, I heard a noise from downstairs, and . . . and that's it. For all I know I could have just slipped and banged my head.'

That might have been more credible if not for the broken front door and ransacked rooms. Whatever had happened to her, it was no accident.

'Your memory might come back in a few days.'

'I don't know if I want it to.' She looked vulnerable lying there in the hospital gown, not at all like the Sophie I remembered. 'The police say I wasn't . . . that it wasn't a sexual assault. But it's horrible thinking that someone broke in and I can't even remember.'

'Have you any idea who it might have been? Anyone with a grudge?'

'No, not at all. I'm not in a relationship now, and haven't been for . . . well, long enough. The police seemed to think it was probably a burglar who thought I was out and panicked when he realized I was in the shower.'

That was news to me. 'Have you spoken to Terry Connors?'

The name seemed to surprise her. 'No. Why?'

'He came to see me.' I hesitated, but she'd a right to know. 'He seems to think it might have been Jerome Monk who attacked you.'

'Monk? That's ridiculous!' She frowned as she looked at me. 'There's something else, isn't there?'

'He told me I was a suspect as well. I was the one who found you and since you can't remember anything . . .'

'You?' Her eyes widened, then she quickly looked away. I felt my stomach dip, wondering if she might believe it herself. But when she spoke again the anger in her voice dispelled it. 'Christ, that's just like him. That's so stupid!'

'I'm glad you think so. Are you OK?' I asked, noticing how pale she'd suddenly become.

'A bit woozy . . . Look, I know I owe you an explanation, but can it wait? I don't really feel like talking about it right now. I . . . I just want to go home.'

'Sure. Don't worry about it.'

'Thanks.' She gave another weak smile, but it quickly faded. 'I think . . .'

She groped for the kidney-shaped cardboard container on the cabinet next to the bed. I reached it first and handed it to her.

'Do you want me to call a nurse?'

'No, I just keep feeling queasy. They tell me it'll pass.' She put her head back on the pillow, closing her eyes. 'Sorry, I think I need to sleep . . .'

The kidney dish toppled slowly from her fingers as her voice tailed off. I stood up, careful not to scrape the chair on the floor. Putting the dish back on the cabinet, I turned to leave.

'David . . .'

Sophie hadn't moved, but her eyes were on me. 'Are you coming back?'

'Of course.'

She gave a slight nod, satisfied. Her eyelids were already starting to droop again, and when she spoke her voice was slurred and barely more than a whisper. 'I didn't mean to . . .'

'Didn't mean to what?' I asked, not sure if I'd heard right.

But she was already asleep. I watched the steady rise and fall of her breathing, then quietly left the ward. As I made my way down the corridor I thought about what Sophie had said. And what she hadn't.

I wondered what she was hiding.

The clouds and rain had lifted next morning, giving way to clean blue skies and bright sunshine. I'd spent the previous night running things over in my mind while I'd eaten a solitary meal in a half-empty Italian restaurant. Even though I was relieved about Sophie, I'd gone to bed feeling flat and restless, convinced there was something I was missing.

But a night's sleep had lifted my spirits, and the bright autumn day made me feel almost optimistic as I checked out of the hotel and set off for my lunch appointment with Wainwright. There was no real need to see him now Sophie was conscious, but having accepted his wife's invitation for lunch I couldn't cry off at short notice.

No matter how much I might want to.

The archaeologist lived near Sharkham Point, a headland on the southern tip of Torbay. It was less than an hour's drive, so I chose a longer route that took in more of the coast. There were high cliffs, beyond which the sun glinted on the choppy sea. Despite the chill I drove with my window down, enjoying the freshness of the breeze. This was a part of the country I didn't know well, but I liked it. Although it was only twenty miles from Dartmoor it seemed a different world; brighter and less oppressive. I didn't blame Wainwright for living here.

The house was easy enough to find: there weren't many others there. It was set back from the road behind a line of tall, bare lime trees, a pebble-dashed 1920s villa criss-crossed with black beams. A long gravel driveway was overhung by more limes on one side, the other flanked by a long expanse of lawn.

A bright blue Toyota was parked outside the double garage. I parked next to it and went up the steps to the front door. An old brass bell was set in the wall. I pressed it and listened to the distant chime coming from somewhere deep in the house. *Here we go.* I straightened my shoulders as brisk footsteps sounded from inside.

The woman who opened the door fitted the voice on the phone too perfectly to be anyone other than Wainwright's wife. Less matronly, perhaps, and wearing a soft crew-necked sweater over a woollen skirt rather than the twinset and pearls I'd imagined. But the perfectly coiffed grey hair and careful make-up were as I'd expected, and so was the steel-trap quality to her eyes.

They were crinkled in welcome now, though, and her smile was surprisingly warm. 'You must be David Hunter?'

'That's right.'

'I'm Jean Wainwright. *So* glad you found us. We're

a little off the beaten track here, but that's how we like it.' She moved aside, still smiling. 'Please, do come in.'

I stepped into the house. The hallway had a beautiful parquet floor and wood-panelled walls. A large vase of white chrysanthemums stood on an antique mahogany bureau, their heavy fragrance fighting with the woman's perfume and face powder. Her low heels clipped out a staccato rhythm as she led me along the hall.

'Leonard's in the study. He's been looking forward to seeing you.'

That was so unlikely I felt suddenly certain I'd made a mistake. Could this be some other Leonard Wainwright after all? *Too late now*. His wife opened a door at the end of the hallway and ushered me in.

After the darkly panelled hallway, the room was dazzlingly bright. Sunlight flooded in through the huge bay window that ran almost its entire length. Bookcases lined the walls, and a handsome, leather-topped desk stood at one side, bare except for another vase of chrysanthemums.

Their scent filled the room, but it was the view that commanded attention. The window faced out over a lawn that ran down to a cliff edge, beyond which was nothing but sea. It stretched out to the horizon, so that the effect was almost like standing on the prow of a ship. It was so breathtaking that I was slow to take in anything else. Then Wainwright's wife spoke.

'Leonard, David Hunter's here. He's an old colleague of yours. You remember him, don't you?'

She'd gone to stand by a wing-backed leather armchair. I hadn't realized anyone was sitting there. It was facing the view, and I waited for Wainwright to get up. When he didn't, I moved further into the room until I could see past the winged sides of the chair.

I wouldn't have recognized him.

The giant of memory no longer existed. Wainwright sat hunched in the chair, staring blankly out at the sea. He seemed to have physically shrunk in on himself, flesh and muscle wasting away. The patrician features were barely recognizable, cheeks caved in and eyes sunken in their sockets, while the once thick mane of hair was thin and grey.

Wainwright's wife had turned to me expectantly. The bright smile on her face now seemed as fragile and transparent as the window itself. I'd stopped dead, shocked, but now I forced a smile of my own as I went forward.

'Hello, Leonard.'

It was the first time I'd called him by his first name, but anything else would have seemed wrong. I didn't bother to offer my hand: I knew there'd be no point.

'Dr Hunter's come for lunch, dear,' his wife said. 'Won't that be nice? The two of you can talk about old times.'

As though finally becoming aware of my presence, the big head turned ponderously in my direction. The fogged eyes looked at me. Wainwright's mouth worked, and for a second I thought he might speak. Then the moment passed, and he turned to gaze back out at the sea again.

'Can I get you a cup of tea, Dr Hunter?' his wife said. 'Lunch will be another twenty minutes.'

My smile felt glued in place. 'Tea would be nice. Can I give you a hand?'

'That's very kind, thank you. We won't be long, Leonard,' she added, patting her husband's hand.

There was no response. With a last glance at the figure in the chair, I followed her back into the hall.

'I'm sorry, I should have warned you,' she said, closing the door. 'I assumed when you rang that you knew about Leonard's condition.'

'I'd no idea,' I said. 'What is it? Alzheimer's?'

'They don't seem entirely sure. I never realized there were so many different types of dementia, but then I suppose one wouldn't. Leonard's developed very quickly, as these things go. The last two years have been . . . quite hard.'

I could imagine. 'I'm sorry.'

'Oh, these things happen.' She spoke with a breezy matter-of-factness. 'I thought seeing a familiar face might help. Our daughters don't live nearby, and we don't get many visitors. He's usually better early on in the day. That's why I suggested you come for lunch. Leonard tends to go sundowning after that. Are you familiar with the term?'

I said I was. As a GP I'd seen how some dementia patients would grow more confused or agitated as the day wore on. No one was entirely sure why.

'Such a lovely phrase for such a cruel thing, I always think,' his wife continued. 'Puts one in mind of cocktails on a summer evening.'

Suddenly I felt like a fraud. 'Look, Mrs Wainwright—'

'Please, call me Jean.'

'Jean.' I took a deep breath. 'Your husband and I . . . Well, to be honest, I'm not sure how pleased he'll be to see me.'

She smiled. 'Yes, Leonard could be quite prickly. But I'm sure he'll be glad of the company. Especially when you've come all this way.'

'The thing is, this wasn't just a social call. I was hoping to talk to him about the investigation we worked on.'

'Then please do. He can be quite lucid sometimes, especially about things that happened in the past.' She opened the study door again before I could protest. 'Now, you two can talk while I get lunch ready.'

There was no way I could refuse. I gave a weak smile and went back inside. The door closed behind me, leaving me alone with Wainwright. *God*. The change in him was shocking. I couldn't help but think about how he'd presented my initial findings at Tina Williams' grave as his own. At the time I thought it was shameless rivalry, but now I wasn't so sure. Perhaps he'd felt the first cracks in his intellect even then and had been trying to hide them.

He gave no sign of being aware of me. He sat in the armchair, gazing out of the window at the sea. I wondered if he even knew what he was looking at.

You're here now. Make the best of it. I moved the chair from the desk until I could see him and sat down, searching for something to say. The point of my visit had vanished along with Wainwright's damaged mind, but I couldn't just sit there. There had been no love lost between us, but I wouldn't have wished this on anyone.

'Hello again, Leonard. I'm David Hunter. We worked together once, on Dartmoor.'

There was no response. I ploughed on.

'It was the Jerome Monk case. Detective Chief Superintendent Simms was SIO. Do you remember?'

Nothing. Wainwright continued to stare at the sea, the heavy features betraying no indication that he'd heard. I sighed, looking out of the window myself. The view was spectacular. Gulls wheeled against the cold blue sky, specks above the marching blue-green waves. Whatever the weather, whatever else

happened, they would always be there. The archaeologist's deterioration was pitiable, but there were
worse places to end one's days.

'I know you.'

I looked up in surprise. The big head had turned
towards me. Wainwright's eyes were fixed on mine.

'Yes, you do,' I said. 'David Hunter. I'm a—'

'Calliph . . . Calli . . . maggots.' The voice was the
same bass rumble I remembered, although more
hoarse now, as though unused.

'Maggots,' I agreed.

'Rot.'

I had to smile. I supposed 'rot' could have referred
to the blowfly larvae's habitat, but I doubted it.
Dementia or not, some things hadn't changed.

His eyes were flicking around now, as though
something inside him had started to wake. The broad
forehead creased in concentration.

'Roadkill . . .'

I just nodded, not having a clue what he meant. His
mind had obviously started to wander. He glared
across at me and thumped his hand down on the
chair arm.

'No! Listen!'

He'd started feebly trying to heave himself up from
the chair. I hurried over. 'It's OK, Leonard, calm
down.'

His arms felt thin as sticks as he struggled to get

191

up, and a sour smell of wasting came from him. But his grip was still vicelike as he seized my wrist.

'Roadkill!' he hissed, spraying spittle into my face. *'Roadkill!'*

The study door was flung open and his wife hurried in. 'Now come along, Leonard, let's not have any nonsense.'

'Bloody woman!'

'Come on, Leonard, behave yourself.' She gently but firmly eased him back into his seat. 'What happened? Did you say something to upset him?'

'No, I was just—'

'Well, something must have set him off. He isn't normally this agitated.' She looked over at me, smoothing her husband's hair as he began to subside. Her manner was still polite but now there was no mistaking the frost. 'I'm sorry, Dr Hunter, but I think you'd better go.'

I hesitated, but there was nothing I could do. Leaving the two of them in the study, I let myself out and went back to my car. The day was still bright and sunny, but the sickly sweet odour of chrysanthemums stayed with me as I drove down the driveway and away from the house.

14

I didn't bother much with the coastal scenery as I drove back to Exeter. I'd promised Sophie I'd call in at the hospital again, and I hoped that would take my mind off the disastrous visit to Wainwright. Seeing the archaeologist reduced like that had been a shock. He'd seemed to recognize me, and although I hadn't intended to upset him perhaps that had been enough to set him off. Years ago I'd taken the Hippocratic oath to do no harm.

I hadn't made such a bang-up job of it today.

It took me almost as long finding somewhere to park at the hospital as it had to drive there from Torbay. When I reached Sophie's ward I saw that the screens had been drawn around her bed. I slowed, thinking a doctor might be with her, until I heard the hushed but angry voices coming from behind them.

'Hello?' I said hesitantly.

The voices stopped. There was a pause and then the screen was pulled back.

The young woman who'd opened it was like a subtly altered version of Sophie. She had the same colour hair, the same shape face and eyes. But although their features were unmistakably cast from the same mould, hers managed to be both sharper and rounder than Sophie's. Right now they regarded me with pinched annoyance.

'Yes?'

'I've come to see Sophie,' I said. 'My name's—'

'David!' Sophie's voice rang out. 'It's all right, Maria.'

The woman's mouth tightened, but she stepped aside to let me pass. Sophie was sitting on the bed, a leather holdall open next to her. She was dressed in a sweater and jeans that somehow didn't look quite right, although I couldn't have said why. She still looked tired, and the bruise on the left side of her face was even more livid than before. But for all that she was clearly much better than the last time I'd seen her.

She gave me a smile that held as much relief as anything. 'Thanks for coming. David, this is my sister Maria.'

Now I saw them together, the differences were more apparent than the similarities. Sophie's sister looked older. She must have been devastatingly pretty as a sixteen-year-old, but it was the plump type of prettiness that didn't age well. The genes that supplied Sophie's slim limbs and bone structure had apparently skipped her elder sibling, and her face was already settling into lines that spoke of disappointment and impatience. As though to make up for it her clothes were smart and expensive, her manicured nails as sharp as blades.

I considered offering my hand, but quickly decided against it. The tension between the two women felt strong enough to arc into life and fry anyone who got in the way.

'David's an old friend,' Sophie said, after an uncomfortable pause.

'Good. Then I hope he can talk some sense into you.'

Sophie looked embarrassed. 'Not now, Maria.'

'Then when? You're in no condition to discharge yourself, never mind stay in that place on your own!'

Sophie gave an exaggerated sigh. 'I'm fine. And "that place" is my home.'

'Where someone was able to walk in and attack you! And now you want to go *back*? You just can't admit you made a mistake, living somewhere so out of the way. I bet you haven't even given any thought to how you're going to get there, have you?'

'David's taking me,' Sophie blurted.

Maria turned to me. 'Really. And will you be staying with her as well?'

I managed to catch my surprise. Behind her sister, Sophie was looking at me in mute appeal. 'For a while.'

'David's a doctor,' Sophie said, smoothly editing the truth. 'See, I told you, I'll be fine.'

'You could have mentioned that sooner.' Maria sighed, reluctantly letting go of her irritation. 'Well, I can see I'm wasting my breath. I hope you have better luck with her, David.'

It seemed safest not to say anything, so I just smiled. This time Maria offered her hand.

'Nice to meet you, anyway. Sorry for seeming a little bossy. I just worry about Sophie.'

'That's all right. It's what big sisters do.'

Her smile was snuffed out. 'You know where I am if you want me,' she snapped at Sophie.

Her heels rapped on the ward floor as she strode out. I turned to Sophie, bewildered. 'Did I say something wrong?'

She'd covered her eyes. 'Maria's two years younger than me.'

The day just kept getting better. 'Oh, God. I should apologize . . .'

But Sophie was laughing. 'Don't worry. She acts like she's older. She always has, that's half the trouble.'

'And the other half?'

'That'd be me,' she said, her laughter drying up. 'She thinks I'm irresponsible and impulsive. Hard to argue, really. We're just different. She's got two lovely kids and a nanny to look after them, and enjoys throwing dinner parties. And that's not me. We don't even like the same clothes.'

She looked down at the jeans and sweater she was wearing. I understood now why they didn't look quite right: they were her sister's.

'So you're discharging yourself?' I asked.

'The doctor wants to keep me in for another twenty-four hours. But all the tests are OK and I feel fine. A little woozy, and I still can't remember what happened, but that's all. I want to go home.'

'You've had a bad head injury. Another twenty-four hours—'

'I'm going home,' she said with finality. 'Look, it's just concussion. I'll take it easy, I promise.'

I let it go. It wasn't my place to argue, and if the hospital and Sophie's sister hadn't managed to dissuade her I doubted I'd have much success.

'Sorry, I didn't mean to snap,' she said awkwardly. 'And thanks for covering for me with Maria. I shouldn't have put you on the spot like that, but she wanted me to go and stay with them. And believe me, that would *not* be a good idea.'

I could imagine. 'So how are you getting home?'

'I'll catch a train,' she said lightly. 'Don't worry, what I said about you staying with me was only for Maria's benefit. And I don't expect you to take me.'

'No, but I will.'

'Oh, no, I couldn't let you do that!'

'I've no choice.' I smiled. 'I gave my word to your big sister.'

Sophie slept most of the journey. For all her bravado she was far from fully recovered, and her eyes had closed even before we'd left the hospital grounds. Her head lolled against the seat rest, but her breathing was strong and regular, rising and falling in the steady rhythm of deep sleep. I drove carefully so as not to disturb her. There were any number of questions I wanted to ask, but they could wait.

Driving out to Dartmoor, with a woman I'd not seen in eight years asleep next to me, I felt oddly at peace. I knew it was only temporary, a brief respite from the real world. Something was obviously troubling Sophie, and her attacker was still out there somwhere. But they were problems for the future. Here in the thrumming cocoon of the car, with the landscape breezing by outside and Sophie's quiet breathing beside me, I felt strangely content.

It was late afternoon when I pulled up outside Sophie's cottage. She woke when I switched off the engine. 'Where are we?' she asked, sitting up and rubbing her eyes.

'Home.'

'God, don't tell me I slept all the way.'

'Best thing for you. How do you feel?'

She thought for a moment, still blinking away sleep. 'Better.'

She looked it. Her colour was normal, except for the shocking bruise on her face. We climbed out of the car. After the tarmac and concrete of the city, the cold autumnal air out here tasted fresh and sweet. The sun was low, casting long shadows across the garden like a spreading stain. Off to one side was the small orchard that had seemed so sinister before. In the daylight it was a little better, although the gnarled old apple trees looked dead and barren.

Behind them, standing almost as tall as the house, was the inverted cone of the kiln. Its dilapidation was more evident now, crumbling bricks seemingly held up by the rusted scaffolding. A pile of unused poles lay nearby, overgrown with grass and weeds: whatever repairs were being carried out had obviously ground to a halt years before.

'That's my pride and joy,' Sophie said, as I opened the garden gate for her. 'It's a Victorian bottle kiln. There aren't many of them left.'

'Does it still work?'

'Sort of. Come on, I'll show you.'

'It's OK,' I said, not wanting her to tire herself.

But she was already following the path towards it. The rickety wooden door squealed as she pushed it open. 'You don't keep it locked?' I asked.

She smiled. 'You're not in the city now. Besides, I don't think thieves would be interested. There's not much of a black market for hand-thrown pots. Unfortunately.'

I followed her inside. There was a damp, dusty smell of old plaster. Light came from small windows set around the circular walls. In the building's centre was the original oven, a giant brick chimney stack that extended through the domed roof. It was scaffolded off, and parts of it were supported by a makeshift assembly of rusted props and timber joists.

'Is it safe?' I asked, looking at the sagging brickwork.

'Safe enough. It was like that when I bought it. It's a listed structure, so I can't knock it down even if I want to. Not that I would. The plan is to get the original oven working again eventually, but that'll have to wait till I get the money. Which won't be any time soon.'

Off to one side stood a smaller, modern electric kiln and a clay-spattered potter's wheel. Workbenches and shelves were arranged around it, stacked with a hap-hazard assortment of pots. Some were glazed, others just baked clay. Even to my unschooled eye they seemed striking: organic shapes that looked as artistic as they were functional. I carefully picked up a large jug whose curving form seemed to flow, as though it had grown naturally. It felt well balanced in my hands, its lines smooth and sensuous.

'I'd no idea you could do this,' I said, impressed.

'Oh, I'm full of hidden talents,' she said, absently running her hand over a large ball of dried clay. It stood on a table littered with half-finished and broken pots. She smiled self-consciously. 'As you'll have noticed, being tidy isn't one of them. Anyway, I hope you can keep a secret.'

Leaving me to wonder what she meant, she went to the kiln's curving wall. Sliding out a loose brick, she reached into the hole and took something out.

'Spare key,' she said, holding it up. 'Always comes in handy.'

Until then I'd not given much thought to the condition of the house, but the sight of the key jogged my memory. *Oh, hell.*

'Wait, Sophie,' I said, hurrying after her as she left the kiln, but by then she'd already seen for herself. She stopped dead on the path.

'Oh, my God!'

When we'd arrived the porch had been shadowed by the dying sun, hiding the damage to the front door, and our attention had been on the kiln. Now we were close enough to see the splintered wood and the way the door hung loosely on its hinges.

I cursed myself. *Idiot! You should have realized!*
The police had made a half-hearted attempt to wedge the door shut, but the hallway was wet where rain had blown in, and muddy footprints criss-crossed the rugs and polished floorboards. There was a rank smell, as if a fox or some other animal had been inside.

Sophie stared in dismay at the scattered contents of the open drawers and cupboards.

'It's not as bad as it looks,' I said feebly, cursing myself for not anticipating this. I should have come here instead of wasting my time at Wainwright's. 'I thought the police would have told you.'

There was no answer. I realized she was crying silently, tears running down her cheeks.

'Sophie. I'm really sorry—'

'It isn't your fault.' She wiped furiously at her eyes. 'Thanks for bringing me home, but I think you'd better go.'

'At least let me—'

'No! It's all right. Really. I – I just want to be on my own. Please.'

I could see she was only holding herself together by force of will. I hated to leave her like that, but I didn't know her well enough to do anything else.

'I'll call you tomorrow. If there's anything else you need . . .'

'I know. Thanks.'

Feeling helpless, I started back towards my car, feet scuffing through the dead leaves that lay on the path. Behind me I heard the door creak in protest as she forced it shut. I got as far as the gate before I stopped, one hand on the weathered wood. The sky was already beginning to darken, the first stars pricking through the cold, deep blue. The ploughed fields and woods were starting to lose their identity in the lengthening shadows. Apart from the sway and rustle of bare branches, there wasn't a sound: no bird or animal to break the solitude. It was a bleak and lonely spot.

I turned and went back to the house.

The door had been pushed to but wouldn't close properly on its sprained hinges. I pushed it open. Sophie was on the hallway floor. She was hugging her knees, head bowed as she shook with silent sobs.

Without saying anything I crouched next to her. She buried her face against me.

'*Oh, G-God, I'm so scared. I'm s-so s-scared . . .*'

'Shh, it's OK,' I told her.

I hoped I was right.

I repaired the front door as best I could, with tools Sophie provided. The lock was broken but I salvaged an ancient iron bolt from the pantry. It wasn't pretty, but it was big and solid, and would serve until a joiner could get here.

At my insistence, Sophie went for a bath while I cleaned up the rest of the mess. Most of the damage was superficial – her belongings had been scattered but there were few breakages. Once I'd cleaned up and opened the windows to clear the musky animal smell, there was little evidence of what had happened.

It was dark outside by the time Sophie came back down. She'd changed out of her sister's clothes into clean jeans and a baggy sweater. Her hair was still damp, brushed and pulled back from her face. Although her cheek was less swollen the skin was starting to deepen into purples and yellows as the bruising ran its course.

'I made some tea,' I said, as she came into the kitchen.

'Fine. Thank you.'

'I've cleared up as best I can but you might want to make sure nothing's missing. Any jewellery or valuables.' She nodded, but didn't seem very interested. 'How's the head?'

Sophie sat down at the scarred pine table, casually folding one long leg underneath her. 'Still aching, but not as much. I took some of the painkillers the hospital gave me.' She avoided looking at me as she reached for the teapot.

'One of yours?' I asked. It was an unusual shape, functional but with clean, elegant lines.

'Just a one-off I tried.' Silence descended. The only

sound was the slow tinkling of the spoon as she stirred her tea. We both watched the spoon going round.

'You'll wear it out,' I said.

'Sorry.' She put the spoon down. 'Look, about earlier . . . I don't usually lose it like that.'

'Don't worry about it. You've been through a lot.'

'Even so, crying all over you like I did. I must have made a mess of your coat.'

'I'll send you the cleaning bill.'

'Yes, please do.'

I sighed. 'Sophie, I'm joking.'

She gave an embarrassed laugh. 'This is really awkward, isn't it?'

'A little,' I admitted. 'Look, you don't have to talk now if you don't want to. It's getting late and I ought to set off soon.'

'You're driving back tonight?' She looked startled. 'I can't let you do that. There's a spare room here.'

'Really, it isn't—'

'You'd be doing me a favour.' She gave me a nervous smile. 'Besides, you promised Maria.'

She was trying hard, but I could see the cracks in her composure. After what she'd been through I didn't blame her for being rattled. 'OK, if you're sure.'

Some of the tension went out of her. 'Are you hungry? I don't have much in but I can rustle something up.'

Whatever was on Sophie's mind, she obviously wasn't ready to talk about it yet. It was best to let her get to it in her own time, though. Besides, I hadn't eaten since breakfast.

I smiled. 'Starving.'

Despite her protests, I made her sit down while I prepared something to eat. She wasn't exaggerating when she'd said there wasn't much in, but I found Cheddar and eggs that I beat into an omelette. There was an old electric range in the kitchen, and while the eggs sizzled in the pan I toasted slices from a stale loaf and slathered them in butter.

'God, that smells delicious,' Sophie said.

But she only picked at her food. The tension edged up between us again as we ate, and it was a relief when we'd finished.

'Let's go into the sitting room,' she said. 'We can talk better in there.'

It was a comfortable room: two big old sofas covered with throws, soft rugs on the polished floor-boards and a woodburning stove. I didn't argue when Sophie insisted on lighting it herself, recognizing it as another delaying tactic.

When it was lit she sat on the other sofa, so that we faced each other across a low coffee table. The flames flickered in the stove, filling the room with a smoky scent of burning pine. It was cosier and more relaxed than the brightly lit kitchen. Sophie and I had never been alone together like this before, and I realized how little we really knew about each other. Sitting with her in the firelight felt strangely intimate.

'Do you want a brandy or something?' she asked.

'I'm fine, thanks.'

She cleared her throat. 'Look, I've been meaning to say . . . I heard about your family. I'm so sorry.'

I just nodded. The wood crackled in the stove. Sophie gave a nervous smile, plucking at her fingers.

'I don't know where to start.'

'How about how you ended up here? Making pottery's a long way from being a BIA.'

She smiled self-consciously. 'Yeah, just a bit. I'd had enough, I suppose. Seeing only the dark side of life, all that pain. And the failures. After the Monk fiasco I lost a lot of my confidence, started second-guessing everything I did. It got to the point where I hated getting up in the morning. So I got out before I burned out.'

Sophie looked around the room as if taking it in for the first time.

'I've been here four . . . no, five years now. God! Pottery used to be a hobby, so when I saw this place for sale I thought why not? I'd always liked Dartmoor and I wanted a fresh start, something completely different. Can you understand that?'

I could. Probably better than she realized.

'The first thing I did was burn all my notes,' she

went on. 'Everything. Every case I'd ever worked on. All of it went on to the bonfire. Except one.'

'Jerome Monk's,' I said.

She nodded. 'I don't know why I didn't get rid of that as well. Perhaps coming out here, not so far from where it all happened . . .' She clasped her hands in her lap, so tightly her knuckles were white. For a few moments the only sound in the room was the muted crackle of fire from the stove. 'Do you ever think about it?'

'Not until Monk escaped.'

'I think about it a lot.' Sophie stared down at her clenched hands. 'We had a golden opportunity to find where Lindsey and Zoe Bennett were buried, and we threw it away.'

I sighed. 'I'm not going to pretend it was a high point for any of us, but sometimes that's how it goes. We did our best. What happened back then wasn't anyone's fault.'

She quickly shook her head, her face shadowed. 'We should have done more. *I* should have done more.'

'Monk had his own agenda for being there, and it didn't have anything to do with taking us to the graves. He only wanted a chance to escape.' *And almost managed it.*

'But that's the thing, I don't think he did.' She waved away my objection before I could make it. 'All right, yes, escaping was part of it. Probably a big part. But I don't think that was the *only* reason he agreed to help. The way he reacted when he saw Tina Williams' grave, I don't think he was putting that on. I'm certain he was genuinely trying to remember.'

She was looking at me earnestly, willing me to believe her. I chose my words carefully. 'Jerome Monk knew that moor better than anyone. He'd managed to hide out on it for months without being caught. If he'd wanted to he could have taken us right to the other graves.'

'Not necessarily. I said back then that finding them wouldn't be straightforward, not after a year, and especially not if he'd buried them at night. And people blank things from their minds without meaning to. Painful memories sometimes, or when their brain has too much to process and just overloads.'

'That might apply to an ordinary man who flipped and lost his temper, but you're talking about Jerome Monk. He's a sociopathic serial killer, a predator. He doesn't have a conscience.'

'On some level he might,' she persisted. 'I'm not defending him or what he did. He's violent and unpredictable, but that doesn't mean he can't be reached. That's why I—'

She broke off, looking down at her hands. An owl hooted outside. 'That's why you what?' I asked.

'That's . . . why I've been writing to him.'

'You've been writing to *Monk*?'

Her chin came up, defiantly. 'Ever since I came here. I write to him once a year, on the anniversary of Angela Carson's murder. We can't say for sure when he killed any of his other victims, so I thought . . . Anyway, once a year I write and urge him to say where the graves are. And I offer to help him.'

I stared at her, aghast. 'Sophie, for God's sake!'

'He's never responded, but all I need is a landmark, some clue of whereabouts they are! And if he needs help remembering, he might be more likely to turn to someone who isn't connected to the police. What harm can it do?'

Christ. I rubbed my eyes. 'Did you put your address on the letters?'

'Well, I . . .' Her fingers clenched and fretted at each other. She gave a guilty nod. 'I didn't know how else could he write back.'

'Do the police know?'

'The police? No, I . . . Well, I didn't think there was much point.'

'Not much *point*? Sophie, you get attacked the day after a rapist and murderer escapes from prison, and you didn't think it was worth mentioning you'd been *writing* to him?'

'I was embarrassed, all right?' she flared. 'And yes, I know how stupid it makes me look, but at least I've tried to *do* something! Every time I see the moor I think that there are still two dead girls – two *sisters* – buried out there somewhere. And no one's doing anything about it. How do you think that makes their family feel? I know how it makes *me* feel, knowing we could have done something about it and didn't!'

There was a tremor of emotion in her voice. I reminded myself she'd been through a lot. This couldn't be easy for her.

'You have to tell the police,' I said gently. 'I can call Terry Connors and—'

'No!'

'Sophie, you don't have any choice. You know that.'

I thought she was going to argue, but the defiance seemed to drain out of her. She stared at the fire flickering in the stove.

'I'll tell the police, but on one condition. I called you to ask for a favour. That still hasn't changed.'

With everything else that had happened I'd almost forgotten why she'd asked to see me in the first place. 'What is it?'

She lifted her head. The flames from the stove tiger-striped her face, masking it in light and shadow.

'I want you to help me find the graves.'

15

The estate was a warren of semi-detached houses. The post-war homes had once aspired to be middle class but now they were beginning to look tired and run down. A few of them had made an effort; neat modern conservatories and new windows amongst the cracked paths and peeling paintwork. But they were the exceptions, lonely optimists in a neighbourhood that had once seen better days.

'Take the next left,' Sophie told me.

She seemed outwardly calm, but there was an underlying nervousness she was trying hard to conceal. I still didn't know where we were going or why, just followed the directions she gave as I drove.

'Why the mystery?' I'd asked.

'No mystery. It's just better if you wait till we get there.'

I hadn't argued. It seemed easier to go along with whatever she had in mind. I'd known Sophie was stubborn, but her determination to find the bodies of Lindsey and Zoe Bennett bordered on obsessional. The night before I'd tried to persuade her it was useless, that the two of us couldn't hope to accomplish anything after a full-scale police search had failed.

I'd wasted my breath.

'We can still *try*,' she insisted.

'Sophie, I wouldn't know where to start. We don't know if Monk buried Zoe and Lindsey anywhere near Tina Williams. And even if he did, grave location was more Wainwright's field than mine.'

I'd told Sophie about the archaeologist's condition. Not that there was much chance she'd have wanted his help anyway. She brushed away my argument.

'Wainwright couldn't see past his own ego. He was more interested in preserving his reputation than anything else. Even back then you were just as capable as he was.'

'I'm flattered you think so, but even if that's true you've got to be realistic. No one enjoys failure, but we did everything that could be done last time.'

'I don't accept that.'

I squeezed the bridge of my nose. 'Sophie . . .'

'Look, I'm not saying we'll be able to actually find them, not by ourselves. All I want to do is try to come up with enough for the police to launch another search. One day, that's all I ask. Give me one day, and if you still think we're wasting our time you can walk away.'

'I just can't see how—'

'One day. Please.'

I should have said no. We couldn't hope to achieve anything in a single day, and there was no point in building up her hopes. The refusal was on my lips, but even in the firelight I could see the need in her eyes. She sat with her hands clenched, waiting for my answer. *This is a mistake.*

'One day,' I heard myself say.

Now I was regretting it. The face in the bathroom mirror that morning had looked like an older, tireder version of me. I'd slept badly, turning restlessly in the small bed in the spare room and determinedly trying not to think about Sophie lying on the other side of the wall. When I'd finally fallen asleep it had been to wake gasping, convinced that Monk was breaking in. But the darkened house had been silent, and the only sound from outside was the cry of an owl.

Before we'd set off on Sophie's mysterious trip, I'd given her the card with Terry's mobile number. She'd promised to tell the police about writing to Monk if I agreed to help her search for the graves, and however much they disliked each other it made sense for it to be him. I'd pretended to need something from my room while she made the call, waiting until her murmured voice had stopped before going downstairs.

'Voicemail,' she said, handing me his card. 'I left him a message.'

Her face was studiedly neutral. I tucked the card back in my wallet without saying anything. Perhaps she had called Terry, but it hadn't sounded like she'd been leaving a message.

It had sounded like a conversation.

We had to wait for a local joiner to come out to repair the front door, so it was early afternoon before we finally set off. The atmosphere in the car was awkward from the outset, and grew more so as we neared wherever it was we were going. Sophie directed me into a cul-de-sac where the road curved round on itself.

'Pull up here.'

I switched off the engine. The semi-detached houses lined both sides of the road. I looked at her, waiting. She gave me a strained smile.

'Just bear with me. Please?'

You've come this far ... I locked the car and followed her through the wrought-iron gate of the nearest house. A short path led to the front door past a well-kept lawn and flowerbeds. Sophie's nervousness was evident as she pressed the plastic doorbell. Westminster chimes sounded from inside, and a moment later the door was opened.

The woman who answered was in her late forties

or early fifties, blond-haired and pleasant-faced but with a drawn look about her. She was smiling, but the expression seemed forced.

'Hi, Cath. Sorry we're a bit later than I thought,' Sophie said.

The woman's hand went to her mouth as she stared at the bruising on Sophie's face. 'Never mind that, what *happened* to you? Are you all right?'

'Oh, I'm fine, I just slipped in the bathroom,' she said quickly. 'Cath, I'd like you to meet Dr David Hunter. David, this is Cath Bennett.'

The name hit me like cold water. Bennett. As in Zoe and Lindsey. Now I knew who Sophie had been talking to on the phone earlier, when she'd pretended to call Terry.

She'd brought me to meet the murdered twins' mother.

The woman turned her brittle smile to me. 'Pleased to meet you, Dr Hunter.'

I murmured something polite. Sophie avoided looking at me as we went inside, but from the flush spreading up her throat she knew how angry I was. I couldn't believe she'd done this, not without warning me first. *You don't meet the families. Ever.* It was hard enough staying objective as it was, without that added emotional burden. Sophie knew that, yet she'd still brought me here.

I wondered what else she might be keeping from me.

I struggled to keep my feelings under control as we went down the hallway. The house was almost obsessively clean, the air sharp with the smell of bleach and air-freshener. Swirling patterns from the vacuum cleaner were carved in the carpet's thick pile, like crop circles in a field of lilac wheat.

The door whispered over them as Cath Bennett led us into a pristine sitting room. A sofa and matching chairs were positioned with clinical precision, the glass coffee table polished to a mirror finish. Ceramic figurines and animals gleamed on the mantelpiece, free from any taint of dust.

Framed photographs of the dead girls were everywhere.

'Please, take a seat,' their mother said, with rigid politeness. 'My husband's at work, but he isn't very good at this anyway. He still can't talk about it. Would you like tea or coffee?'

Sophie was still avoiding looking at me. 'Some tea would be lovely.'

'And how about you, Dr Hunter?'

I managed a smile. 'Same for me, please.'

She bustled out, leaving us alone with the photographs of her murdered daughters. They smiled at us from all over the room, two identically pretty, dark-haired girls. I tore my eyes from them and stared at Sophie.

'Please don't be mad,' she said in a rush. 'I'm sorry

to spring it on you, but I knew you wouldn't come otherwise.'

'You're right. What the hell were you *thinking*?'

'I wanted to remind you what's at stake. What all this is really about.'

'You think I don't already *know*?' I made an effort to calm down. 'Sophie, this is wrong. We shouldn't be here.'

'We can't go now. Just half an hour. Please?'

I didn't trust myself to speak. We sat in silence until Cath Bennett returned, carrying a tray set out with tea things. Best cups and saucers, and a plate of neatly arranged biscuits.

'Help yourself to milk and sugar,' she said, taking a seat on the sofa. 'Sophie says you're a forensic anthropologist, Dr Hunter. I'm not sure what that is, exactly, but I appreciate what you're doing.'

What you're doing? Sophie flashed me a look of mute appeal. 'David was involved in the original search on the moor eight years ago,' she said quickly.

'Eight years.' Cath Bennett reached for a framed photograph on the mantelpiece. 'I still can't get used to how long it's been. They'd have been twenty-seven this year. In May.'

She handed me the photograph. I took it reluctantly, feeling as though I were accepting a pact. It wasn't the same picture that had been used in the newspapers, which I'd seen again on the internet only days before, but it looked to have been taken around the same time. Not long before the two seventeen-year-olds had been abducted and murdered by Jerome Monk, less than three days apart. Both sisters were in it, side by side, each an almost perfect reflection of the other. But there was still a subtle difference between them. Although both were laughing, one of them was grinning brazenly at the camera, shoulders thrown back as she stared at the camera with a look of challenge. By contrast her twin seemed more subdued, head a little downcast, with a self-conscious look about her.

'They had their dad's colouring,' her mother went on. 'Zoe took after Alan in most ways. Always an extrovert, even when she was a little girl. She kept us busy, I can tell you. Lindsey was the quiet one. They might have looked the same, but they were like chalk and cheese in every other way. If they'd—'

She stopped herself. Her smile was tremulous.

'Well. No good playing "what if". You've met him, haven't you? Jerome Monk.'

The question was aimed at me. 'Yes.'

'I wish I'd had the chance. I always regretted not going to the trial. I'd like to have stood in front of him and stared him in the eye. Not that it'd have done much good, by all accounts. And now he's escaped.'

'I'm sure they'll catch him soon,' Sophie said.

'I hope they kill him. I know you're supposed to forgive and move on, but I can't. After what he did, someone as evil as that, I just hope he suffers. Do you have any children, Dr Hunter?'

The question caught me by surprise. I felt the weight of the photograph in my hand.

'No.'

'Then you can't know what it's like. Jerome Monk, he didn't just murder our daughters, he killed our future. Seeing Zoe and Lindsey married, grandchildren, it's all gone. And we don't even have a grave we can take flowers to. At least Tina Williams' parents have that.'

'I'm sorry,' I said, although I didn't know what I was apologizing for.

'Don't be. I know you did your best to find them eight years ago. And I appreciate whatever you can do now. We both do. Alan . . . well, he doesn't like to talk about it much. That's why I told Sophie to call during the day, while he's at work. Nothing can bring our girls back, but it'd be a comfort to both of us to know they're somewhere safe.'

I set the framed picture down on the coffee table. But I could still feel the dead girls' eyes on me, staring from every photograph in that sad and spotless room.

There was an icy gulf between Sophie and me as we drove back to Dartmoor. I felt furious with her, with

Monk, with myself. And behind the anger was the rawness opened by Cath Bennett's unwitting words.

Do you have any children? Then you can't know what it's like.

The streets and houses gave way to country roads before Sophie broke the silence.

'I'm sorry. It was a bad idea, OK?' she blurted. 'I got in touch with her a few months ago, and . . . well, I thought if you met her . . .'

But I was in no mood to let her off that easily. 'What? That I wouldn't be able to say no?'

'I didn't commit you to anything, I only said you *might* be able to help. She must have just assumed—'

'What did you *expect*? Her daughters were murdered! There isn't going to be a day goes by when she doesn't wonder if she'll hear they've been found. Raising her hopes like that's just cruel.'

'I was only trying to do the right thing!' she flashed. 'I'm sorry, all right?'

I bit back my response. The car fishtailed slightly on a muddy stretch of road as I took a bend too fast.

'Careful,' Sophie said.

I eased my foot off the pedal, letting the speed bleed off. Some of my anger went with it. Of all people, I should have known better than to lose control when I was driving.

'I shouldn't have shouted,' I said.

'It's my fault.' Sophie stared out of the window,

rubbing her temple. 'You're right, I shouldn't have done it. I thought . . . Well, it doesn't matter.'

'Is your head hurting?'

'No.' She dropped her hand. We were approaching a turn-off for Padbury. 'Go straight on here,' she said, as I indicated to take it.

'Aren't we going back to your house?'

'Not yet. There's one more place I'd like to go first. Don't worry, it doesn't involve meeting anyone else,' she added when I gave her a look.

I'd assumed Sophie's attempt to persuade me had ended with the visit to meet Cath Bennett. It was only when we passed the overgrown earthworks that once housed the old tin mine's waterwheel that I realized where we were heading.

Black Tor.

Where Tina Williams had been buried.

I took the turning without having to ask. It was like driving back in time. I passed the point where the policewoman had stopped me eight years ago and parked at the end of the dirt track that cut across the moor to the tor. The last time I'd been here this whole area had bustled with trailers, vans and cars. Now, except for a few distant sheep, the moor was empty.

I switched off the engine. 'Now what?'

Sophie gave a weak smile. 'I thought we'd take a walk.'

I sighed. 'Sophie . . .'

'I just want to go and see where the grave was. That's all. No more surprises, I promise.'

Resigned, I got out of the car. A cold breeze plucked at my hair. The air was fresh, underlaid with a faintly sulphurous whiff of bog. I felt the past overlay the present as I looked out at a landscape I'd last set eyes on nearly a decade before. The moor stretched for miles, a wintry patchwork of gorse, heather and dead bracken. There was no corridor of police tape, no distant blue forensic tent. But for all that it was hauntingly familiar. Here was the same pattern of rocky tors, the same undulating hummocks and troughs. The years still seemed to fall away, leaving me feeling hollow at how long had passed since the last time I'd stood here.

And how much had changed.

Beside me, Sophie stood with her hands jammed in her coat pockets, eyes scanning the moor. If she felt at all daunted by it, she gave no sign.

'It's a long walk. Are you sure you're up to it?' I asked. Coming here had snuffed my earlier anger. As perhaps she'd hoped it would.

'I'm fine.' She looked up at the grey sky. 'We'd better hurry. It'll be dark soon.'

She was right: the afternoon was already shading into a dusky twilight. A thin mist was starting to form, rising from the ground like steam from a horse's back. Before I locked the car I took the torch from the glove compartment. We should be back long before dark, but I'd been lost on a moor at night once before. It wasn't an experience I wanted to repeat.

We set off along the track that led to Black Tor. About halfway along it she stopped, turning to face the moor off to our left.

'OK, this is where the police tape was strung out to the grave.'

'How can you tell?' As far as I could see, nothing about where we stood looked very different from anywhere else.

Sophie gave me a sideways glance, mouth quirking in a smile. 'What's wrong? Don't you trust me?'

'I just don't see how you can remember. It all looks the same to me.'

She leaned nearer to me, her hand resting lightly on my arm as she pointed. 'The trick is to memorize landmarks that aren't going to change. See that other tor about two miles away? That should be at right angles to where we are now. And then if you look over there . . .'

She turned, standing close against me so I turned with her. 'There's a sort of cleft in the ground. If we're at the right place the end of it should line up with that hummock with the flat rock on top. See?'

I nodded, but I wasn't really concentrating on what she'd said. She was still pressed against me. She brushed a windblown strand of hair away from her face as we looked at each other, then she moved away.

'Anyway . . . this is a natural entry point into the moor as well,' she said. 'There's a steep bank running along most of the track, but it's easier to negotiate just here. Shall we?'

'OK.'

I was glad to start walking again. *Keep your mind on what you should be doing.* The embankment running down from the track might not be so steep here, but it was a lot more overgrown than I remembered. I scrambled down, then turned to help Sophie. She came down in a rush, flashing me a self-conscious smile as I steadied her.

'Are you sure you can find where the grave was without a map?' I asked as we started picking our way across the tangled heather.

'I'm sure,' she said.

It was hard going. Even when the heather gave way to spiky marsh grass it was still impossible to see where we were treading. My boots alternatively squelched into mud or twisted on some hidden rock or hole. But Sophie seemed confident of where she was going, skirting the clumps of thorny gorse and boggier patches of ground as if following an invisible path. It took me a while to realize that she wasn't just reading the landscape any more.

'You've been here recently, haven't you?' I asked.

She pushed her hair out of her eyes. 'Once or twice.'

'Why?' There couldn't be anything to see, not after all this time.

'I don't know. It feels ... *sanctified*, almost. Knowing what happened, that someone was buried here. Can't you feel it?'

I felt something, but it was more of a prickling sense of unease. *Like we're being watched.* That was stupid, but I was uncomfortably aware of how alone we were, how far we'd come from the road. And the light was still dropping, wisps of wraith-like ground mist obscuring the dips and hollows. I found myself glancing at the nearest patches of gorse and rocks.

'How much further?' I asked.

'Not far. In fact it's just . . .' She tailed off, staring directly ahead.

The moor was pitted with holes.

They'd been hidden by the grass and heather until we were right on top of them. I counted half a dozen, each one about eighteen inches deep and about twice that long, roughly hacked out with clods of peat scattered around them. They seemed to have been dug at random, with no pattern or scheme.

I looked at Sophie. 'You didn't . . .'

'No, of course not! They weren't here last time I came!' Her indignation was real: this wasn't another of her surprises. 'Could an animal have dug them?'

I crouched down by the nearest hole. It was a little smaller than the rest, as though it had been abandoned partly dug. Its edges were marked with clear vertical cuts, and a neatly severed earthworm coiled blindly in the bottom. I could almost hear Wainwright's voice: *Lumbricus terrestris. Overcomplicate at your peril.*

'These were dug with a spade,' I said, straightening. 'Where was Tina Williams buried?'

'Just over there.' Sophie pointed. The patch of ground was undisturbed, overgrown with heather. The holes were unevenly spread out all around it.

'Are you sure?'

'I'm sure. The first time I came back out here I brought the original Ordnance Survey map I'd marked the coordinates on. I didn't need it after that.' She came and stood closer. 'It was Monk, wasn't it?'

I didn't answer: we both knew there was only one person who would have done this. None of the holes was big enough to be a grave. They were more like crude attempts at the exploratory trench Wainwright had dug when we'd found the dead badger.

'I don't understand. Why would Monk have been digging out here?' Sophie asked, glancing round uneasily.

'It has to be for the graves. You always said he might be telling the truth about not being able to remember where they were. Perhaps you were right.'

Her forehead wrinkled. 'That's not what I meant. I'm not surprised he couldn't find them after all this time, if that's what he was doing. But why would he *want* to?'

That hadn't occurred to me. It wasn't unheard of for killers to dig up their victims and rebury them, sometimes more than once. But that was usually done out of panic, a paranoid urge to hide the evidence. That didn't apply here. Monk had already confessed to the murders, and Zoe and Lindsey Bennett's graves had lain undetected for years.

So why dig up half the moor looking for them now?

I found myself looking down at the earthworm again, wriggling in its stubborn attempt to burrow into the soil. Something about it was nagging me. Then I realized.

Worms, even cut ones, don't stay long on the surface. Either they burrow back underground or they're eaten. Yet this one was still here. And the hole it was in was smaller than the others, as though whoever had dug it had broken off or . . .

'We need to go,' I said.

Sophie didn't move. She was staring across the moor. 'David . . .'

I followed her gaze. No more than a hundred yards away a motionless figure stood watching us. It seemed to have appeared from nowhere: there were no bushes or rocks nearby where it could have hidden. In the fading light it was little more than a silhouette, motionless in the rising ground mist. But there was a breadth and bulk about it that had an awful familiarity.

Topping the broad shoulders was the pale globe of a head.

There was an instant when everything seemed frozen. Then the figure started towards us. I took hold of Sophie's arm.

'Come on.'

'Oh, God, that's him, isn't it? It's Monk!'

'Just keep walking.'

But that was easier said than done. Heather clutched at our feet like barbed wire, and white tendrils of mist spread across the darkening moor like a vast cobweb. At another time I might have appreciated the sight. Now it made each step potentially treacherous. If either of us fell or turned an ankle . . .

Don't think about that. I kept my grip on Sophie's arm, urging her back towards the track. The car was just visible on the distant road, a tiny block of colour disappearing into the dusk. I felt sick at how far away it looked. It was tempting to ignore the track and cut straight across the moor, but even though that was the shortest route it would mean slogging over rough heather and bog. That would take even longer, and in the fading light we daren't risk it.

Both of us were already out of breath as I took another glance behind us. The figure was nearer than before, steadily closing the gap. *Don't get distracted. Keep going.* I turned away, and focused on the track ahead of us. It was no use phoning for help. Even if there was a signal no one would get here in time.

We stumbled over tussocks of reed-like marsh grass, boots squelching into the mud and water concealed underneath. I took another look back and saw that the figure wasn't following us any more. Instead of trying to catch us before we reached the track, he was cutting across the moor towards the road.

He was going to try to beat us to the car.

Sophie had seen him as well. 'David . . .' she panted.

'I know. Just keep going.'

The track was tantalizingly near, but once we reached it we still had to get back to the road. The figure didn't have nearly so far to go. He was moving across the moor in a steady, unhurried stride. *God, we're not going to make it.* The ground rose more steeply as we reached the bank immediately below the track. Sophie was struggling now, and I had to help her scramble up the last few yards, clutching at handfuls of heather to pull ourselves up.

Then we were on the track's firmer surface. My chest was burning as I tugged Sophie into a lumbering run. 'Come on!'

'Wait . . . get my breath . . .' she gasped. Her face was white and slick with sweat. She shouldn't have been exerting herself so soon after coming out of hospital, but there was no choice.

'We need to run,' I told her.

She shook her head, pushing me away. 'Can't . . . I can't . . .'

'Yes, you can,' I said, tightening my arm under her shoulders and almost dragging her down the track.

My legs felt like water as we lurched towards the car. The figure was no more than thirty or forty yards away, off to one side and slightly below us as he slogged over the rugged moor. But he'd begun to slow now himself. The pale head turned towards us as we stumbled the last few yards. He'd stopped, barely a stone's throw away. I could feel his eyes on us as I fumbled for my key fob and unlocked the car. Sophie collapsed inside while I ran round to the driver's side, conscious of the shadowy figure watching from the knee-deep mist.

He'd beaten us. Why did he give up? I'd no idea and didn't care. Slamming the door, I turned on the engine and stamped on the accelerator. As the car roared away I looked in the rear-view mirror.

Both the road and moor behind us were empty.

16

I didn't slow for two or three miles. Only when I was certain no one was following did I began to relax. Reaction was setting in, leaving me wrung out and clammy as I let the car's speed ease back to normal.

'Are we safe?' Sophie asked. She was still breathing heavily. The bruise looked worse than ever against the pallor of her face.

'I think so.'

She closed her eyes. 'I'm going to be sick.'

I pulled over. Sophie stumbled out of the car almost before we'd stopped. Leaving the engine running I waited nearby, keeping one eye on the surrounding moor. Despite my assurances I'd be happier when we were far away from this place. The dusk was thickening and the rustle of wind through the heather only emphasized the loneliness. We could have been the only living things out there.

But we weren't. As I waited for Sophie, I checked my phone and saw with relief that there was enough signal to make a call. I dialled Terry's number, willing him to pick up. It seemed to ring for a long time, but just when I thought it was going to go to voicemail he answered.

'This better be good.' He sounded slurred, as though he were either very tired or drunk. But I couldn't see even Terry drinking in the middle of an investigation like this.

'We're at Black Tor. We've—'

'Who's "we"?'

'Sophie Keller. She discharged herself from hospital yesterday and—'

'Keller? What are you doing there with her?'

'Does it *matter*? Monk's *here*!'

That seemed to get through. 'Go on.'

I kept it brief, conscious of the fading light. 'So you didn't actually see him up close?' Terry said, when I'd finished.

'Look, it was Monk! I didn't see another car, so he can't have got far.'

I heard a rasp of bristles as Terry rubbed his hand across his face. 'OK, leave it with me.'

'Do you need us to hang around?'

'I think we'll cope.' His tone was heavy with

sarcasm. 'If I want you I'll know where to find you.'

The line went dead. Feeling the familiar irritation, I put the phone away and went over to Sophie. She gave me a wan smile. 'Sorry. False alarm.'

'How're you feeling?'

'My head's throbbing a little, but it isn't too bad. Did you call the police?'

'I've just spoken to Terry Connors. He's getting things moving.'

Her mouth tightened at the mention of Terry, but for once she didn't criticize him. 'Do we have to wait here?'

'He says there's no need.'

I'd been expecting that we'd have to stay until the police got there, but I wasn't about to argue. I looked out at the moor. The light was dropping quickly, and a haze of mist blurred the edges of the little we could still see. Sophie shivered, and I knew what she was thinking.

Monk was still out there.

I put my arm around her. 'Come on, I'll take you home.'

The mist had thickened to a full-blown fog by the time we reached Padbury. I was forced to slow to a crawl, my headlights almost useless against the white gauze. I didn't even realize that we'd reached the village until the shadowy outline of the old church loomed up out of the fog.

I pulled into the lane at the bottom of Sophie's garden and switched off the engine. In the ticking silence as it cooled we might have been at the bottom of the sea. I found myself glancing around uneasily as we went up the path, straining to hear. The fog wrapped round us, making everything more than a few feet away all but invisible.

'You should get security lights,' I said, as the conical shadow of the kiln took form on one side, towering over the spectral branches of the orchard.

'I don't need them out here,' Sophie said, reaching in her bag for the house keys. She faltered as she realized the irony of what she'd just said. 'Not usually, anyway.'

But the front door was still intact, the new lock fitted by the joiner reassuringly solid. When Sophie opened it and flicked on the hall light, the house looked exactly as we'd left it that morning.

I hadn't realized till then how tense I'd been.

From the deep sigh she gave as she shot home the new bolts on the door, it seemed that Sophie felt the same way.

'How are you holding up?' I asked as she tiredly pulled off her coat.

'I've had better days.' Her smile was unconvincing. 'Look, about what happened earlier with Cath Bennett . . . I'm sorry, I didn't think it through.'

After what had happened that no longer seemed

important. 'Forget it. Anyway, you were right. Monk wouldn't have dug those holes without a good reason. There must be at least one other grave round there. The police'll have to search the whole area again.'

She looked as though that hadn't occurred to her. 'You think so?'

'I don't see that they've any choice. Monk's as good as told us where to look. That's what you wanted, isn't it?'

'Yes, of course.' She sounded doubtful. 'God, I really need a drink.'

So did I, but not yet. 'I think it might be a good idea to stay somewhere else tonight.'

Sophie was sitting on the stairs, unfastening her muddy boots. She stopped to look up at me, her face closed. 'No.'

'You could book into a hotel—'

'I'm not going anywhere.'

'You've already been attacked here once, and we still don't know who by. If it was Monk—'

'If it was Monk I'd be dead. You know it as well as I do. If you want to run away you can, but I'm not going to!'

I stared in surprise. *Where did that come from?*

Sophie sighed. 'I'm sorry, you didn't deserve that. It's just . . . I – I'm scared and confused, and this is my *home*. If I leave now I'll never feel safe here again. Can't you understand that?'

I could. That didn't mean I agreed, but there was no point arguing. 'OK.'

'Thank you.' She came over and gave me a hug. I held her for a moment, feeling the warm pressure of her body before she stepped back. 'I can be a cow sometimes, but I appreciate everything you're doing. And I wouldn't blame you if you decided to go anyway.'

The opening was there if I wanted to take it. I could walk away now, go back to London and let Sophie and the police handle it from here.

But that wasn't going to happen. Whatever was going on, it had its roots in what happened eight years ago. I'd been involved then, and I still was.

I gave Sophie a smile. 'You mentioned something about a drink.'

We shared the cooking that night. Dinner was grilled lamb chops from the freezer with minted potatoes and frozen peas. Not haute cuisine, perhaps, but it was simple and satisfying. Sophie produced a bottle of wine, and gave it me to open while she defrosted the chops.

'Padbury doesn't have much of a wine merchant's,' she apologized, pouring two glasses.

'It'll be fine,' I said. And it was. The alcohol took the edge off any remaining awkwardness, and I didn't argue when Sophie suggested leaving the dishes till morning. Taking what was left of the wine with us, we went into the sitting room. I put more logs in the stove and built up the fire using kindling and old newspaper from the wicker basket. *You're getting good at this.*

Soon bright flames were dancing behind the smoky glass panel, driving the chill from the room. Sophie and I sat at either end of the sofa. We didn't talk, but the silence was comfortable. I took another drink of wine and stole a look at her. She was drowsing, legs curled up on the sofa, head fallen back to expose the slender line of her throat. Her face was peaceful and relaxed, the firelight softening the bruising so it could almost have been shadow. The intervening years had been good to her, I decided. She wasn't conventionally beautiful, but the strong features would still turn heads. They would still look good in another eight years' time. Or eighteen.

She was breathing with the slow, steady rhythm of deep sleep, the almost empty wine glass still held loosely in her fingers. It had fallen slightly to rest lightly between her breasts. I was loath to disturb her but it was starting to slip, each breath dislodging it a little more.

'Sophie . . .' I said gently. There was no response. 'Sophie?'

She came awake gradually, eyes staring at me blankly before blinking as awareness returned.

'Sorry,' she apologized, sitting up. 'Please tell me I've not been drooling.'

'Only a little.'

She smiled and swatted at me. 'Pig.'

'Why don't you go to bed?'

'Not much of a host, am I?' she said, but she didn't argue. She stood up and put her hand on my shoulder as she swayed unsteadily. 'Whoa . . .'

'Take it easy,' I said, getting up to support her. 'Are you OK?'

'Just tired, I think. Must have stood up too quickly.'

She was still holding on to me. I had my hands on her waist, standing close enough to feel the warmth coming from her. Neither of us moved. Sophie's eyes were big and dark as she leaned into me. A smile curved her face.

'Well . . .' she said, and something hit the window with a *bang*.

We jumped apart. I rushed to the heavy curtains and yanked them open, half expecting to see Monk's nightmare face glaring back at me. But the window was unbroken and empty. All I could see beyond it was an amorphous sheet of white fog.

'What was it?' Sophie asked, standing close behind me.

'Probably nothing.'

It was an inane thing to say, especially when my

own heart was pounding. *Monk can't have followed us back here. Can he?* But he didn't have to follow us. Not when Sophie's address had been on her letters.

'Stay here,' I told her.

'You're not going *outside*?'

'Only to take a look.' The alternative was cowering inside all night, wondering what had hit the window. If it was nothing then we could relax. If it was Monk . . .

Then it wouldn't make any difference.

I took the heavy iron poker from beside the glowing stove and went into the hall. Sophie hurried into the kitchen and returned with a lantern-style torch.

'Lock the door behind me,' I said, taking it from her.

'David, wait—'

But I was already sliding back the bolts on the front door and stepping outside. There was nothing to see but fog. The air was damp, scented with loam and rotting leaves. I shivered, wishing I'd thought to grab my coat. The fog soaked up the lantern's beam. Keeping close to the side of the house, I began making my way towards the sitting room. The poker felt flimsy in my hand, and I was already beginning to think this wasn't such a good idea. *What are you going to do if there is someone out here? What if it's Monk?*

But it was too late now. Up ahead I could see a

misty glow that must be the sitting-room window. I picked up my pace, keen to get it over with.

And something moved on the ground at my feet.

I stumbled backwards, raising the poker as I thrust out the lantern. There was another flurry of movement, and then the light and shadows resolved themselves.

Caught in the lantern's beam, an owl blinked up at me.

I lowered the poker, feeling stupid. The bird was ghostly pale, its face almost white. It was hunched on the grass below the window, wings splayed out awkwardly at its sides. The dark and alien eyes shuttered in another slow blink, but it made no attempt to move.

'It's a barn owl,' Sophie said from behind me.

She startled me: I hadn't heard her approach. 'I thought you were waiting inside?'

'I didn't say that.' Sophie had more sense than me, enough to pull on a coat. She crouched beside the injured bird. 'It's lucky the window didn't break. Poor thing. The fog must have confused it. What do you think we should do?'

'It's probably just stunned,' I said. The bird was staring straight ahead, either determined to ignore us or too dazed to care. 'We shouldn't move it.'

'But we've got to do something!'

'If it struggles we might hurt it even more.' Besides,

injured or not, the bird was still a predator. Its beak and claws were no less sharp.

'I'm not leaving it out here,' Sophie said, in a tone I was beginning to recognize. I sighed.

'Have you got a blanket or something?'

The owl flapped a little as I cautiously covered it with an old towel, but quickly subsided. Sophie suggested leaving it just inside the kiln, propping the door open so it could fly out when it had recovered.

'What about your pots?' I asked.

'They're insured. Anyway, it's an owl. It can see in the dark.'

The bird was surprisingly light as I carried it into the kiln, the rapid tattoo of its heart thrumming under my hands. Inside was damp and musty with the smell of old bricks. My footsteps echoed as I set the owl on the floor and removed the towel. We hadn't turned on the light, and its pale feathers were almost luminous in the darkness.

'Do you think it'll be all right?' Sophie asked as we returned to the house.

'We can't do any more tonight. If it's still there in the morning we can call a vet.'

I locked and bolted the front door, giving it a tug to make sure. Sophie shivered as she rubbed her arms.

'God, I'm frozen!'

She was standing very close. Looking at me. It would have been natural to take hold of her.

'It's late,' I said. 'You go on up, I'll see to things down here.'

She blinked, then nodded. 'Right. Well . . . goodnight.'

I waited while she went upstairs, then went through the rooms, angrily turning off the lights. I told myself I'd done the right thing. Sophie was scared and vulnerable, and things were complicated enough already.

But I wasn't sure whether I was angry because of what had almost happened, or because I hadn't let it.

I lay awake in the single bed, listening to the nighttime silence of the house and thinking about Sophie. I finally fell asleep, only to be half-woken by a noise from outside, the sharp cry of either predator or prey. It didn't come again, and as sleep reclaimed me I forgot all about it.

17

Next morning I woke early and padded downstairs in the cool and quiet house while Sophie slept. I made myself a cup of tea as the sky gradually lightened, thinking about the past twenty-four hours. Normally I'd have turned on the radio to listen to the news, or gone online. But I didn't want to disturb Sophie and the house didn't have Wi-Fi. Instead I sipped my scalding tea at the kitchen table and watched the day slowly begin.

The morning chorus of birdsong reminded me of the owl. Pulling on my coat and boots, I went outside. The fog had lifted, although there was still an early haze, part drizzle, part mist. It frosted the branches of the apple trees, beading the cobwebs with quicksilver as I crossed the wet grass.

The sitting-room window had a dusty smeared

mark where the owl had flown into it, but the only other sign of the bird was a few delicate pale feathers on the floor of the kiln. They could have been dislodged by the impact, although there was another, less happy explanation. There was no shortage of foxes around here. With the kiln door left open the injured predator could easily have become prey.

I wandered around the kiln. The scaffolding and props wedged against the walls had been here so long they might almost have grown out of the structure. Some sections of brickwork had been repointed with fresh mortar years ago, or even decades by the look of things. But most of it had been left to crumble away, and I guessed that the loose brick where Sophie kept her key was only one of many. Renovating the kiln, let alone getting it working again as she hoped, would be a big and expensive job.

She would have to sell a lot of pots.

Still, she was obviously talented. The crockery, bowls and vases stacked on the shelves were all simple yet striking designs. I ran my hand across the mound of hard clay on the workbench. It was made up of unused scraps that Sophie had slapped together and left to dry, but even that could have been an abstract piece of art.

I gave it a pat and went back into the house.

Sophie still wasn't up, which was good: she needed the rest. I was hungry and debated making breakfast but decided to wait for her. I was only a guest and wasn't sure how she'd feel about my making myself at home.

It was late before I heard her moving about upstairs. By the time she came down I'd put the kettle on and had a mug of tea waiting.

'Morning,' I said, handing her the mug. 'I wasn't sure if you were a tea or coffee person first thing.'

She looked bleary-eyed and a little self-conscious. She was wearing an oversized sweater over her jeans, hair pulled back and still damp from the shower. 'Tea's great. I save my real caffeine fix till I'm working. Did you sleep well?'

'Fine,' I lied. 'How are you feeling?'

'My cheek's still sore, but other than that I'm OK.'

'Can you remember anything yet about what happened?'

'What? Oh . . . no, still blank.' She went to the fridge. 'How about the owl? Is it still there?'

'No, I checked earlier. It's gone.'

She grinned. 'See? I told you it'd be all right in the kiln.'

I didn't mention the feathers on the kiln floor. If Sophie wanted a happy ending I wasn't going to spoil it for her.

'No bread for toast, I'm afraid, but I can offer you bacon and eggs,' she said, opening the fridge. 'Scrambled all right?'

I said it was. 'I thought I'd set off back before lunch,' I told her, as she cracked the eggs into a bowl.

She paused, then continued beating the eggs. 'You're leaving?'

'I might as well. The police'll have to relaunch the search for the Bennett twins now Monk's been digging on the moor.'

I was surprised they hadn't contacted us already. Even if they hadn't found Monk after our sighting the day before, I'd have expected someone to have been in touch to take our statements.

'I suppose so,' Sophie said. 'Not as if there's anything keeping you here, is there?'

She had her back to me. The frying pan clattered on the range. The silence stretched and grew heavy.

'I can stay longer. If you're bothered about being here by yourself, I mean.'

'Why, just because someone attacked me?' She slapped rashers of bacon into the pan, the hot fat setting up an angry hissing. 'I expect I'll get used to the idea. I don't have much choice, do I?'

'It was probably just a burglary that went wrong, like the police said.'

'Well, that makes me feel much better, doesn't it?' She stabbed a fork into the bacon and flipped it over as though it were to blame. 'I used to feel safe here. Even though it was the middle of nowhere,

I never once felt threatened like I did living in a city. But that's my problem, not yours.'

'Look, I know how you must feel—'

'No you don't.'

I hesitated. This wasn't something I'd planned to go into, but I knew that if Sophie wasn't careful the assault could become a trauma she'd never recover from.

'Actually, I do. I was stabbed after a case the other year.'

She turned to look at me. 'You're not serious?'

So I told her about the events on Runa, and how Grace Strachan had turned up on my doorstep months later, returning from the dead to plunge a knife into me.

'And they never caught her?' Sophie asked, her eyes wide. 'She's still out there?'

'Somewhere. The police think she left the country soon afterwards. She and her brother were rich, so she probably had access to bank accounts no one knows about. Chances are she's in South America or somewhere by now.'

'That's awful!'

I shrugged. 'Looking on the bright side, she probably thinks I'm dead. So there's no reason for her to try again.'

I felt a superstitious unease as soon as I'd spoken. *Don't tempt providence.*

Sophie had moved the pan from the heat. She looked down at it, troubled. 'I'd no idea. And now I've dragged you into all this.'

'You didn't drag me into anything. And the reason I'm telling you this is because everything points to your attack being a one-off. Whoever did it can't have really wanted to hurt you, or . . . Well, you'd have got more than a fractured cheek.'

'I suppose.' She looked thoughtful, but there was still a shadow in her eyes. Abruptly, it was gone. She turned the heat back up under the pan and gave me a mischievous grin. 'Anyway, let's have breakfast. Then before you go you can show me your scar.'

But her good mood didn't last. She grew distracted again, pushing the food around listlessly on her plate. I offered to help with the dishes, but she declined. I got the impression she wanted some time to herself, so I left her in the kitchen and went to shower and pack my things.

I wondered if it was only now dawning on her that she wouldn't be part of any search operation this time round. For whatever reason, finding Zoe and Lindsey Bennett's graves had become a personal crusade, but Sophie wasn't a BIA any more. Her involvement had effectively ended the moment we'd found the holes left by Monk at Black Tor. Now the police would take over and she'd be nothing more than an onlooker.

Letting go was never easy.

I took my bag downstairs. The radio was playing when I went into the kitchen. Sophie was standing by the sink, her hands motionless in the water.

'Is there anything—' I began.

'Shh!' She silenced me with a quick shake of her head. For the first time I paid attention to what was being said on the radio.

'. . . *police haven't released the victim's identity, although they confirm the death is being treated as suspicious. In other news . . .*'

Sophie's face was white. 'Did you hear?'

'Only the last part.'

'There's been a murder. They haven't said who it is, but it's in Torbay. Near Sharkham Point. Isn't that . . .'

I nodded, realizing I wouldn't be leaving yet after all.

That was where Wainwright lived.

18

It was less than an hour's drive to Sharkham Point from Padbury. Sophie had insisted on going, and I didn't put up much of an argument. I wanted to find out who the victim was just as much as she did. I'd called Terry straight away, but he wasn't answering his phone. That wasn't surprising: odds were he'd have been called out to the scene. I told myself it might not have anything to do with Wainwright. Murders happen every day, and so do coincidences.

But I couldn't quite believe it.

Two days before when I'd driven to Torbay there had been a vaulting blue sky and bright autumn sunshine. Now grey clouds turned the countryside drab and colourless. The fields we passed were shorn to an untidy stubble or ploughed into muddy ridges of soil, while the dead leaves that clung to the bare trees gave them the ragged appearance of scarecrows.

Neither Sophie nor I spoke much during the journey. She sat staring out of the window, as wrapped up in her thoughts as I was in my own. Only when we reached the coast and saw the distant bellying of the sea beyond the cliffs did she stir. I knew what she was thinking: we'd know soon, one way or another.

Then we were passing a signpost for Sharkham Point. Not far ahead of it we could see a fairground strobing of blue lights on the road.

Sophie's hand went to her throat. 'Oh, God. Is that Wainwright's house?'

A heaviness settled in my stomach. 'Yes.'

A cordon of police tape stretched across the road, fluttering in the wind. Beyond it police cars and trailers were parked on either side of the gates, along with a few press and TV vans. An ambulance was on the driveway outside the house, but the absence of flashing lights or sirens testified that there was no longer any urgency.

I parked a little way before the cordon. 'What should we do?' Sophie asked. Her usual confidence seemed to have abandoned her.

'We've come this far. No point going back now,' I said, and climbed out of the car.

There was a stiff wind blowing from cliffs overlooking the sea. It carried a faint hint of saline, tainted by exhaust fumes. I could hear the chug of a generator from somewhere nearby. A policeman in a bright yellow reflective jacket moved to block us as we approached.

'The road's closed.'

'I know. My name's David Hunter. Is DI Connors here?' I asked.

He regarded us for a few seconds, then spoke into his radio. 'Got a David Hunter here, asking for . . .'

'DI Terry Connors,' I said as he looked at me for confirmation.

He repeated it and waited. The pause seemed to go on a long time, then there was a crackling voice. He lowered the radio.

'Sorry.'

Sophie spoke up before I could say anything. 'Does that mean he isn't here or he won't see us?'

The policeman regarded her stonily. 'It means you're going to have to leave.'

'Who's dead? Is it Professor Wainwright or his wife?'

'Are you relatives?'

'No, but—'

'Then you can read about it in the papers. Now, last time: go back to your car.'

'Come on, Sophie,' I said, taking hold of her arm. I knew the police well enough to know we weren't going to get anywhere like this.

She pulled free, facing up to the PC. 'I'm not going anywhere until I know what's happened.'

I'm not sure how it would have gone, but at that moment there was a flurry of activity from the house. A group of police officers came down the driveway. At their head was a man whose smart uniform and peaked cap marked him as police hierarchy. The uniform was new, and the hair and moustache were more grey. But the chipped ice of the eyes was the same, and the bland, unlined features hardly seemed to have aged.

Simms didn't so much as glance in our direction as he strode towards an unmarked black BMW, but someone else did. One of his entourage was staring at us: middle-aged, overweight and balding. It was only when I saw the prominent teeth that I realized it was Roper.

He hurried over and spoke to his superior. Simms stopped, his pale eyes turning to us. *Now for it*, I thought as they came over, Roper trailing behind like a pet dog.

The PC who'd stopped us stood rigidly to attention. 'Sir, I was just—'

Simms paid him no attention. His eyes touched on Sophie without interest or recognition before pinning me again. There had always been an aura of arrogance about him, but it was more pronounced now. His insignia identified him as an Assistant Chief

Constable, a rank few CID officers ever made. I wasn't surprised. If ever a man had been born to wear a uniform, it was Simms.

Roper also seemed to have prospered. The crumpled suits had been replaced with well-tailored clothes and the nicotine-stained teeth had been artificially whitened. He'd put on weight, too, at least from the waist up. While the DC's upper body had the paunchy, well-fed look of a man who took his food and drink seriously, his low-slung trousers still flapped loosely around skittle-thin legs.

Neither of them seemed pleased to see us. Simms had a pair of black leather gloves clenched in one hand, tapping them impatiently against his thigh.

'Dr Hunter, isn't it?' he said. 'May I ask what you're doing here?'

Sophie didn't give me a chance to answer. 'What happened? Who's been killed?'

Simms regarded her for a beat, then pointedly turned to me again. 'I asked what you were doing here.'

'We heard about the murder and wanted to find out if Professor Wainwright and his wife were involved.'

'And that concerned you how, exactly?'

ACC or not, his attitude was beginning to rankle. 'Because I thought Jerome Monk might have killed them.'

Roper glanced uneasily at Simms. The ACC's expression didn't change but his eyes were glacial.

'Let him through,' he told the PC.

I hid my surprise and ducked under the tape. Sophie moved to do the same.

'Just Dr Hunter,' Simms said.

The PC stepped in front of her. 'Oh, come *on*!' Sophie protested.

'Dr Hunter's a police consultant.' Simms gaze lingered dispassionately on her bruised cheek. 'As far as I'm aware you no longer are.'

Sophie drew herself up to argue. 'I'll see you back at the car,' I said quickly, knowing Simms wouldn't change his mind. She shot me a furious look, then snatched the keys off me and strode back down the road.

Simms was already heading towards the house, polished black shoes crunching on the gravel driveway. Roper fell into step beside me. The wind plucked at his thinning hair. He still used too much aftershave, but like everything else about him it was more expensive now.

'Turning into quite a reunion, isn't it?' His grin was almost a nervous tick. He motioned with his head back at Sophie. 'Not happy, is she? What happened to her face?'

I was surprised he didn't know. But then I'd no idea

if he and Terry still worked together. 'Someone broke into her house and attacked her.'

'She needs better locks. When was this?'

'Four days ago.'

The grin left his face as he made the connection: four days made it right after Monk's escape. 'Did they get who did it?'

I'd all but forgotten Terry's warning – or threat – that I might be a suspect myself. It wasn't a comfortable thought. 'Not yet. She can't remember much about what happened.'

'Was she raped?'

'No.'

'Anything stolen?'

'No.'

Roper gave a huff of amusement. 'Bloody lucky, eh?'

I changed the subject. 'When did Simms make ACC?'

'Must be ... oh, four or five years ago now. Around the same time I made DI.'

He gave me a little sideways look as he said it. *Roper? A detective inspector?* I wouldn't have thought he'd have made detective sergeant. Hitching his wagon to Simms' star obviously hadn't done his career any harm.

'Congratulations,' I said. 'Who's SIO here?'

'Steve Naysmith. He's a bit of a highflier, only

made Detective Chief Super last year.' Roper's tone made it clear he didn't approve. I took that as a point in Naysmith's favour. 'But the ACC's taking a very personal interest. The SIO's got to run everything by him.'

Naysmith must love that. But then Simms had known Wainwright well. He wasn't about to sit this one out.

Especially if Monk was the main suspect.

Simms had stopped by the entrance to the house, where a trestle table had been set up with boxes of protective gear.

'I wasn't anticipating having to do this again,' he said irritably, tearing open a sealed packet of overalls. 'I don't have long to spare. I have a press conference soon.'

Some things don't change. I didn't know why Simms was doing this, but I doubted it was just for my benefit. As he struggled into the overalls I thought he looked even less comfortable in them now than he had eight years ago, and suddenly I realized why. The smooth features were so bland that it was only his clothes that gave them character. The white, all-in-one suits robbed him of that, making him look peculiarly unfinished.

'Need me for anything else, sir?' Roper asked.

Simms didn't so much as glance at him as he pulled on overshoes and gloves. 'Not right now, but stay here until Dr Hunter and I have finished.'

Without waiting to see if I was ready, he went inside.

The genteel quietude of the house I remembered had been shattered. White-suited CSIs were packing away equipment, but evidence of what had happened was everywhere. Every surface was finely coated with fingerprint powder, as though the house had been gathering dust for years. Glass from a broken window was scattered on the parquet floor amongst the spilled soil from an overturned potted plant. The house still smelled of chrysanthemums, but beneath it was a faint taint of faeces and drying blood, a lingering essence of violent death.

'The intruder forced open the kitchen door,' Simms told me, skirting a line of muddy footprints that were being photographed by a CSI. 'No attempt at concealment, as you can see. We've also found several patches of sputum, which should enable a DNA analysis.'

'Sputum?'

'It appears the killer spat on the floor.' He was walking down the hallway in front of me, blocking my view. Now he stepped aside, and I saw Leonard Wainwright.

The forensic archaeologist looked pathetic in death. Dressed in pyjamas and an old striped bathrobe, he lay crumpled near the foot of the stairs, amongst the shattered remains of a glass-fronted china cabinet. Blood from where he'd been cut by the broken glass had dried blackly, splashed across the floor. But there wasn't enough of it for him to have bled to death. His face was obscured by a tangle of grey hair, through which the slits of his bloodshot eyes were visible. His head was twisted impossibly far to one side, almost resting on one shoulder. *Broken neck*, I thought automatically. For no reason I found myself staring at Wainwright's bare feet. They were calloused and yellow, and the ankles that protruded from the pyjama bottoms were an old man's, thin and hairless.

He'd have hated anyone seeing that.

I hadn't expected to find the body still there. I'm no stranger to either crime scenes or violent death, but this was different. Forty-eight hours ago I'd been talking to Wainwright, and the sight of him on the hallway floor caught me unprepared.

A diminutive figure in baggy overalls was kneeling beside his body, humming absently to itself as it took a reading from a thermometer. The tune was perky and familiar: one of Gilbert and Sullivan's, though I couldn't name it. The white-gloved hands were as small as a child's, and although the face was all but obscured by a hood and mask, I recognized the gold half-moon glasses straight away.

'Nearly done,' Pirie said without looking up.

I was surprised to see him. I'd have thought the pathologist would have retired by now. 'You remember Dr Hunter, George?' Simms asked.

The pathologist raised his head. The eyebrows bushed above the glasses like grey spider legs, but his gaze was as bright and intelligent as ever.

'Indeed I do. A pleasure as always, Dr Hunter. Although I wouldn't have thought your skills were needed in this instance.'

'He isn't here in an official capacity,' Simms told him.

'Ah. Nevertheless, if you'd care to lend a hand you'd be very welcome. I recall you extended the same courtesy to me. I'd be happy to return the favour.'

'Perhaps another time.' I appreciated the offer, but post-mortems weren't my field. 'I'd have thought the body would've been taken to the mortuary by now.'

Simms's face was impassive as he stared down at the body of his friend. 'We had to wait for Dr Pirie to finish another job. I wanted someone I knew working on this.'

'What about his wife? I asked. There was no sign of Jean Wainwright, and the news report had only mentioned a single death.

'She's been hospitalized. Hopefully only from shock, but she wasn't well herself, even before this.'

'So she wasn't actually hurt?'

'Not beyond witnessing her husband's murder. Their cleaner found them both this morning when she let herself in. Jean was in a . . . confused state. She hasn't been able to tell us much so far, but I'm hoping she'll be able to answer questions later.'

'So she hasn't said who did it?'

'Not as yet.'

But I didn't think there was much doubt. First Sophie, now Wainwright. Perhaps Terry was right after all . . .

'Have you found anything?' I asked Pirie.

The pathologist considered, the thermometer held aloft like a conductor's baton. 'First impressions only. Rigor and livor mortis suggest he's been dead for between eight to twelve hours, as does the body temperature. That puts the time of death between one and five o'clock this morning. As I'm sure you can see for yourself, his neck has been broken, which at this stage seems the most probable cause of death.'

'It would take a lot of force to do that,' I said, thinking how Monk had killed the police dog on the moor eight years ago.

'Oh, undoubtedly. For anyone to break a grown man's neck deliberately would have taken a huge degree of strength—'

'Thank you, George, we won't disturb you any longer,' Simms said. 'Please keep me informed.'

'Of course.' Pirie's expression was hidden by the

mask. 'Goodbye, Dr Hunter. And should you change your mind my offer still stands.'

I thanked him, but Simms was already heading back down the hallway. As soon as we were outside he began stripping off his overalls, his dark uniform emerging from them like an insect from a chrysalis.

'Are there any other witnesses apart from Jean Wainwright?' I asked, unfastening my own.

'Unfortunately not. But I'm hopeful she'll be able to provide us with a detailed account before much longer.'

'It looks like Monk, though, doesn't it?'

Simms snapped off his surgical gloves and dropped them into a large plastic bin already half full of other discarded forensic gear. 'That remains to be seen. And I'd thank you not to speculate at this stage.'

'But you heard what Pirie said about the killer's strength. And spitting on the floor sounds like a sign of contempt. Who else could it be?'

'I don't know, but at the moment there's no firm evidence to suggest that Jerome Monk had anything to do with it.' Simms spoke with controlled anger. 'Hopefully Jean Wainwright will be able to tell us what happened. Until then I will not have needless scaremongering. The last thing I need is for the press to start running with unfounded rumours.'

'Hardly unfounded. It's a matter of record that Wainwright headed the search team. The press are bound to make the connection before long.'

'By which time Monk will hopefully be back in custody. So until then, or we have evidence to the contrary, I'll continue to treat this as I would any other murder investigation.'

I understood then. For someone as PR-conscious as Simms it was bad enough that Monk had escaped. The last thing he wanted was for stories to circulate that the escaped killer was on some sort of vendetta. That was exactly the sort of publicity an ambitious ACC could do without.

'Jean Wainwright called me two days ago,' Simms said. 'She told me you'd been here, and that Leonard had become very agitated. Care to tell me what that was about?'

I suppose I should have expected Wainwright's wife to tell him about my visit. 'I wanted to talk to him about Monk. I didn't know about his condition. If I had—'

'Jerome Monk doesn't concern you, Dr Hunter. And now you've put me in the embarrassing position of having to ask where you were this morning between one and five o'clock?'

But I'd been waiting for that. 'I was in bed at Sophie Keller's house. And no, she can't vouch for me. As for Jerome Monk, you can't seriously think I'm not going to ask questions after what happened yesterday.'

'What are you talking about?'

'When Monk came after us on the moor.' Simms was looking at me as though I were mad. I tugged the gloves from my hands and threw them into the bin. 'Oh, come on, Terry Connors must have told you!'

Simms had gone very still. The only sign of emotion on the wax-like face was the compressed line of his lips.

'Terry Connors isn't involved in this investigation. He's been suspended.'

19

It started raining as I drove out to Black Tor. The water came down in sheets, so that the windscreen wipers were hard-pressed to clear the glass. It was earlier than when Sophie and I had come out here the day before, but by the time I reached the overgrown mine workings the sky had darkened so much that it seemed almost night.

Now, though, it was Roper who sat in the passenger seat, smelling of aftershave and onions. He was as disgruntled at the arrangement as I was, but Simms hadn't given either of us any choice. He'd told me to make Roper my first point of contact rather than Naysmith, suggesting there was no love lost between him and the SIO. Sophie was still back at Wainwright's, giving her statement. At least I assumed she was: I hadn't had a chance to speak to her before we'd left. Roper had returned my keys and assured me that someone would take her home, and then a procession of cars had set off for Dartmoor.

Up ahead the blurred tail lights of the ACC's black BMW were screened by a fine mist of spray thrown up by its tyres. The press conference had been postponed so that Simms could come out here. He'd demanded to hear everything, starting from when Terry appeared on my doorstep on the morning of Monk's escape. I'd kept nothing back, not even Sophie's letters to Monk. I'd felt guilty about that, but we'd gone beyond keeping secrets.

Simms' pale-blue eyes had blazed, but it wasn't until I described finding the holes dug on the moor the day before, and the scrambled chase that followed, that he became incandescent.

'This was twenty-four hours ago and I'm only just *hearing* about it? God *Almighty*!'

I couldn't blame him. I was still trying to take it in myself. Not only was Terry suspended, he wasn't even a DI any more. Simms had told me he'd been demoted to detective sergeant the previous year.

Terry, what the hell are *you playing at?* I still had the card he'd given me: *Detective Inspector Terry Connors*. Still, it explained why he'd told me to call him on his mobile rather than at headquarters. *I'm never there*, he'd said.

At least that much had been true.

In a way I could almost understand him lying about his rank and suspension: pride had always been one of Terry's sins. What was inexcusable was that rather than admit to his charade he'd thrown away a chance to capture Monk. Now Wainwright was dead, and his killer was still on the loose.

There was no going back from that.

Beside me, Roper stifled a belch. Not very successfully. 'Pardon,' he muttered, baring his teeth in a sheepish grin. He looked out at the rainswept moor. 'Christ, it's really coming down. Couldn't have brought us here on a sunny day, could you?'

'I'll try harder next time.'

'Good one,' he said, with a snickering laugh. He stared at the rain beating against the car windscreen and sighed. 'Bloody Connors. He's shafted himself this time. And us.'

I knew an invitation when I heard one. 'Simms said he'd been demoted.'

'Stupid sod got caught altering an evidence log.' He shook his head in disgust. 'Wasn't even anything important, just got his dates mixed up. If he'd owned up he'd have been slapped on the wrist and that would have been it, but no. The golden boy from the Met couldn't admit he'd made a mistake.' He didn't try to hide his satisfaction.

'And his suspension?' I asked.

Roper sucked his teeth, as though debating

whether or not to tell me. 'He assaulted a police-woman.'

'He what?'

'Nothing violent, thank God. He was just too pissed to take no for an answer. Typical Connors, thought he was God's gift. Never could keep his fly zipped.'

I realized I was squeezing the steering wheel. *No, he couldn't.* I forced myself to relax my grip.

'So he was drunk?'

'Drunk? He's a piss-head, he's hardly been sober for years. Don't get me wrong, there's nothing wrong with a beer or two, I'm the first to admit that.' He patted his distended stomach. 'But some people can handle it and some can't. And Connors couldn't. He was on borrowed time even before he got knocked back to DS, and it was all downhill from there.'

I remembered how Terry had sounded on the phone when I'd told him about Monk. 'What'll happen to him?'

'If he's lucky he'll just be kicked off the force, but he could be looking at criminal charges. Bloody idiot. If I'd had his opportunities I wouldn't have pissed them away, I can tell you.' His regret was trans-parently false. He gave me a sideways look. 'How come you don't know about this? I thought you two used to be friendly.'

'We lost touch.'

'If I were you I'd keep it that way.' He fell silent. I heard him sucking his teeth again. He stopped, embarrassed, when he realized. 'So, tell me more about this attack on Miss Keller.'

I ran through what had happened. Roper listened with his hands folded on his paunch. I was starting to revise my opinion of the man. Terry had always been dismissive of him, treating him as Simms' lapdog. But whatever else Roper might be, I didn't think he was anyone's fool.

'So the locals think it was a burglary, eh?' he said.

'That's what they say.'

'They're probably right. Single woman, living on her own in the sticks. Asking for trouble, really. And you say she's a potter now?' He smirked, shaking his head. 'Well, well.'

We didn't have much to say to each other after that, but we were almost at Black Tor. Several cars and a dog van were already waiting by the end of the track when we arrived, close to where I'd parked the day before. A mix of uniformed police and CID stood by them, coat collars turned up against the rain. None of them looked happy and several of them were drawing on cigarettes as if their lives depended on them.

But they were hastily thrown down and trodden on as Simms got out of his car, shrugging on a thick coat. One of the plain-clothes officers stepped forward to speak to him.

'That's Naysmith, the SIO,' Roper muttered as we went over.

Naysmith was a keen-looking man in his early forties, gaunt and raw-boned. He glanced in my direction but Simms made no attempt to introduce us. I wasn't close enough to hear what was said, but Naysmith gave a terse nod before moving away. The group was all business now as it prepared to go out on to the moor. The air was split by barking as a dog-handler took a German shepherd from a van and clipped a coiled length of rope to its harness.

I hoped it had better luck than the last one.

Roper had gone to talk to a small group of plain-clothes officers, so I stood on my own nearby, feeling like I didn't belong as rain dripped from my coat hood.

'Been a while, Dr Hunter.'

I looked around at the burly man who'd approached. He wore a reflective waterproof coat, and I had to peer at the face inside the hood before I recognized Jim Lucas, the POLSA from the original search. He'd never been slim, and the intervening years had given him the ruddy nose and cheeks that spoke of either outdoor work or high blood pressure.

But his handshake was as firm as ever, and his eyes crinkled with the same warmth I remembered.

'I didn't realize you were advising on this,' I said, pleased to see a friendly face.

'For my sins. Have to admit, I'd have been happy not to set eyes on this godforsaken spot again.' His eyes roved round the moor. 'Bad business about Wainwright.'

I nodded. There was nothing to say.

'The sooner we get Monk back behind bars the better. I hear you and Sophie Keller had a run-in with him yesterday.'

The memory was already starting to seem unreal. 'I think so. We didn't get a close look at him.'

'If you had you wouldn't be here. Either of you.' He let that sink in for a second, then smiled. 'How is Sophie these days?'

'She's fine.' This wasn't the time to go into details.

'Jacked it in to make pots, didn't she? Good for her. I retire myself next year.' He scowled at the foul weather. 'Can't say I'll be sorry. I'm getting too old for this game. And the job's changed since I started. All paperwork and bureaucracy now. Speaking of which . . .'

He looked behind me as Simms' clipped voice rang out.

'When you're ready, Dr Hunter.'

The ACC had put on a pair of brand new wellingtons. The shin-high rubber boots looked ridiculous with his tailored overcoat and uniform, but not everyone there was so lucky. I saw Roper looking disconsolately at his thin-soled shoes as we set off along the muddy track. The dog-handler, a swarthy man with a shaved head, walked slightly ahead of the rest of us, feeding out the rope attached to the harness as the German shepherd snuffled the ground.

'Will the rain make any difference?' I asked him.

He answered without taking his eyes from the dog. 'Not unless it really pisses it down. It's the peat that'll be a problem. Soaks up water like a sponge, and if it gets too boggy it doesn't hold the scent.'

'It's pretty boggy where we're going.'

He gave me a look as though I'd questioned his dog's ability. 'If there's a scent to be found, he'll pick it up.'

The rest of us waited as the handler and his dog searched the area where Monk had stood watching while Sophie and I drove away. Or at least as near to it as I could recall: they found nothing, and eventually Naysmith called them back. Perhaps it was my imagination, but I thought a few cool glances were sent my way after that. As we continued along the track I found myself wondering if perhaps we really had overreacted the day before.

God, please don't let me be wasting everyone's time.

The rain darkened the squat tower of Black Tor in the distance, making the boulders live up to their name. We cut off the track at about the same point that Sophie and I had the day before and began trekking across the moor. Lucas had a compass and map, but either his sense of direction wasn't the equal of Sophie's or the whole area had become more waterlogged overnight, because it seemed a lot harder going this time. I stared ahead anxiously, searching for any sign of the holes. But the moorland seemed untouched, a sea of drab greens and browns that I began to feel was mocking me.

Then, just as had happened the day before, the heather and grass around us was suddenly pockmarked with muddy craters.

I felt irrationally relieved: I'd almost begun to think we wouldn't find them. Everyone stopped. The only sound was the drip and patter of rain on our coats, then one of the policemen broke the silence.

'Bloody big moles they've got round here.'

Nobody laughed. Naysmith motioned the dog-handler forward. The German shepherd strained on its line, nose pressed to the ground. Almost straight away it began following something.

'He's got a scent,' the dog-handler called, but even as he did the dog changed direction and began zigzagging aimlessly between the holes. 'It's all over.'

'I can see someone's been here. I want to know where he went,' Simms snapped.

The handler gave Naysmith an uneasy glance. The SIO nodded. 'Try to find a trail leading away.'

As the dog-handler moved off, Simms went to the nearest hole. 'Dr Hunter, can you say if anything was buried in any of these?'

The holes were all too small to have held a human body, but other than that I couldn't say. 'No. I doubt it, but you should have a cadaver dog check them anyway.'

'Well, looks like the other graves must be somewhere nearby.' Naysmith was squatting by one of the holes. 'Wouldn't be much point him digging like a dog for a bone otherwise.'

'We searched this entire area last time without finding anything,' Roper said. 'He could have hidden a stash of cash or something. Makes more sense than wanting to dig up bodies that have been safely buried for eight years.'

He had a point, but Simms was having none of it. 'Monk wouldn't have buried money. That'd involve planning ahead, and he doesn't think like that. No, this was about finding the Bennett girls. Dr Hunter, where was Monk when you first saw him?'

I scanned the moor. Without the ground mist everything looked different, and there were no convenient landmarks to help me pinpoint where I'd first seen the figure. This was Sophie's speciality, not mine, but in his wisdom Simms had made her stay behind.

Still, I felt reasonably confident as I pointed. 'Over there. About a hundred yards away.'

Rain dripped from the rim of his hat as Simms looked dubiously at the unremarkable patch of moor. There wasn't much to see, no tor or hummocks large enough to have concealed anyone as big as Monk.

'He can't have appeared from nowhere. Where did he come from?'

'He was just standing there when we saw him. That's all I can tell you.'

Simms' gloved fingers drummed against his leg, like a restless cat twitching its tail. 'Bring the dog,' he said, and started walking.

The moor became boggier as we headed further out: patches of viscous black mud pooled with oily water. Several times we had to detour where it was too thick to cross, Roper muttering under his breath as he slithered about in his city shoes. Twice the dog seemed to catch an elusive trace of scent, but both times its handler shook his head after it lost it again.

It was only as we neared the spot where I'd seen Monk that I realized we were retracing our steps from years before. This was where he'd claimed the other graves were, before Sophie's discovery of the badger sett had diverted us. I considered mentioning it, but Simms was sceptical enough already. *Don't push your luck.*

I stopped and looked around, trying to gauge how far we'd come.

'Well?' Simms prompted.

'Around here somewhere, but it's hard to say where exactly.' I was uncomfortably aware that everyone was watching me. 'Over there, I think.'

The patch of moor looked no different from any other. Just grass and heather, shivering slightly from the beating of the rain. There was no sign that anyone had ever been here.

'You said he came after you. Which way did he go?' Simms asked.

I tried to visualize it, but it wasn't easy from this new perspective. 'To start with he followed us towards the track, but then he headed across the moor for the road to cut us off.'

Naysmith motioned to the dog-handler. 'See if you can find anything.'

The handler began casting round with his dog in an attempt to pick up Monk's trail. But they floundered straight away, the German shepherd's paws sinking into black mud. The dog thrashed and whined as its handler hauled it out, only for it to become stuck again moments later.

'It's too wet,' he called, heaving it back on to firmer ground. 'It's like a quagmire round here.'

'Keep trying,' Simms told him.

The handler's face made it clear what he thought of that. The dog's paws plunged deep into the soft mud, bogging it down. It had to be pulled free several more times, until both dog and handler were filthy and out of breath. Finally, it seemed to catch a scent on a stretch of firmer ground. Its ears pricked up in interest as it began to follow it, only to suddenly whine and back away.

'Now what?' Simms demanded as the dog sneezed and pawed its nose.

'Ammonia,' the handler said, sniffing with distaste. The pungent chemical smell was bad enough for humans; to a dog's sensitive nose it would be actively painful. He patted the German shepherd, giving Simms a reproachful look. 'The rain's washed some of it away but someone was expecting us. We're done here.'

Simms seemed about to insist but Naysmith intervened. 'It's going to be dark soon. We can bring more dogs out tomorrow, organize a proper search. There's not much more we can do tonight.'

He stared levelly back as the ACC glared at him. Simms' hand tapped impatiently at his side before he gave a grudging nod.

'All right. But first thing tomorrow—'

'*Over here.*'

The shout came from Lucas. While the dog had been struggling through the mud, the search advisor had wandered off by himself. He stood on a low hummock, looking down at something on its far side. Simms' wellingtons slapped against his legs as he went over, leaving the rest of us to follow.

The ground dropped away behind the hummock, so that it was lower than it first appeared. The concealed side was camouflaged with scrubby gorse, except for where rocks broke through the vegetation on the slope like the scalp of a bald man.

Caught in the angle where several rocks leaned against each other was a sheer black hole less than a metre across.

'Christ, is that a cave?' Naysmith asked.

Lucas was studying his map. 'There aren't any caves on this part of the moor. They're all in the limestone further out, like the ones at Buckfastleigh. It's all granite round here.' He folded up the map. 'No, it's an adit.'

'A what?' Simms demanded.

'An old mine entrance. This used to be tin-mining country until about a hundred years ago. Small-scale stuff, mainly. Most of the tunnels were filled in or sealed off, but not all of them. Some are still there.'

I thought about the grassed-over waterwheel and mine workings near the turn-off for Black Tor. It was just another part of the moor's landscape. I'd driven past it any number of times without really noticing it.

Or given a thought to what might lie below the surface.

Naysmith bent over the opening. 'Looks deep. Anyone got a torch?' There were mutterings and exchanged glances. 'Oh, for Christ's sake, *somebody* must have brought one!'

'I've got this.' A CID officer sheepishly offered a small penlight.

Naysmith shook his head in disgust as he took it. He shone it into the opening and peered inside. His voice sounded hollow.

'Can't see much. Goes back a long way.'

'Get the dog over here,' Simms said.

The handler was tight-lipped as he brought the German shepherd forward. Its coat was black with mud and steam curled from its lolling tongue, but it had recovered from the ammonia. When it neared the opening its ears abruptly snapped up. It snuffled intently at the rocks, then lurched towards the open hole. Its paws scrabbled as the handler hauled it back.

'OK, good boy.' He fussed and patted it as he looked up at Simms. 'No two ways about it. Either he came out of here or he went down. Or both.'

There was a silence as that sank in. It was Roper who spoke first.

'Well, now we know why Monk wanted to come out here eight years ago. And why he's so hard to find.' The DI's prominent teeth were bared in a grin that was almost a snarl. 'The bastard's gone to ground.'

20

The lights were on in Sophie's house when I pulled up in the lane. I switched off the car engine and sat in the darkness, enjoying the few moments of peace. The rain had all but stopped while I'd been driving, but puddles still gathered on the roads, sluicing up a steady spray from the tyres.

I put my head back against the seat rest, taking a moment to savour the quiet before I went inside. I'd had no choice but to come back. For one thing my bag was still here: after hearing about the murder I hadn't taken it when we'd rushed off to Sharkham Point. But I wanted to check on Sophie anyway: I hadn't had a chance to speak to her since we'd split up at Wainwright's.

A lot had happened since then.

Lucas had told me more about the mines as we'd

walked back to the cars. Naysmith had stationed two police officers at the adit in case Monk resurfaced there, although that wasn't likely. The remains of old tin mines could be found across Dartmoor. Not all the tunnels had survived, and those that had weren't always safe even for cavers to go down. The more accessible entrances were sealed behind locked gates and steel bars, but adits like the one we'd found still existed on the moor, overgrown and all but invisible unless you knew what to look for.

Monk obviously did.

'We knew about the mines, but they weren't considered a serious option,' Lucas told me. 'Monk was a loner who spent a lot of time on the moor, but as far as we knew he didn't have any caving experience. And believe me those mines are scary places. You don't want to go down them unless you know what you're doing.'

'So they weren't checked at all?'

'Only enough to rule them out. The bigger ones were searched after the girls went missing, in case Monk had dumped the bodies in them. But we didn't go very far down, and after that we just had dogs sniff around the main entrances. We didn't find anything, so that was that.' The search advisor puffed out his cheeks. 'If Monk's been using them Christ knows where he is. Some of those mines are a couple of hundred years old, and I'd bet not all the old adits will be shown on maps. Monk could go down one hole and surface God knows where.'

That was an unsettling thought. 'Are there any mines near Padbury?'

'Padbury?'

'That's where Sophie lives.'

'Let's take a look, shall we?' Lucas unfolded his map, stubby finger tracing a path as he consulted it. 'Nothing nearby. The closest would be Cutter's Wheal Mine, about three miles away, but that's sealed off.'

I was glad of that much, at least. Locking the car, I pushed open the creaking gate and walked up the path to the house. After the rain the air was earthy and fresh, scented with wet grass. The light from the windows made the nearby kiln seem darker by comparison. I paused outside the front door, took a deep breath and then knocked.

Nothing happened for a while, but just when I was about to try again I heard the bolts being shot inside. The door opened on its newly fitted chain and Sophie looked out at me from the gap. She didn't say anything. The door closed in my face, then there was a rattle as the chain was unfastened and it was opened again.

Without a word, she went back down the hallway. I heard the sound of vegetables being chopped as I closed and bolted the door. *Doesn't look good.*

I pulled off my muddy boots and hung up my coat, then followed her into the kitchen.

She had her back to me, thick hair screening her face. The knife thumped on to the chopping board.

'Roper said someone would bring you home,' I said.

Sophie answered without turning round. 'They did. About two hours ago.'

'How did it go? Your statement.'

'As you'd expect.'

The line of her back was stiff and uncompromising. She scraped the sliced carrots into a pan and began cutting potatoes.

I took a deep breath. 'Look, I'm sorry. I told Simms about your letters to Monk. I didn't have any choice.'

'I know.'

She said it indifferently; I'd been steeling myself for more than that. 'I wasn't sure how you'd feel.'

'I told them myself. I'm not a complete idiot, I know I couldn't keep it a secret. I even printed them copies from the computer.'

'So you're OK about it?'

'Why shouldn't I be? It isn't against the law to write to someone. Even Monk.'

She didn't turn to look at me. The knife sliced up and down, a staccato rapping on the board.

'So what's wrong?'

'What's *wrong*?' She slammed down the knife.

'They took me away like a – a *criminal*! No one would tell me anything! I didn't even know you'd gone until some hatchet-faced policewoman said she was bringing me home. I felt *useless*!'

'I'm sorry.'

She sighed and shook her head. 'Oh, I know it isn't your fault. First there was the shock of Wainwright being murdered, and then ... then I had the door closed in my face. It's the first time it's really been brought home to me that I'm not a BIA any more, I'm just a civilian. I *hated* being left out! But I shouldn't take it out on you.'

'Don't worry about it. It's been a rough day for everyone.'

'That's no excuse.' She put her hand on my arm, and suddenly there was a tension between us. It broke when Sophie lowered her hand, turning quickly back to the worktop. 'So what happened after I'd gone?'

I told her about Wainwright, and the adit we'd found. 'The police are sending down a cave team, but Lucas doesn't think Monk will still be there. Once we'd seen him yesterday he'd have realized we'd find the mine.' *That one, at least.* From what Lucas said there were plenty of others.

'So that was why he said he'd take us to the graves. He just wanted to get close to the mine so he could escape.' She sounded bitter. 'God, I really made a fool of myself, didn't I?'

'You weren't to know. And there's something else.'
I told her about Terry.

'He's *suspended*?' Sophie looked stunned. 'I'd no idea.'

'There's no reason you should have. By the sound of things he's in denial himself. He's got a drinking problem and his career's on the skids. Simms wants us to let Roper know if we hear from him again, but after what happened to Wainwright I don't think he'd dare.'

'You don't think . . .'

'What?'

'Nothing. It doesn't matter.'

But I guessed what she'd been about to say. 'You're wondering if Terry had anything to do with Wainwright?'

'I know it's stupid, but with everything else he's done . . .' She looked scared.

'I can't see it. Terry might have gone off the rails, but there'd be no reason for him to do something like that. Simms might not want to admit it, but I don't think there's any doubt it was Monk.'

Are you sure? I couldn't pretend to know what Terry was capable of any more. But the brutal nature of Wainwright's death, even down to the sputum left contemptuously on the floor, had all the convict's hallmarks.

Which brought me to another problem.

I took a deep breath. 'I think you should reconsider staying somewhere else until this has blown over.'

Sophie's mouth set stubbornly. 'We've already been through this.'

'That was before Wainwright was killed.'

'We don't know for sure that was Monk, and even if it was, why would he want to hurt me? I didn't do anything to him.'

You didn't have to. You're an attractive woman. For a behavioural specialist, she could be obtuse when it suited her.

'All Wainwright did was insult him eight years ago, but he's still dead,' I said, trying hard not to lose my patience. 'We don't know what's driving Monk. Perhaps Terry's right and he's going after anyone from the original search team. But even if he's not you still brought yourself to his attention by writing to him. It isn't worth the risk.'

She was still scared, I could see that. But her chin had come up in the now familiar gesture of defiance.

'It's my decision.'

'Sophie—'

'I told the police the same thing this afternoon. I can look after myself. No one's asking you to stay.'

God, but she could be infuriating. I was almost tempted. My bag was packed, and I was under no illusions as to my chances if Monk did turn up. But I knew I wasn't going to leave her there alone. Not because she was attractive, or even because I was very aware of the spark between us. No, my reason was simpler than that.

We have to be able to live with ourselves.

I sighed. 'I'm not going anywhere.'

She gave me a tired smile. 'Thank you.'

'Just promise me you'll at least think about it.'

'I promise,' she said, and I was forced to settle for that.

Dinner was a vegetable curry, thrown together from what little was left in Sophie's pantry and fridge. The meal was a subdued affair. I was acutely conscious of how isolated we were out there, and despite her bravado I think Sophie was too. The past few days had taken their toll. She insisted the headache she'd mentioned was just tension, but she looked exhausted. When I told her I'd clear up while she went to bed she didn't put up much of a fight.

'If you're sure . . . Help yourself to whatever you like. There's brandy and whisky in the sitting room.'

I was tired myself, but I knew if I went to bed I'd only lie awake, listening to every creak and bump in the old house. After Sophie had gone upstairs I washed and dried the dishes, then went to hunt down a drink. The whisky was a generic blend, but the brandy turned out to be a fifteen-year-old Armagnac that had hardly been touched.

I poured myself a healthy measure, threw another log into the stove and sank back on to the sofa. I considered turning on the TV for the news, but I doubted there'd be anything about the investigation I didn't already know.

Instead I just sat in the quiet, staring at the flames and listening to their muted crackle. Even without her, Sophie's presence filled the room. Her ceramics stood on the low table, with a couple of larger vases on the floor, and the stripped-pine furniture and rugs had the same unfussy style as she had herself. I could smell a faint trace of her scent on the cushions. I sipped the Armagnac, puzzling again over her stubbornness . . .

The ringing of the phone woke me. I bolted upright, hastily setting the glass aside. The extension was on a chest of drawers. I snatched it up before it could ring again, glancing at my watch. Half past two.

No one called at that time for anything good.

'Hello?' There was no answer. *Please yourself*, I thought irritably, about to hang up. Then I heard a sound down the line. Adenoidal and laboured, the wheeze of someone breathing.

Suddenly I knew it was Monk on the other end.

The hairs on my forearms prickled as they stood up. I found my voice.

'What do you want?'

Nothing. The breathing continued. The moment stretched on, then there was a soft *click* as the connection was broken.

I realized I'd been holding my own breath. I lowered the handset. The house was silent: I'd answered the phone before it could wake Sophie. I hurried into the kitchen, searching through drawers for a pen and paper before playing back the caller's number and scribbling it down.

From the code it looked like a local landline. I stared at the piece of paper, slowly sliding down from the rush of adrenalin. Dazed, I called Roper and left a message on his voicemail. I'd no proof it was Monk, and an anonymous phone call was hardly going to impress him.

But I knew.

I made sure the front door was still locked and bolted, then went from room to room to check the windows. They seemed old and flimsy. The wooden frames wouldn't keep anyone out, but at least I'd hear if they broke in. I went back into the sitting room and stoked the embers in the stove before adding more kindling and another log. As the flames crawled over it, I closed the stove door and laid the poker within easy reach.

Then I settled down to wait for morning.

21

Even though I'd left a message for Roper, he wouldn't have been my first choice of police officer to call. But I didn't have Naysmith's mobile number, and I doubted the SIO would be at his desk in the middle of the night.

I waited until a reasonable hour before trying him, only to be put through to yet another answering service. I briefly explained what had happened and gave Sophie's number rather than trust the poor mobile reception.

Having done all I could, I set about trying to wake myself up. Despite my best intentions, I'd fallen asleep on the sofa as the chorus of birdsong had begun to sound outside. The hour's uneasy rest had left me feeling groggy and put a crick in my neck. Leaving Sophie to sleep, I stood under a hot shower until I began to feel a little more human.

She was in the kitchen, wrapped in a thick towelling bathrobe, when I went downstairs. 'Morning. We're down to cereal today. I really have to go shopping later.'

'Cereal's fine.'

She rubbed her eyes. 'God, I feel wrecked. I bet I look it, too.'

I'd been thinking just the opposite. Even with her sleep-tousled hair and loosely tied bathrobe there was a natural poise to her. She caught me looking.

'What?' she asked, smiling.

The harsh ring of the phone brought me round like ice-water. *Damn.* I'd been hoping to tell Sophie about the anonymous call before Roper or Naysmith phoned.

'That might be for me,' I said quickly, but she'd already answered it.

'Yes . . . Oh.' She made a moue of distaste and mouthed *Roper*. 'Yes, he is. Just a second.'

She gave me a questioning look as she passed me the handset. I was uncomfortably aware of her standing there as I told Roper about the phone call.

'What makes you think it was Monk?' he asked.

'The fact he didn't speak, for one thing. People normally apologize if they call the wrong number, and . . .' I stopped, glancing at Sophie.

'And?' Roper prompted.

Oh, hell. I could feel Sophie's eyes boring into me. 'It was only an impression, but I thought he was . . . surprised. As though I wasn't who he'd expected.'

'All this from a silent phone call?' I could hear his scepticism. But I'd had a lot of time to think it through while I'd been waiting for daylight. 'How do you even know it was a man on the other end?'

'The breathing was too deep to be a woman's. And I could hear him wheezing, as though he were out of breath or asthmatic.'

'Heavy breathing, eh? You sure this wasn't just a dirty phone call?'

My hand had tightened on the receiver. 'Monk was having a suspected heart attack when he escaped. Perhaps he wasn't faking being ill.'

I couldn't believe even Monk could have escaped if the attack had been genuine, but something must have convinced the prison doctors. An odd noise came down the line as Roper considered: he was tapping his teeth with a pen.

'Can't hurt to check the number, I suppose,' he said. 'Tell you what, I'll call round and take your statement myself.'

'Don't go to any trouble,' I said, my stomach sinking.

Roper gave his nasal chuckle. 'Oh, it's no trouble, Dr Hunter. I'm in the area. And the ACC wants me to keep an eye on you and Miss Keller.'

Which could be taken two ways, I thought as I hung up. Sophie was glaring at me, hands balled on her hips.

'Monk rang *here*? And you didn't *say* anything?'

'It was the middle of the night. I didn't want to disturb you.'

'Don't you think I might have liked to *know* about it?'

I was on a short fuse myself. 'Fine! If he rings again I'll ask him to wait while I come and get you!'

'You know what I mean! This is my house, I don't need protecting!'

'I wasn't—' But I stopped myself: there was no point in arguing. 'Look, I'm sorry. I was about to tell you when Roper called. And I'm only guessing that it was Monk.'

'God.' She pushed her hands through her hair, troubled. 'Could it have been Terry Connors?'

'I don't think so. If it was Terry why didn't he say something?'

'Why does he do anything?' she said dully, rubbing her temple. She made an attempt to smile. 'Terry Connors or Jerome Monk. Talk about spoiled for choice.'

'There's more good news. Roper's calling round later.'

Sophie stared at me, then burst out laughing. 'Right, just for that you get to make breakfast.'

It was late morning by the time Roper arrived. We were in the kiln, Sophie having decided she needed to work. 'I haven't done anything for days. I'm supposed to have an order for a restaurant finished by the end of the month.'

I watched as Sophie started the potter's wheel. She wore a pair of men's work overalls, faded and streaked with clay. Her hands were strong and dexterous as she worked on the wheel, manipulating the clay so easily it seemed to form shapes of its own volition.

'Do you want to try it?' she asked.

'No thanks.'

'Coward.'

She trimmed the loose edges from the rim of the plate she'd just thrown and slapped them on to the big clay ball on the workbench.

'What's that?' I asked.

'This?' She gave an embarrassed laugh, smoothing in the lump of clay she'd just added with her thumb. 'Nothing. Just a bad habit. I used to throw all the waste into a bin, but then I got lazy. And it sort of grew. I quite like it, though. It isn't trying to be anything, and it's always changing. Plus it's therapeutic.'

She gave it a hard slap, then wiped her hands on a cloth she'd hung from the end of a scaffolding pole.

'Now, I need to get on.'

I took the hint and left her to it, going back out

into the garden. A thin haze of mist and drizzle hung in the air. I cut across the wet grass to the small orchard. The trees were gnarled and ancient, probably as old as the house itself. One or two wizened fruit still hung like forgotten Christmas ornaments from the bare branches, unpicked and forlorn. The grass underneath was dappled with windfall apples, sweetening the air with the cider scent of their rot.

The distant drone of a car engine broke the stillness. I waited for it to appear as it slowly grew louder, the sound deceptive in the mist. A flash of grey appeared through the hedgerows higher up the lane, and then the car was pulling up at the bottom of the garden.

Roper climbed out, squeezing out from behind the seat with a grunt. 'Thought I was never going to get here,' he grumbled, pushing open the gate. 'Not an easy place to find, is it?'

'I thought you were in the area?'

He bared his teeth in a grin, but his eyes were taking in the house and surroundings. 'Relatively speaking, Dr Hunter. Where's Miss Keller? Or should I say Trask these days?'

I ignored the jibe. 'In the kiln.'

He looked doubtfully at the rusting scaffold protruding from the old brickwork. 'Is it safe?'

'So long as you don't sneeze.'

We started towards the entrance, but Sophie came out before we reached it, wiping her hands on the cloth.

'Afternoon, Miss Keller,' Roper said, looking beyond her into the kiln. 'Interesting workplace you've got here.'

She pulled the ill-fitting door shut behind her, cutting off his view. 'I'm busy at the moment. Is it just David you need to talk to?'

'Actually, it was both of you.' Roper's grin flickered out. 'There's been a bit of a development.'

The visit wasn't just about the phone call, I realized. 'What's happened?'

The DI looked uncomfortable. 'Wainwright's wife gave us a description of the man who killed her husband. It was Monk.'

'I'm not going!'

Sophie stood in the kitchen, arms folded in front of her like a barred gate. She was still wearing her work overalls, three empty mugs next to her waiting for water from the cooling kettle. I didn't think they were going to be filled any time soon, but right now that was the least of anyone's problems.

Roper wore the dogged expression of a man at the end of his tether. 'It'll only be for a few days. You can come back as soon as Monk's in custody.'

'Last time it took you three months to catch him,'

Sophie retorted. 'If you think I'm going to put my life on hold until then you can forget it.'

Roper looked as if he could have cheerfully strangled her himself. For once I couldn't altogether blame him. Jean Wainwright had recovered from shock enough to relate what had happened. She'd been woken in the middle of the night by a commotion inside the house. She and her husband slept in separate rooms, the sort of personal detail I imagined she would hate to reveal. Thinking he was wandering – something that many dementia sufferers were prone to do – she'd thrown on a dressing gown and hurried on to the landing. She'd turned on the light to find Wainwright lying at the foot of the stairs, in the wreckage of the china cabinet.

Standing over him was Monk.

She'd passed out, and had still been only semiconscious when the cleaner arrived. Preliminary forensic tests had confirmed her story. Monk's fingerprints were all over the house, and DNA from the sputum found on the floor had also matched the convict's. It was hard to see that as anything other than a clear statement of contempt. Monk had made no attempt to cover his tracks.

He'd gone beyond that.

None of which would have involved Sophie, except for the anonymous phone call to her house. It had been made from a lonely public phone box on the outskirts of Princetown, a small town surrounded by high, open moors. It was also the site of Dartmoor prison, where Monk had spent the early years of his sentence. That could have been a coincidence, but there was a more compelling reason why the location might have appealed to him.

There was an old tin mine nearby.

The cave team who had gone down had reported that, like the larger mine at Black Tor, it was flooded and impassable after the recent rains. Even so, it still had to be checked out.

'Wouldn't surprise me if the bugger made the call from there deliberately, knowing we'd waste time. He conned us into taking him out on the moor looking for graves, so he's not as stupid as he looks,' Roper said. 'There's only so many mines he can go down, though, and now we know what he's up to he's on a hiding to nothing. It's only a matter of time before he's caught. The question is what sort of damage he can do before then.'

Which was the real reason for his visit. After what had happened to Wainwright, Monk's attempt to contact Sophie was being taken seriously. So seriously that Simms had arranged for her to stay at a police safe house. Or perhaps 'instructed' was more accurate.

The conversation had gone downhill from there.

'We don't suggest this sort of thing for fun,' Roper persisted. 'It's for your own good.'

'I'll decide what's for my own good, thanks. I'm not going to some grubby safe house because of some . . . some stupid phone call you don't even know for sure was *from* Monk. This is my *home*!'

'That didn't stop someone from waltzing in and knocking you unconscious a few days ago.' Roper raised his eyebrows in mock enquiry. 'Don't suppose you've remembered anything about that yet, have you?'

Sophie's hand made an involuntary movement towards the bruise on her face. She lowered it. 'Don't you think I'd have told you if I had? Anyway, that was nothing to do with Monk. The police said it was just a burglary.'

'Yes, so I gather. Except I don't think you've reported anything stolen, have you?'

Sophie opened her mouth, then closed it. 'There was some cash I'd left lying around and a few pieces of cheap jewellery. It didn't seem worth bothering with.'

That was news to me: she hadn't said anything was missing. Roper regarded her for a moment.

'Look, love—'

'I'm not your "love". And I'm not leaving. You can't expect me to just drop everything, I've got a business to run!'

'You should have thought about that before you chose a murderer as a pen pal,' Roper snapped. 'To someone like Monk that's as good as an invitation.'

Sophie folded her arms. 'I'm not going.'

Roper sighed, looking at me as though to say, *Well?* 'He's right,' I told her. 'It doesn't have to be a safe house. Like I said, we could go to a hotel for a few days. Or you could stay at your sister's—'

That was a mistake. 'Oh, no! No way.'

'It would only be for—'

'No. I'd rather face Monk.' She turned to Roper. 'Sorry you've had a wasted trip. Now if you don't mind I've got work to do.'

She banged out. Roper stared after her. 'Well, that's that.'

'Isn't there something else you can do?' I asked.

He pulled at his lip unhappily. 'I suppose I can see about having a panic button installed. Not that it'll do much good, the time it'll take a response team to arrive.'

'Can't you arrange for police protection here?'

'We're not a private security service. She's been offered a safe house, but if she wants to stick her head in the sand that's up to her.' He got to his feet, shaking his head. 'The ACC isn't going to like this.'

'He's going to like it even less if Monk hurts anyone else.'

Roper gave me a sharp look. 'I'm sure he'll take that under consideration, Dr Hunter.'

I saw him out, watching as he drove away, then I

fetched my coat and went across to the kiln. I could hear the whirr of the potter's wheel before I opened the door. Sophie sat behind it, intently shaping a bowl from a piece of wet clay.

'I'm not going to change my mind,' she said, without looking up.

'I know. I just wanted to see if you were all right.'

'I'm fine.' The bowl on the wheel was uneven, but she didn't seem to notice.

'You didn't say anything before about money and jewellery being missing.'

'There was nothing valuable. It wasn't worth mentioning.'

I waited. She kept her attention on the wheel. 'If there's anything you need to tell me . . .'

'I just need to be alone for a while, OK?'

The bowl had begun to wobble and lose its shape. It was beyond salvaging, but Sophie carried on as though it might somehow correct itself. Not knowing what else to say, I went out. The damp and misty air caught my throat as I headed back to the house.

I couldn't understand why Sophie was being so stubborn. But then I didn't really know her. *So why are you staying? Just for her?* That was part of it, although there was another reason as well, one that had been nudging at me ever since I'd heard about Monk's escape. And perhaps even longer: it had been lying dormant but this went back eight years, to the abortive search on the moor.

I wanted answers.

I'd just reached the house when my phone beeped with an incoming message. The signal was unreliable around here, subject to the vagaries of weather and geology, but something had obviously got through. I took it out and saw I'd got a text. It was short and to the point.

Trencherman's Arms, 2pm.

It was from Terry.

22

The mist thinned as I neared the higher ground at Oldwich, but as though to compensate the drizzle gave way to rain. It was the sort of monotonous downpour that seemed as though it could go on for ever, making the moor look lifeless beneath the incessant grey sky.

The Trencherman's car park was empty except for one other car. I didn't know if it was Terry's or not, but the grubby paintwork and litter-strewn interior made me doubt it. Although the yellow Mitsubishi must have been long gone by now, Terry had always been as fastidious about his car's appearance as he was about his own.

But when I went into the pub and saw he was the only customer I realized the car must be his after all. He was sitting at a secluded corner table. His clothes were crumpled and unwashed, and even from across the room I could see the untidy stubble on his chin. He stared into his half-empty beer glass, an expression on his face I'd not seen before. It was one I didn't associate with Terry.

He looked lost.

Then he noticed me and it vanished. His shoulders straightened as I went over. He sat back, regarding me with something more like his old arrogance.

'I wasn't sure you'd come.'

I almost hadn't. The sensible thing would have been to tell Roper, or to ignore the message altogether. I'd considered both, but whatever mess Terry had got himself into was a disciplinary matter rather than a criminal one, and running to Simms went against the grain.

Besides, I wanted to hear what he had to say.

I pulled up a chair and sat opposite him. A sour smell of sweat and unmetabolized alcohol came across the table. 'What did you want to see me about?'

'Aren't you having a drink?'

'I won't be staying long.'

I'd told Sophie I was going to buy food. That was no lie: I'd stopped off at a local shop on my way here to stock up on groceries. I didn't like leaving her alone at the house, but after Roper's visit we both needed some time to ourselves. Still, I didn't plan on being away any longer than I had to.

'I think we've had this conversation before.' Terry took a drink himself. 'You tell anyone where you were going?'

'No.'

'How about Sophie?' His grin was vicious. 'Don't tell me you've not got your feet under that table. Sympathetic shoulder and all that. Or are you still pretending to be just good friends?'

'Why don't you tell me what you want, Terry?'

'More than friends, eh? That didn't take long.' I stood up to go. He held up his hands. 'All right, all right. Christ, I'm only joking.'

I sat down again. 'Either you tell me what's going on or I'm leaving.'

'OK.' He drained the rest of his beer and set his glass down. 'I heard about Wainwright. Monk doesn't mess about, does he?'

'How did you know?' There had been no mention of Monk being a suspect on the lunchtime news, so I guessed Simms was still stalling for time.

'Same way I know about him hiding down the mines. I've still got a few friends left on the force.' Terry sounded bitter. 'I expect you've spoken to Simms.'

'He told me you'd been suspended.'

'Did he say why?'

'No, but Roper did.'

That provoked a sour smile. 'Yeah, I bet. Two-faced little bastard.'

'He said you'd assaulted a policewoman.'

'I didn't *assault* her, it was only a bit of fun. All right, I might have had a few beers, but she didn't mind. Not until people started telling her that I'd abused her rights. Her *rights*. Christ.'

But I wasn't interested in Terry's excuses. 'You let me think you were part of the investigation. Sophie too, even after she'd been attacked. Why?'

He reached for his glass before remembering it was empty. He kept hold of it, as though he felt more comfortable with it in his hand. 'It's hard to explain.'

'Try.'

He frowned into his glass. 'I've made a mess of everything. My marriage, my family, my career. The works. All the opportunities I used to have . . . it's all gone. The last time I did anything I was proud of was when I tackled Jerome Monk out on the moor. You remember that?'

His mouth quirked into a grin at the memory. It didn't last long.

'When he escaped . . . well, it brought a lot of things back. Suspended or not, I'm still a police officer. I couldn't just sit at home listening to the news reports. And I know how Simms' mind works. He made his name from putting Monk away, and he won't want anything to tarnish that. He's going to have his own agenda.'

'You're saying he doesn't want to see Monk

caught?' I didn't like Simms, but I couldn't believe that even of him.

'No, just that his first priority's going to be covering his own back. Especially now Wainwright's been murdered. That's going to open a whole can of worms, and you can bet he's going to do his best to keep a tight lid on it. He might dress it up as not wanting a media frenzy to interfere with an investigation, or whatever, but that's just PR bollocks.'

It was near enough to what Simms had said to me himself to strike a chord. Terry gave a lopsided grin.

'Had this conversation with him already, have you? Then you know I'm right. Wainwright and Simms were friends, as far as bastards like him can have any. And it's going to look pretty bad if an ACC can't even protect his old cronies. Especially if people start asking why Monk went after Wainwright in the first place.'

'Perhaps he remembers how Wainwright treated him.' *To think society wastes money keeping animals like this alive.* 'You said yourself he might have grudges against anybody involved in the search. Or were you making that up as well?'

'No, but there's got to be more to it than that. Monk's a rapist, and he's been locked up for the last eight years. You seriously think he doesn't have more important things on his mind than offing a senile old archaeologist who hurt his feelings?'

'Then why did he kill him?'

'To get back at Simms.' Terry leaned forward, growing intent. 'Think about it. Simms didn't just put Monk behind bars, he made it a personal *crusade*. Well, now the boot's on the other foot, except Monk knows he'd never get anywhere near him, not with all the protection Simms will have. So he's trying to humiliate him instead, going after easy targets like Wainwright to stir up as much shit as possible before he's caught. He knows he's never going to be released again, not after killing that other inmate earlier this year, so what's he got to lose?'

There was a perverse logic to it, I supposed. I'd wondered myself if Monk could have killed Wainwright because of some warped vendetta. But something didn't quite ring true.

'Why are you telling me this? What can I do about it?'

'For a start you can get Sophie away from her house. I've not been there, but I'd guess it's pretty isolated.' *That's an understatement*, I thought, as he went on. 'Now Monk's killed Wainwright the gloves will be coming off. One way or another this'll be over in the next few days, but more people are going to get hurt before it's done. Take her somewhere safe until Monk's behind bars again. Or dead.'

'I've tried. I don't know if it's because she doesn't

want to leave her home or her work, or if she's just being stubborn.'

'Her work?' Terry looked startled, as though that hadn't occurred to him. 'Yeah, of course. Her bloody pots.'

'Simms sent Roper to persuade her to go to a police safe house, but she wouldn't listen. I asked for police protection at her house, but it doesn't look like it's going to happen.'

He seemed distracted, but then his mouth curled in contempt. 'Simms must be running scared to even offer a safe house. He's a politician, he's worried how things *look*. If he starts putting people under close protection it'll be as good as admitting what Monk's doing. He'd be leaving himself wide open to accusations that he should have done something before Wainwright was killed. As far as Simms is concerned this isn't a manhunt any more, it's damage limitation. All he can do now is spin the murder as a one-off and hope Monk's stopped before he kills anyone else.'

It sounded plausible, but then Terry was good at that. 'Why didn't you tell me any of this to start with? Why all the pretence?'

'What, you think I was going to turn up on your doorstep and admit I'd been knocked back to detective sergeant? It was hard enough coming to see you as it was. But I'd got an idea how this might play out and I wanted to warn you. I thought I owed you that much.' Terry looked down at his empty glass. 'I've made enough mistakes. I didn't want to make another.'

He looked across at me, almost daring me to doubt him. But I'd known him too long to be taken in so easily.

'If you're so concerned about catching Monk, why didn't you tell Naysmith or Roper that we'd seen him on the moor? This could have been over by now.'

'That was a bad call, I admit. I thought you must be exaggerating. I suppose I might have had a bit too much to drink, as well.' He sighed. 'God knows, I've been regretting it ever since.'

I shook my head. 'Nice try, Terry.'

'What do you mean?'

'You're not doing this out of concern for Sophie's welfare. I don't know what you want, but Simms isn't the only one with an agenda, is he?'

He tried to laugh it off. 'Christ, you're a suspicious sod, aren't you? Come on, give me a break. Everybody deserves a second chance. Even me.'

No, they don't. Not unless they've earned it. I didn't say anything, just looked at him. His expression didn't exactly alter, but somehow the angles of his face hardened. He gave a tight smile.

'So that's how it is, eh? I thought you might have

got rid of that chip on your shoulder by now. Looks like I was wrong.'

I wasn't going to waste my time arguing. I'd come here hoping for answers, but I obviously wasn't going to get any. I pushed my chair back and headed for the door, but Terry hadn't finished.

'Give my regards to Sophie!' he called after me. 'And don't fall for that vulnerable routine. She used that on me as well!'

It was cold and raining outside but I barely noticed. Starting the engine, I drove away from the village without giving any thought to where I was going. When I came to a narrow road I took it. A little way along was an overgrown gateway to a field where a few Dartmoor ponies grazed in the rain. I pulled over and stopped.

Sophie and Terry?

They'd never even *liked* each other. On the search operation they'd barely spoken, and when they had it was a struggle for them to be civil.

And why was that, do you think? Because there was nothing between them?

I felt as though the world had subtly shifted. It was no good telling myself that Terry was lying. There had been a sneering triumph in his voice, as though he'd been waiting for his moment. Sophie's past was nothing to do with me. I'd no right to judge her, and even less to feel jealous. But this was different. We were in the middle of a murder investigation, and it wasn't just anybody.

It was Terry Connors.

One of the ponies had come to the gate beside the car, potbellied and muddied. It leaned its head through the bars, staring at me with dark-eyed curiosity. There was a white blaze on its forehead, slightly off-centre. I felt a vague recognition, until I realized it was in roughly the same place as the dent in Monk's skull.

Stop brooding. There are more important things to think about. I switched the engine on and drove away. I hadn't been paying attention to where I was going, and I had to drive until I saw a signpost before I realized where I was. I'd been heading away from Padbury, and had to backtrack through Oldwich to pick up the right road.

I drove past the pub without looking to see if Terry's car was still there.

The mist began to close in again as I left the high moor behind. Soon it had thickened to a blank fog, hazing my vision like cataracts and forcing me to slow down. By the time I reached Sophie's house twilight was gathering, the windows glowing like lighthouses through the gloom.

There was another car parked behind Sophie's in the lane.

Leaving the groceries I'd bought in the car boot, I

hurried up the path and tried the front door. It was locked. I banged on it and waited, straining for any sound from inside. I heard the bolts being shot back, and then the door was opened.

'There's a car in the lane—' I stopped. The chain was on but it was a man's face that stared at me through the gap.

'That'd be mine. Can I help you?' he said.

Before I could answer Sophie's voice came from behind him. 'It's all right, Nick, let him in.'

The man looked past me, scanning the path and garden before closing the door and slipping off the chain. He opened it and stood back, a fit-looking man in his early thirties, wearing jeans and a faded sweatshirt. He didn't take his eyes off the path as I went in. As soon as I was inside he closed and bolted the door again.

Sophie was in the hallway, smiling. A pretty blonde woman stood next to her; short, but with the compact muscularity of a gymnast. There was a poised watchfulness about her, and as the man finished locking up I saw her hand move away from her hip.

There was a gun holstered there.

'David, meet Steph Cross and Nick Miller.' Sophie's smile broadened. 'They're my bodyguards.'

23

If I hadn't been told that Miller and Cross were police I'd never have guessed. Both were specialist firearms officers, trained in close protection work, but there was nothing about their appearance or attitude to suggest it. In their casual clothes they might have been teachers or medics.

Except for the guns, of course.

'What made Roper change his mind?' I asked. We were in the kitchen, sitting round the table while Sophie unpacked the groceries I'd fetched from the car and began preparing dinner.

'Roper?' Miller was crunching a strip of raw pepper.

'DI Roper. He's on the ACC's staff.'

'Bit too high and mighty for us, then,' Miller said. 'Our orders came from Naysmith, but I can't tell you

315

any more than that. We were told to pack our bags for a trip to the country, so here we are. Ours not to reason why, and all that.'

He was the more outgoing of the two, laid back and with a ready grin. His short hair was prematurely grey, although somehow it didn't age him. Cross was a few years younger, probably still in her twenties. Although she was quieter than her partner, there was an air of unruffled competence about her that was reassuring.

At least Naysmith was taking Sophie's safety seriously.

'How long will you be staying?' she asked them, scraping chopped onion into a pan. I hadn't realized how tense she'd been until now. The pair's arrival seemed to have lifted a weight from her, so that she seemed almost drunk with relief.

'Long enough,' Miller said, peering at the bolognese sauce Sophie was preparing. 'Don't worry, we won't get under your feet. Just keep us fed and watered and you won't even know we're here. Although you might want to sauté the onions a bit longer before you add the meat.'

Sophie put down the spoon, mock-indignant. 'Do you want to do this?'

'Naw, cooking's not part of my job description. But I'm a quarter Italian, I know these things. I'd go easy with the salt, as well.'

Sophie appealed to Cross. 'Is he always like this?'

The blonde policewoman gave the impression of smiling even though her mouth didn't actually move. Her cornflower-blue eyes were serene and watchful. 'You learn not to take any notice.'

Miller looked hurt. 'I'm just saying, that's all.'

It was almost possible to forget why the pair were there, which was probably the idea. It was easier to guard someone if they were relaxed rather than jumping at shadows.

And Sophie had certainly relaxed. Her objection to staying in a safe house didn't extend to other types of protection. I was glad about that, but the meeting with Terry still preyed on my mind. I'd called Roper to let him know, and been relieved to go straight to his voicemail. I'd left a short message without going into details. If he wanted to know more he could call me back.

But I still hadn't had a chance to talk to Sophie about it. Miller and Cross must have picked up on the atmosphere, because after a while they made an excuse and left us alone. Sophie was on such a high that even then she didn't notice.

'They're really nice, aren't they? Not at all like the armed police I used to know,' she said, stirring the simmering pasta sauce. The kitchen smelled of tomato and garlic. 'They turned up about an hour or so after you'd left. I don't often get customers stopping by, so I thought they'd got lost at first, or they were trying to sell something. Then they flashed their ID and said Naysmith had sent them. Did you know he was going to?'

'No.'

Sophie broke off to look at me. 'I thought you'd be pleased. Is something wrong?'

'I saw Terry Connors this afternoon.'

She went very still, then turned back to the saucepan. 'What stone did he crawl from under?'

'He said he wanted to explain.'

'Oh?'

'I didn't know there'd been anything between you.'

She had her back to me, her face hidden. The only sound was the spoon rattling against the pan. 'There's no reason why you should.'

'Don't you think you should have mentioned it?'

'It isn't something I like to talk about. It was a mistake. A long time ago.'

I said nothing. Sophie put the spoon down and turned to face me.

'Look, it doesn't have anything to do with what's going on now.'

'Are you sure about that?'

'It's in the past, all right?' she flared. 'It's none of your business anyway. I don't have to tell you everything!'

She was right, she didn't. But she was wrong about

its being none of my business. It had become that when she'd asked for my help. And whatever game Terry was playing affected us both. The sauce popped and bubbled in the pan.

'You need to stir that,' I said, and went upstairs.

My bag was back in my room. I threw the rest of my things into it. The last thing I felt like was a long drive back to London. But Sophie was safe with Miller and Cross there. There was no longer any reason for me to stay, and I'd had enough of feeling used.

I'd finished packing when I heard a noise from the doorway. Sophie was watching me.

'What are you doing?'

I zipped the bag shut. 'It's time I left.'

'Now?' She looked surprised.

'You've got two armed guards. You'll be fine.'

'David . . .' She closed her eyes, fingers rubbing her temple. 'God, I can't believe Terry Connors can still cause trouble after all this time! All right, I know I should have said something, OK? I'm sorry. I was going to, just . . . not yet. It isn't something I'm proud of. I was going through a bad patch and . . . it sort of happened. It didn't go on for long, not much more than a fling, really. He told me he was separated, that he was waiting for his divorce to come through. As soon as I realized he was lying I ended it. And that's it.' She was watching me nervously, her expression sincere.

'Had you been seeing him recently?' I asked.

'No, I swear.' She came over, but stopped just in front of me. 'Stay tonight. If you still feel the same way tomorrow, then I promise I won't try to stop you. But don't leave like this. Please?'

I hesitated, then put down my bag. Sophie hugged me, her body tight against mine. 'I'm not always a very good person,' she said, her voice muffled.

For once I didn't want to believe her.

Dinner was surprisingly relaxed. That was largely down to Miller. He kept up a flowing banter, so that the meal seemed more like a social occasion than guard duty. Cross said little, smiling at her partner's jokes but content to leave the conversational running to him. Sophie had opened a bottle of wine to go with the lasagne she'd cooked – largely ignoring the suggestions from Miller – although only she and I drank any. The police officers declined without making a big deal of it, and I noticed that neither of them ate much either. They were there to do a job, and full stomachs slowed reflexes.

I hoped they wouldn't need them.

Naysmith had phoned earlier to check on us. The SIO was brisk and businesslike when I took the phone from Miller to speak to him.

'Is there any news about Monk?' I asked.

'Not yet.'

'I just wondered if something had happened to make you put Sophie under close protection. DI Roper didn't seem keen on the idea earlier.'

'DI Roper isn't the SIO, I am,' he said. 'We found Monk's fingerprints on the phone box, which confirms he's tried to contact her. As far as I'm concerned that justifies taking whatever measures are necessary.'

'I'm not complaining. I'm just surprised Simms approved it.'

There was a pause. 'As I said, I'm SIO. The ACC is too busy to be bothered with every operational detail.'

In other words the decision had been Naysmith's, not Simms'. Tensions between the SIO and his immediate superior were nothing new on any investigation, but I hoped they wouldn't get in the way.

'You've got two good officers there,' Naysmith went on. 'Their orders are not to take any chances, so whatever they tell you to do, you do it. No arguments, no debates. Clear?'

I said it was.

Monk wasn't mentioned during dinner, but despite Miller's best efforts the convict's presence loomed over the table like an unwanted guest. The police officers had checked the entire house, closing all the curtains so that anyone outside wouldn't be able to see in. And I noticed how they'd subtly engineered the seating so that they flanked Sophie, with Miller closest to the door and Cross between her and the window.

It was only afterwards, when the empty dishes had been stacked in the sink, that the reason for them being there was finally addressed.

Sophie reached for the bottle of wine. I shook my head when she made to refill my glass; she poured what was left into her own and set the bottle down with a thump.

'So how long have you two been doing this?' she asked, taking a drink.

'Too long,' Miller said. Cross just smiled.

'Do you always work together as a team?'

'Not always. Depends on the job.'

'Right.' Sophie was unsteady as she set down her glass. Suddenly she seemed drunk. I hadn't been paying attention, but she must have had more wine than I'd thought. 'So are the two of you . . . you know . . . an item?'

For once Miller seemed lost for words. It was Cross who answered. 'We just work together.'

'Right. Colleagues.' Sophie waved her hand at the guns holstered on their hips. 'Aren't you uncomfortable wearing those?'

Miller had regained his poise, but there was a faint blush on his cheeks. 'You get used to it.'

'Can I take a look?'

'Best not.' He said it lightly enough, although it was obvious that he wasn't happy. Cross was watching Sophie with her usual Zen-like calm, the blue eyes unreadable. But the atmosphere around the table had abruptly changed.

Sophie seemed oblivious. 'Have you ever used them?'

'Well, they like us to know which end the bullets come out of.'

'But have you ever *shot* anyone?'

'Sophie . . .' I began.

'It's a legitimate question.' She stumbled over 'legitimate'. 'If Monk walked in here, now, would you be able to kill him?'

Miller exchanged a quick look with Cross. 'Let's hope it doesn't come to that.'

'Yes, but if he did—'

'Who'd like coffee?' I said.

Miller seized on the opening. 'Sounds good. I'm ready for a caffeine fix.'

Sophie blinked, as though she were struggling to keep up. 'Coffee? Oh . . . right, sorry.'

'I'll get it,' I offered.

'No, it's OK.' She stood up but clutched the table as she suddenly swayed. 'Whoa . . .'

I reached out to support her. 'Are you all right?'

Her face had paled but she tried to smile as she straightened. 'God . . . what was in that wine?'

'Why don't you go to bed?' I said.

'I . . . I think I'd better.'

I went upstairs with her. 'How are you feeling?' I asked when we reached the bedroom.

'Just a bit woozy.' She was still pale but looked better than she had downstairs. 'My own fault. All that wine when I've hardly eaten all day.'

Reaction was probably as much to blame as the wine. She'd been through enough to affect anyone, but I was mindful that she was still recovering from concussion.

'Are you sure you're OK?'

'I'm fine. You go back downstairs.' She smiled tiredly. 'I really am a rotten host.'

I went down to the kitchen. I could hear murmured voices but they fell silent as I approached. Miller was by the window, the curtain swinging as though it had been disturbed. Cross was leaning against the table, the denim of her jeans tight against her muscular legs. They regarded me with professionally bland faces.

'How is she?' Miller asked. I noticed he had his radio in his hand.

'Just tired. Has something happened?'

'Naw, I'm just checking in.' He slipped the radio away. 'That offer of coffee still on?'

I put the kettle on to boil and spooned instant coffee into three mugs.

'Not for me, thanks,' Cross said.

'Steph doesn't do tea or coffee,' Miller told me. 'Caffeine's poison, and don't even mention refined sugar. Two in mine, please.'

It had the sound of an old argument neither of them took seriously. Cross pushed herself off the table as I poured boiling water into two mugs.

'Time to do the rounds.'

I watched her go, then turned to Miller. 'She isn't going outside by herself ?'

'No, just seeing that everything's locked up.'

'I thought you'd already checked?'

'Never hurts to make sure.' He said it lightly, but I realized it was in case Sophie or I had unlocked anything. They weren't leaving anything to chance.

I passed him a mug. 'Can I ask something?'

'Fire away.'

'What happens if Monk does come?'

He blew on the coffee to cool it. 'Then we get to earn our wages.'

'You know how dangerous he is?'

'Don't worry, we've been briefed. And we've heard the stories about him.'

'They aren't stories.'

'We won't underestimate him, if that's what you're worried about. If he tries anything, we stop him. Simple as that.'

I hoped it would be. Miller took a sip of coffee,

pulling a face at the heat. 'If it's Steph that's bothering you, don't let it. She can look after herself.'

'I'm sure she can.'

'But you'd have been happier if it was two men?'

I didn't like to admit it, but he was right. I didn't consider myself a chauvinist but Cross was half the convict's size. 'You haven't met Monk. I have.'

'And he's a rapist and a monster and all the rest. I know.' Miller's usual brashness had gone. 'Steph's a better shot than I am, she's faster and she could take me in a fight any day. When she was in uniform a crackhead decked her partner one night and pulled a knife on her. I've seen the file. He was six two and thirteen stone. She took the knife off him, put him on the floor and cuffed him without any back-up. And that was before she got her third dan in karate.'

There was a half-smile on his face as he spoke, but I don't think he was aware of it. I thought of how he'd blushed when Sophie had asked if he and Cross were an item. Perhaps not, but they were certainly more than colleagues.

At least as far as Miller was concerned.

'We're not here to arrest Monk, our job's to protect Sophie,' he went on. 'At the first sign of trouble we're getting you both the hell out of here. Failing that . . . Well, I don't care how big he is, he's not bullet-proof.'

He gave a cheerful grin that wrinkled the corners of

his eyes. Perhaps because I was looking for it I saw the hardness behind them now.

'Do you want a hand with the dishes?' he asked.

It wasn't much longer before I went to bed myself. I left Miller and Cross sitting at the kitchen table, comfortable in each other's company. The only spare room was the one I was in, but Miller assured me neither of them would be sleeping.

I was glad they were there, but it felt strange going to bed and leaving them downstairs. I paused outside Sophie's room, considering knocking to see if she was all right. But there was no sound from inside, so I guessed she was asleep.

I went into my own room and crossed to the window without turning on the light. The fog made the starless night doubly impenetrable. I tried to make out shapes in it until the cold radiating from the glass made me lower the curtain.

I was tired but I didn't think I'd be able to sleep. There was too much adrenalin racing through my system. I should have felt relaxed with the two armed officers downstairs, but instead I felt restless and pensive. As though I were waiting for something to happen.

If it does it'll all be over before you can do anything about it. Miller was right: no matter how dangerous Monk might be, he wasn't bullet-proof.

Even so, instead of getting undressed I lay on the bed fully clothed. *Christ, what a day.* I stared at the darkened ceiling, thinking about Monk, about Simms and Wainwright. And about Sophie and Terry. As my eyelids grew heavy it seemed there was a connection there I could almost see, a tenuous link that hovered frustratingly out of sight . . .

Someone was shaking me. I woke in a panic to find Miller standing by the bed with a torch in his hand. If he thought it was odd to see me lying there fully dressed he gave no sign.

'Get up, we need to go.'

The last rags of sleep fell away. Blinking against the brightness, I swung my legs off the bed.

'What's happened?'

There was nothing affable about Miller now. His face was grim as he headed back towards the landing.

'Monk's coming.'

24

I hurried after him. The torch beam made the landing and stairs unfamiliar in the darkness.

'What do you mean?'

'He's on his way.' Miller didn't slow. 'Grab your coat but don't turn on any lights. We're leaving in two minutes.'

As he went to the window at the end of the landing the door to Sophie's room opened and Cross emerged. 'She's getting dressed,' she told him. Miller gave a nod, easing back the curtain to peer out of the window as she went downstairs.

I was struggling to take it all in. 'How do you know he's coming?'

He spoke without turning, eyes scanning the fog-thick darkness. 'He called again.'

'I didn't hear the phone.'

'We unplugged the upstairs extension so if he rang we could answer it ourselves.' Miller let the curtain drop. 'We're trying to get a location but it'll take time. So we're getting you both out.'

'Just because he phoned again?'

'No, because he thought Steph was Sophie. He told her he was in Padbury and said he was on his way.'

'Why would he warn her?'

'No idea. Could be a bluff but we aren't going to stick around to find out.' He handed me the torch. 'Go and get Sophie. Thirty seconds and we're out of here whether she's dressed or not.'

My mind still felt sluggish. *Come on, wake up!* I hurried into the bedroom, expecting to find Sophie dressed and ready. But in the light of the torch I found her sitting on the edge of the bed, the duvet draped loosely around her as she held her head in her hands.

'Come on, Sophie, we've got to go.'

'I don't want to.' Her voice was sleepy and muffled. 'I don't feel so good.'

I began searching round for her clothes. 'You can rest later. Monk could be here any second.'

She shielded her eyes from the torch. 'God, how much wine did I have?'

'Sophie, we need to leave.' I handed her the clothes I'd snatched up. 'I know you don't want to but we don't have any choice.'

I half expected her to refuse, that we would get into

the safe house argument again. But she meekly took her clothes and stood up, letting the duvet fall. She was wearing a T-shirt but I looked away as she began to get dressed.

Cross appeared in the doorway. 'Ready?'

'Nearly.'

She waited for us as Sophie finished pulling on her clothes. Miller was waiting by the front door when we went downstairs, the hallway still in darkness. I gave him back the torch.

'We're just going to walk out to our car, nice and quiet,' he said as I pulled on my boots and fastened my coat, then helped Sophie fumble into hers. 'I'll go first, then you two. Nice and fast but don't run. Steph'll be right behind you. Get in the back of the car and lock the doors. OK?'

Sophie gave an uncertain nod, leaning against me. Miller tried to slide back the bolts quietly, but they still sounded like gunshots in the quiet. Drawing his gun, he opened the door in one smooth movement.

Cold, damp air rolled into the hallway. Outside it was pitch black. The beam from Miller's torch bounced back from the thick fog that had closed in around the house. I felt Sophie's hand tighten on mine.

'Stay close,' Miller said, and started down the path.

Mist blanketed everything. Even Miller was just a dark shape, silhouetted against the glow from the torch as he led us towards the gate. The fog seemed to soak up noise as well as light. Only the deadened scuff of our footsteps told me we were still on the path. When I glanced back at Sophie I could barely make out her face, even though she was right behind me.

The gate creaked as Miller held it open, and then we were on the lane. The hazy outline of their car took shape in front of us, its lights flashing with an electronic squawk as he unlocked it.

'OK, get in.'

The car's interior was cold as I slid into the back seat beside Sophie. Cross shut the door behind me and climbed into the front as Miller started the engine. There was a *thunk* as the locks engaged and then we were accelerating away, the headlights showing a wall of grey fog.

No one spoke. Cross murmured briefly into her radio, then fell silent again. Miller sat forward in his seat, trying to make out the road. Padbury lay behind us, but it was impossible to get any sense of where we were. It was like driving on the sea bed. The fog swirled like plankton in the headlights, half-seen shapes emerging briefly before disappearing again.

For all that, Miller kept up a good speed, shoulders hunched with concentration. After a few miles the sense of tension in the car began to ease.

'Well, that was fun,' Miller said. 'You OK back there?'

'Where are we going?' Sophie asked. She sounded exhausted.

'We're going to take you to a safe house for the time being. Only temporary, but we can sort out what's happening after that tomorrow.'

They'd obviously had a contingency plan worked out. I waited for Sophie to object, but she seemed past caring. In the darkness of the car I could just see her rubbing her head.

'Sophie? Are you all right?' I asked.

'I don't—' she began, and then Miller yelled, '*Shit!*' as a figure materialized from the fog in front of us.

There was a glimpse of outstretched arms and flapping coat, then Sophie was flung against me as Miller braked and swerved. But not in time. We hit the figure full on, but instead of the expected *thud* of impact it disintegrated in a blizzard of fragments and cloth. The car slewed, throwing me hard against the side window as Miller fought for control.

He almost made it. Fragments of glass peppered us as he punched a hole through the windscreen, letting in a cold blast of air. The car briefly seemed to level out, and I had time to think, *Thank God*. Then there was a crunching jolt and everything tipped sideways. The car seemed to hang weightless, then something slammed into me. The world became a tumbling confusion of darkness and noise. I was flung around without any sense of up or down.

Then there was stillness.

Gradually, sounds and sensations began to reassert themselves. A faint ticking, the steady drip-drip of rain. I could feel it against my face, along with cold air, but it was too dark to see. I was sitting upright but at an angle. Something was constricting my chest, making it hard to breathe. I groped at it with hands that felt leaden and clumsy. I was coated with a fine powder: residue from the airbags. They'd deflated now, draped out like pale tongues. But the seatbelt still held me in place, stretched taut across me like an iron band. I fumbled to unfasten it, shedding pebble-like pieces of broken glass, and slid down the seat as it slithered free.

'Sophie?' I tried to make her out in the darkness. Relief flowed through me as she stirred. 'Are you hurt?'

'I . . . I feel sick . . .' She sounded dazed.

'Hang on.'

There was movement in front of us as I struggled with Sophie's seatbelt. I heard Cross groan.

'You two all right?' she asked.

'I think so.' I tugged at the catch to Sophie's seatbelt. 'What did we hit?'

But Cross gave a cry and began scrambling over to Miller. 'Nick? *Nick?*'

He was slumped in his seat, not moving. I hurriedly freed Sophie's seatbelt. 'Can you get out now?'

'I – I think so . . .'

The door on my side was jammed. The hinges screeched in protest as I kicked it open. My legs almost gave way when I climbed out of the car. I leaned on to it for support, light-headed and aching all over. The car had come to rest at the bottom of a shallow embankment. It was upright but canted on one side, the bodywork scraped and mangled. One headlight was smashed and the other gave only a sickly glow, shining sadly into the ground like a blinded eye. The fog was tainted with the smell of petrol, but there was no sign of fire.

Crystalline pieces of shattered glass crunched underfoot as I limped around to the driver's side, slipping on the torn earth and grass. The car was more badly damaged here. The roof had crumpled, buckling the door shut. I tried forcing it open but it was useless: it would have to be cut away before anyone could get to Miller.

Cross was still inside the car next to him, talking urgently on the radio. She'd propped a torch on what was left of the dashboard, and I could see Miller hanging limply in his seat, held in place by the belt. Blood smeared his face and matted his hair, black and shiny in the torchlight.

I reached through the jagged hole where the window had been and felt for the carotid artery in his neck. There was a pulse but it was weak.

'Is he all right?'

Sophie had climbed out of the car and was gingerly making her way towards me.

'We need to call the paramedics,' I said. Even if we could have got him out of the car, moving him ourselves could do more harm than good. 'How about you?'

I could feel her shivering as I put my arm round her. She leaned against me. 'Bit dizzy, and my head's splitting.'

I would have asked more, but at that moment the car creaked as Cross forced her way out.

'Help's on its way,' she said, facing us across the car roof. She'd regained some of her calm. There was blood on her face, either her own or Miller's. 'They're going to try to send an air ambulance but I don't think it'll be able to get to us in this.'

Neither did I. The fog was as thick as ever, and even if there was somewhere for a helicopter to land I doubted it would attempt it.

'What happened?' Sophie asked. She still sounded dazed. 'God, did we hit someone?'

In the turmoil of the crash I'd forgotten about that. 'I'll go and look.'

'No.' Cross was firm. 'No one's wandering off. We'll wait for help to arrive.'

I saw with surprise that she'd taken her gun from its holster. But I was already replaying the snatched images of the figure caught in the headlights, recalling how it had come apart when we hit it. Not like there'd been flesh and bone inside the coat, more like . . . branches.

A scarecrow.

'She's right,' I said. 'We should stay here.'

'We can't just leave them there!' Sophie protested.

Cross was staring into the darkness, but now she turned to face Sophie across the car. 'Yes, we can. If you want to do something, there's a blanket—' she began, and then a shadow charged at her out of the fog.

Miller hadn't lied about how fast she was. The torch beam spiralled as she flung herself backwards. The figure was almost on top of her but she lashed out with a side kick at the same time as she swung the gun up. I heard a thump as the kick landed but her attacker swung a savage backhanded blow that caught Cross in the face. There was a meaty, bone-on-bone impact, and the policewoman pitched to the ground like a broken toy.

Sophie's scream freed me from my shock. 'Run!' I yelled, scrambling around the car, and throwing myself at the figure.

It was like hitting a brick wall. An arm swung, batting me against the car. The breath burst from me but before I could cry out a hand clamped around my throat. Calloused fingers dug into my neck, pinning

337

me against the bonnet as stars burst in my vision.

In the light from the fallen torch I found myself looking into the Halloween mask features of Jerome Monk.

He stared down at me with eyes that were dead and black. I flailed at him, but the arm beneath the greasy jacket was as solid as a tree trunk. His hand was jammed like a vice under my jaw. I could taste the stink of him, foul and feral as an animal's cage. My head felt about to burst. My sight was going now, the fog seeming to thicken around me. Through it I saw him look over his shoulder, heard the clumsy snap of branches as Sophie stumbled away.

God, no! I tried to shout out but I couldn't breathe. Monk jerked the arm holding me, slamming me back against the car. The air burst from my lungs as something rammed into my stomach. Abruptly the pressure was gone from my throat and I felt myself falling.

Then I hit the ground and the fog closed in completely.

25

I passed out, though only for a few seconds. I found myself in the mud, eyes pulsing with blood and my head throbbing as I tried to draw breath. There was a rushing in my ears.

Through it, as though from a long way away, I heard Sophie scream.

I tried to stand, but my body wouldn't respond. *Get up! Come on, move!* I clambered on to my hands and knees, mud and water soaking into my clothes. But my vision was clearing now, the blood-red mist lifting. I retched as my diaphragm spasmed. Sucking in ragged breaths, I used the car to drag myself to my feet.

I took a step and clutched at the car again as my legs almost gave way. Cross's torch had rolled against a front tyre, throwing a flat white light across the grass. In it I saw the policewoman. She lay sprawled in the grass, in the same broken posture as she'd fallen. There had been a horrible finality to the sound Monk's fist had made on her jaw.

But there was nothing I could do for her, or for Miller either. Snatching up the torch, I flung open the car boot. The cabin light was broken, but the dim yellow glow might act as a guide when the back-up arrived. I paused just long enough to grab the blanket from inside and throw it over Cross.

Then I went after Sophie and Monk.

I'd only a vague idea of which way they'd gone. The car had crashed on the edge of a wood, and the gnarled trees hemmed me in as I broke into a shambling run. The ground beneath them was a jumble of moss-covered rocks and bog grass which I skidded and slipped on. I slowed, shining the torch around.

'SOPHIE!'

My shout was soaked up by the fog. There was no answering cry, no sign of a struggle. The only noise was my own hoarse breathing and the dripping rustle of wet branches. Monk had planned this, I thought bleakly. Either he'd been watching the house and known Sophie had a police guard, or he'd anticipated it. The phone call had been to herd us away from Padbury, towards where he was waiting. Even the fog had worked in his favour, obscuring the scarecrow or dummy he'd set up in the road until we were right on top of it.

It was still working for him now, making it impossible to see more than a few yards. I looked desperately for any sign of which way they'd gone, but all around me was a shadowy warren of crooked trees.

I'd lost them.

I stood there while the stark fact sank home. It was hopeless. There was no point in carrying on, not when each step could be taking me further in the wrong direction. All I could do now was go back to Miller and Cross and wait for help to arrive.

Numb with defeat, I began to retrace my steps over the moss-covered rocks. I wasn't even sure where the car was, but in the light from the torch I saw the muddy tracks I'd gouged in the soft moss. I started to follow them before I realized. Heart thumping, I swept the beam back and forth in a wide arc across the ground.

Off to one side, just visible in the fog, another muddy trail had been ploughed through the soft ground.

I'd no way of knowing if it was that of Monk and Sophie, but I doubted many people came in here. The moss covered the rocks like seaweed at a low tide as I set off in the new direction. Whoever had come this way had slipped on it just as I had, smearing it off to reveal the dark, wet stone underneath. If this was Monk he was making no attempt to hide their tracks.

Either he didn't expect anyone to follow them or he didn't care.

A little further on the tree line abruptly ended. I found myself on an overgrown trail, one that was obviously used by walkers. The ground was churned to black mud in both directions. I stared at it, panting. *Come on, which way?*

Unless I'd become completely turned around, the road lay off to the left. If Monk had stolen a car then that would be where he'd have headed. Yet I hadn't heard an engine, and in the silence the sound would have carried even in this fog.

I hobbled into a run and followed the path deeper into the woods.

The torch beam pitched drunkenly as my boots squelched in the sludge. Then, as though the fog were solidifying, a craggy rock face loomed in front of me. The light fell on a barred iron gate set over a gaping cave mouth. No, not a cave, I realized.

A mine.

Lucas had mentioned an old tin mine a few miles from Padbury, but he'd said it was sealed off. *Not any more.* The rusty gate hung open, a broken padlock half buried in the trampled mud in front of it.

I took hold of the gate. The iron bars were cold and

rough. There was a metallic groan as I swung it open and shone the torch inside.

A tunnel of rock ran down into blackness.

My breath swirled in the fog as I stood there. *Now what?* I hurt all over. I'd chased after Sophie and Monk without giving any thought to what I'd do if I caught them, but I hadn't expected this. The sight of that dark opening in the rock touched on a primal fear that made the hairs on my neck stand on end.

But I had no choice. The blue display of my phone lit up like a beacon in the darkness, showing me what I'd already guessed: no signal. And I'd wasted enough time. Taking out my wallet, I dropped it by the gate so that the police would know where I'd gone. *You hope.*

Wiping the clammy sweat from my hands, I gripped the torch and started down the mine.

The shaft was barely high enough to stand upright. The air had the cold, dank smell of an old cellar. Water dripped from the roof timbers and trickled in runnels across the sloping floor. My footfalls echoed as I scuffed through it. The shaft began to drop more steeply, a rough-hewn wormhole hacked out by long dead miners. It fell away in front of me, vanishing beyond the reach of the torch.

I'd been walking for about five minutes when the ground began to level out. The shaft opened up, vaulting to twice its height as the walls drew back on either side. But directly ahead my light showed a tumbled mound of rock and shale. At some time in the past the entire roof had come down: jagged timbers protruded from between slabs of granite like broken bones.

The mine was blocked.

Water had formed a shallow pool where the rock-fall had partially dammed the run-off trickling down the shaft. I splashed through it, shining the torch around in the hope of finding a way past. There was nothing. I couldn't understand: I'd been certain Monk had brought Sophie down here. But I'd seen no tunnels leading off the main shaft, and the cave-in was impassable.

Or was it? I shone the torch over the blocked shaft one more time. The shadows from the rocks and shattered timbers jerked in the beam, but the fall looked solid. Then I moved the torch again and my breath caught in my throat.

One shadow didn't shift with the rest. It was in the angle where the uppermost rocks met the roof, a patch of impenetrable darkness. I picked up a stone and threw it. Instead of a clatter, it vanished silently inside.

Not a shadow. A hole.

It made sense. Monk wouldn't let himself be boxed in, and with the mine entrance sealed and the main shaft blocked for decades it was possible no one even knew this was here. As long as the gate remained padlocked, Monk could have had the run of the place.

But what lay on the other side?

I tested the nearest rock. It didn't budge. Neither did any of the others. The torch beam cast angled shadows as I carefully hoisted myself up. I reached for another handhold and felt something give beneath my foot.

There was a loud *crack*.

I froze. When nothing happened I shone the torch down. One of the rotten timbers sticking out from the rocks had snapped. *God*. I took a moment to let my heart rate slow, then levered myself the rest of the way. Now I could see what had caused the hole. A slab of granite had fractured from the top of the tunnel, leaving a gap high up in the angle between roof and wall. All but invisible from the ground, it was like a toothless mouth, perhaps three feet wide and two high.

Cold as it was, I was sweating as I shone the torch inside. The hole extended for a few yards before the beam vanished into darkness. It was wide enough to crawl through, though not to turn round. The only way to get back would be by shuffling backwards, feet first.

And praying I didn't get stuck.

I lowered my forehead on to the edge of the hole. The granite was grainy and cold against my skin. *I can't do this.* I thought about the weight of ancient rock suspended inches above me. The roof had collapsed once already. Even if I wasn't crushed I'd no idea what lay on the other side. If I crawled through I might not be able to get back. *You've done all you can. Let the police come down here with a proper search team.* A craven part of me whispered that it was the best thing to do. No one would blame me: I didn't even know for sure that Monk had brought Sophie this way. And even if he had, what good could I do? The sensible thing would be to go back for help.

And what'll happen to Sophie then? What's happening to her now, while you're dawdling here?

Without giving myself time to think, I pushed myself into the hole. The rough granite grated like sandpaper as I wriggled my way inside, the cold rock striking through my clothes. There was more space than I thought, but then there'd have to be for Monk to get through. *If he did. You still don't know for sure.* But I was committed now. My breath steamed in the light from the torch as I crawled awkwardly along the rock's dark length. It seemed to take an age before I reached the other end. Panting, I shone the beam into the dark.

I'd emerged at the top of a long, low cavern. It sloped away to one side, ending in a drop-off from where I could hear the gurgle of running water. Whatever this was, I didn't think it was part of the mine. It was little more than a horizontal crack in the rock, barely high enough to stand. *Well, you wanted to see what was here: now you know.*

Getting out of the hole was difficult. I'd gone through headfirst, so I had to wriggle around before I could swing my legs free. My boots scrabbled on rock, then I dropped down to the slanting floor. The low roof meant I had to stoop as I held the torch in front of me. The cavern's broad expanse sprang to life, deep shadows stretching away beyond the limits of the beam.

'*Sophie?*' I called. '*SOPHIE!*'

My shout rang out, echoing into oblivion. The only response was the chunter of the underground stream, invisible in the shadows. Aiming the torch into the darkness at the far side, I started across.

I had to bend almost double. According to Lucas, there weren't any cave systems in this part of Dartmoor. Yet this was obviously a natural formation, not man-made. *Looks like he got it wrong*, I thought, and as I did I banged my head on an outcrop of rock. I reeled back, more startled than hurt.

And dropped the torch.

No! I grabbed for it but missed. It clattered on to the rock, the light flickering as it hit. I tried to trap it with my foot but it pitched past, skittering and bouncing down the slope towards the drop-off. Its beam threw crazy patterns as I scrambled after it, but it was rolling too fast. Then it reached the edge, and as though a switch had been flicked I was plunged into darkness.

I didn't move. The enormity of what had happened stunned me. I stared into the blackness where the torch had disappeared, hoping to see a faint glow. There was nothing. The dark was so complete it seemed to have depth and weight. Now I couldn't see it, the vast weight of rock all around me seemed even more oppressive.

The heavy silence was broken only by the splash of unseen water. *Don't panic. Think it through*. My hand was unsteady as I reached into my pocket for my phone. I gripped it tightly as I took it out and thumbed a key.

A blue glow threw back the dark as the phone's display sprang to life. *Thank God*. It wasn't as bright as the torch but right then it seemed beautiful. Holding it up like a miniature lantern, I began edging towards the drop-off that the torch had rolled over. It was possible the fall had just loosened a connection: if I could find it I might be able to get it working.

I'd only taken a few more steps when the blue light suddenly winked out.

I felt a stab of panic as blackness engulfed me again. But the display had only gone on to stand-by: it lit up again when I pressed a key. Weak with relief, I carried on. The sound of the underground stream grew louder, moistening the air with a damp chill. I was forced to bend almost double as the roof became even lower, but I didn't have much further to go.

I was almost there when my phone rang.

The piercing *beep* was shockingly loud. For an instant I felt a surge of hope, before I realized no one could call down here. What I'd heard wasn't the ringtone.

It was the low-battery warning.

I'd been meaning to charge the phone for days. The last time was before I came to Dartmoor, but with reception so patchy I'd hardly used it. It hadn't seemed important.

It did now.

Oh, Christ. I stared at the flashing battery icon. As though to prove a point, the screen went out again. My fingers trembled as I pressed a key. The phone lit up but beeped again almost immediately. There was no way of knowing how much longer the battery would last, and using the display would drain it faster than ever.

I took a final, agonized look towards the drop-off. It was only a few yards away, but there was no guarantee I'd be able to retrieve the torch. Or that it would still work if I did. There was no longer any question of going on. I needed to get out and fetch help while I still could. Once I was back in the mine the shaft ran straight to the surface. I'd be able to follow it out even if the phone died. But if it failed before then . . .

Don't think about that.

I tried to steady my breathing, resisting the urge to rush blindly back towards the hole. I went as fast as I could, but my back was aching from being stooped over and my progress still seemed agonizingly slow. The phone's display went out twice more as I crabbed back up the slope. Each time I froze, hardly daring to breathe as I pressed a key to bring the screen back to life.

I was perhaps halfway across when the screen went dead for the fifth time. I quickly thumbed a key. Nothing happened. I pressed another. And another. The screen stayed dead. The darkness seemed to thicken as I jabbed the keypad in desperation, praying for just a few more seconds of light.

But it didn't come. The blackness seemed to press against my eyes. I lowered the phone.

I wasn't going anywhere.

26

It was cold down there. I started to shiver soon after the phone gave out. The air was damp and frigid, and once I'd stopped moving the cavern's chill soon cut through my clothes. I'd settled down on to the rock surface, first squatting on my haunches then sitting down when my muscles became cramped. Cold or not, I dared not go any further when I couldn't see anything. I'd been lost once at night on a Scottish island. I'd thought that was as bad as it could get.

This was worse.

My first instinct was to try to feel my way to the hole I'd crawled through. I knew the opening had to be tantalizingly close. Negotiating the rockfall in the dark wouldn't be easy, but once I was back in the mine my chances of making it to the surface would be much better.

If I'd been able to fix the hole's position in my mind I might have tried. But I'd be groping my way blindly, unable to see any falls or projections of rock. Even if I didn't crack my head open, it would be all too easy to become disorientated. And if I found an opening I'd have no way knowing if it was the right one: I could end up crawling deeper into the cave system without realizing it.

No, like it or not, my only option was to stay where I was. The police would find the broken gate and my wallet, and then it was only a matter of time before the mine was searched. If I could find the opening that led here then surely they would as well.

And if they don't?

Sooner or later if no one came I knew I would have to make a decision. But I wasn't ready to think about that yet. I tried my phone again, hoping some residual charge would light the screen for a few seconds. It didn't. Now I'd time to think, coming down here seemed unbelievably stupid. Even if I'd caught up with Sophie and Monk, what would I have done? Fought him off? The idea was laughable. It hadn't occurred to me to bring Cross's gun, and if I had I wouldn't have known how to use it. No, I should have stayed with the car, done what I could for her and Miller until back-up arrived. Instead I was trapped underground in a cavern no one might even know existed, while Monk and Sophie . . .

I couldn't bear to even think about that.

I put my head on my knees, wrapping my arms round them to hug what little heat I could to myself. The cold ached into my bones, but I hardly cared. There was no way of even knowing how long I'd been down there. I couldn't see my watch face, and in the dark I'd lost all track of time.

Huddled and shivering, I strained to hear anything that might indicate help was on its way. Once I thought I did: the echo of a far-off clatter drifted through the cavern. I shouted into the blackness until I was hoarse and my throat hurt. But when I stopped to listen the only sound was the fluid ripple of unseen water.

Feeling as useless as I'd ever been in my life, I closed my eyes and tried to rest.

At some point I must have dozed. I wouldn't have thought it possible, but I was aching and exhausted. Without being aware of it, I drifted into an uneasy sleep.

And then, suddenly, I was awake. For a few seconds I had no idea where I was. Panicking, I narrowly avoided banging my head on the low rock as I started to lurch to my feet. I lowered myself back down on to the cold rock as the bleakness of the situation sank in. My legs had cramped. I stretched out first one, then the other, massaging the muscles to ease them.

That was when I heard the noise.

It sounded like the far-off skitter of a falling rock. I froze, listening. After a moment it came again, and this time it didn't stop. It grew louder, the unmistakable echoing scrape of someone's approach.

'*In here!*' I yelled. '*I'm in here!*'

The cramp was forgotten as I stared into the darkness, relief and adrenalin making my heart thump. It seemed to take a long time before a light appeared in the blackness.

Thank God. 'Over here!'

The light began to move in my direction, the dancing yellow beam of a torch. It was only as it grew larger that I realized it was coming from the wrong direction. Whoever this was they were approaching from the far side of the cavern, not the opening from the mine. And there was only a single light instead of the massed torches of a rescue party.

The shout died in my throat. A sick resignation spread through me as the torch came closer. Beyond the glare I could make out a bulky figure and the pale dome of a bald head, stooped and hunched beneath the bellying rock. It stopped a few feet away. I smelled something rank and animal.

Monk lowered the torch. The filthy combat jacket looked too small across the massive shoulders and arms. The button eyes regarded me as his chest rose and fell, each breath accompanied by a low wheeze.

'Get up.'

The cave system was an underground maze, but Monk seemed to know exactly where he was going. He squeezed through narrow crevices, crawled along water-dripping passages that bent and wormed their way through the rock. He didn't hesitate, slithering through gaps I would never have dared risk by myself. But despite his size he never once got caught or stuck. On the surface he might be a freak; here, in the subterranean tunnels, he seemed in his element.

After that single, terse instruction he hadn't spoken again. Ignoring my frantic questions about Sophie, he'd simply turned and headed back the way he had come, as though he didn't care if I followed or not. Bewildered, I stayed where I was. It was only as the shadows flowed back into the cavern, rushing to fill the vacuum left by the receding torch, that I forced myself to move.

Monk never so much as glanced round, though he must have heard me. I felt utterly lost. None of this made sense, not the fact that he'd come back nor why – or where – he was leading me. The thought of going deeper into the caves appalled me, yet what else could I do? He could have killed me already if that was all he wanted.

And I had to find Sophie.

The passage we were in abruptly opened into a space large enough to stand. Monk started across without pausing. I took the opportunity to catch up. 'Where is she?' I panted.

He didn't answer. He was obviously feeling the exertion, each breath a thick, wet rattle, but he didn't slow. When I grabbed hold of his arm it felt like a piece of teak under the oily cloth.

'What have you done with her? Is she hurt?'

He jerked his arm free. He didn't seem to put any effort into it, but I was yanked off my feet. I sprawled on my hands and knees on the rock, hard enough to skin them.

'Shut the fuck up.'

His voice was a hoarse rumble. He turned to carry on, but doubled up as a coughing fit seized him. He leaned against the rock face, huge shoulders shaking from the violence of the spasm. It sounded as though his lungs were full of fluid as he spat a gob of phlegm on to the floor. Breathing heavily, he passed a hand across his mouth before continuing on as though nothing had happened.

After a moment I went after him. But I was thinking now about the ragged breathing I'd heard over the phone, and the sputum the police had found at Wainwright's house. Everyone had assumed that was a gesture of contempt, but I was no longer so sure.

Monk was ill.

Not that it made him any less dangerous, or slowed him down. I had to push myself to keep up, knowing that if I didn't I'd be left stranded. All I could do was fix my eyes on Monk's broad back, silhouetted by the torch beam, and trust that there was some purpose to this.

I'd been trailing behind him, sloshing ankle-deep through water that ran down the sides of a narrow, upward-sloping passage, when the light suddenly went out. I stopped dead, fighting panic, wondering if all this had been a sadistic trick to abandon me down here.

Then I heard a muted noise coming from nearby, and at the same time made out a faint glow coming from one side of the passage. I edged towards it and found myself at a cleft in the rock. The scrape and grunt of Monk's laboured progress came from inside, and I could just make out the flickering beam of his torch.

The cleft climbed at a steep angle. I had to haul myself up, clambering after the receding light. I went as fast as I could, but it still grew dimmer. The rough grain of the rock scraped against my coat, pressing in closer. Soon I couldn't make out any light at all, or even hear him. I tried to swallow the fear and bile that rose in my throat. *Stay calm. Just keep going.*

Then the passage kinked in a sharp dog-leg, and I saw a glow up ahead. Following it, I found myself in a small, natural chamber in the rock. I halted, dazzled after the darkness by the dim light from a lantern on the floor. The air was fetid and sour, a mineral dankness fighting with an animal reek. A hissing gas heater threw out a warmth that seemed stifling after the cold of the caves. As my eyes adjusted I took in a jumble of bags, bottles and cans scattered on the floor. Monk was crouched on a rumpled blanket, looking at me with that not-quite-smile and dead eyes.

Huddled as far away from him as she could get was Sophie.

'*Oh, God, D-David . . . !*'

She flung her arms around me as I knelt by her. I stroked her hair as she buried her face in my shoulder, feeling her body trembling through her coat.

'Shh, it's OK.'

It was far from that, but the relief I felt at seeing her swamped everything else. Her face was pale and streaked with tears, the bruise still livid. There was something else about her, something that wasn't right, but I was too overwhelmed by finding her to follow up the half-formed thought. She bent her head to wipe her eyes and it went from my mind.

'Are you all right? Has he hurt you?' I asked.

'No, he didn't . . . I – I'm fine.'

She didn't look or sound it, but I felt my relief edge up another notch. Whatever Monk had in mind, Sophie had fared better than his other victims.

So far.

He was still on the blanket, watching us, with his big hands dangling from his knees, scabbed and bruised. The low yellow light from the lantern made the indentation in his forehead into a shadowed pit. Squatting there, he could have been a throwback to a more primitive age, a pale, hairless ape hunched in its cave.

But he seemed even more ill than I'd thought. The massive shoulders were slumped with exhaustion, and the skin was drawn tight across the heavy bones of his face, tinged with a sickly, jaundiced cast. His mouth hung open as he breathed, a sibilant wheeze sounding with every rise and fall of his chest. He obviously had a serious respiratory infection, maybe even pneumonia, and living in these conditions wouldn't have helped. Monk looked like a man at the end of his physical limits.

Except that Monk wasn't a normal man. And ill or not, the dark eyes watching us were bright and unblinking.

I made myself look back: it was like staring down an attack dog. 'You don't need two hostages. Let her go.'

'I don't want a hostage,' he said, his voice sounding raw. His mouth twitched in a sneer. 'Think I don't remember you from before? Not so fucking smart now, are you?'

No, not so smart at all. 'So why've you brought us here?'

'I brought her. You just followed.'

'Then why did you come to find me?'

Monk turned his head to hawk into the corner of the chamber, then sank back against the rock. His breathing had steadied, but still sounded like air escaping from a broken bellows.

'Ask her.'

I turned to Sophie. I could feel her trembling against me. 'I . . . We heard you shouting. Sound carries down here. When it went quiet, I thought . . . I thought . . .' She gave me a desperate look. Again I felt a sudden disquiet that had nothing to do with Monk, but her next words drowned it out. 'I told him . . . I – I said you'd be able to help.'

'I don't understand.'

Sophie glanced nervously across at him. 'He . . . he says he can't—'

'No, he doesn't *say*, I don't fucking *say*! I *can't*!' His shout reverberated in the small chamber. 'I try but I *can't*! There's nothing there! It didn't matter before, but it does now!'

Monk ran his scabbed hands over his skull, rasping them on the stubble that had started to grow there. His mouth worked, as though the next words were being torn from him.

'I want to know what I did.'

* * *

Time didn't seem to exist in the cramped chamber. I'd broken my watch at some point, shattering the face so that the glass had turned crystalline. Beneath it the hands were motionless, frozen at between two and three o'clock. Not that it made much difference down here. The light from the lantern gave the small chamber an otherworldly quality, intensified by the soporific warmth from the hissing gas heater. The fumes wouldn't help Monk's breathing, but there was enough air current down here to stop the build-up from becoming toxic.

I sat on a wadded-up plastic sheet, my back against the rock, with Sophie curled against me. Monk had subsided after his outburst. He seemed exhausted, slumped forward with his head hung between his raised knees, hands wrapped protectively around it. The posture made him look oddly vulnerable. He hadn't moved in a while, and the steady whistle of his breathing made me think he was asleep. But I still watched him carefully as I lowered my head to Sophie's.

'What did he mean?' I whispered.

'I – I don't know . . .'

I pitched my voice low, not taking my eyes from Monk. 'He must have said *something*. Why does he want help? Help for what?'

'I don't *know*! I – I feel so sick, and the light's too bright.'

I shifted so my body shielded her from the lantern. 'Sophie, this is important. You need to tell me.'

She massaged her temples, glancing fearfully across at Monk. 'He . . . he says he can't remember killing those girls. Not just burying them, any of it! He wants . . . he thinks I can help, because I said I could help him find the graves, even if he'd forgotten where they were. But I didn't mean I could help him get his *memory* back! Oh, God, this can't be happening!'

I could feel her shaking. I hugged her to me. 'Go on.'

Sophie wiped her eyes. 'That's why he was digging round Tina Williams' grave. He thought . . . he thought if he found the graves, saw the bodies again, it'd make him remember. That's why he came after us when he saw us out there, he knew it had to be me. But I – I can't do anything like that, that's not what I *meant* !'

'Shh. I know.' I stroked her back, warily watching Monk. 'What did he mean when he said it didn't matter before, but it does now?'

'I – I don't know. But I told him . . . I said you could help. When I heard you shouting, it was the only thing I could think of. God, I'm so sorry, this is all my fault!'

I held her as she cried herself into an exhausted sleep. I was shattered myself, bone-weary and aching, but I had to stay awake. I stared across at Monk's unmoving form, desperately trying to think what to do. Everyone had always assumed he'd been lying when he'd said he couldn't remember where the Bennett sisters were buried. Now . . . I didn't know.

Not that it made any difference. Even if Monk really was suffering from some sort of amnesia there was nothing Sophie could do about it. She'd been a BIA, not a psychiatrist. She was no more able to help him recover his memories than I was. Sooner or later he was going to realize that, and when he did . . .

I had to get her out of here.

Monk still hadn't moved, and if the deep, wheezing rhythm of his breathing was anything to go by, his sleep was deeper than ever. But I doubted it was deep enough for us to slip out without disturbing him. *So what, then? Club him while he's asleep?* Even assuming I could do something so cold-blooded – and that he didn't wake and tear me apart – I'd no idea how to get back to the surface.

I looked around the chamber, hoping to see something that might help. The floor was piled with empty water bottles and food wrappers, discarded gas canisters and batteries. Some of them were years old, probably dating to the last time Monk had hidden out here. Near me was a tattered phone directory and a more recent pile of boxes, ripped open to spill cough linctus, foil packets of antibiotics and small brown bottles I recognized as smelling salts, clearly raided from some chemist's. The smelling salts puzzled me, until I made the connection with the police dog that had tried to track him a few days earlier.

Smelling salts contained ammonia.

The only other thing nearby was a plastic bag filled with foul-smelling earth. The musky odour was somehow familiar, but I couldn't place it. Still watching Monk, I tried to see what else was hidden among the debris. I gently moved a box aside and stiffened when I saw what lay behind it.

The black cylinder of a torch.

It was just out of reach. For all I knew it could be broken, and even if it wasn't we'd still have to get past Monk before we could use it. But at least it offered a small hope, and right now I needed every little I could get. Careful not to disturb Sophie, I leaned towards the torch, stretching as far as I could. My fingers were only inches away from it when I felt a change in the chamber. The hairs on my arms prickled, as though the air had suddenly become charged. I looked up.

Monk was staring at me.

Except he wasn't, not quite. His eyes were fixed on a spot just off to one side. I moistened my mouth, trying to think of something to say. Before I could he jerked his head spastically to his right, mouth curling in a one-sided sneer.

Then he began to laugh.

It was an eerie, phlegm-filled chuckle. It grew louder, rising in pitch until his shoulders were shaking with the force of it. I flinched as he suddenly lashed out with a scabbed fist, smacking it sideways into the rough wall beside him. If it hurt he gave no sign. Still laughing, he thumped his fist into the rock again. And again.

Sophie stirred and gave a restless moan. Without taking my eyes off Monk I put my hand on her shoulder, willing her to keep still. She subsided, too exhausted to fully wake as Monk's manic laughter began to die down. At any moment I expected those dead eyes to turn to us, but it was as though we weren't even there.

The last bubble of laughter escaped from his chest, and his breathing slowed back into the raw wheeze of before. He sat quiescent, blood dripping from the hand he'd been slamming into the wall, mouth hanging slack as though he were drugged.

Christ! I'd no idea what had just happened. I knew Monk was unstable, but this . . . this was something else. It had seemed involuntary, as though he hadn't even been aware of it himself. Or even really conscious. From nowhere, something Roper had said all those years ago suddenly came back to me: *He kicked off on one last night . . . One of his party pieces, apparently, having a tantrum after lights out. That's why the guards call him laughing boy.*

Monk was starting to stir, blinking slowly as though he were waking up. Another coughing fit racked him. When it passed he cleared his throat and spat on to the floor. It seemed to exhaust him. He rubbed a hand over his face, the same one he'd punched the wall with. He frowned when he saw the blood on it, then realized I was watching.

'The fuck you looking at?'

I quickly looked away. Trying to sound unconcerned, I picked up one of the foil packs of antibiotics that lay on the floor nearby. 'These won't do your chest infection any good.'

'How would you know?'

'I used to be a doctor.'

'Fuck off.'

I dropped the tablets back into the mess. 'OK, don't believe me. But they're for bladder infections, not respiratory tract.'

Monk's dark eyes glittered. He looked down at where Sophie's head lay on my lap.

'What this?' I asked quickly, nudging the soil-filled bag with my foot. It was the first thing that came to mind.

He seemed to debate whether to answer, but at least it shifted his attention from Sophie. 'Fox piss.'

'Fox . . . ?'

He raised a booted foot. 'For the dogs.'

That explained some of his stink, at least. Foxes used their pungent urine to mark their territory: Monk must have been smearing himself with soil from a den, hoping to mask his own scent. Once again I felt there was something I should remember, but I was too distracted to worry about it.

'Does it fool them?' I knew it wouldn't, but I wasn't about to tell him that.

'Not the dogs. The handler.'

I'd underestimated him. Police dogs would be able to track him regardless of what he used. But if an inexperienced handler caught the distinctive smell of a fox they might think the dog was on the wrong trail.

'What is this place?' I asked. 'I didn't think there were any caves round here.'

'Nobody does.'

Including the police. 'Is this where you hid last time?'

His head snapped up. 'I don't fucking hide! I've always come down here.'

'Why?'

'To get away from people like you. Now shut the fuck up.'

He rummaged in the rubbish on the floor and produced a bar of chocolate. Ripping it open, he tore into it as though he were famished. When it was gone he twisted the top from a bottle of water and tilted his head back to drink. I was aware of my own parched throat as I watched his Adam's apple bob up and down.

Monk tossed the empty bottle aside. He nodded down at Sophie. 'Wake her up.'

'She needs to sleep.'

'You want me to do it?'

He reached his bloodied hand towards Sophie. I acted instinctively, knocking it away. Monk became very still, his eyes burning into me.

'She's hurt,' I said. 'If you want her to help you she needs to rest. She's just been in a car crash, for God's sake.'

'I didn't know it'd roll like that.' He sounded sullen. He looked down at Sophie again, this time taking in the fading bruise on her cheek. 'What happened to her face?'

'Don't you know? Someone broke into her house and attacked her.'

Something seemed to flicker in those dark eyes. The broad forehead creased into deep lines. 'It was all smashed up. She wasn't there. I didn't . . . I can't . . .'

He folded his hands over his shaved head, his voice dropping to an inaudible mumble.

'Can't what?' I pushed, forgetting myself.

'I can't fucking *remember*!' His shout reverberated inside the small chamber. He banged the heels of his hands against the sides of his head, as though trying to drive them through. 'I try and try, but there's *nothing*! You're supposed to be a doctor, what's wrong with me?'

I couldn't begin to answer that. 'I was only a GP, but there are specialists—'

'Fuck 'em!' Spittle sprayed from his mouth. 'Pricks in white coats, what do they know?'

This time I had enough sense to stay quiet. Some of the heat seemed to go from him. The big hands opened and closed as he looked at Sophie. She hadn't woken, even now.

'You and her . . . She's your girlfriend.'

I was about to say no, but something stopped me. Monk didn't seem to expect an answer anyway.

'I had a girlfriend.' He clasped both hands round the back of his head. His mouth worked. 'I killed her.'

27

By the time he was fifteen, Monk's life was set in stone. Orphaned since birth, he'd grown up doubly excluded, shunned for his physical defects and feared for his abnormal strength. The few families that fostered the surly, freakish boy soon sent him back, shaken by the experience. By the time he reached puberty he was stronger than most grown men, and violence and intimidation had become second nature.

Then the blackouts started.

To begin with he didn't realize. Most came at night, so his only awareness of them was a feeling of haziness and lethargy next day, of inexplicable bruises or bloodied hands. The problem only came to light in a young offenders' institution, when his nocturnal behaviour terrified the other inmates. Monk would throw tantrums, laughing like a lunatic and reacting to any attempts to subdue him with devastating, frenzied violence. Next morning he wouldn't recall any of it.

At first he believed the accusations and subsequent punishments were just new forms of victimization. He reacted by becoming more insular and aggressive than ever. It never occurred to him to ask for help, and he would have rejected any had it been offered. Not that it was. Prison psychologists spoke of anti-social behaviour, of impulse-control disorders and sociopathic tendencies. One look was enough to confirm anyone's worst suspicions. He was a freak, a monster.

He was Monk.

As he grew older he took to wandering on the moor. The ancient landscape, with its rocky tors and thorny gorse, had a calming effect. More importantly, it allowed him to be on his own. One day he came across an overgrown hole in a hillside. It was an old mine adit, although he didn't know that at the time. It opened, quite literally, a new world for him. He began seeking out the old mines and caves that lay below the surface of Dartmoor, exploring and even sleeping in them whenever he could. He spent as much time down in the cold, dark tunnels as he did in the run-down caravan he called home. They were a reassuring constant, indifferent to day or night and untouched by weather or seasons. They made him feel secure. Stilled.

Even the blackouts seemed less frequent.

He was on his way to the moor one night when he saw the gang. He'd been away from it for almost a week, labouring on a building site for cash in hand. Now, with money in his pocket, the need to get back made his skin prickle and itch. He felt as if nails were being scratched on blackboards inside him, and there was a muzziness in his head that often presaged an impending blackout.

At first he ignored the hooded youths huddled under a broken streetlight. They had something down on the floor, trapping it like a pack of animals. Monk wasn't interested, and would have gone on by if it hadn't been for their laughter. Vicious and cruel, it throbbed behind his eyes like an echo of childhood. The gang had scattered after he'd knocked two or three of them away, leaving a lone figure on the floor. The tendons in Monk's hands had ached with the need to hit something else, but the girl on the ground had looked up without fear. She gave him a shy smile.

Her name was Angela Carson.

'You *knew* her?'

The question spilled out before I could stop it. According to the reports I'd read, witnesses had seen Monk in his fourth victim's neighbourhood before the murder, but it was assumed he'd simply been stalking her. There was never any suggestion that he'd *known* Angela Carson, let alone that they'd had any sort of relationship.

The look in Monk's eyes was answer enough.

After that first, accidental meeting the pair had been drawn together. Both were lonely. Both, in different ways, excluded from society. Angela Carson was almost completely deaf, and it was easier for her to sign than speak. Monk didn't know how, but the two of them still managed to communicate. In the plain young woman he finally found someone who was neither terrified nor repulsed by him. For her part, it wasn't difficult to imagine that she found his strength comforting. He took to visiting her after dark, when there was less chance of being seen by neighbours.

It wasn't long before she asked him to stay the night.

The blackouts had been less frequent since they'd met. He'd been calmer, less agitated. He'd allowed himself to believe they were over. Even so, he hadn't meant to fall asleep.

But he had.

He claimed to have no recollection of what happened, only that he found himself standing by the bed. There was a pounding on the door as the police tried to break in. All was noise and confusion. His hands were covered in blood, but none of it was his.

He looked down and saw Angela Carson.

That was when Monk lost what little control he had left. When the police burst into the room he attacked them in a frenzy. Then he ran until his legs gave way, futilely trying to escape the images of that bloodied room.

Without even thinking about it, he'd gone out on to the moor.

And gone to ground.

That the police would be looking for him didn't really enter into his thinking: he was trying to escape from himself, not them. Cold and hunger drove him up after a few days. He'd lost all sense of time, and it was night when he emerged. He stole clothes and food, and what equipment he needed, and was back in his sanctuary before dawn.

Over the next three months he spent more time underground, beneath the gorse and heather of Dartmoor, than he did in the outside world. He only emerged into fresh air and daylight to move to another system of tunnels, or to steal or forage fresh supplies and check the traps he'd laid for rabbits. The surface reminded him of who he was and what he'd done. Underneath the dark rock he was able to bury himself away.

And forget.

Indifferent to his own safety, he was able to find places and worm into tunnels that no one else would dare to enter. Twice he had to dig himself out when the roof collapsed; another time he was almost drowned when the system he was in flooded after heavy rains. Once he sat unseen, hunched in the shadows as a group of cavers clattered by only yards away. He let them go, but afterwards sought out a less public refuge.

The blackouts continued, but down there he was only vaguely aware of them. Sometimes he would wake in a different cavern or tunnel from the one he remembered, with no memory of how he had got there. He took to sleeping with a torch in his pocket for when that happened.

Then one day he found himself walking on the roadside in broad sunlight. He felt confused, his thoughts as muddy as his clothes, with no idea of where he was or what he was doing. That was how the police found him.

The first time he heard of Tina Williams or Zoe and Lindsey Bennett was when he was charged with their murders.

'Then why did you plead guilty?' I asked.

Monk absently rubbed at a spot between two of his knuckles, the button eyes staring at nothing. I'd always thought they were empty: now I wondered how I could have missed the pain in them.

'Everyone said I'd done it. They found their stuff at my caravan.'

'But if you couldn't remember—'

'You think I fucking cared?'

He glared at me, but even that seemed too much effort. He convulsed as another coughing spasm took him. It was even more violent than before, and when it passed it left him gasping.

Without thinking, I reached out for his wrist. 'Here, let me check your pulse—'

'Touch me and I'll break your arm.'

I lowered my hand. Monk sat back against the rock, regarding me with suspicion. 'If you're a doctor, how come you dig up bodies? Think you can bring them back to life?'

'No, but I can help find who killed them.'

I wished the words back as soon as they were out, but it was too late. When Monk started wheezing I thought it was another coughing fit until I realized he was laughing.

'Still a fucking smartarse,' he rumbled.

But he soon broke off. Each breath was a ragged whistle, and there was a sheen of sweat on his face. The black eyes seemed sunken into his skull as it pressed through the yellow skin.

'The heart attack wasn't faked, was it?' I said.

Monk stroked his hand back and forth over his head, his thumb fitting disconcertingly into the depression in his skull. It seemed to calm him.

'It was charlie.'

It took me a moment to understand. 'You over-dosed on cocaine? Deliberately?'

The big head nodded. His hand continued to rasp over it.

'How much?'

'Enough.'

It explained how Monk had fooled the doctors. As well as sending his blood pressure sky high, a cocaine overdose could trigger tachycardia, making his heart-beat dangerously fast and irregular. The symptoms could easily be mistaken for the onset of a heart attack, and prove just as fatal. Judging from Monk's condition I guessed he'd suffered cardiovascular damage at the very least, perhaps even heart failure. Throw in a respiratory infection and it was a miracle he wasn't dead. No wonder we'd escaped from him out at Black Tor.

He'd been too sick to catch us.

'You could have killed yourself,' I said.

His mouth curled. 'So what?'

'I don't understand. You waited eight years, why escape now?'

His mouth twitched in what at first I mistook for a smile. Then I saw the look in his eyes and realized it was anything but.

'Because the bastards stitched me up.'

I'd been on the verge of believing him until then. Even, God help me, pitying him. Monk was capable of a lot of things but acting wasn't one of them. But while I'd have sworn the bizarre seizure I'd witnessed was genuine, this was pure paranoia. I must have let my thoughts show.

'You think I'm a psycho, don't you?'

'No, I—'

'Don't fucking lie!'

He was glaring at me, big head jutting forward. *Careful*. 'Why do you think you were set up?'

He glared at me for a moment longer, then examined his scabbed fists. Blood still dripped from the one he'd hit against the rock, but it didn't seem to bother him.

'I got word that this new cunt was saying he'd seen someone poking around under my caravan before it was raided. They pulled a warrant card on him and said it was police business. Told him to fuck off, that if he told anyone he'd get banged up on paedo charges and thrown to the nutjobs. Said he'd be doing himself a favour if he kept his mouth shut. So he did. Never told anyone until he got sent to Belmarsh and wanted to big himself up to the hardmen.' Monk turned his head and spat. 'Like I wasn't going to find out.'

This wasn't the paranoid rant I'd been expecting. It had been the discovery of Zoe Bennett's lipstick and hairbrush under his caravan that had confirmed Monk's guilt. He would have known that, of course, but even so . . .

'This prisoner . . .' I said.

'Walker. Darren Walker.'

'Did he tell you the policeman's name?'

'He said it was some bastard called Jones. A DI.'

The name meant nothing to me, but there was no reason it should. 'He could have been lying.'

'He wasn't. Not after what I did to him.' Monk's face was pitiless. His lips twitched back in a snarl. 'Should've said something sooner.'

Terry had told me about Monk beating another inmate to death when he'd broken the news of his escape. *Put two wardens in hospital when they tried to pull him off. Surprised you didn't hear about it.* I tried to swallow: my mouth was so dry it took me several attempts. I pointed at a pack of unopened water nearby.

'Can I have a drink?'

He hitched a slabbed shoulder in a shrug. I opened one of the bottles, conscious of my hands shaking. But the water eased my parched throat, and the fact he'd allowed it was something in itself.

I drank half, saving the rest for when Sophie woke. 'How does Wainwright fit into this?' I asked, capping the bottle again. 'Why did you kill him?'

I half expected Monk to say he couldn't remember that either. He dredged something up from his lungs and hawked on the floor before he answered.

'I didn't kill him.'

'His wife identified you, and your DNA was all over the house.'

'I didn't say I wasn't there, I said I didn't kill him. He fell downstairs. I never touched him.'

It was possible, I supposed. Wainwright's body had been lying near the foot of the stairs: he could have broken his neck falling down them. Finding Monk in your home would have been terrifying for anyone, let alone someone with dementia.

'Why did you go to their house anyway? You can't have thought Wainwright had anything to do with setting you up.'

Monk had clasped both hands on his head as he looked at Sophie. She stirred in her sleep, frowning as though she could feel his eyes on her. 'Didn't know what else to do when I couldn't find her. I thought he might know where she was. Or know something. I tried digging holes on the moor like I saw him do, see if that'd make me remember. Didn't expect you and her to turn up, though.'

He gave a death's-head grin.

'Weren't expecting me either, were you? You were so scared I could practically smell you. If I wasn't knackered from digging them fucking holes I'd have caught you.'

So instead, frustrated, that night he'd sought out the only other person he could think of. Someone who was easy to find, with his name in the phone book.

'Wainwright was ill. He couldn't have helped.'

Monk's head snapped up. 'I didn't know that, did I? You think I'm sorry he's dead? Stuck-up bastard treated me like scum, I've not forgotten that! I'd have broken the fucker's neck anyway!'

'I don't—' I began, but it was as if a switch had been flicked.

'*The bastards stitched me up!* Eight years I thought I was too cracked to remember what I did! *Eight fucking years!*'

'If you didn't kill the other girls—'

'I don't give a fuck about them! But if I was set up then I could have been for the rest of it. For Ange!' The dark eyes were fevered and manic. His head jerked, an unconscious twitch of his jaw. 'The fuckers could've tricked me, made me think I killed her as well! You get it? I might not have done it, *and I need to fucking remember!*'

Any hope I'd had of reasoning with him died then. Monk wasn't interested in retrieving any lost memories, only in absolving himself of guilt over Angela Carson. But that wasn't going to happen. Whatever the fate of the other victims, whether he'd intended it or not, he'd killed her himself.

And nothing Sophie said could alter that.

'Look, whatever you did, if it happened during a blackout then you're not fully responsible,' I said. 'There are types of sleep disorders that—'

'*Shut the fuck up!*' He surged to his feet, fists clenched. 'Wake her up!'

'No, wait—'

He moved so fast I didn't see it coming. It was little more than a backhand cuff, but it snapped my head to one side as if I'd been hit with a plank. I fell on to the debris littering the floor as Monk grabbed hold of Sophie.

'Come on! Wake up!'

Sophie moaned feebly, her body still limp. I lunged at him, grabbing hold of his arm as he drew it back to slap her. He thrust me away and I slammed into the rock.

But Monk made no further attempt to hit Sophie. He was staring at his fist as if he'd only just become aware of it. It was the one he'd struck against the rock, and as he looked at the blood on it the rage left him as quickly as it had arrived.

He lowered his arm as Sophie stirred.

'David . . .'

'I'm here.' There was blood in my mouth, and my jaw and teeth throbbed as I went to her. This time Monk didn't try to stop me.

Sophie rubbed her head, brow creased in pain. 'I don't feel so good,' she said, her voice slurred, and then she vomited.

I supported her until the spasm had passed. She gave something between a groan and a sob, shielding her eyes from the lantern light. 'My head . . . it really hurts.'

'Look at me, Sophie.'

'Hurts . . .'

'I know, but just look at me.'

I smoothed the hair back from her face. She squinted, blinking as she opened her eyes. Shock ran through me. While her left pupil was normal, the right was dilated and huge. *Oh, God.*

'What's wrong with her?' Monk demanded. He sounded suspicious, as though this were some sort of trick.

I took a deep breath as Sophie tried to huddle away from the light. *Keep calm. Don't lose it now.* 'I think it's a haematoma. '

'A what?'

'A haemorrhage. She's bleeding inside her skull. We need to get her to a hospital.'

'You think I'm fucking stupid?' Monk said, and seized hold of her arm.

'Don't touch her!' I snapped, shoving him away.

At least, I tried to: it was like pushing a side of meat. But he stopped, his eyes unblinking as they stared at me. There was the same stillness about him that I'd witnessed earlier, a sense of poised violence barely held in check.

'There's blood collecting inside her head,' I said, my voice unsteady. 'It could be from the car crash or before. But if the pressure isn't released . . .' *She'll die.* 'I have to get her out of here. Please.'

Monk's mouth twisted in frustration, his wheezing breaths growing even more ragged. 'You're a doctor. Can't you do something?'

'No, she needs surgery.'

'Fuck!' He slapped his hand against the wall. In the small chamber it echoed like a pistol shot. *'Fuck!'*

I ignored him. Sophie had slumped against me. 'Sophie? Come on, you have to stay awake.'

If she lapsed into unconsciousness down here I'd never be able to get her out. She stirred feebly. 'Don't want to . . .'

'Come on, I need you to sit up straight. We're getting out of here.'

Monk's hand thrust against my chest. 'No! She said she'd help me!'

'Does she look like she can help anybody?'

'She's staying here!'

'Then she's going to die!' I was shaking, but from anger now. 'All she's done is try to help you. Do you want more blood on your hands?'

'Shut UP!'

I saw his fist coming but I had no chance of avoiding it. I flinched as it whipped by my face, his coat sleeve skimming my cheek as he punched the rock by my head.

I didn't move. The only sound was Monk's ragged

wheezing. His breath stank in my face. Chest heaving, he dropped his arm and stepped back. Blood dripped from his hand. He'd struck the rock full on this time: it had to be broken.

But if it hurt he gave no sign. He looked at the swollen knuckles as though they didn't belong to him, then down at Sophie. For all his size, there was something pathetic about him. Beaten.

'She couldn't have helped anyway, could she?' he asked. 'It wouldn't have made any difference.'

I tried to think of a safe answer, then gave up. 'No.'

Monk lowered his head. When he raised it again the gargoyle face was unreadable.

'Let's get her out.'

I used one of the bottles of smelling salts to rouse Sophie. She moaned in protest, trying to move her head away. The ammonia was a temporary measure at best, but it wouldn't make her any worse. And I needed her as aware as possible.

We didn't have much time.

There was always a risk of haematoma after a head trauma. Some developed very quickly, others could take weeks, slowly swelling blood blisters inside the skull that put pressure on the brain. Sophie's must have been building up for days. Either it had been too small to be detected by the hospital scans or she'd discharged herself before anyone had picked it up.

Either way I should have realized. The signs had been staring me in the face, and I'd missed them. I'd put her slurred speech down to alcohol and fatigue, dismissed her headache as a hangover.

Now she could die because of me.

Sophie barely knew where she was. She could walk, but not without support. By the time Monk had helped me manhandle her from the chamber it was obvious we wouldn't be able to go back the way we had come, with its narrow tunnels and crawlways.

'Is there another way out?' I asked as she slumped against me.

In the torchlight Monk looked terrifying, but I was more frightened for Sophie now than of him. His breathing sounded worse than ever. 'There is, but . . .'

'What?'

'Doesn't matter,' he said, and set off down the passage.

The world shrank down to the rough rock above me and on either side, and Monk's broad shoulders in front. I'd brought the torch from the floor of the chamber. The beam was weak but at least it threw back the darkness enough to see where we were going. If I fell now I'd drag Sophie down with me.

I had my arm around her, taking as much of her weight as I could. She was weeping with pain, her voice weak and slurred as she begged me to let her lie down and sleep. When she started to flag too much I held the smelling salts under her nose, trying not to think what would happen if she collapsed down here. Or that both our lives depended on a killer we'd no reason to trust.

Away from the airless warmth of the chamber it was freezing. My teeth chattered from the cold, and Sophie was shivering beneath my arm. Water streamed along the uneven floor of the passage. I thought about the stories I'd heard of cavers drowning in flooded tunnels. There had been a lot of rain over the last few weeks, but I told myself that Monk knew what he was doing.

The walls of the passage opened out into a vaulted cavern, where a fine, cold haze filled the air with a mineral tang. In the confined space the sound of falling water was deafening. The light from the torch showed it pouring down the rock walls, shattering into cascades before tumbling into the turmoil of a pool. Nearly all of the cavern was flooded, but Monk picked his way along a bank of shale that skirted its edge. At the far side the rock was split by a narrow vertical fissure, just above the water level. My heart sank when he stopped by it.

'Through there.'

He had to raise his voice to be heard above the water. Supporting Sophie, I shone the torch into the fissure. If anything it narrowed even more the further in it went.

'Where does it go?'

'Comes out in a passage that goes to the surface.' I could hear the wet tear of Monk's breathing even over the splash of the water. In the low torchlight the misshapen bones of his face made him look like a walking corpse.

'Are you sure?'

'You wanted another way out. That's it.'

With that he turned and started back along the shale bank, sloshing through the edge of the water. 'You're not just going to leave us?' I yelled after him.

There was no response. The torch beam bobbed as he made his way back across the flooded cavern. The level had risen while we'd been standing there.

'David . . . wha's . . .'

Sophie was leaning heavily against me. I swallowed the fear that had risen in my throat. 'It's OK. Not much further.'

I'd no idea if that was true or not. But we'd no choice. Shining the torch ahead of us, I hugged her to me and edged sideways into the narrow gap. It disappeared into darkness above our heads, but there wasn't much more than eighteen inches clearance between the rock faces. I fought down a wave of claustrophobia as they seemed to squeeze tighter with each shuffling step.

My breath steamed in the weak light from the torch. Its pale beam showed where the fissure twisted out of sight further along. After a few yards I looked back but the flooded cavern was already lost from view. Not that we could have gone back now anyway. There was no room to turn round, and I couldn't back up with Sophie tucked under my arm. I was almost dragging her now, struggling to support her as I took one crablike step after another.

How much further? I told myself it couldn't be far. The fissure was growing narrower, the sides pressing in closer the deeper we went. I could feel it, solid and unyielding against my chest, restricting my breathing. *Don't think about it. Just keep moving.* But even that was becoming more difficult. The irregular rock underfoot threatened to trip me and the gap continued to narrow. There wasn't enough room for us both to get through, not while I was holding Sophie.

I willed myself to stay calm. 'Sophie, I've got to free my arm. I need you to stand by yourself for a few seconds.'

My voice echoed oddly, flattened by the rock. She didn't respond.

'Sophie? Come on, wake up!'

But Sophie didn't move. Now I'd stopped she was a dead weight against me, and it was growing harder to hold her upright. If not for the walls of the fissure holding her in place I doubt I could have. I groped one-handed for the bottle of smelling salts in my pocket, desperate not to drop either them or the torch. I opened the bottle with my teeth, my eyes watering from the reek of ammonia even though I held my breath, then struggled to reach around to hold it under Sophie's nose. *Come on. Please.*

There was no reaction. I tried for a little longer, then gave up. *OK, don't panic. Think.* The only option was for me to squeeze through the narrow section first and somehow pull her through after me. But if I let go of her and she collapsed . . .

There's no room for her to fall, and you can't stay here. Just do it! My arm was growing numb. I began trying to ease it from beneath her shoulders. *You can do it. Nice and easy.* My coat sleeve rasped on the rough rock but Sophie's weight pinned me in place. No matter how hard I tried I couldn't prise myself loose. I twisted round to get more leverage and felt the rock faces clamp around my upper body like a vice. For a second I couldn't move, then I wrenched myself back to my original position, skinning my knuckles in the process.

Oh, God! I closed my eyes, fighting for breath. There didn't seem to be enough air. Stars sparked in my vision. I tried to steady my breathing, realizing I was starting to hyperventilate. *For Christ's sake don't pass out!* Gradually, my heart slowed. I opened my eyes. Lit by the torch from below, the rock wall was inches from my face. I could see its granular texture, smell its damp, salty hardness. I moistened my dry lips. *Come on, think!* But I didn't have any options left. My arm felt completely dead. Sophie was unconscious, wedged against me more tightly than ever. I couldn't go any further, nor could I back out, not with her blocking the way.

We were trapped.

There was a glow off to one side. I looked over Sophie's head and saw a torch beam lighting the fissure behind us, throwing the irregularities of the rock into sharp relief. There was a slow scraping, accompanied by the rasp of laboured breathing.

Then Monk edged into view. He was jammed sideways into the narrow gap, mouth contorted as he forced himself towards us. It had been tight enough for me: I couldn't imagine what it must be like for him.

He didn't speak until he'd reached Sophie. Still holding the torch, a massive hand snaked out and gripped her shoulder.

'Got her . . .'

His voice was a strained gasp, but I felt most of her weight lift from me. I slid my arm from behind her, smearing more skin from my knuckles on the rock, and then I was free. I flexed my fingers, gritting my teeth as my arm blazed with returning circulation.

'Go,' Monk wheezed.

He kept Sophie upright while I squeezed between the rock faces. My coat snagged as they gripped tighter than ever, then I'd scraped through and the fissure widened. I sucked in air, giddy with relief as I shone the torch back on to Monk and Sophie.

His mouth was open in a rictus, his breathing agonized as the rock constricted his massive chest. But he said nothing as I reached back through the narrow section, grabbing a handful of Sophie's coat in one hand and protecting her head with the other.

The close walls of the fissure helped us now, holding her in place as Monk propped her up on one side while I pulled her through the narrow section from the other. Heaving her arm around my shoulders so her head was cradled against me, I took her weight and straightened. Then I shone the torch back on to Monk.

He'd worked his way even further in to help me with Sophie. Now he was wedged impossibly tightly into the gap, squashed between the rock. His mouth worked like a grounded fish as he fought for breath.

'Can you get back?' I panted. There was no way he could make it through any further.

It was hard to tell but I thought he grinned. 'Bulked out . . . since last time . . .'

It sounded painful for him to even talk. *Christ, he's not going to be able to get out of there.* 'Listen, I can—'

'Fuck off . . . Get her out.'

I hesitated, but only for a second. He'd survived

down here well enough without my help, and Sophie was my priority. I began half carrying, half dragging her away. I glanced back once, but could see only darkness. There was no sign of Monk or his torch.

He must have gone back, but I couldn't spare any thoughts for him. It was a little wider here but Sophie was a dead weight. It was all I could do to support her. Water was streaming down the uneven base of the fissure now, flowing over my boots and making it impossible to see where I was treading. I stumbled repeatedly, our coats scraping and snagging on the rock that still pressed in on us. I kept on, knowing that if we became trapped now we were on our own.

Then the walls suddenly opened out. Gasping for breath, I shone the torch around a low passage. It was only a little higher than my head but wide enough for us to stand side by side. If Monk was right, then this must be the way to the surface.

It sloped uphill at a steep angle. I started up but I was stooped under Sophie's weight, my legs leaden and shaking. I couldn't go any further, not without a rest. Lowering her to the floor, I knelt beside her and stroked the tangle of hair from her face.

'Sophie? Can you hear me?'

There was no response. I checked her pulse. It was too fast. When I checked her eyes the right one was more dilated than ever. It didn't change when I shone the torch into it.

I struggled to lift her again, but there was no strength in my limbs. I took a few faltering steps and almost fell. I lowered Sophie back to the ground. *This is hopeless.* I bowed my head, almost weeping. I'd no idea how far there was to go, but I couldn't carry her any further. If she was going to have any chance of surviving, there was only one thing I could do.

I had to leave her behind.

Don't waste time. Do it. I stripped off my coat, gently wadding the sleeves under her head and wrapping the rest around her body. The cold bit into me straight away, but I didn't care. I looked down at her, feeling my resolve weaken. *God, I can't do this.* But I didn't have a choice.

'I'm coming back, I promise,' I said, my voice shaking from the chill.

Then I turned away and left her in the darkness.

The passage began to climb more steeply. Before long I was having to use my hands to clamber upwards. The walls and roof closed in, until it was little more than a tunnel. The torch revealed nothing except a black hole surrounded by rock. It seemed endless. Exhaustion made me dizzy. My senses began playing tricks on me, so that I began to think I was heading downwards, crawling deeper underground instead of towards the surface.

Then something scratched my face. I jerked away, yelling out as something snagged my hair. I shone the torch at it and saw spiky branches. *Plants?* I thought, dumbly. I felt water dripping on to my face, but it was only when I noticed the cold wind on my cheek that I realized it was rain.

I was outside.

It was dark. In the torch beam I saw that the passage had emerged in a clump of gorse that clung to a sloping rock face. I had to crawl underneath the spiky, dripping branches, tugging myself free when they snagged my skin and clothes. I slithered the last few yards and splashed feet first into a freezing stream.

Shivering in the cold, I shone the torch around as I climbed out. The fog had cleared but rain fell in a sullen, steady downpour. I was on the moor, at the foot of a small tor. It was overgrown with gorse that completely hid the cave mouth. There was light on the horizon, but I'd no idea if it marked dawn or dusk, or even where I was. I tried to force my numbed mind to work. *Which way? Come on, decide!*

A faint noise came to me on the wind. I tilted my head, trying to catch which direction it was coming from. It faded, and for a moment I was afraid I was imagining it. Then I heard it again, stronger this time.

The distant whickering of a helicopter.

I clambered up the side of the tor, fatigue and cold forgotten as I waved the torch over my head.

'*HERE! OVER HERE!*'

I shouted myself hoarse, oblivious of the gorse tearing at me as I hauled myself on to the crest of the tor. I could see the helicopter's running lights now, bright specks of colour perhaps half a mile away. For an awful few seconds I thought it was going to fly straight by. Then it banked and came towards me. As its lights grew in size I could make out the police markings on its side, and when I saw that the last of my strength went. My legs gave way and I slumped on to the cold stone, willing the approaching machine to fly faster.

28

I seem to have spent an disproportionate amount of my life in hospitals. I've become too familiar with the slow tick of time passed on hard plastic chairs, the anxiety and frustration.

The waiting.

The past twenty-four hours seemed unreal, like a bad dream I couldn't shake off. That was partly due to the hypothermia I'd developed, not severe but bad enough to leave me still feeling chilled and slightly detached, as though I were watching events happening to someone else. The pale light in the sky I'd seen when I'd emerged from the cave had been morning. It felt like I'd been underground for days, but it was only hours since the car crash.

In the police helicopter I'd been wrapped in a blanket and given chocolate and hot tea from the pilot's Thermos. I'd been shivering uncontrollably by then, but I wouldn't let them take me to hospital. I was frantic to go straight back down for Sophie, but there was no question of that. When the rescue team arrived there was a bad moment when they couldn't find the cave. It had seemed like an age until a yell from deep in the thicket of gorse announced that the entrance had been located.

The next hour was one of the longest of my life. Sitting in the cramped plastic and leather cabin of the helicopter, woozy from exhaustion and nauseated by the smell of aviation fuel, I was free to replay all that had happened. In the cold dawn light everything I'd done, every decision I'd made, now seemed wrong.

Sophie was alive but unconscious when they brought her out. By then the gorse bushes immediately around the cave entrance had been hacked away, enough for the stretcher to be carried to the waiting air ambulance. I went with her, knowing better than to ask the paramedics questions they couldn't answer. When the helicopter landed at the hospital a team of nurses and doctors rushed her away, crouching beneath the whirling rotors.

I was taken more sedately to Emergency, where I was given a robe and put on an IV drip. My cuts and abrasions were cleaned, the worst of them dressed with antiseptic-smelling gauze. I told my story again and again, to a succession of first uniformed and then

CID officers. Finally, after I was moved to a curtained cubicle, I was left alone. I can't remember ever feeling so tired. I was sick with worry for Sophie, but none of the police officers who'd questioned me seemed to know anything. Intending only to rest for a moment, I put my head back and was instantly asleep.

The whisk of the curtains being opened woke me. I sat up, disorientated and aching all over as Naysmith stepped into the cubicle.

The tall SIO's throat was mottled with fresh razor burn and his eyes were red and lined with fatigue, but he seemed tense and alert.

'How's Sophie?' I asked before he could speak.

'Still in surgery. There's a build-up of blood on her brain, so they need to release it. Other than that, I can't tell you.'

Even though I'd expected it the news hit me hard. There were different types of haematoma, but recovery – and survival – depended on how quickly surgery was carried out. *This is your fault. You should have realized sooner.*

Naysmith fished something wrapped in plastic out of his pocket. 'You might need this,' he said, setting my muddy wallet on the bedside trolley. 'We found it a couple of hours ago. We were just about to send a search team down the mine when the helicopter picked you up.'

'What about Miller and Cross?'

If he blamed me for abandoning them he didn't show it. He pulled up a chair and sat down. 'Miller's got a fractured skull, busted ribs and some internal bruising. He's unconscious but stable. Cross has a broken jaw and concussion. She was already conscious when the back-up arrived, so she could tell them what happened. Sort of.'

I was relieved. It could have been a lot worse, although I wasn't sure the injured police officers would agree. 'And Monk?'

'Nothing yet. We're sending teams down and we've got police guarding both entrances. But there could be others we don't know about. Cutter's Wheal Mine's been sealed up for years, and no one had any idea there were any caves connected to it. From what we've seen it's a big system, almost as big as Bakers Pit at Buckfastleigh. If Monk's still down there we'll find him eventually, but it's going to take time.'

And if he isn't he could be anywhere by now. Naysmith crossed his legs, a man getting down to business.

'So, do you want to tell me what happened?'

I knew he'd have been briefed already, but I went through my story again. He listened without comment, even when I told him about Monk's claim that he'd been framed by a police officer. When I finished he heaved a long sigh.

'Well, he was telling the truth about Wainwright, at

400

least. He broke his neck falling downstairs. The post-mortem found carpet burns from the stair carpet and there were patches of his blood and hair on the banister. Either he took a tumble in the dark or missed his footing from the shock of seeing Monk. Can't say I'd blame him.' He paused, his face expressionless. 'How much of the rest of it did you believe?'

It was hard to say any more. The whole of the previous night had begun to take on a surreal quality. I made an effort to focus.

'I believe what he said about the blackouts. And about his relationship with Angela Carson. He was too ill to pretend, and the seizure or whatever it was I saw him have, that was real.'

'You really think he might have killed her during one?'

'From what I saw I'd say it could have happened like that.'

'What about the other girls?'

'I don't know. I suppose it's possible he killed them all during blackouts, but I think that's stretching it. He'd have to have disposed of their bodies as well, which doesn't seem likely. He genuinely doesn't seem able to remember anything about them, but that isn't what bothers him.'

'Monk's a callous bastard. That's not new.'

'No, I mean he isn't interested in clearing his name or even having his sentence reduced. That's what makes me think he's telling the truth. The only reason he escaped was because he's desperate to convince himself he didn't kill Angela Carson.'

'He was found in a locked flat with her body, blood on his hands and her face pulped in. I don't think there's much doubt, do you?'

'Not about that, no. But for the past eight years he's had to live with knowing he killed the only person he's ever been close to, and he can't even remember doing it. He's not the most stable of personalities anyway. Can you blame him for clutching at straws?'

Naysmith was silent for a moment. 'What about this story about him being framed?'

Now we're coming to it. I sighed. Hearing Monk tell it in the caves was one thing; discussing it in the cold light of day was something else entirely. It would have been easier to dismiss it as the rambling of a deranged mind, or the invention of a guilty one.

The problem was I couldn't believe it was either.

'I don't think he was making it up,' I said.

'That doesn't mean Darren Walker wasn't. There's no record of any DI called Jones, either now or eight years ago. Walker could have been spinning him a line, trying to fob him off. Christ, if I was cornered by Monk I'd probably do the same.'

'Why would Walker spread a story like that in the first place?'

'A petty thief like him would be out of his depth

with the hardcases in Belmarsh. He wouldn't be the first to make something up to bolster his reputation.'

'Monk believed him. And from what he told me I don't think Walker would have been in any condition to lie.' *Not after what I did to him.*

'There's still nothing to corroborate any of this,' Naysmith said irritably, as though he'd been arguing the point with himself. 'We've only Monk's word to go on, since he conveniently beat Darren Walker to death. And you'll have to forgive me if I don't put much faith in that, or believe that a police officer planted evidence on the say-so of a lowlife like Walker. I checked his records. He was suspected of any number of thefts and burglaries but he had more lives than a bloody cat. Always managed to slip off, until last year. And why wait till then before he started mouthing off?'

I didn't know. I couldn't quite believe myself that I was defending Monk. But I'd had time to think as I lay on the hospital trolley. I might not like the new picture that was emerging, but I couldn't ignore it.

'Perhaps because he *had* been caught. You said yourself Walker would be out of his depth somewhere like Belmarsh. People can do anything when they're scared.'

'Doesn't necessarily follow,' Naysmith said. 'Where would this phantom DI have got anything belonging to the Bennett twins from anyway? There's no way he could have lifted evidence from a high-profile murder investigation without it being noticed. Especially not if it turned up again at Monk's caravan.'

'Unless he didn't get it from the evidence locker.'

The words lay heavily in the small cubicle. Naysmith looked at me for a long while, his eyes lidded. 'You know what you're saying, don't you?'

'Are you telling me it hasn't occurred to you as well?'

He didn't answer. He didn't have to. We'd skirted around it so far, but I knew the same question would be preying on his mind as on mine.

If Monk didn't kill the other three girls, who did?

Naysmith kneaded the bridge of his nose. 'We're going to want to talk to you again. What are your plans when you're discharged? Will you be going back to London?'

I hadn't given it much thought. 'Not yet. I'll probably pick up my things from Sophie's and book into—'

The curtain was suddenly swept aside as Simms stepped into the cubicle. With his crisply braided uniform and peaked cap, the ACC looked ridiculously smart in the drab hospital setting. But the wax-like features were flushed a deep crimson, and his mouth was set in a thin line.

Naysmith warily got to his feet. 'Sir. I didn't know you were—'

Simms didn't look at him. He clenched his black

leather gloves so tightly in his fist it looked like he was choking them.

'I'd like to speak to Dr Hunter. Alone.'

'He's already been interviewed. I can—'

'That'll be all, Detective Chief Superintendent.'

Naysmith looked furious but managed to restrain himself. He gave me the barest nod before brushing out. The distant sounds of the hospital only heightened the silence inside the cubicle. Simms glared at me.

'What the *hell* do you think you're trying to do?'

I wasn't in the mood for another inquisition. I felt drugged with fatigue and worry and was very conscious of lying propped up in the ridiculous hospital gown.

'I *was* trying to sleep.'

The pale eyes were cold and hostile. 'Don't think you're going to come out of this with any credit, Dr Hunter, because I can assure you that you won't.'

'What are you talking about?'

'I'm talking about these . . . these wild allegations you're making! That Jerome Monk is innocent, that a police officer fabricated evidence against him. You can't seriously think anyone will *believe* that?'

'They aren't my allegations. And I didn't say—'

'In the past week Monk has caused the death of a helpless man and almost killed two police officers. Or have you forgotten that?'

I felt a stab of guilt. 'There was nothing I could—'

'A former police consultant is fighting for her life because of him, yet you still seem intent on exonerating a convicted rapist and murderer. It's no secret that people around you have a habit of getting hurt, Dr Hunter, but I never expected this sort of recklessness, even from you!'

I must have pushed myself upright in the bed but I couldn't recall doing it. 'I'm not trying to exonerate anyone. I'm just saying what happened.'

'Oh, yes, this "fit" that Monk conveniently threw in front of you. I supposed it never occurred to you that he might be doing it deliberately? Or that he'd already fooled the prison doctors into believing he was having a heart attack?'

'What I saw wasn't faked. And he didn't fake the cardiac symptoms either: he induced them. There's a difference.'

'You'll have to forgive me if I don't share your credulity, Dr Hunter. It's obvious Monk manipulated you. He spoon-fed you this . . . this cock and bull story and then let you go, hoping you'd do exactly this!' He slapped the gloves against his thigh. 'Have you any idea of the *damage* this could do?'

'To your reputation, you mean?'

I regretted losing my temper straight away, but the words were out. Simms' pale eyes bulged. The hand clutching the gloves twitched, and for a second I thought he might actually strike me. But when he spoke his voice was controlled.

'I apologize, Dr Hunter. Perhaps I should have waited to see you. You're obviously overwrought.' He pulled on his gloves as he spoke, working his fingers into the tight leather. 'I hope you'll give some thought to what I've said. We're on the same side, and it'd be a shame for a professional disagreement to get out of hand. People are quick to talk, and I know police consultancy work is hard to come by.'

His face was completely expressionless as he stared down at me. Using the sleeve of his coat, as though even his gloves weren't proof against contamination, he swept aside the curtain and went out.

I watched it swaying behind him as his footsteps receded into the background hubbub. *What the hell was that supposed to mean?* I was too tired to care very much.

But I knew a threat when I heard one.

29

It was late afternoon before I was discharged. I'd managed to sleep after Simms left, but only fitfully, slipping in and out of wakefulness in the small cubicle. Still, I felt better for it, more alert if nothing else. At some point my clothes had reappeared, unwashed but dried and neatly folded in a plastic bag. The mud and bloodstains were proof that the previous night had been real, much as I might wish otherwise.

No one could tell me anything about Sophie, but I persuaded one of the nurses to check. She reported that she was out of surgery but still critical. I told myself that was only to be expected after an emergency craniotomy: the doctors would have had to remove a flap of bone from her skull to drain the build-up of blood.

But the news did nothing to lift my spirits. I dressed and sat fretting in the cubicle until a junior doctor finally told me I could go.

'Where's the ICU?' I asked her.

The intensive care unit was quieter and less bustling than Emergency, with an air of strained urgency about it. The desk nurse wouldn't let me in to see Sophie, but given the state of my torn and dirty clothes I probably wouldn't have either. Feeling a sense of déjà vu, I explained that I only wanted to find out how she was. It made no difference: the nurse was adamant she could only give out information to next of kin.

'If you told me you were her husband or fiancé, perhaps . . . ?' she added pointedly. It was a deliberate opening, but I hesitated.

'Dr Hunter!'

The voice was Sophie's. I turned, ridiculously hoping to see her miraculously recovered. But it was another woman who was walking down the corridor towards me. Her face was blotched from crying, so that it took me a moment to recognize Sophie's sister.

'What are you doing here?' she demanded, without giving me a chance to speak. She was quivering with emotion, her hands white-knuckled on the wadded-up tissue she clenched.

'I wanted to find out how Sophie is—'

'How she *is*? My sister's lying in intensive care!

They cut open her *skull*, that's how she is!' Her face crumpled. 'There could be brain damage, or . . . or . . .'

'I'm sorry—'

'*Sorry*? Don't you *dare*! You said you'd look after her! I wanted her to come home with me, where she'd have been safe. Instead she's . . . she's . . .' She turned on the desk nurse. 'I don't want this man going near my sister! If he comes back, don't let him in!'

She spun round and hurried back down the corridor. The nurse looked embarrassed.

'Sorry, but she's next of kin . . .'

I nodded. There was nothing else I could do there. The heavy doors to the ICU swung shut behind me with finality as I headed back to the main wards.

There was one more person I had to see.

I was batted between wards before I finally found where Cross had been taken. At first I thought the policewoman was asleep. She had her eyes shut, and a cowardly part of me was relieved. But as I approached her bed she opened them and looked directly at me.

She looked a mess. The blonde hair was plastered darkly against her head. Her face was even more shockingly bruised and swollen than Sophie's had been, and a painful-looking assembly of wire and screws clamped her jaw shut.

Now I was there, I didn't know what to say. We

410

just looked at each other for a moment, then she reached for something on the bedside table. It was a writing pad: she wrote briefly and then turned it round for me to see.

Looks wrse than it is. Morphine great.

I wouldn't have thought I could laugh, but I did. 'I'm glad to hear it.'

More slow scribbling, then the pad was turned round again. *Sophie???*

I chose my words. 'Out of surgery. She's in intensive care.'

The pen scratched once more. *Miller conscious. Nrses say making bad jkes.*

I smiled. It was the first good news I'd had in what seemed an age. 'That's great.' I took a deep breath. 'Look, I . . .'

But she'd started writing again. It was more laborious this time as she began to tire. When she'd finished she tore out the sheet from the notepad and folded it in half. Her eyelids were already starting to droop as she held it out for me. I think she was asleep again before it left her hand.

I waited until I was in the corridor before I opened it. Cross had written just a short message: *U did right thing.*

My eyes blurred when I read that. I had to pause for a while before I tucked it away. I desperately wanted to get out of the hospital, to breathe fresh air and clear my head, but that would have to wait.

There was something else I needed to do first.

My car was still at Sophie's with the rest of my things. I could have phoned for a cab, but I decided to pick one up outside. The walk would do me good, and I didn't want to stay at the hospital any longer than I had to.

A receptionist directed me to the nearest taxi rank, but I hadn't gone far from the entrance before a car pulled up alongside. I looked round as its window was wound down.

It was Terry.

'Thought I might find you here,' he said. I carried on walking. 'David! Jesus, hang on a minute, will you?'

The car pulled forward until it was alongside again.

'Look, I only want to talk. I heard what happened last night. How's Sophie?'

Reluctantly, I stopped. No matter what I thought about him, Terry had once had a relationship with her. Feelings don't stop just because it's over.

'She's in intensive care. I don't know any more than that.'

'Christ.' His face had paled. 'I know I'm the last person she'd want to see. But she's going to be all right?'

'I don't know.'

He looked stunned.

'Where are you going?' he asked, subdued.

'I need to collect my things from Sophie's.'

He leaned over and opened the passenger door. 'Come on. I'll give you a lift.'

I didn't want to spend any more time in Terry's company, but talk of Sophie made my anger against him seem unimportant. The past was the past. Life was too short to bear grudges. Besides, I was so tired I could hardly stand.

I got in.

Neither of us spoke for the first few miles. It was only as the city and suburbs gave way to open countryside that he broke the silence.

'Do you want to talk about it?'

'No.'

He fell quiet again. I stared out of the window as the moor began to swallow us up. The car heater was on, and the warmth and drone of the engine began to take effect. I felt myself start to drift off.

'At least we know now who attacked Sophie the other day,' he said.

I sighed: Terry never could take no for an answer. 'I still don't think that was Monk.'

'What, even after this?'

'He admitted going to her house but she was already in hospital by then,' I told him. 'I thought an animal had got in when I took her home, because he was using soil from a fox den to mask his scent. It was hard to miss. If he'd been there before, when I found her in the bathroom, I'd have noticed.'

'Fox piss? Crafty bastard.' Terry sounded almost admiring. 'There's lots of rumours flying around. Talk that he was having a relationship with Angela Carson. That he might not have meant to kill her.'

I rubbed my eyes. 'It's possible.'

'You're not serious?'

I didn't feel like talking but I couldn't blame Terry for wanting to know. And there didn't seem any reason not to tell him. 'Before I left the hospital I spoke to a neurologist. He told me about a condition called frontal lobe syndrome. It happens sometimes when the front of the brain is damaged.'

'So?'

'That dent Monk has in his skull?' I tapped my own forehead. 'It was caused by a bad forceps delivery. Monk's mother died giving birth and I think his frontal lobe was damaged at the same time. That can cause violent and unpredictable behaviour and difficulty remembering things. Very occasionally it causes what are known as gelastic seizures, where people laugh or scream, and lash out at things that aren't there. It's a type of epilepsy, but because it tends to happen during sleep it's often undiagnosed. Usually it's put down to night terrors. Or someone "kicking off", like the prison guards said Monk did.'

Terry shrugged. 'Big deal, so he's got this frontal lobe thing. That doesn't excuse what he's done.'

'Not all of it, no. But it's starting to look as though he didn't rape and murder Angela Carson. They were in a relationship, and he killed her during a seizure after they'd had sex. If she'd tried to restrain him it would only have made things worse, and with someone as strong as Monk it wouldn't have made much difference if it was intentional or not.'

Terry gave an incredulous laugh. 'Oh, come *on*! Even you can't expect anyone's going to believe that!'

I wasn't surprised Terry was sceptical. Even now I wasn't sure how much of what Monk had told me could be believed. He was still a violent, dangerous man, and the memory of the car crash and the nightmare journey through the cave would haunt me for a long time.

But the picture wasn't as simple as everyone had assumed. And neither were Monk's actions. Simms might argue that the convict had his own motives for letting us go, but I remembered how he'd squeezed himself into the fissure to help me with Sophie, when he could have left us both to die down there.

That wasn't the act of a conscienceless killer.

'I think we looked at Monk and saw what we wanted to see,' I said. 'Everyone thought he was a monster because he raped a deaf girl and beat her to death. Take that out of the equation and it changes everything. Like whether he really murdered Tina Williams and the Bennett twins.'

'He *confessed*, for Christ's sake!'

'He was punishing himself.' I remembered the deadness – and pain – in Monk's eyes. Whatever revulsion society felt towards him, it was nothing compared to what he felt for himself. 'He'd killed Angela Carson during one seizure; for all he knew he might have killed the others as well. But I really don't think he cared by then.'

Terry snorted. 'If you believe that, then Monk wasn't the only one who got a knock on the head.'

I was too tired to argue. 'It doesn't matter what I believe. It's a physiological condition, not a mental illness. That's why the psychiatrists who examined him didn't pick up on it. But it'll be different now they'll know what to look for.'

'You're serious, aren't you?' Terry gnawed his lip. 'So if he claims he didn't kill the other girls, who did?'

I shrugged, fighting a wave of fatigue. 'Have you ever heard of a DI called Jones?'

Terry braked as the car in front slowed. 'What's this prick doing?' he muttered. 'Jones? Don't think so. Why?'

That was something else I'd had time to think about. If Monk – and Walker – were telling the truth, then the policeman who'd planted the dead girls' belongings at the caravan was an obvious suspect. Except that, according to Naysmith, Jones didn't exist.

But I'd said enough. 'It doesn't matter. Just something Monk said.'

Terry glanced at me. 'You look done in. We'll be another half-hour yet. Why don't you get your head down?'

I was already putting my head back and closing my eyes. Jumbled images flashed through my mind: the cave, the car crash, the way the shadows had filled the indentation in Monk's skull. I saw the mangled body of Tina Williams, clogged with oozing mud, and heard Wainwright's booming laugh. I felt the scrape of a spade cutting through wet peat, and then the car went over a bump and I woke up.

'Back with us?' Terry asked.

I rubbed my eyes. 'Sorry.'

'No worries. We're just about there. '

I looked out of the window and saw we were almost in Padbury. The day had turned while I'd slept, the light thickening to dusk. It felt like I'd spent all my time lately in darkness. After this I promised myself a holiday. A proper one this time, somewhere hot and sunny. Then I remembered Sophie lying in hospital, and any thoughts of going away vanished.

Terry pulled up at the bottom of the garden, behind where my car was parked. He stared up at the house, leaving the engine running. 'Well, here we are. Do you want me to stick around?'

'No, I don't plan on staying.' I paused, my hand on the door handle. 'What about you? What are you going to do now?'

A shadow crossed his face. 'Good question. Take my lumps from Simms and then . . . I'll see. Try to get my act together, I suppose.'

'Good luck.'

'Thanks.' He looked through the windscreen. 'So. Are we OK, then. Me and you?'

It occurred to me that I probably wouldn't see Terry again after this. Although I wasn't exactly sorry, it meant another chapter of my life was ending. There was no need for it to be on a bad note.

You have to bury the past sooner or later.

I nodded. He held out his hand. I only hesitated a moment before I shook it. 'Look after yourself, David. I hope Sophie's all right.'

There was nothing more to say. I climbed awkwardly out of the car and watched as Terry pulled away, his car's tail lights disappearing down the lane. The wind was getting up, and the sound of the engine was quickly lost, leaving only the rustle and sway of the trees.

I massaged my back. Everything ached, and my muscles had stiffened up on the journey. Rousing myself, I started up the path. The house was in darkness. The curtains were drawn, as we'd left them when we rushed out, giving it a closed, untenanted look. I was only going to collect my bag and then leave. I didn't much feel like driving anywhere, but I wasn't comfortable with the idea of staying here on my own. Even though Sophie wouldn't mind, it wouldn't have felt right.

I got as far as the front door before I realized I didn't have a key. I tried it anyway, but it was locked: either Miller or Cross would have seen to that the night before. I slumped against the door, feeling totally defeated. Then I remembered the spare Sophie kept hidden in the kiln. She'd had a new lock fitted but I hoped she'd have replaced the hidden key as well. *Please let it be there.*

The dilapidated brick tower loomed ahead of me as I crossed the overgrown path, its scaffolding standing out against the darkening sky like a gallows. The unlocked door creaked as I pushed it open and felt for the light switch. Nothing happened. I flicked it a few times, but the bulb must have blown. *Great.* There was a torch in my glove compartment, but of course the car keys were inside the house: I'd left them there in the rush the night before.

Pushing back the door as far as it would go, I went into the kiln. In the dying light it was like stepping into a tomb. The loose brick where Sophie had hidden the spare key was near the scaffolded central chimney. The brick dust and smell of damp plaster tickled the back of my throat as I walked across. There was another scent mingled with them, sharp and familiar, but I'd only just noticed it when something crunched under my boots. As my eyes adjusted I saw that the floor was littered with broken pottery. My sluggish brain was still trying to process that when I recognized the out-of-place smell.

Aftershave.

I stopped dead, the hairs on the back of my neck prickling. I turned round. The dim twilight from the doorway didn't reach far into the kiln. The shadows were impenetrable. I stared at where they seemed to coalesce. There was a rustle of movement.

'Is that you, Dr Hunter?' Roper said.

30

Roper peered into the gloom, trying to make me out. In the kiln's dark interior he couldn't see me any better than I could him.

'Glad you're none the worse after last night,' he said. 'Lucky escape you had, by all accounts.'

My heart was still thumping as I tried to unscramble my thoughts. 'What are you doing here?'

I heard rather than saw him shrug. 'Oh, I just came to check on things. Miss Keller really should have a lock fitted. Unless she wants people to be able to walk in here, of course.'

The notion seemed to amuse him.

'I didn't see your car,' I said.

'I left it in a lay-by further up the road. Thought the walk would do me good.'

And prevent anyone from seeing he was here. I was

starting to think more clearly now. Starting to think that Darren Walker could have been telling the truth about the police officer at Monk's caravan. DI Jones might not exist, but that didn't prove anything.

Whoever he was, he'd hardly have given his real name.

I tried to sound unconcerned, gauging my chances of getting past Roper to the door. 'Did Simms send you?'

'The ACC's got enough on his plate as it is at the moment. No, this was just to satisfy my curiosity, you might say.' There was a click and the lamp on the workbench came on. It had been knocked on its side; Roper stood it upright, tutting as he looked round. 'Somebody made a mess, didn't they?'

The light revealed a scene of devastation. Sophie's bowls and dishes had been swept from the shelves to break on the floor. Even the heavy electric kiln had been pushed on to its side, its door hanging open.

'Looks to me like someone was searching for something, wouldn't you say?' Roper was smiling but his eyes were sharp and appraising. 'Mind telling me what you're doing here yourself, Dr Hunter?'

'I've come to collect my car.'

'Funny place for a garage.'

'My bag's in the house. Sophie keeps a spare key in here.'

'Does she, indeed?' He scanned the kiln. 'Good at

hiding things, Miss Keller. But then a former BIA like her should be. Comes from knowing where to find them, I expect.'

I lost patience. There was no point playing games. 'Did you find what you were looking for?'

'Me?' Roper seemed genuinely shocked. 'I think we're getting our wires crossed, Dr Hunter. I didn't do this.'

He sounded offended. I wasn't entirely convinced, but I felt my suspicions begin to recede. 'Then who did?'

'Well, now, that's the question, isn't it?' Roper considered the wreckage, absently scratching his stomach. 'How well do you know Miss Keller?'

'Why?'

'Because I'm trying to decide if you're involved in this.'

There was a sudden edge to his voice, and my last doubts about him disappeared. I'd never really taken Roper seriously before. He'd always seemed like an appendage of Simms, promoted for loyalty rather than ability. Looking at him now I began to wonder if there was more to him than that.

Perhaps Sophie wasn't the only one good at hiding things.

'Until this I hadn't seen her in eight years,' I said carefully.

'You sleeping with her?'

I bit back the urge to tell him to mind his own business. 'No.'

He gave a grunt of satisfaction. 'Tell me, Dr Hunter, doesn't the timing of all this strike you as a bit odd? Terry Connors crops up out of the blue to warn you you're at risk from Monk. Asking if you've heard from any of the old search team. Then Miss Keller – or Miss Trask as she's started calling herself – calls you asking for help. She turns up unconscious and her house is trashed. Except that the burglar didn't bother to take anything.'

'She said some money and jewellery were missing.'

He waved that away. 'You don't believe that any more than I do. And I'm not convinced by her "amnesia" either. Someone breaks into her house and knocks her out, and she can't remember anything about it? Please.'

'That can happen.'

'I'm sure it can, but she didn't seem too worried about it. So why did she lie? Who was she protecting? Herself or somebody else?'

I opened my mouth to object, but he was only saying what I'd thought myself. I just hadn't wanted to accept it. 'What's your point?'

'My point is I don't believe in coincidences.' He prodded a piece of clay with his foot. 'If you've something valuable you want to hide there's two ways to go about it. One is to put it somewhere really safe, where no one will ever be able to find it. The trouble is if you can think of it, chances are somebody else will as well. The other way is to put it somewhere no one will ever think to look. Somewhere so obvious they won't even realize it *is* a hiding place. Preferably where you can see it every day.'

I stared at the workbench where Sophie had built up the mound of clay scraps. *Just a bad habit.* I remembered how she'd come in here as soon as we'd got back from hospital, claiming she was looking for the spare key. How she'd run her hand across it, as though to reassure herself. Right out in the open but too big to move.

No wonder she hadn't wanted to go to a safe house.

'I think she was hiding something in a ball of dried clay,' I said. Sophie hadn't even bothered to put a lock on the kiln door, practically announcing that there was nothing of value inside.

Roper smiled. 'I'm less interested in where it was hidden than in what it was. All this started when Jerome Monk escaped, so there has to be a connection. And whatever was here, it was important enough for Miss Keller to risk facing him rather than leave it untended.'

And important enough for someone to knock her unconscious and leave her for dead while they searched the house. My mind was whirring now, the last cobwebs of fatigue dropping away.

'Terry Connors tried to persuade me to take Sophie away yesterday afternoon,' I said. 'That's why he wanted to see me.'

'Did he now? Then perhaps Monk did him a favour. Got her out of the way long enough for him to find what he was looking for.' Roper considered the debris littering the floor, a smile playing round his mouth. 'For someone who's suspended he seems to be taking an unhealthy interest in this case. I think it's time we had a serious talk with DS Connors.'

A cold feeling was forming in the pit of my stomach. I'd been too tired to wonder why Terry was waiting for me outside the hospital. I'd put his questions down to curiosity, but that wasn't what struck me now. He'd claimed he didn't know where Sophie lived, yet I hadn't told him how to get here.

He'd already known the way.

'I've just seen him,' I said. 'He gave me a lift.'

Roper's smile vanished. 'Connors was *here*?'

'He dropped me off and then went.'

'Shit!' Roper reached in his pocket for his phone. 'We need to go. I should—'

But before he could finish a shadow stepped through the doorway behind him. There was a sickening *thunk* of metal on bone as something swung against the back of his head, and Roper pitched face first on to the ground.

Breathing heavily, Terry stood over him with a

short length of scaffold gripped in his hands. His mouth stretched into a snarl as he looked down.

'Bastard had that coming for a long time.'

It had happened so quickly there was no time to react. I stood there, stunned by Terry's appearance as much as by the sudden violence. There was a wildness about him, a look of fevered desperation. His once-neat hair had been snagged by branches, and his shoes and trouser bottoms were splashed with mud. Panting, he wiped his mouth on his sleeve as he lifted his gaze to me.

'Jesus, David. Why couldn't you just have got your things and left?'

My mind was starting to function again. I hadn't heard a car engine: Terry must have parked and doubled back across the fields. Perhaps when he saw Roper's car in the lay-by. The policeman lay where he'd fallen. Dark blood glistened on his head, nearly black in the lamplight. I couldn't see if he was breathing or not.

Terry raised the pole threateningly as I started towards them. 'Don't try it!'

I stopped, keeping out of reach. 'Put the pole down. Just think what you're doing.'

'You don't think I have? Christ, you think I *want* this?' A spasm of anguish crossed his face. He lashed out and kicked a piece of clay. It ricocheted off the scaffolding that propped up the curving wall of the kiln and skittered off into darkness. 'You want to blame somebody, blame Keller! This is her fault!'

I thought about what Roper had said. About the ball of clay, now in fragments on the floor. 'What was she hiding that was so important?'

At first it seemed he wasn't going to answer. He shook his head, but his grip on the scaffolding pole seemed to loosen.

'Zoe Bennett's diary.'

It took me a moment, but then I began to understand. Zoe, the extrovert of the two Bennett twins, who, unlike her sister, preferred partying to studying. And Terry, a womanizer still smarting after being forced to transfer from the Met in disgrace. What better way to salve his ego than with a pretty, vivacious seventeen-year-old with aspirations to be a model?

'Your name was in it,' I said.

His shoulders slumped. The scaffolding pole had sunk lower, almost forgotten.

'I'd been seeing her for a couple of months. The photos don't do her justice; she was a real looker. Trouble was she knew it. She'd got it all worked out: how she was going to go to London, sign up with a big model agency. She was impressed because I'd been with the Met, could tell her stories about Soho and all the rest.'

He grinned at the recollection, but it quickly faded. His mouth twisted.

'Then I saw her with someone else. Some cocky young bastard in his twenties, flash car. You know the sort. We had a row. Things got out of hand. I hit her and she went mental. Screaming at me, saying she'd see to it I got sacked, that she'd say I raped her. We were in my car and I was scared people would hear. I just wanted to shut her up, so I got hold of her throat, and . . . and it was just so fucking *quick*. One minute she was struggling, and the next . . .'

I looked down at Roper, dead or unconscious at his feet. 'Jesus, Terry . . .'

'I *know*! You think I don't *know*?' He'd lowered the scaffolding pole altogether, but still gripped it in one hand. He ran the other through his hair, his face stricken. 'I'd got a lock-up, so I hid her body in there. I thought . . . I thought if I didn't do anything it'd be treated like just another teenage runaway. Zoe was always saying how she was going to go to London.'

'She was *seventeen*!'

'Oh, don't start,' he snapped, with a flash of his old temper. 'What was I going to do? Give myself up? That wouldn't bring her back! I'd got Debs and the kids to think about. What was the point in spoiling their lives?'

I felt sickened. 'Did you kill her sister as well?'

Terry seemed to flinch. He no longer looked at me, but there was something like shame in his eyes. 'Lindsey found Zoe's diary,' he said dully. 'There was my phone number, details of how often we'd met. What we'd done. She didn't tell anyone because she didn't want to hurt Zoe's reputation. She thought because I was a police officer I might be able to help find her.'

Christ. So she'd gifted Terry with the only piece of evidence that could implicate him in her sister's death. And, in the process, made herself the only witness.

'Don't look at me like that!' Terry yelled. 'I *panicked*, all right? If that had come out it would have been all over! I couldn't afford to be questioned. And she looked so much like Zoe, just seeing her was like she was accusing me!'

'And Tina Williams? Why did . . .' I broke off as I realized. *Another teenager, dark-haired and pretty.* 'She was just a decoy, wasn't she? So it'd look like a serial killer and take attention off the twins.'

A strange look came over Terry's face, as though he was confronting a part of himself he barely recognized. He shrugged, but he still wouldn't look me in the eye.

'Something like that.'

The shock had gone now, replaced by anger and disgust. 'I *saw* her, Terry! I saw what you did! For Christ's sake, you *stamped* on her face!'

'She was already dead!' he yelled. 'I lost it, all

430

right? Jesus, you think I wanted to do it? Any of it? You think I *enjoyed* it?'

It doesn't matter: they're still dead. But it explained a lot of things. Like Terry's behaviour during the search, especially when Monk inexplicably offered to take us to the graves. Pirie had been closer to the truth than we'd realized when he'd said that Tina Williams' horrific injuries might be an expression of her murderer's shame, an attempt to erase his own guilt. That hadn't made sense when we'd thought Monk was the killer, but it did now.

No wonder Terry's life had fallen apart.

Through the doorway behind him I saw it was growing darker outside. The lamp cast a cocoon of brightness, beyond which the kiln's gloom seemed to deepen. I'd no idea how long I'd been there, but I couldn't expect any help. Roper still hadn't moved, and from what he'd said no one knew where he was. Somehow I had to get past Terry, although I'd no idea how. There was nothing nearby to use as a weapon except broken pottery.

'Was DI Jones the best name you could come up with?' I asked, stalling.

'Worked that out as well, did you?' Terry actually smiled. He seemed calmer, as though relieved to be finally confessing what he'd done. 'It was either that or Smith. Monk was too good an opportunity to miss. I'd still got some of Zoe's things hidden away,

431

but I had to move fast before his place was swarming with SOCOs. I wasn't as careful as I should have been. Almost fell over Walker. But I flashed my warrant card and put the fear of God into him. Said if he kept his mouth shut I'd look after him.'

And for eight years Terry had been as good as his word. *More lives than a bloody cat*, Naysmith had said. *Always managed to slip off.* Small wonder when there was a police detective on his side, making sure any evidence was conveniently lost or mislabelled. Only when Terry had been suspended himself, and DI Jones finally let him down, had Walker broken his silence.

And Monk had beaten him to death for it.

Terry would have guessed why. He must have been frantic when Monk escaped. Especially when there was still one piece of evidence that could link him to Zoe Bennett.

'How did Sophie get the diary?' I asked.

'Nosy bitch went snooping through my things. It was about a year after the search. Debs had kicked me out so I was renting a flat. Me and Sophie had got together again. I always meant to get rid of the diary, but I never did. Stupid really. I'd hidden it, but Sophie always was good at finding things.'

He sounded bitter. Part of me registered that their relationship wasn't the fling Sophie had claimed, but now wasn't the time to dwell on that. I thought I saw

Roper's hand moving, but kept my attention on Terry.

'How much did she know?'

'Only that I'd been screwing Zoe, the diary made that much obvious. She was more pissed off because it was while I'd been seeing her than anything. She went ballistic. She wouldn't tell me what she'd done with the diary, only that it was somewhere "safe".' His face turned ugly at the memory. 'It didn't matter so much when Monk was in prison. She couldn't tell anyone without admitting she'd been withholding evidence. But when Monk escaped . . . That changed everything.'

'That's why you panicked and came to see me. To see if Sophie had told me anything.'

'I didn't *panic*. I just wanted the fucking diary back! And I know Sophie. If she was going to go running to anyone from back then, I knew it'd be you.'

He's jealous? There was a bubbling groan from the floor. Terry looked down at Roper in surprise, as though he'd forgotten him. The policeman twitched, his eyes fluttering.

'Don't!' I shouted, as Terry hefted the scaffolding pole.

He paused, the pole still raised. I thought there might be something like regret in his face. 'I really was going to let you go until I saw Roper's car. You know I can't now, don't you? You know that.'

I did. And I didn't know what I was expecting. 'What about Sophie?'

'What about her? She can't do anything without the diary.'

'Don't you even care what you've done to her?'

'What *I've* done to *her*? Jesus! The blackmailing bitch's made my life hell for years!'

'She was scared. And she's in hospital now because of you!'

He stared at me, Roper momentarily overlooked. 'What are you talking about?'

'Monk didn't cause the haematoma. You did, when you forced your way into her house looking for the diary.'

'Bullshit! I don't believe you!'

'It's a contrecoup injury from where she hit her head on the bathroom floor when she fell. She discharged herself from hospital before they could pick it up. She obviously wanted to come home to see if the diary was still safe. And even then she didn't tell anyone what had happened. She was terrified, but she still protected you!'

'She was protecting herself! She was looking out for herself, the same as she always does!' He levelled the scaffolding pole at me. 'You think you're going to make me feel guilty about her? Forget it, she brought it on herself!'

'And if she dies it'll be just another accident? Like Zoe Bennett?'

The way he stared at me told me I'd gone too far. The only sound was the mournful sigh of the wind outside the kiln. Terry shifted his grip on the pole.

'At least tell me where they're buried,' I said quickly.

'What for? You had your chance eight years ago.' His face seemed to close down, blank of expression. 'Let's get this over with.'

He started towards me, then suddenly staggered. I thought he'd tripped until I saw that Roper had clutched hold of his leg. The lower half of the policeman's face gleamed wet with blood in the lamplight, and his front teeth were snapped off at the gum. But his eyes were bright and full of malice as he tried to drag himself to his feet.

'Fucker!' Terry yelled. He lashed out with the scaffolding pole as I rushed at him. I ducked back, falling against the kiln's central chimney, and felt something grate beneath my shoulder. Wrenching his foot free, Terry kicked at Roper's head as if it were a rugby ball. There was a sound like a dropped watermelon and Roper flopped limply. As Terry came at me again I grabbed the loose brick where Sophie hid her spare key and flung it at him. He tried to block it, but it caught him a glancing blow in the face before clumping to the floor.

'Bastard!' he spat, spraying blood and spittle, and swung the length of scaffolding at my head.

I managed to get an arm up but the metal pole smashed into my chest. My breath exploded as I felt ribs break. Agony burst through me, and as I crashed to the floor Terry stepped up and whipped his foot into my stomach.

I doubled up, unable to breathe. *Move! Do something!* But my limbs wouldn't obey. Terry stood over me. He was gasping for breath himself, his face slick with sweat. He touched his fingers to his scalp where the brick had struck him and stared at the blood on them. His features contorted.

'You know what, Hunter? I'm glad you didn't go when you'd got the chance,' he panted, and raised the length of metal over his head.

The kiln door banged shut behind him.

Monk, I thought instinctively. But the doorway was empty. The door flapped loosely in the wind, and as Terry spun round to face it Roper lurched into him.

He was barely able to stand, but he caught Terry off balance. His momentum carried them past me and slammed them into the ancient scaffolding against the kiln's wall. The rickety structure shuddered under their weight, ringing like a giant tuning fork as loose spars clanged to the floor. It swayed drunkenly from the impact, and for a second I thought it would hold. Then, as though in slow motion, the entire scaffold gave a creaking groan and collapsed on top of them like a stack of cards.

I thought I heard a scream, though I couldn't tell who from. I tucked into a tight ball, covering my head as planks and steel poles came crashing down. The air was filled with a clamour like insane bells that seemed to go on and on.

Then silence.

My ears rang as the echoes died away. Slowly, I unwrapped my arms from around my head. The air was thick with dust. The kiln was in darkness: the falling scaffold had knocked out the lamp. I coughed, gasping as pain shot through my broken ribs. The floor was littered with scaffolding and broken timbers. I made my way across them, relying on touch to guide me.

'ROPER? TERRY?'

My shout died away. A brick thumped down in the darkness, jangling the fallen poles like discordant wind chimes. In its wake I heard only the pitter-patter of falling mortar. Sophie had told me the scaffolding had been shoring up the kiln's unstable chimney and outer wall for decades.

Now there was nothing to support it.

There wasn't anything I could do by myself: I needed to get to a phone. I could just make out the light from the door through the murk. I picked an unsteady path across the tangle of scaffolding towards it. The air outside was sweet and clean. A last faint light remained in the sky as I hobbled towards the house, arm pressed to my injured ribs.

I was almost there when I heard a rumble behind me.

I looked back in time to see the kiln collapse. It seemed to sag and then, without fuss, simply toppled in on itself. I stumbled further away, shielding my eyes as a billowing cloud peppered me with grit. Then all was quiet again.

I lowered my arm.

A skein of dust hung like smoke over what was left of the kiln. Half of the brick cone was gone, leaving a jagged ruin against the evening sky. The section of wall with the door was still intact. I limped back to it, covering my mouth and nose with my sleeve as I peered through the doorway. It was partially blocked with bricks that spilled out from inside.

This time I didn't bother to shout. A final brick tumbled down on to the rubble with a sound like falling skittles, then there was nothing. Not a sound, nor any sign of life.

The kiln yawned in front of me, dark and silent as a grave.

31

The police found Monk three days later. In the aftermath of everything else that had happened, the search for the convict was stepped up still further. But even then events hadn't quite run their course.

It took the emergency services eight hours to dig out Terry and Roper from underneath the kiln's walls. By the time the remaining structure had been made safe enough to start shifting the rubble, everyone knew it was a recovery operation rather than a rescue.

I wasn't present, but I'm told there wasn't a sound from the rescue teams and police who'd assembled at the scene. When the last bricks were removed Roper was found lying on top of Terry. The post-mortem showed later that he'd died almost immediately, which was no surprise given the injuries he'd already sustained. Terry wasn't so lucky. Roper's body had partially protected him from the falling debris, and there was enough brick dust in his lungs to suggest he hadn't been killed outright. Although there was no way of knowing if he'd been conscious or not, the cause of death was suffocation.

He'd been buried alive.

My own injuries were painful but not serious: three cracked ribs from where I'd been hit with the scaffolding pole, plus cuts and bruises. For the second time in twenty-four hours I found myself back in hospital, though this time in a private room rather than a curtained cubicle, where the press could more easily be kept away.

'You've opened up an unholy mess,' Naysmith told me. 'You know there's going to be hell to pay over this, don't you?'

I supposed there would be, but I couldn't get too worked up over it. Naysmith was watching me carefully.

'Are you sure you've told us everything? There's nothing you've missed out?'

'Why would I leave anything out?'

When I left the hospital and stepped outside into the daylight everything felt slightly unreal. I'd been told Sophie was stable but still unconscious, although I hadn't been allowed to see her. I couldn't face going back to her house again so I booked into a nearby hotel. For the next two days I hardly left it, ordering room service I barely touched and watching the story break on the news. Monk still hadn't been caught, and there was fevered speculation about where he might be, and why the police hadn't captured him.

I knew from the updates I received from Naysmith that it wasn't for lack of trying. The rain continued to fall, and the teams going down into the cave system where Monk had taken Sophie were hampered by flooding. The discovery of a third entrance disheartened everyone. For a time it looked as though he might have escaped to some other refuge, or even fled Dartmoor altogether.

He hadn't. When the flood waters receded enough to allow the search team deeper into the dripping tunnels, they found Monk still in the narrow fissure where I'd last seen him. He'd been dead for some time, wedged so tightly between the rock faces that it took the best part of a day to get him out. Although the fissure had flooded he hadn't drowned. The strain of forcing his massive frame into that small space had proved too much even for him, as I think he'd known it would. When I couldn't see his torchlight behind us I'd assumed it was because he'd managed to free himself. But the searchers found the torch in his pocket, switched off. He'd died alone in the dark, far away from daylight or human contact.

He'd made his choice.

The cause of death was heart failure and pneumonia after a cocaine overdose, which was as I'd expected. But the post-mortem produced two notable findings. On most people the striations where the muscle fibres anchor to the long bones of the arms and legs are quite delicate. On Monk they were unusually deep, more in keeping with the dense musculature of a beast than a man.

That explained his abnormal strength, but it was the other finding that was most significant. There were massive lesions in his brain, corresponding to the depression in his skull. They were in the orbitofrontal cortex, where even mild trauma can cause behavioural problems and frontal lobe epilepsy. The likelihood was that they'd been caused by the forceps delivery that had killed his mother. Monk had been born damaged, a freak but not a monster.

We'd made him into one of those ourselves.

News of his death deepened my feeling of being stuck in limbo. Every time I closed my eyes I was back in the caves with Sophie and Monk. Or hearing the awful hollow impact as the scaffolding pole clubbed the back of Roper's head. My thoughts would run off at a tangent, as though trying to pick their own way through my mind. I felt as though there were something I should remember, something important.

I just didn't know what it was.

When I finally fell into a fitful sleep that night it

was only to wake suddenly in the early hours with Terry's voice echoing in my head, as though he were in the room with me.

You had your chance eight years ago.

It was something he'd said in the kiln, but it had been buried along with everything else until my subconscious spat it out. I thought it through, fitting it in with everything else till I was sure, and then called Naysmith.

'We need to go out on the moor.'

The first frost of the season crisped the coarse grass in the hollow as the CSIs began digging into the mound that Sophie had led us to years before. Naysmith and Lucas stood beside me, watching in silence as the dead badger was once again exposed to daylight. Preserved by the peat, the animal was hardly any more decomposed than it had been last time. But as more of the mound was cleared away the remains could be seen to be flattened and crushed, the splintered ends of broken bones protruding through the peat-clogged pelt.

'Where do you think Connors got the badger from?' Naysmith asked as a CSI carefully removed it from the hole.

'Roadkill,' I said.

Wainwright had told me as much when I'd visited him, but I'd dismissed it as rambling. I was wrong.

The discovery of the badger had appeared to explain both the cadaver dog's reaction and the disturbance to the soil. It had seemed a literal dead end, its presence enough to deter us from digging any deeper.

But no one thought to question why an animal that preferred dry, sandy conditions should have dug its sett in waterlogged ground. Monk's abortive escape had distracted us, but there were other clues we'd overlooked. Animal bones had also been found at Tina Williams' shallow grave, and the coincidence alone should have alerted me. As should the smell of decomposition: faint or not, it was stronger than it should have been in peat conditions.

Most obvious of all, though, was the broken bone that Wainwright had exposed. It was a comminuted fracture, a fragmented break typically caused by deliberate or accidental violence. A fall, say, or being hit by a car. An animal that had died in its burrow had no business with an injury like that.

There was no way of knowing when Wainwright had realized. It was possible he'd known for years, and elected to keep quiet to protect his reputation. But dementia sufferers often live more in the past than the present. Perhaps the knowledge was waiting in his subconscious, trapped there until it was brought to the surface by some random misfire of failing synapses.

I should have realized myself. And on some level I

had. Even back then, when the search reached its violent denouement, I'd felt the familiar itch that told me I was overlooking something. But I'd let it go. I'd been so sure of myself, so confident in my abilities, that I hadn't thought to second-guess my findings. I'd seen only the obvious, blithely putting the Monk case from my mind as I got on with my life.

And for years I hadn't thought about it at all.

We found Zoe and Lindsey Bennett only a little deeper than the badger carcass. Whether from sentiment or convenience, he'd buried the sisters in the same grave. The pressure of earth had contorted their limbs, so it looked as though they were embracing each other, but the peat had still worked its arcane magic. Both bodies were remarkably preserved, the skin and muscles uncorrupted, the hair still plastered thickly to their heads.

Unlike Tina Williams, they had no visible injuries.

'Wonder why he didn't inflict the same sort of damage on them?' Lucas asked, looking at the undamaged, peat-stained flesh. 'A mark of respect, you think?'

I doubted respect had anything to do with it. Terry hadn't beaten Tina Williams out of contempt for her, but for himself. It had just taken that long for him to see what he'd become.

The police found Zoe Bennett's diary in his car, wrapped in a clay-coated plastic bag. He'd sold the bright yellow Mitsubishi years ago, but even the minor mystery of the white car seen when both Lindsey Bennett and Tina Williams had disappeared was now explained: at night, especially on monochrome CCTV footage, it was almost impossible to distinguish yellow from white. From what Naysmith told me, the diary contained nothing very incriminating, beyond the simple fact of Terry's name. It showed the seventeen-year-old wasn't as worldly as she'd tried to pretend, thrilled at having a police detective as a lover. Terry would have been flattered by some of what she said.

Perhaps that was why he'd kept it.

'It isn't right, what Simms is doing,' Lucas said, as we left the CSIs to complete their work and headed back to the cars. 'Makes me glad I'm retiring. You should be given credit, not treated like you've done something wrong.'

'It doesn't matter,' I said.

The search advisor gave me a sideways look, but said nothing. With no one left alive to corroborate my story, Simms was doing his best to discredit my account of what had happened. Not only had he built his reputation on wrongly convicting Monk, but now it emerged that he'd entrusted the real killer with responsibility for searching for the missing victims. The press were clamouring for blood, and for probably the first time in his life Simms was reluctant to appear in front of TV cameras. With his career at stake he'd even suggested that I might be suffering from post-traumatic stress after my recent experiences, and was therefore an unreliable witness. So far none of the mud he'd thrown had stuck, but it was clear I'd outstayed my welcome. He'd seen to it that I'd been shut out of the investigation, and it was only as a courtesy from Naysmith that I'd been allowed to accompany them on the moor that morning.

But I was long past caring about Simms. I'd just arrived back at the hotel when my phone rang. The woman's voice at the other end was instantly recognizable.

'It's Marie Eliot, Sophie's sister.' She sounded tired.

I tensed, my hand gripping the phone. 'Yes?'

'She's awake. She's asking to see you.'

Even though I'd known what to expect, Sophie's condition was a shock. The thick mane of hair had been shaved off, replaced by a white dressing. She looked thin and pale, and her arms where the tubes fed in and out were emaciated and wasted.

'Bet I look a mess . . .'

Her voice was a whisper. I shook my head. 'You're OK, that's the main thing.'

'David, I . . .' She took hold of my hand. 'I'd have died if not for you.'

'You didn't.'

Her eyes filled with tears. 'I know about Terry. Naysmith told me. I – I'm sorry I didn't tell you everything. About the diary. I need to explain . . .'

'Not now. We can talk later.'

She gave a faint smile. 'At least we got Zoe and Lindsey back . . . I was right after all.'

Her eyes were already closing. I waited till her breathing showed she was asleep, then gently disengaged my hand. Sophie looked peaceful, the stress of the past week smoothed from her features. I sat beside the bed for a while, watching her.

Thinking.

It was still unclear whether she'd face charges for withholding Zoe Bennett's diary. Although she'd kept its existence from the police, even by Terry's admission it hadn't come into her possession until after Monk was convicted of – and had confessed to – the murders. There was nothing in the diary to undermine that, so technically it could be argued it wasn't even evidence at that point. She would have to answer some awkward questions, but from what Naysmith had told me it was unlikely she'd be prosecuted.

It wasn't as if she'd actually committed a crime.

She regained her strength quickly. The doctors expected her to make a full recovery, with no long-term impairment. After what she'd been through, they said she'd been incredibly lucky.

I agreed. Even so, I waited until I felt she was well enough to have the conversation I'd been putting off. My footsteps rang on the hospital floor as I followed the corridor to Sophie's room. It seemed a long walk. A nurse was in there with her, one of the regulars I'd seen before. They were both laughing as I went in. The nurse gave Sophie a dimpled grin, making me wonder what they'd been talking about.

'I'll leave you two to it,' she said, going out.

Sophie sat up, smiling. The dressings were off her skull and her hair was already growing out to an auburn stubble, blunting the sutured, horseshoe-shaped scar. She was starting to look more like her old self. Like the person I remembered from eight years ago. It was as though a weight had been lifted from her.

'Marie's spoken to the insurers,' Sophie said. 'They've agreed to pay out for all the stock and equipment I lost when the kiln collapsed. We're still haggling about the building itself but I'll get more than enough to set up again. That's great, isn't it?'

'Yes,' I said. I'd only been back out to the house once, to collect my car. The sight of the ruined kiln, the bricks now pulled from it and scattered over the garden by the rescue teams, had been depressing. I'd been glad to leave.

Sophie's smile faded. 'What's wrong?'

'There's something I need to ask you.'

'Oh, yes?' She tilted her head quizzically. 'Go on.'

'You knew Terry killed them, didn't you?'

I watched the swift play of emotions on her face. 'What? I don't understand . . .'

'You knew he'd murdered Zoe and Lindsey Bennett, and probably Tina Williams. I just can't make up my mind if you stayed quiet to protect him, or because you were scared what he'd do to you.'

She drew back slightly as she stared at me. 'That's an awful thing to say!'

'I'm not saying you had any proof. But you knew, all the same.'

'Of course I didn't!' Patches of colour had flushed her cheeks. 'You really think I'd have kept quiet if I'd known Terry was a *murderer*? How can you even *think* something like that?'

'Because you're too intelligent for it not to have occurred to you.'

That took the heat from her. She looked away. 'I'm obviously not as clever as you think. Why would I have bothered writing to Monk, asking where the twins' graves were, if I knew he hadn't killed them?'

'I wondered about that. I thought it was just lucky you'd kept copies of the letters, but I don't think luck had anything to do with it. You wanted them to prove you really thought Monk was guilty, in case something like this happened. You just never expected him to call your bluff.'

'I don't believe this! Look, if this is because of the diary I've already told the police everything. They know all about it!'

'Then why don't you explain it to me?'

She looked down at where her hands were clasped together on the bed, then back up at me. 'All right, I lied about me and Terry. It was more than just a fling. We'd been seeing each other on and off for a couple of years while he was in London. There was even talk of him divorcing his wife at one point.'

Another minor piece of the puzzle slipped into place. 'Were you still seeing him during the search?'

'No, we'd split up before then. He was . . . well, it was always pretty heated between us. We'd row a lot. About him seeing other women.' She didn't seem to notice the irony of what she was saying. 'It wasn't until months after the search that we finally got back together again. He promised he'd changed. Like an idiot I believed him.'

'Was that when you found Zoe Bennett's diary?'

'His wife had thrown him out by then. He got called out on a job and left me alone in this squalid little flat he was renting. I was bored, so I started tidying things away. Half of his things were still in boxes. The diary was buried under a pile of papers in one of them. God, when I realized what it was . . . You can't imagine how that felt.'

No, I didn't expect I could. 'Why didn't you tell

anyone? You'd got proof that Terry had been having a relationship with a murdered girl. Why would you keep quiet about something like that?'

'Because I thought Monk was guilty! Everyone did!' She was looking at me earnestly. 'What was the point of stirring up a lot of needless trouble? Not so much for him but for his family. I'd done enough to them already without that. And I'd found things left by his girlfriends before. Cheap jewellery and make-up in his car. Underwear. I thought the diary was just more of the same.'

'Sophie, you were a behavioural specialist! You're telling me you never once thought it was more than that?'

'No! I wanted to hurt him, that's why I took the diary. I knew he'd been sleeping with her, but I never suspected anything else!'

'Then why were you frightened of him?'

She blinked. 'I . . . I wasn't.'

'Yes, you were. When I took you home from hospital you were terrified. Yet you still pretended you couldn't remember who'd attacked you.'

'I – I suppose I didn't want to get him into trouble. You can't switch off your feelings for someone, even if they don't deserve it.'

I passed a hand over my face. My skin felt grainy. 'Let me tell you what I think,' I said. 'You took the diary on impulse, to hurt Terry like you say. You were angry and jealous and it gave you a hold over him. It was only after you'd taken it that you realized the danger you'd put yourself in. But by then you couldn't go to the police without getting yourself into trouble. So you hid it and kept quiet, and hoped the threat of it would stop him from killing you as well.'

'That's ridiculous!'

But there was a defensiveness behind her indignation. 'I think you blamed Terry for spoiling your career,' I went on. 'It must have been hard, helping the police to expose other people's secrets when you'd one like that of your own. So you stopped working as a BIA and tried to make a fresh start. Except that takes money, doesn't it?'

For a second Sophie looked afraid. She hid it behind bluster. 'What are you trying to say?'

I'd had plenty of time to think it through over the past few days. Terry had called Sophie a blackmailing bitch, and while I didn't give much credence to what he said it had started me thinking. That didn't mean I liked what I was about to do. But we'd gone too far to stop now.

'The cottage you're living in, it can't be cheap. And you said yourself the pottery doesn't sell. Yet you still seem to make a decent living.'

Sophie's expression was defiant but brittle. 'I get by.'

'So you never asked Terry for money?'

She looked down at her hands, but not before I saw that her eyes were brimming. The door opened and the nurse who'd been there earlier came in. The smile died on her face.

'Everything all right?'

Sophie nodded quickly, her face averted. 'Thanks.'

'Let me know if you want anything.' The nurse gave me a cold look before she went out again.

I didn't say anything else. Just waited. I could hear footsteps and animated voices from the corridor, but in that small room there wasn't a sound. The noise and energy of the hospital outside seemed like another world.

'You don't know what it was like,' Sophie said eventually, her voice cracked. 'You want to know if I was scared? Of *course* I was scared! But I didn't know what else to do. I took the diary without thinking. I – I was just so bloody *mad*! He'd been screwing that . . . that teenage *slut* while he'd been seeing me! But I swear at first I still thought Monk had killed her. It was only later that . . . that I . . . Oh, Christ!'

She covered her face as the tears came. I hesitated, then passed her a tissue from the bedside table.

'I didn't want to believe it was Terry. I kept telling myself Monk really had killed them. That's one reason I started writing to him, trying to convince myself. I was wrong.' She broke off to wipe her eyes. 'But I was angry as well. I'd given up everything because of Terry. My career, my home. He was the reason I moved out here. The least the bastard could do was help me start again. I didn't ask for much, only enough to help set me up. I thought . . . I thought as long as I'd got the diary I'd be safe.'

Oh, Sophie . . . 'But you weren't, were you?'

'I was until Monk escaped. I hadn't heard anything from Terry in over a year. Then he phoned up, ranting and threatening what he'd do if I didn't give him the diary. I'd never heard him like that before, I didn't know what to do!'

'So you phoned me,' I said tiredly. Not to help her find the graves, or at least not only that. She'd wanted someone with her in case Terry tried anything.

'I couldn't think who else to call. And I knew you wouldn't say no.' She plucked at the damp tissue. 'Next day I was getting ready to meet you when he hammered on the door. When I wouldn't let him in he . . . he broke it down. I ran upstairs and tried to lock myself in the bathroom, but he forced his way in there as well. I got hit by the door.'

Her hand went automatically to the fading bruise on her cheek. I remembered seeing the stairs were wet when I'd found her. If I'd given it any thought I might have realized she hadn't been surprised in the bathroom as she'd claimed.

'Why didn't you say something then?'

'How could I? I'd been hiding evidence for years! And I'd no idea Terry had been suspended. When you said he'd been to see you . . .'

A shudder ran through her. Instinctively I started to reach out, but stopped myself.

'I didn't really do anything *wrong*!' she blurted. 'I know I made a mistake, but that's why I wanted to find Zoe and Lindsey's graves so badly. I thought at least if I could do that much it might make up for . . . for . . .'

For what? Protecting their killer? For letting the wrong man stay in prison? Sophie looked down at the shredded tissue in her hands.

'So what now?' she asked in a small voice. 'Are you going to tell Naysmith?'

'No. You can do that.'

She took hold of my hand. 'Do I have to? They already know about the diary. It won't change anything.'

No, but it'll end eight years of lies. I set her hand on the bed and stood up.

'Bye, Sophie.'

I walked out into the corridor. My footsteps rang on the hard floor as the clamour of the hospital enveloped me. I felt an odd detachment as I walked through it, as though I were encased in a bubble separating me from the noise and life around me. Even the fresh, cold air outside didn't dispel it. The bright autumn sunlight somehow seemed flat as I went back to my car. I unlocked it and stiffly lowered myself into the seat. My cracked ribs were manageable but still painful.

I closed my eyes and put my head back. I felt empty. The idea of driving back to London didn't appeal, but I'd been here long enough. Too long, in fact. The past was beyond reach.

Time to move on.

Rousing myself, I reached into my pocket for my phone, wincing as my ribs protested. I'd turned it off in the hospital and when I switched it back on it *beep*ed straight away. For an instant I was back in the darkness of the cave, then I shook my head.

I had a message waiting. Or rather messages: I'd missed three calls, all from the same number. It wasn't one I recognized. I frowned, but before I could play any of them my phone shrilled again. It was a call this time, from the same number as before. I straightened. *Something urgent.*

I felt the familiar quickening of interest as I answered.

Acknowledgements

As ever, I couldn't have written this book without the help of other people, especially the real-life experts who were generous enough to help with the often thorny issue of research. In no particular order, thanks are therefore due to Tony Cook, Regional Major Crime Advisor with the National Police Improvement Agency; Dr Markus Reuber, Academic Neurology Unit, University of Sheffield; forensic ecologist Patricia Wiltshire; Dr Tim Thompson, Senior Lecturer in Crime Science at the University of Teesside, and Dr Rebecca Gowland, Department of Archaeology, Durham University, for allowing me to take their Body Location and Recovery course; Doug Bain, retired dog-handler and CSI; Professor Sue Black and Dr Patrick Randolph-Quinney of the

University of Dundee's Centre for Anatomy and Human Identification; Professor John Hunter, Institute of Archaeology and Antiquity at the University of Birmingham; Dave Warne, chairman of the Plymouth Caving Group, and the Ministry of Justice Press Office.

The ratio of decomposition is taken from W. R. Maples' and M. Browning's *Dead Men Do Tell Tales*, Doubleday, 1994.

Thanks also to Hilary for her unfailing support, to Mom and Dad for never doubting, to Ben Steiner, SCF, Simon Taylor and the team at Transworld, my agents Mic Cheetham and Simon Kavanagh, all at the Marsh Agency, and to the translators who have introduced David Hunter to a wider audience.

Finally, I owe a huge debt of gratitude to my international rights agent Paul Marsh, whose death in 2009 was a loss to publishing as well as to everyone who knew him.

Simon Beckett, August 2010

THE CHEMISTRY OF DEATH
Simon Beckett
A David Hunter thriller

Living in a quiet rural backwater, Dr David Hunter felt he might at last have put the past behind him. But then they found what was left of Sally Palmer . . .

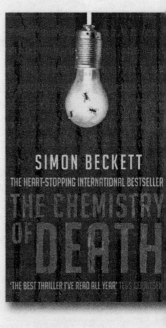

It isn't just that she was a friend that disturbs him. Once he'd been a high-profile forensic anthropologist, all too familiar with the many faces of death, before tragedy made him abandon this previous life. Now the police want his help. But to become involved will stir up memories he's long tried to forget. Then a second woman disappears, plunging the close-knit community into a maelstrom of fear and paranoia. And no one, not even Hunter, is exempt from suspicion . . .

Gruesome and gripping, this startling British crime thriller has an unnerving and original twist.

Shortlisted for the CWA Duncan Lawrie Dagger for Best Crime Novel of the Year

'Spine-tinglingly frightening, but also poignant and caring . . . hits the bull's eye from the word go!'
INDEPENDENT ON SUNDAY

'Very distinctive . . . a cut above the average, with a convincing central character, a gripping plot and a fine store of morbid information'
OBSERVER

'In the mould of Patricia Cornwell, but by a Brit . . . brilliant'
DAILY MIRROR

WRITTEN IN BONE

Simon Beckett

A David Hunter thriller

'I took the skull from its evidence bag and gently set it on the stainless steel table. Tell me who you are . . .'

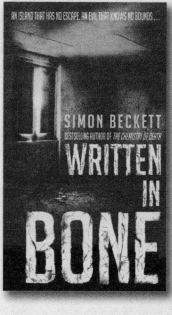

On the remote Hebridean island of Runa, a grisly discovery awaits the arrival of forensic anthropologist Dr David Hunter.

A body – almost totally incinerated but for the feet and a single hand – has been found. The local police are quick to record an accidental death but Hunter's instincts say otherwise: he's convinced it's murder. Indeed it appears Runa might not be such a peaceful community after all – and a burned corpse but one of its dark secrets.

Then an Atlantic storm descends, severing all power and contact with the mainland. And as the storm rages, the killing begins in earnest . . .

Powerful, unpredictable and shocking, Written in Bone is a nerve-shredding crime thriller from a brilliant British storyteller.

'Beckett cranks up the suspense . . . unexpected twists and a gory climax'
DAILY TELEGRAPH

WHISPERS OF THE DEAD

Simon Beckett

A David Hunter thriller

'In plain black letters were the words Anthropological Research Facility, but it was better known by another, less formal name. Most people just called it the Body Farm . . .'

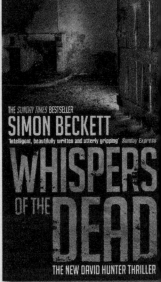

In America to escape the violence that nearly killed him, forensics expert David Hunter needs to know whether he is still up to the job of confronting death in all its strange and terrible forms.

Then a body is found in a remote cabin out in the woods. And then another . . .

Pushed deep into the heart of a terrifying manhunt, Hunter begins to wonder if they're on the trail of a maniac who simply cannot be stopped.

This is a shocking, cunning and heart-stoppingly exciting crime thriller from a No.1 international bestselling storyteller.